T
THIN
WOMAN

An utterly charming English country house murder mystery

DOROTHY CANNELL

An Ellie Haskell Mystery Book 1

JOFFE BOOKS

Revised 2023 edition
Joffe Books, London
www.joffebooks.com

First published by St Martin's Press in 1984

This paperback edition was first published
in Great Britain in 2023

Cover art by Dee Dee Book Covers

ISBN: 978-1-80405-856-5

NOTE TO THE READER

Please note this book is set in the 1980s in England, a time before smartphones, and when social attitudes were quite different.

CHAPTER ONE

Nice people everywhere know that family reunions are occasions of wholesome pleasure, more innocently rewarding than lavender-scented sheets in the airing cupboard or fresh pots of homemade bramble jelly cooling on a marble pantry shelf. I hope, therefore, that posterity will not judge me harshly when I confess I read the invitation to Merlin's Court with the same panic I would have accorded a formal notice that I was to be executed at the Crown's convenience. The gently worded letter on thin violet writing paper summoned me to a gathering of the clan at the ancestral home of an aged uncle. My horror lay in the knowledge that I could no longer conceal my disreputable secret from the relations I had cleverly avoided the past few years. Advertising campaigns describe such as I in soothing terms — full-figure girls. But who are we kidding? One simple three-letter word says it all.

Camouflage might help. Not the new outfit kind (I no longer put faith in clothes), but a broad-shouldered man to stand behind. Ideally what I needed was a handsome, devoted spouse and a circle of adorable golden-haired children, who always ate with their mouths closed and never swore in public. Surrounded by all that moral support I might feel better equipped to look my wretchedly beautiful cousin Vanessa in the eye. Daydreamer! I was, needless to say, single, and unless Zeus came down from Olympus and made me an offer, likely to remain so.

The weather that evening matched my mood. It was bleak and blustery, typical of late January in London. I had returned from work, my face rubbed raw, to find the letter on the doormat. My flat was at the top of a gaunt Victorian house, run by a phantom landlady who was never to be found when the taps leaked but materialized the instant the rent was due. Having hung my coat on the peg by the front door, I arranged my umbrella so it could rain over my geranium plants, and headed for the kitchen, where I did what I always did in times of trial — opened the refrigerator door. This time I was tempted to climb inside, blotting out the intrusive world. But that would have solved nothing. The ensuing scene would have been a remake of Pooh Bear getting stuck while visiting Rabbit, and no one was going to use my legs for towel racks. So I did another comforting Pooh-Bearish thing. I filled a plate with a loaf of French bread and six chocolate éclairs, tucked a pot of Mrs Biddle's Best Strawberry Jam under one arm and grabbed the butter dish. Planting my loot on the scrubbed wood table next to the African violet the cat had knocked over, and the morning newspaper ringed with coffee stains, I stuck a candle in a Coke bottle and lit it with a flourish. I downed two éclairs and four slices of crusty bread lavish with sweet yellow butter; thus strengthened, I reread the invitation to Merlin's Court — my nickname for my antiquated relation's abode. The real name was something prosaic like The Laurels or Tall Chimneys, not at all in character with the whimsical quality of the house.

The letter, of course, was not penned by the great man himself. Such attention might have given me an undue sense of my own importance. Aunt Sybil, who lived with the old dear and doted on his every whim, had scratched the missive in her quaint Victorian hand, all wispy loops and curls like fallen eyelashes. I was afraid to breathe on the paper in case the writing disappeared. The weekend party was to commence on the evening of Friday, the thirteenth of February, and to conclude (promptly, no doubt) on the Sunday after four o'clock tea. Refusal of this genteel invitation was obviously deemed unthinkable. I was demurely asked to apprise Aunt Sybil if I would be escorted by a gentleman friend so that a separate bedroom could be prepared.

What a lovely word: *escorted!* It makes one think of seaside promenades, top hats and twirling canes, and delicious young men with evil on their minds. The last escort I had was the ward orderly who wheeled me into Outpatients the night I twisted my ankle running for a taxi. "Have another éclair, Ellie!" "I don't mind if I do." The thick yellow cream oozed between my fingers. I wiped a splotch off the newspaper, and there it was in big bold black letters, shouting just for me! *ELIGIBILITY ESCORTS, MALE AND FEMALE. A HIGHLY LEGITIMATE SERVICE. DON'T GO ALONE! PICK UP THE PHONE.*

"And get murdered," said a little voice in my ear.

"What for?" said another little voice. "You don't have any money. You're not gorgeous."

I finished the last éclair and wished I hadn't. How much would it cost to rent a man for the weekend? A packet, no doubt. But I had Mother's money. I rarely bought clothes or furnishings for the flat. As an interior designer, I got my kicks doing up other people's houses. Being selective was my business. I could apply those same professional skills to choosing a man, the kind who would enhance any drawing room décor. He would be tall and elegant, with finely moulded features and a pair of darkly arched sardonic eyebrows. I had met such paragons often, between the pages of Regal Romances; they were suavely named Julian St. Tropé or Eduard Van Heckler and were the perfect accessory for a girl wanting to make a nice impression.

"Fool." I crumpled the paper and picked up the empty plate. "You'd land up with someone called Fred Potts who moonlights selling floor polish door to door." As if on cue, the doorbell trilled. It was my roommate, Tobias Feline. A very conventional cat, he refused to come up the fire escape and through the window. Perched on the hall table outside my door, he would nudge the bell until I got the message and opened up. Tobias was not alone. My neighbour Jill, from downstairs, followed him in, which did not please him. Tobias hates company. His scowl said, "Kick the witch out." Sniffing disgustedly at his food dish, he stalked off to sharpen his claws on the sofa in my tiny sitting room. Poor Jill *was* looking a little witchy. She had dyed her short spiky hair once too often (she uses the every-other-day kind), and it was now a sullen-looking green, which clashed with her eyebrows. I've tried to hate Jill because she is tiny with a capital *T* — four foot ten, weighs less than I did at birth, and always sucking in her non-existent stomach, saying she simply must go on a diet. But she is also nice with a capital *N*. Dropping down on a kitchen chair, she kicked off her Cinderella-sized shoes and rolled a bottle of plum wine onto the table, stretched her skinny little arms above her head, and said she was exhausted. I wasn't surprised. Jill teaches self-defence to women who are afraid to go out alone at night, and she has a judo chop that would send Mr Universe through three floors and bounce him back up again.

"Wooh! What a night. That wind. I practically flew home. Time for a warm-up. Fetch a couple of mugs, Ellie dear, and I'll pour us each a slug of plum yum-yum."

"Do you mind drinking alone?" I reached into the cupboard and came back to the table with a glass marked Present from Blackpool. "Sorry, but I don't want to curdle my éclair."

"What's up? You look a little sour already." Jill topped up her glass and looked at me intently. Priding herself on being an amateur psychiatrist, she has been thumbing her way through my neuroses for the past three years. So far she has prescribed group therapy, meditation, macramé, yoga, and a pen friendship with a guru. I handed her the invitation and poured myself a double Andrews Liver Salts.

"So? It doesn't sound like the most exciting bash of the season, but it's a weekend at the seaside. Boring probably, but harmless."

"You haven't met my aunt Astrid or her dear, delectable daughter, Vanessa — the girl designed with men in mind — not a brain in her head, but who notices?"

"Meow!" Jill ran a finger round the rim of her glass and poured herself another shot.

Tobias cocked an ear round the corner, decided he wasn't being spoken to, and retreated.

"Cattiness is one of my few pleasures in life — I don't smoke, I don't drink (much), and I don't have sordid affairs with men lusting after my body."

"If you didn't eat for six you might have a hope. Stop feeling sorry for yourself. I keep telling you, I'll go on a diet if you will. We'll make it a team effort. An early morning jog down to the station and back, calisthenics while you're working, and three teeny-weeny meals a day — no cheating!"

"Thanks a lot, Jill, but I couldn't take that tomato, vinegar, and stale cake routine again. Besides, it's all too little, too late. The gala event is only three weeks away. And don't suggest my refusing the invitation. They would all guess why I didn't dare show."

"Even though they haven't seen you for over two years? You weren't as heavy then as you are now."

"No, but I was always chunky. When I was a teenager, Aunt Astrid predicted I would end up as big around as the dome of St. Paul's. My failure to answer all letters and Christmas cards will have confirmed their worst suspicions."

"Didn't you tell me your uncle Merlin is a recluse, that he hasn't seen you since you were a child? Why this sudden yearning to entertain his kith and kin?"

"Goodness knows. Perhaps the old boy is about to kick the bucket, although the last I heard he was threatening to live to be a hundred. You know the type — hasn't seen a doctor in fifty years and never gets a cold. Anyway, Uncle Merlin isn't my problem; he's not interested in women. He can sit on his mothballs until he croaks. It's the others I'm worried about, not just gorgeous Vanessa and Mummy, but Uncle Maurice, Aunt Lulu, and my cousin Frederick. I don't want them asking what a nice girl like me is doing in a body like this!"

"Being flip isn't helping, Ellie. You've got to come to terms with whatever is driving you to destroy yourself. Probably some trauma at an early age . . ."

"All right! But miracles sometimes take time, which I do not have. What I do have is this!" Pushing the newspaper across the table, I pointed to the ad for Eligibility Escorts and awaited her reaction. If Jill scoffed . . . but she didn't.

"Ellie, this is super! Will you try it? You're always so hide-bound."

"Only if I can feel safe that the agency is legitimate. A lot of these places are cover-ups."

"For immoral purposes? You're afraid they'll interview you for a post as lady of the night? Ellie, you'd never get the job."

"Thanks a lot!"

"Not just because you're, hmmm, large. It's your depressing aura of blatant respectability." Jill poured another drink and waggled it in front of my face. One of the reasons I liked her was that she didn't skim over the subject of my weight. "Here's to Ellie! I wonder how this outfit works? Do you rent the man by the hour, the day? In your case I would ask about their special weekend package deal!"

"You are ridiculous." I was hungry again but decided to try the last of the wine instead. "I'll ring them tomorrow. Nothing definite; just a few discreet enquiries. If the person on the other end sounds sane, I will ask for an appointment. I can always decide not to go at the last minute."

"You'll go. Come to think of it, my cousin Matilda went there or to a similar place. She was between husbands at the time. She literally cannot stand up if she doesn't have a man's arm to clutch. She decided if the groom could rent a suit and a top hat it was perfectly proper for her to rent a man. I believe he was mistaken for the father of the bride or the maitre d', one or the other."

"Let us drink to presentable men, however they come," I cried, raising my glass. "Whatever the price."

* * *

The next day I did not feel quite as swingingly sophisticated. I put off telephoning Eligibility Escorts until late in the afternoon. Going into the back area of the showroom where I worked, I poured a cup of coffee from the electric pot perched dangerously on a packing case, sharpened three pencils until they were lethal, sat down behind the desk, stood up, organized a box of paper clips, picked up the phone, put it down, and finally dialled the number. It was engaged. Five minutes later I got through and was informed by the anonymous voice at the other end of the wire that appointments were not necessary. Office hours were 8.30 to 5.30, and I would be expected to provide three references, type-written, in triplicate. *Click*.

Not very friendly, but definitely businesslike. I began to feel better. Cancelling my late afternoon appointment with a woman who wanted her suburban three-bedroom, pre-war house turned into a French château, I took the tube to the Strand, checked the address in my purse for the fourth time, and began the ten-minute walk to Goldfinch Street.

My feet slowed it to twenty. They also walked me into Woolworth's, where I bought a lipstick I didn't need in a colour I would never wear, and a bag of potato crisps which I tucked into my bag for a little security.

Unfortunately, I had no trouble finding the building that housed Eligibility. No one could miss it. The architect had not bypassed an innovative trick. Riding the lift — a glass funnel revolving on its own axis with no visible means of support — through a jungle of hothouse plants was an experience in itself. My only hope was that some exuberant tenor would not forget himself, burst into song, and with one glorious ping splinter the lot of us. I kept my eye on a stout, swarthy gentleman with a black operatic beard and silently dared him to breathe. In the nick of time the great globular machine drifted to a halt, hung in the air for a second, then, in a silent yawn, opened its doors. Briefly I considered making an immediate return voyage. But I despise cowards, even if I am one most of the time.

Turning a corner, I found myself immediately in front of a glass door proclaiming in blazing letters Eligibility Escorts. Underneath was a nauseating little etching of two hearts entwined.

Scrambling in my bag, I fished out a pair of dark glasses, and turned up the collar of my camel coat. Who was I hiding from? Me? My insides plummeted; I did a bit of Lamaze breathing I had picked up on the telly and opened the door.

As is often the case when one expects the worst, nothing sinister lurked inside. It was the usual kind of reception room where exorbitant fees are collected: bleached bone walls, bamboo window blinds, and a sparing, eclectic use of accessories. The room's focal point was a silicone-upholstered blonde, cleverly disguised as the receptionist. Seated behind a crescent-shaped orange Formica desk, she was filing her already razor-sharp nails and genteelly chewing gum, blowing cute little bubbles which exactly matched her candy-pink lipstick. She didn't look up as I came in on waves of Johnny Mathis crooning enticingly.

I cleared my throat and noisily swallowed my voice. "Excuse me?"

"Yes?" Blondie Locks sucked in the neat little dollop of gum and managed, if possible, to look more bored than ever. "If you've come about the job" — the emery board continued to hum — "it's taken. Sorry, but first come, first served."

"Job?"

She looked blank. "Janitor, male or female, no experience necessary, no fringe benefits, age forty-five and" — she paused — "you mean you didn't want it?"

Surely I could not have aged that rapidly since morning? This bottle-blond, sugar-coated idiot was going to be a real treat. From her X-ray stare I might have been a maggot crawling out from a silver tray of neatly trimmed cucumber sandwiches. Nerves be damned, I was not going to be treated like the cat's lunch.

I took off the dark glasses and put them in my pocket. "I'm here as a client, not as a full-time employee. You may remember" — I cast a glance round the empty waiting room — "I rang up this afternoon, and you told me I could come in without an appointment. I hope I haven't wasted my time? I have clients of my own that I have neglected for this." Take that, I thought, feeling her mean little eyes work slowly up and down taking in my parachute-shaped coat and serviceable shoes. Why had I done this to myself?

"Management requirements are, I am afraid, very exacting—"

"Exactly what are these requirements? If I'd known you wanted 36–24–35, I wouldn't have eaten lunch."

"Look, miss, I don't make the rules. Life isn't always fair."

Profound thought for the day.

"Listen, if I looked the way you think I should, I wouldn't be here. Now can you help, or may I speak to someone who will?"

Her sigh rattled the paper clips. "I don't make the decisions for E.E. . . . Oh well, Mrs Swabucher will want these completed before you go in." A sheaf of application forms, miniature hearts stamped in each top right-hand corner, and stickily clipped together with a bent paper clip, was thrust into my hands. "Go into that little cubbyhole near the window."

Blondie Locks did not bother to get up; she just waved a packet of gum. "You'll find what you need, pens, pencils, and an adding machine."

I heard a door open and close at the far end of the room but not before I caught the words, "Wooh, we've got Miss World out there." Always before, I had rather enjoyed filling out application forms. They assert in nice clear print that I am a person with past accomplishments, ideas, and goals

— all neatly tabulated. Check Box A, B, or C, sign on the dotted line. Never much room for soul-searching. I have not been arrested, practised bigamy, or belonged to a far-out tropical religious cult. But this interrogatory was obviously the brainchild of some Freudian disciple who wanted me to dig my own grave and lie in it.

When using the bathroom, did I always close the door?
Did I smoke other people's cigarettes?
What kind of nightwear did I prefer?

Somewhere between these skilfully dotted lines lay boo-by traps to be detonated by the unwary. Having chewed off the ends of two pencils and decided that if this drivel did not finish me off, lead poisoning would, I skipped a few lines and came to a question in large type, several times under-scored. This was obviously the biggie. "What did I want most out of life?"

A. A fulfilling sexual relationship.
B. Money.
C. Approval of one's peers.

I was tempted to respond, "Fish and chips with plenty of vinegar and peas, a large Coke, and a chocolate ice-cream sundae with extra cream, two cherries, no nuts."

An alarm went off, puncturing my right eardrum. Blondie Locks was back, holding a natty-looking timepiece expertly between her cherry-ripe claws.

"You'd better see Mrs Swabucher now. She leaves for a conference the day after tomorrow." From her smirk, Blondie Locks had apparently decided I was Joke of the Day. Everyone hold your sides and roll in your seats; here comes Miss Woollen Underwear looking for Mr Right.

The inner sanctum was like a great big powder puff, all fluffy and pink and softly scented. Everything was pink — the carpet, the wallpaper, the curtains, the lampshade that looked like a parasol; even the large desk in the centre of the room was a pearly pink, heart-shaped of course. Behind this sat a fluffy elderly lady, who looked a bit like a powder puff herself. In that rosy light her hair had a pinkish glow.

"Miss, er, Ellie Simons." Blondie Locks plopped down my test papers on the desk and skittered out on her nine-inch pencil heels.

"Come in, come in, my dear. My! You look scared to death, poor pet." Mrs Swabucher came trotting out from behind the desk, and I was amazed to see she was wearing cosy bedroom slippers with large silk pink pompoms, which quite cancelled the effect of her rose wool suit.

She caught my eye and gave an improbable wink. "I know, I know they make me look like an old tabby cat, but I do suffer so with my feet, and my daughter Phyllis gave them to me last Christmas. She's the tall girl in this photo, the one standing next to the boy with the hamster — my grandson Albert. Let me take your coat, dear, pull that chair up so we can have a really jolly natter. How about some coffee?"

This was the master-mind of E.E.? I noticed with mild surprise that my hands had stopped shaking. I was able to hold the delicate coffee cup with its gentle tracing of tiny rosebuds quite steady. The room was deliciously warm despite the rain prattling down outside. I might have been spending a quiet evening with an elderly friend or relative, except that my relatives were all as warm as snakes.

"Has that girl been giving you a hard time?" Mrs Swabucher sat down again behind the photograph frames and sipped her coffee. "I knew she was wrong the minute I set eyes on her. But what can one do? It's absolutely impossible to find good help these days: sloppy, rude, and dreadfully under bred. Now you, Miss Simons, I can see, are a lady."

"About the test?"

"Oh, don't worry your head about that nonsense for a minute. That was my son Reginald's idea. He's an accountant, and you know how they are — 'Mother, you must be efficient, up to the minute, go by the book.' What I do go on is instinct, and I'm never wrong. That's how I got into this business in the first place. I understand people. My dear late husband always said I was a born match-maker, and when he passed on . . . what else did I have to do?"

She ran down momentarily like an old watch, and I murmured something about not requiring anything quite as permanent as a husband.

Mrs Swabucher beamed at me. "One never can tell! Have a chocolate, all soft centres. I order them specially."

I eyed them hungrily, but refused.

"Worry about your weight, don't you, dear? Shouldn't. At your age it's probably just puppy fat."

"I'm twenty-seven."

"Dear, oh dear! About to die of old age, are you!" Mrs Swabucher chuckled throatily. "Come on, be a devil. Enjoy yourself! Ah! You're afraid — you think this is another test, like that rubbish outside. Let's get one thing straight, Miss Simons. I'm not devious, not clever enough for it. Now eat up, and we'll get down to business. Tell me all about yourself."

It was easy. I had one chocolate, two chocolates. Mrs Swabucher handed me the box and told me to keep it on my lap. She kept pouring me coffee. I told her about the invitation to Merlin's Court, described Vanessa and how dreadfully inadequate I felt in her presence, how I hated my weight but felt powerless to control it, and how I thought even a make-believe relationship would give me the confidence to get through the big weekend.

By the end of my recital Mrs Swabucher had tears in her eyes and was blowing noisily into a pink silk handkerchief. "What a pity my youngest boy, poor William, never had a chance to meet you."

I had visions of an early and tragic death. But Mrs Swabucher explained that last June her offspring had married a very undeserving liberated person who believed in separate holidays and disliked children.

I, however, was the present and could be helped. The dear lady began taking copious notes in a peculiar-looking shorthand interlaced with blots and arrows: Jobs, hobbies, likes, and dislikes all went into the pot, where they would be allowed to stew for a while, said Mrs Swabucher. In the meantime, she would examine her files and put on her thinking cap. Somewhere out there was the man whose life would briefly touch mine.

"Aren't you going to a conference in a couple of days?" I asked, suddenly realizing how late it was. I had been sitting in this room for two hours.

"That girl can't tell the truth to save her life. Conference indeed! Sounds grand, doesn't it? What I'm really doing is visiting my grandchildren for a few days. But business before pleasure. Before I go anywhere I am going to find that man for you."

We lifted our coffee cups and drank a toast to Mr Right, wherever he was.

CHAPTER TWO

During the week following my visit to Eligibility Escorts I tried to console myself with the old adage that no news is good news, but even to my ears the cliché rang hollow. Either Mrs Swabucher was unnecessarily choosy or so far her scouting expedition had met with dismal failure. I had given her Jill's number, having finally thrown my telephone out. Ideally, I should have sent it to a monastery. Each time I heard Jill's footfall on the stairs I held my breath until my cheeks turned blue. Usually she was just coming up to borrow an egg. Her latest fad was mixing one in a glass of salt water for a late-night gargle. The only telephone calls she reported were three obscene ones from a lady in Knightsbridge who thought Jill was her paper boy. On Wednesday she did call me down and handed me the receiver. He sounded dreamy! False alarm, it wasn't him, just Mr Green from the cleaners at the corner, jubilantly reporting he had found the belt to my blue-and-white-spotted silk dress. I was tempted to tell him to keep it for a clothesline, but he was a kind little man supporting an aged mother.

Saturday arrived, and Jill insisted on a shopping spree. I absolutely must have a new outfit for the weekend. Bleating miserably that He was bound to ring up the moment my back was turned, I trudged after her into a decrepit little boutique in Soho. We were greeted with repellent ecstasy by the owner herself: a frowsy-looking woman with matted shoulder-length hair and a tattoo of a headless chicken on her left wrist. Serena would transform me. The question was, into what? Against my insistence that I did nothing for it at all, I was bullied into purchasing a full-length purple silk caftan sporting pearl beading round the neckline and gold braid round the sleeves and hem. Serena and Jill insisted I looked opulent. The term I would have chosen was Arabian Fright. But I did feel I had preserved a small measure of integrity in rejecting the gold cloth Aladdin slippers with the raised pointed toes.

"What's that burbling noise?" I asked, when we finally reached Jill's door, drenched from the rain that had met us when we came out of the tube. "Sounds like Tobias trapped somewhere. I think he's suffocating."

Jill got out her key. "That's not Tobias. You know how irritated Miss Renshaw, from the basement, gets if the phone rings all day and no one answers it. Now when I go out for any length of time I shove it under a beanbag."

Her hand paused at the lock. We looked at each other. "The phone!" we screeched in unison. "It's ringing!"

I grabbed for the key. Jill dropped it, and we heard the soft metallic *thud-thud* as it went flipping across the dark linoleum floor. "Idiot," we said together. Getting down on our hands and knees, we crawled in circles, rear-ending each other every now and then in our panic.

"Too late!" cried Jill.

"Has it gone down a crack?"

"No! Drat you. The phone's stopped. Ah! Found it!" She held the key as far away from me as possible and dared me to move until she safely unlocked the door.

"What do you expect me to do? Stay down here forever? I'm getting lockjaw in my knees."

Jill made a throaty little growl as I staggered up and followed her inside. We both stood disconsolately in the middle of the floor, still in our wet coats; the telephone squatted on its haunches saying nothing at all.

"Ring, you big black toad," I ordered, and obediently it did.

"You answer." Jill peeled off her coat. "And if it's that laboratory person again asking if I will donate my body for experimentation, say I give while I'm alive."

"Riverbridge 6890," I croaked. How can a woman's voice break at twenty-seven?

"Ellie Simons?" An accusing voice came from the other end.

"Um, ah, what, who is . . . ?"

"Bentley Haskell. I've spent half the day on the phone trying to reach you. I understood from Mrs Swabucher at the service that this was some kind of emergency. If you have perhaps made other arrangements that's fine with me, but I do like to know where I stand on these assignments."

"Yes, quite! Naturally I do understand your position." In my terror I dropped the phone and it went down with a rattling thump.

Jill perched on a stool by my left ear. "Stop grovelling."

"Shush." I yanked the cord away from her and spoke into the mouthpiece. "Don't worry, that was the phone I dropped, not my false teeth."

Impatient breathing came over the wire. "Miss Simons, I only take a couple of appointments a month. Escorting unattached females is not a full-time profession with me so I endeavour to set up my calendar as much in advance as possible. Exactly how much time are we talking about, and when?"

"When?" I echoed. "I thought Mrs Swabucher would have — just a moment, please. I'm so sorry about all this. I know I have the invitation right here, somewhere, in my bag. You want to know the dates?"

"You don't suffer from amnesia, do you, Miss Simons?"

"Oh, how amusing, Mr., eh . . . !" I did a Blondie Locks titter. "I always enjoy men — people — with a sense of humour." Covering the receiver, I mouthed frantically at Jill, "When am I going?"

She closed her eyes in pain. "Do black cats and ladders strike a chord? Friday the thirteenth! And stop whimpering at his feet. It's dehumanizing."

Jill was right. Enough of this nonsense! Squaring my shoulders I did an impersonation of my bank manager when he is letting me know he can bounce my cheques with one hand. "Mr Hammond, I have all the information right here at my fingertips. The dates are February thirteenth to the fifteenth."

"Haskell. Bentley T. Haskell. I gather from our mutual associate Mrs Swabucher that your situation is somewhat unusual, that you are looking for more than a mere escort. You wish me to pose as the devoted gentleman friend?"

"Will there be an extra charge? No problem. You may have the money in cash if you prefer."

"Thank you, and in unmarked bills if you can arrange it."

Funny man. Did he despise his work, find it demeaning? He sounded in a hurry to move on to whatever eligible men do for indoor entertainment on dreary winter evenings.

"Shall we arrange a meeting before we make this trip?" he asked. "That way you can fill me in on the details."

"No, I don't think that will be necessary." No point in giving this already hostile male an excuse to back out. Mrs Swabucher's kindly description of me might not match the truth. "If you give me your address, Mr Haskell, I will send you an agenda — time of departure, destination, etc."

"Thank you, but direct all correspondence to the agency. I don't give out my home address to clients."

Was the man afraid I might appear on his doorstep one dark and stormy night and try to rape him?

"Perfect!" What was I thinking of? "Like you, Mr Haskell, I want to keep this matter strictly business." I gave a little trill of laughter aimed at showing him how amusing I found all this.

"Am I interrupting your dinner?"

"No." Was he going to let down his defences and ask me out?

"I thought you were choking."

So much for the light approach! Before he hung up I mentioned transportation. I had thought we would travel by train, but when he suggested our taking his car I found the offer irresistible. Immediately I envisioned us sweeping regally between the iron gates at Merlin's Court.

"Fine," I told Mr Haskell. "Add petrol expenses to the bill."

He assured me he would and rang off.

I sat by the phone staring at the ceiling and holding my knees together. They were chattering worse than my teeth.

"What's his name?" asked Jill.

I told her.

"Sounds like a car," she said.

"Jill, you know I am very sensitive about name jokes."

"Sorry. I forgot that Ellie is an abbreviation. How about cracking a bottle of rhubarb wine in celebration?"

The evening was a good one, once I came out of shock. In doing an instant replay of the telephone conversation, I deluded myself that anyone as rudely abrupt as Bentley Haskell had to be a dish. Lesser men always try harder. Every gothic hero encountered between the pages of a paperback romance started out hostile, until the heroine got her silky little paws on him. I toyed with a mental image of Mr Haskell sporting an interesting limp, and a scar trammelling one swarthy cheek — injuries suffered in the traditional hunting accident.

By my third glass of wine I was feeling pretty chipper. But the next morning, sober once more, I remembered those heroines all looked like Vanessa. If I were ever cast in a gothic plot, it would be as buxom Dame Goody trundling through life in the devoted service of others. This is the real world.

The next week passed in an orgy of indecision. I used up my entire supply of writing paper, presents from three years back, drafting letters to Mrs Swabucher instructing her to cancel the order, all of which got savagely ripped apart and cremated in my kitchen stove. Tobias, that fearless specimen of feline life, was afraid to say "Meow" to me. I was snappy with Jill. All in all, I was a wreck and getting fatter by the minute. Time was growing short. I wrote to Aunt Sybil saying I would be escorted and I sent the agenda to the agency asking that it be passed on to Mr Haskell.

When the fateful day arrived, my eyes were bloodshot and my skin — my one prized feature — was a beehive of angry red blotches. Minutes ticked fiercely by, bringing the phantom Mr Haskell ever closer. I couldn't find the keys to my suitcase, and the oatmeal-egg white face mask Jill had slapped on me from the neck up had set hard as concrete. For a while we were afraid we would need to summon someone from the local petrol station to come and chisel me out.

"It's a shame this isn't a masquerade do," sighed Jill. "You could go as a lump of petrified rock."

Fortunately I laughed and the rock crumbled. Now came another risky procedure — squeezing me into a new pair of panty hose without popping them like overblown balloons.

Over the head with the purple caftan.

"Are you sure this outfit is suitable?" I was fumbling with a recalcitrant pearl earring.

"Sure!" Jill was trying to pry my left foot into a black grosgrain shoe I hadn't worn in years.

"Nowadays, you can wear a brown paper bag and no one will bat an eye."

"What time is it?" I was searching for my small gold watch. My usual Big Ben-sized one would not go with this rig. "He's due here at three-thirty."

"You're fine! Although I wish you wouldn't always wear your hair in that dowdy bun, or at least do something about the colour. Mid-brown isn't in this year." Jill had moved on to the right foot. "Ten more minutes." The doorbell buzzed and Jill nearly lost her hand as I backed up.

I hate early birds. Punctuality comes high on my list of unforgivable sins. The bell buzzed again, insistently. Jill opened the door while I hovered between the bedroom and the sitting room like a great purple moth.

"Miss Simons?" He sounded pleasant and something else — relieved?

"No, Jill, a friend from downstairs; Ellie's in here."

Fanfare and drum roll — my wretched knees knocking again. We were face to face at last. He wasn't tall, dark, and handsome, but two out of three wasn't bad. His height was nothing more than average, perhaps five nine, an inch taller than me in heels. His hair was dark and curly, almost black. With his olive skin his eyes should by rights have been brown but they were a vivid blue-green. He wore wire-rimmed glasses that didn't lose him any points at all (I later found out he wore them only for driving), and he was thin, thin, thin. Perhaps not theoretically handsome but decidedly attractive. Noting his well-cut coat over the dark wool suit, white shirt, and striped silk tie, I knew what I looked like — a fairground fat lady, bawdy, vulgar, grotesque.

Poor man, what a way to earn a living. I'd be nice to him. Tomorrow I would return to my tweeds and when the weekend was over I'd give him a really decent tip so he could take his mother or girlfriend — or wife — out for dinner. Was there any law that said escorts had to be single?

Tying on my best smile, I came forward to shake hands. He had a nice strong clasp, but his eyes were coldly impersonal. Irrationally I resented that. No one had twisted his arm to bring him here.

He spotted my suitcase and swung it up lightly in one hand, saying, "I'll take this down to the car while you finish dressing."

I stared frostily at the man. "You are looking at the finished product."

Those brilliant blue-green eyes took in every inch of purple; his lips curled. "You must forgive me," he said, "ladies' apparel has always been beyond me. I thought that was a dressing gown. Are you ready?"

"Not quite." My voice hit a false octave but to hell with that. "I'd like to explain something before we leave. Mr Haskell, you are here to do a job, just like any other employee. Nothing wrong with that, most of us are forced to earn our daily bread. I have worked with some people I wouldn't ask to tea if I were stranded with them on a desert island, but I have learnt one very important truth."

"Yes?"

"Always try and please the boss, because if you don't you may not get paid, by cheque, in cash, at all."

His brows had drawn into one long black line. For a moment I thought he might pitch the suitcase at me and, athletic as he undoubtedly was, he would have hit target — on the nose.

"Have a wonderful time!" chirruped Jill, handing me my coat.

We were on our way.

CHAPTER THREE

Not having been outside, or even drawn back my curtains that day, I was unprepared for the grim discovery that it was snowing. Large soft swirls like soapflakes powdered the air. Seaside weather? Apparently Bentley Haskell's car laboured under the misconception that it was. The badly scarred rusty-grey vehicle was parked tight against the kerb and the top was down. I knew convertibles went in for that sort of thing, but with discretion. Not in the midst of snow flurries churning in from the east. Mr Haskell had tucked my case inside the boot and was holding open the near-side door.

"Do you need help getting in my dear?" He smiled grimly. "Just practising."

"No. What I do need is for you to put the lid on this thing."

"Impossible, I'm afraid. The hinges have been rusted out for years. Don't worry — you won't get wet."

As I sat down in astonishment on a very damp seat, he placed a scarlet-and-white-spotted umbrella in my hand, pressed the catch, and a giant fairy toadstool bloomed overhead. My feet found sudden and welcome warmth from a hot water bottle wrapped in the remains of an old grey cardigan. But I was not appeased. I could have been chugging along in a snug train compartment waiting for an attendant to announce dinner was being served in the dining car. Only one explanation made any sense: The man sitting calmly at my side, reading a road map, was an escapee from Dartmoor. In this instance Mrs Swabucher should have listened to son Reginald, the accountant, and done her homework.

"You'll find a couple of travelling rugs on your lefthand side." Folding the map neatly and returning it to the leather pocket under the dashboard, Mr Haskell set the monster in gear. It answered with a whine that turned to a snarl. We shot forward, clipped past a head-scarfed woman on a wavering bicycle, inched round a huge lorry and a double-decker bus, and were moving swiftly with the evening flow of traffic fighting to be clear of London before dark.

"Comfortable, my dear?" He had small, very white teeth. One overlapped slightly, emphasizing the evenness of the others.

"Frozen."

"Tuck that other rug round you. My problem is I find this weather bracing. I forget others may not share my enthusiasm for nature in the raw."

"The train would be too hot, no doubt?"

"Stifling."

Was this how I would make my sweeping entrance down the carriageway at Merlin's Court? Unable to pry my icy fingers free from this ridiculous umbrella? Prematurely aged with my snow-white hair? Men! To think I had hankered after one all these years.

"Try to keep moving," he said, eyes fixed steadily on the road.

"Great! I'll get up and jog around the back seat. Don't stop if I topple overboard. I really do prefer a quick hit-and-run to dying of frostbite by inches."

"I meant wiggle your toe, flap your hands about — not the one with the umbrella." He winced. "I need both eyes for this drive — visibility is getting poor."

"You noticed?" I closed my eyes and my lids immediately became heavy. It was snow that weighed them down, not sleep. Huddled under my blankets I could not reach the large bar of hazelnut chocolate hidden in my bag that was beginning to call to me in a plaintive voice.

"Can a person," I asked, "contract rigor mortis while still alive?"

He snorted irritably, then added quite mildly, "It might help if we talked."

Was the iceberg melting?

"To be convincing," he continued, "I need to know something about who's who at the country estate. Is this a mansion we are visiting?"

"More like a castle. Not the bona fide kind, of course," I added hastily as I saw his eyebrows escalate. "A miniature reproduction, built well over a hundred years ago by Uncle Merlin's grandfather. Family legend claims that he was senile when the plans were drawn. Only a person in the throes of second childhood would possess that sort of imagination. The house is straight out of a fairy tale — turrets galore, ivy-crusted walls, a moat no bigger than a goldfish pond, and even a teeny portcullis guarding the front door, though they keep that open now."

"Sleeping Beauty revisited?"

"Exactly. The castle even has an official curse. Though, for a change of pace, we have a wizard instead of a witch."

"Let me guess, Uncle Merlin himself?"

"Naturally! His wickedness lies in what he has done to the place, or rather not done. He's allowed it to moulder away. Strictly speaking, he isn't an uncle — more of a cousin several times removed — but my mother was a practical lady. She insisted on keeping up the connection with our one wealthy relative. As a child I was forced to knit bedsocks for him each Christmas and only twice got invited for a visit. Both times I was sent packing within the week. He said I was eating him out of house and home and he'd be on bread and margarine for a year making up for it."

"I sincerely hope those won't be our rations for the weekend." Bentley Haskell guided the car around a slick curve. We were approaching the outskirts of London. I changed umbrella arms and sank as far as possible into my blanket cocoon. My companion unfortunately showed no signs of frosting up.

"What other fascinating characters may I expect to meet?"

"All kinds." I shivered. "A wife-swapping foursome from the East End, a witch doctor who recently had his licence revoked for . . ."

"If you are going to be silly," said Mr Haskell through his nose, "I'll merely concentrate on driving."

Effectively squashed, I sat looking like a big round jelly shivering on its plate. Magnanimously he proffered an olive branch.

"Just family, I suppose?"

"We have Uncle Maurice," I parroted like a child reciting. "He's a stockbroker in his fifties — paunchy and not very tall, wears what hair he has left glued down with heavily scented hair cream. One can smell Uncle Maurice all over the house."

"The perfect murder clue. He is not, I suppose, the type to bludgeon the butler to death?"

"Unlikely. If he had any flair for murder he would have done in his wife, Aunt Lulu, years ago. She's a doorbell."

"A what?"

"A ding-a-ling. Aunt Lulu could have a complete brain removal and no one could tell the difference once they put her hair back on. She waxes her floors hourly, irons her lavatory paper before she hangs it up and exists for her thrice-weekly appointment with her hairdresser. She and Uncle Maurice have a son named Freddy. Nothing like either of them. Freddy is a free spirit: prides himself on never washing, wears his hair in a pony tail, and sprouts a beard that resembles a dish-cloth that went down the rubbish disposal. A very hip fellow, our Freddy — rips about the countryside on a motorbike, has one ear pierced, and smokes pot like a dragon."

"Sounds more of a conformist than his father." Bentley Haskell squinted through the scurrying snowflakes at a half-obscured signpost, hooked a right where the road forked, touched a patch of ice, swerved briefly, and we were on course again. I felt like a block of ice cream, frozen so solid it would bend the spoon that dared to take a poke at it.

"Freddy is a musician," I chattered, "with one of those makeshift groups composed of scrubbing boards, nutcrackers, and electric hair dryers. At the moment he is resting. According to Aunt Astrid's latest Bad News Bulletin the cuckoo has returned to the nest and Mama and Papa bird don't have the strength to shove him out."

"Aunt Astrid?" Mr Haskell's black brows drew into a line of intense concentration as we slid into the small town of St. Martin's Mill and skated past a row of half-timbered cottages peering at us through the gathering dusk. The snow had stopped at last.

Lowering the umbrella I tenderly flexed my arm muscles. "Aunt Astrid is a widow, always dresses for dinner, and is never seen without her pearls. I believe she considers herself the reincarnation of Queen Victoria — you'll note the use of the royal 'we.' Always looks like she just sat down on a red-hot poker. She has a daughter — Vanessa," I mumbled. Mr Haskell was pulling off the road so I was spared a description of Vanessa in all her femme fatale glory.

"Time for a fill up," he said.

"Petrol or food?"

"Neither," said Bentley Haskell repressively, as visions of egg and chips danced in my head. "I thought you might appreciate having your hot water bottle warmed up."

"So I would," I shot back at him. "It reverted to a tombstone hours ago. But if that's a pub hovering about over there I am going inside to thaw out over a thick juicy steak and oceans of steaming coffee. You can suit yourself, stay out here and turn into Frosty the Snowman or join me."

Poor Mr Haskell, he looked outraged and tempted all at the same time. The flesh was weak, for he drew up under the creaking inn sign, aptly named The Harbour, yanked the water bottle from my grasp, and banged open his door.

"I hope you are paying for this!" he snarled, slapping the snow from his arms as he stamped round to help me out.

"Do I have a choice? You are getting to be a very expensive commodity, Mr Haskell." My dignity was somewhat lessened by having to cling tightly to his arm to prevent my legs sailing off on their own. "This coat" — it was ten years old — "is quite ruined, and if it wasn't for your hare-brained notion of travelling in your ventilated car we would both be toasty warm at Merlin's Court tucking into one of Aunt Sybil's marvellous dinners."

"Really? From your description of the place I gained the impression we would be fishing very dead bats out of very cold soup."

His vision was close to the truth, which further fired my wrath. Glaring, we made for the door. Once inside we ignored each other and informed the nervous girl behind the bar, as we stood making puddles on the floor, that we wanted a table for two. The echo was annoying but I looked straight ahead.

Soon we were seated by a roaring fire in a room gleaming with well-tended brass and ornately carved wainscotting. It was impossible not to mellow a fraction in the midst of this eighteenth-century charm. I decided not to treat Mr Haskell like the worm he undoubtedly was.

"Cosy, isn't it?"

"A bit overdone — this Ye Olde Worlde bit. Why is that ludicrous girl wandering around in a nightgown and curler cap?"

"The waitress? That's the Nell Gwyn look. Are you afraid she will go tripping off to bed before we have time to order?"

We both decided on steak and mushrooms. Refusing potatoes was hard, but I wanted him to think my problem was glandular. Our food came, sizzling and spitting on earthenware trenchers.

"Miss Simons," he said, picking up his fork, "I suggest we practise using first names so we don't slip up upon arriving at the castle."

I carefully speared a mushroom. "Your attention to detail is most impressive. Very professional. Are you always called Bentley, or do you shorten it? Benny?"

"Ben," he said frigidly, "and Ellie, what would that be, Ellen?"

I cut a piece of beef, moved it around my plate, then cut it again.

"Not Ellen, I gather."

"If we are supposed to be close friends you will have to know. My full name is Giselle." I looked up in time to see his lips twitch. Would the waitress notice if I stabbed the man with my fork and got blood all over the clean white tablecloth? Surprisingly his face smoothed out and he reached over, touching my hand.

"Parents can be very juvenile. These flights of fancy do very well for infants gurgling and bouncing around in their high chairs, but Petal and Daffodil have to grow up. Names should be given out on approval — exchangeable at the age of reason."

"Thanks." My voice came out gruff. I am uneasy when people, especially men, are kind to me. "Poor Mother, she meant well. She had visions of me following in her footsteps, fluttering around in a frothy pink tutu."

"Your mother is a dancer?"

"Was. Only in the corps de ballet, strictly small town. All those pirouettes and arabesques and she tripped running down a flight of stairs at the railway station; like me she was always late. Anyway, she died ten years ago."

"I'm sorry. And your father?"

"Off finding himself. At the moment he's farming in New South Wales. When last I heard, he had two — sheep, not farms — and if I know Daddy's luck the ewe undoubtedly is on the pill. He's great really; next year he may decide to be a fireman, or a circus clown."

"Which validates my theory that lovable as they may be, parents are the real children." Ben accepted a cup of coffee from the mob-capped waitress who was twitching round him in a disgustingly familiar way. Time for Mr Haskell to remember he had a living to earn. I had provided him with all the scintillating details of my family history, bar Vanessa; now Bentley T. Haskell — This Is Your Life.

He began by informing me that he had been disinherited, disowned, and dispatched to the devil by his parents. Another ancestral home gone west? This one turned out to be a greengrocer's shop in Tottenham.

I could picture those poor parents, hands gnarled by hard honest work, pelting the prodigal out the door with handfuls of carefully trimmed cabbages, then bolting the door and hanging up the Closed sign. But why?

His offence was interesting. Mum and Dad had not taken kindly to the idea that their son was a practising atheist.

"Practising?"

"I helped stage a rally outside the Hallelujah Revival Chapel, one of those narrow, venomous sects that still believe in burning heretics at the stake. In this instance they had refused to bury a small child in consecrated ground. If that kind of piety is religion I don't need it."

"Your parents are very devout?"

"Very. Dad is an orthodox Jew and Mother a staunch Roman Catholic. To give the old folks their due, they have a great marriage. They have spent the last forty years consumed with missionary zeal, each trying to convert the other. We have a mezuza by the front door and a statue of the Blessed Virgin on the mantelpiece. Mother told me she baptized Dad years ago while washing his hair, and he continues to introduce her to his friends as Ruth, although her name is Magdalene."

"Then I'm surprised they gave up so quickly on you. There must be more to your eviction than the Hallelujah Revival March. What other sins did you commit?"

Peering round for the waitress who had gone in search of the bill, Ben said in quite an amiable tone, "I'm surprised you don't trip over your nose going down the street. What makes you so sure my misdeeds were many?"

Fascinated, I watched as, with the merest flick of one finger, he brought Nell Gwyn trotting to heel. She picked up the money, which I had laid on the table, with maddening slowness and finally padded off again, wagging her tail.

"Out with it!" I exclaimed. "The suspense is giving me indigestion. What did you do, kidnap the mayor's daughter? Forget to return your library books?"

"My primary mistake was being born an only child. My parents put all their eggs in one basket. Mother was nearly forty when I was born. She never could have any more children."

Probably afraid to, poor woman, I thought. "Your mother must be getting up in years," I suggested slyly.

"Nearing seventy."

Which made Ben about thirty, one of my favourite ages for other people, particularly single men.

"Go on," I said.

"All right, if you must know, I wrote a book — a very graphic book — modern." He searched for a word suitable for ladies' ears. "Robust?"

"That's an adjective favoured by wine connoisseurs and girls with my kind of figure. Wouldn't pornographic be more apt?"

"Not in my opinion." His black brows came down again in that haughty manner that immediately turned those paper-back heroes into swashbuckling demons. Bentley Haskell looked like a kid who couldn't get his ball back.

"Has this masterpiece been published?"

"Don't sneer. I'm now well into my second draft."

"Aha! In other words you are not yet a household word. Why couldn't you wait until the thing came out in hardcover before dumping it in your parents' laps? What's so admirable about that kind of honesty? Were you trying to teach two old people a new set of dirty words?"

Ben looked injured. "I thought they'd like it! Besides, I had to get Mother and Dad off my back. They kept pushing me to go to work for my uncle Solomon. He owns a restaurant near Leicester Square."

"Sounds a fine opportunity, a nice family business."

"Sure, at one time it was what I wanted. I trained as a chef in some of the best hotels in Europe and the United States; but then the writing bug bit me while I was working in Paris last year and I turned my creativity in another direction. Bending over a hot oven for the rest of my life no longer appeals."

A cook? Could I never escape from food?

Sympathizing with someone who could blithely turn his back on Cordon Bleu was not in my nature. "I suppose," I said tartly, "that working for Uncle Solomon, even part-time, would have meant compromising the integrity of your artistic aspirations. Do you live in a garret?"

Ben folded his serviette and dropped it on the table. "I'm not starving, thanks to good old Eligibility Escorts and women like you."

"You mean 'robust' old maids." I lumbered to my feet and grabbed my bag. "But you are too wishy-washy to damn well say so."

"What foul language!" His shocked voice followed me out into the entry-way. "My mother never permitted me to mix with girls who swear."

The man was not even mildly funny. We stepped out the pub door into biting cold, in silence more frigid than the weather. We were on the road when he remembered the hot water bottle, jerked the car round, and disappeared back into the pub.

The second half of the drive was twice as miserable as the first. Night had clamped down and even with the car's brights piercing the swirling vapours it was impossible to see ten feet ahead. Ben was an expert driver, but I could sense he was having trouble staying out of ditches. As we drew nearer the coast, the wind striking our faces was harsh and stinging with salt. Snow was blowing off the trees, drifting into big white bolsters. Perhaps it was as well Ben and I were not talking. Aunt Sybil expected us around seven. The hour was now nearly 9.30. We drove through the town of Walled Minsterbury and kept moving northeast.

"Once we reach the village of Chitterton Fells, will you be able to give me directions to your uncle's house?" Ben's voice broke our long silence with such a rasp that I, drowsy with cold, lurched sideways against the steering wheel, sending us into a spin.

Ben took a word out of his own book (I couldn't blame him for being upset), elbowed me roughly aside, and with some difficulty straightened the front wheels.

"Before killing both of us — do you know the way?"

If ever a girl needed to redeem herself, this was the time. But I am one of those unfortunates who under normal circumstances cannot find their way to their own front gate without a road map, and these circumstances were not normal. I couldn't see Ben, let alone a signpost.

"You are not going to like this," I remarked chattily, "but I haven't been there since I was twelve. . . . Don't snarl at me!" I glowered into the dark. "In weather like this, people put out a hand and never see it again."

"Thanks a lot," sneered the invisible man.

The car did a bounce, a skid and, like a revolving door, slid very slowly into a tree, or a telegraph pole, or some other vertical obstruction that had no business standing around in the thick of drifting fog and whirling snow.

Not often, but occasionally, being heavy is a definite plus. I now did my fair share of pushing, shoving, and cajoling that car out of the ditch. My efforts earned me a reluctant word of praise from Ben. He called me a "pal." One hour later, my feet now slabs of frozen fish, we had that empty-headed vehicle back on the road. Huffing and puffing, my companion-of-the-night and I climbed back aboard.

I was prepared for the fact that my hot water bottle had died of exposure; the shock was finding the battery was about to do the same. The engine gave one brief bronchial cough, sputtered twice, and wheezed its last breath. My horoscope had not predicted my day would end this way. But there I was crunching down a barren country road, torn and muddy silk skirts lashing about my ankles under a coat that didn't do the job, and clinging to the arm of a man who hours earlier had been a total stranger.

"Keep going," Sir Galahad muttered through clenched teeth, "we are bound to reach a village or at least a house before the turn of the century."

A tree loomed up — one of its scraggy branches reached out to claw my cheek. It was all too much. I was finished — a broken woman.

"Light ahead!" shouted Ben. He went into a wild war whoop that nearly knocked me over, but this was no time to pick an argument. To our right I saw the house emerge like a dark apparition with blinking yellow eyes. Involuntarily I turned, and Ben's arm moved around me in the embrace of comrades who together have come through direst peril.

"Let's go, Ellie!" He squeezed my hand and we ploughed on, arriving within minutes at a pair of drunken iron gates.

"Civilization!" he yelped.

"Better than that," I said. "A pair of homing pigeons couldn't have done better. This is Merlin's Court."

CHAPTER FOUR

"One would think," grumbled Ben, "that a house this size could afford the luxury of a doorbell."

"Patience! Uncle Merlin's grandfather — builder of this mediaeval fantasy — disliked the obvious." I came squelching up behind him across the narrow moat bridge, feeling like a deep-sea diver trying to retrieve his land legs. "Somewhere to the left of you is a gargoyle. He's the knocker."

"This? I thought the house was sprouting fungus! What do I do? Belt him one?"

"Moron! You yank his tongue out and watch his eyes roll round."

Ben grimaced and did as he was told. We stood huddled on the step, stamping our feet, listening to the unholy din clamouring inside the house, like a shower of falling crockery.

"Who's out there?" queried a distrustful voice from beyond the door.

"Aunt Sybil? It's me, Ellie!"

"You go first," said Ben at his most gentlemanly. "Then if something dark and rubbery hits you over the head, I can run for help."

A bolt creaked and a wedge of pale light gradually widened. "My dear! We had quite given up expecting you.

Merlin went up to bed an hour ago." Aunt Sybil peered short-sightedly out into the night. "And this must be your gentleman friend. Come in, come in, before that wind takes off the door. My gracious! You look . . ."

"Please" — Ben extended a hand to my bewildered great-aunt — "don't put it into words. Ellie and I both know we look like visiting vampires." We were now in the hall, a shadowy cavern lit by a couple of bilious, wall-mounted gas lamps which threw into ghastly relief a pair of moth-eaten fox heads grinning hungrily at us.

"Dear, oh dearie me." Aunt Sybil gave me one of her slack kisses. "A hot bath for each of you would seem best, but we are having trouble with the boiler. Old Jonas, the gardener, who is supposed to see to such matters, is a little poorly at present. A nuisance, but then every cloud . . . we might have had him planting himself, muddy boots and all, in the drawing room, just like one of the family. Doesn't know his place and Merlin is too soft with him. Now let's see, do either of you need to go upstairs" — she paused delicately — "or would you prefer coming straight to the drawing room fire?"

Remembering, despite the years since I had visited, the ghastly chill of the upper regions, I voted for instant warmth.

"Good idea," agreed Ben, removing his coat and adding it with mine to the tumbled array atop the trestle table. "I think I am beginning to mildew."

"Merlin will be so disappointed to have missed your arrival." Aunt Sybil went ahead of us. From the rear she looked rather like a small disapproving rhinoceros, her dark silk dress riding up over her rump in a concertina of wrinkles. Bad weather was no excuse for unpunctuality with Aunt Sybil.

When I was a child the drawing room had always reminded me of a funeral parlour. Time had not improved it. Here, as in the hall, the lighting flickered dimly, produced by one gas lamp and a scattering of candles. Dark, cumbersome furniture crowded every patch of floor space. A nicely morbid addition was the picture over the mantel — a young maiden on her deathbed, lips serenely smiling, a rose clasped in one waxen hand while the Greek chorus sobbed in the background. My relations were arranged in a semicircle before the fireplace looking for all the world like players in a Victorian melodrama. But that was the wrong way round. They were the audience — Ben and I the actors.

"Good gracious, Ellie!" snorted Aunt Astrid, as stiff-necked as her boned taffeta blouse. "What have you done to yourself?"

"Looks like a very large drowned rat," supplied Freddy unimaginatively. He should talk. Leaning up against the mantelpiece, he could easily have been mistaken for a dirty floor mop except for the gold skull and crossbones puncturing his ear.

I decided to cut corners. "Okay!" I said, yanking Ben into the middle of the room. "So I'm soaked through and, unfortunately, I did not shrink in the wash. Now can we all say hallo nicely?"

"Must you be so belligerent, darling!" Vanessa uncoiled herself like a skein of silk from the chair closest to the fire and fixed her luminous topaz eyes on Ben, who I am ashamed to say was grinning foolishly. "Aren't you going to introduce us to your delightful friend?" she pouted. "Or am I jumping to conclusions? Even wringing wet, he doesn't seem your usual type, Ellie dear."

As the only man with whom Vanessa had previously seen me was a porter at Charing Cross Station, I decided to maintain a dignified silence. Let Ben introduce himself. He was quite happy to do the talking. Shaking hands all round, he agreed that the weather was shocking and then, like the pendulum of his namesake, swung back to my lovely and unprincipled cousin. Ben would have to be reminded at a very early date that chatting up the enemy was not in his contract.

My rescuer was bland, paunchy Uncle Maurice. He reached for a decanter of port and poured some into a rather grimy glass, wondering in his rather booming voice whether it had been two years or three since he had last seen me. I wasn't paying attention. The man from E.E. was embarking on a witty account of our journey, in which I did not figure strongly. Vanessa has a sneaky habit of being a superb listener when a man is doing the talking.

The fire, like a tired old volcano, belched forth more smoke than heat. But standing as close to it as he was, Ben's trouser legs were beginning to steam, and from the smouldering light in his eyes, so were his thoughts. Aunt Sybil murmured something a little harried about roast beef sandwiches and tea, and took off for the kitchen — not quite closing the door behind her.

"That draught" — Aunt Astrid winced — "will be the death of me."

"Oh, come now, Auntie!" Freddy had shrunk down into a crouching position and was bouncing off the soles of his feet. "If your sciatica, lumbago, heartburn, and other assorted ailments have not finished you off yet, a little chill won't do the trick. Didn't Mum say something last month about your having a nasty case of piles?"

"Must you be so vulgar!" Aunt Astrid drew herself up in fury.

"Sorry, Auntie! Should have known you wouldn't take that one sitting down," Freddy replied cheerily, while pulling at the tufts of his beard with both hands.

"For heaven's sake, Frederick," snapped Uncle Maurice, "stop tweaking yourself. One would think you were moulting. And if it is not too much to ask, either stand up or sit down properly. Stop bobbing about like a jack-in-the-box! You make me feel seasick."

Freddy did stand up but remained unrepentant. He gave me a playful poke in the middle. "Ever tried losing weight, Ellie?"

"Ever tried finding a job, Freddy?"

He looked reproachful. "*Certainement!* But employers are never prepared to meet my conditions — that I work from twelve to one with an hour for lunch."

"What a great grief your son and heir must be to you, Maurice, and our poor Lulu," interjected Aunt Astrid bitingly.

"Speaking of the fond mother," I said, looking round, "where is Aunt Lulu?"

"Upstairs, chasing bedbugs around her room to relieve the tension. The old girl's in a bit of a state." Freddy rolled his eyes and thumped a resounding fist against his chest. "As you might guess, it's all my fault. Vanessa has shown me up again, may her teeth rot! There she goes telling your boy friend all about her current success. Mother just couldn't take it."

"Lulu went up to bed with a migraine," bristled Uncle Maurice. But no one paid him any attention.

"What's the scoop, Vanessa?" My voice was supposed to portray inviting curiosity, but I am not much of an actress. Didn't anyone want to hear that I had recently designed a Danish sunroom for Mrs Hermione Boggsworth-Smith?

"Oh, Mummy, why did you go and tell them! You know I hate all this fuss." The beautiful hypocrite sank down on the arm of the sofa. Lifting her lovely supple arms above her head, she ran long slim fingers through the heavy waves of chestnut hair in a gesture both tentative and beguiling.

"Liar." Freddy cheerily spoke my thought out loud.

Aunt Astrid and (worse) Ben were both eying Vanessa with the besotted adulation properly reserved for little gold idols and fatted calves. Speaking of cattle, where were those roast beef sandwiches?

"Vanessa," intoned Aunt Astrid reverently, "has been formally asked to model for Felini Senghini."

"Who?" I croaked over Freddy's guffaw.

Ben's appalled expression informed me he considered me public embarrassment number one. "Ellie, you must be joking! Everyone has heard of Felini Senghini!"

"I never joke on an empty stomach." My voice rose dangerously, but reminding myself that this man was supposedly my sweetheart, I put my arm possessively through his and bared my teeth in a friendly smile. "Is he the man with the olive oil complexion whose face is on the box of spaghetti?" I asked hopefully. "No, I've got it! He's the opera star who brought down the house singing *Figaro* wearing only his moustache and a bowtie."

Like her heroine, Queen Victoria, Aunt Astrid was not amused. Nobody made cracks about Vanessa and her career.

"I realize it must be difficult for you, Ellie, having a cousin like Vanessa," she grated, looking above my head, "but spitefulness is never becoming."

Freddy winked at me. "I like Ellie when she's feisty. What is unbecoming is that frightful purple get-up. Looks like you just escaped from a harem, or did the sheikh run first?"

Aunt Astrid was talking over us. "Felini Senghini is considered by people in the know to be the couturier of this century."

"Ellie, dear," mewed Vanessa, "aren't you going to congratulate me?"

I was spared this fate worse than death by the arrival of Aunt Sybil with the supper tray. Finding a vacant spot to set it down took a little ingenuity. Ben came to the rescue, clearing a space on the buffet between two brass candlesticks and a tarnished silver bowl filled with hair clips, sugar cubes, and a knot of grey wool.

"What's up with you?" he breathed in my ear. "I'm beginning to enjoy myself."

"Don't get in the habit," I replied through clenched lips.

"Meaning?"

"Meaning — if you don't stop cuddling up to Vanessa you can kiss your pay cheque goodbye."

Ben had the audacity to look surprised. Before he could reply Freddy crept up behind us. "Let's talk about you two, all the gory details — where you met, etc."

Ben and I watched each other, momentarily united in an uneasy truce. "Where was it, Ellie?" mumbled my conspirator through a mouthful of stale sandwich. "We've known each other . . . a while, and with everything else . . . the details rather . . ."

And the man considered himself a creative genius!

"Singles club?" suggested Freddy.

I trod down hard on Ben's foot to let him know he could safely leave the story-telling to me. His subsequent gasp might have been from relief or agony, but his eyes were a little glazed when I looked soulfully up into them. For added reassurance I gave his hand a tender squeeze, which produced a silent *ouch* and a flash of white teeth, hastily converted into a beaming smile for Freddy's benefit.

"Ben really doesn't have amnesia on the subject," I said, "but our meeting came under rather unhappy circumstances. We met at a rally, protesting cruelty to children outside the Hallelujah Revival Chapel."

"Met at church!" Aunt Sybil handed me a jug of lukewarm water to heat up the coffee pot. "How very nice. Such a change from all those discos and swingles places. What denomination are you, Mr Handel?"

"*Haskell.* A confirmed ath . . ."

"Every child should be confirmed," intruded Aunt Astrid portentously letting Ben know he had won no points with her. "Why can't everyone be Church of England? What's good enough for Her Majesty is certainly good enough for me!"

I carefully avoided looking at Ben. "Aunt Sybil," I asked, "when will we see Uncle Merlin?"

"Probably not until tomorrow evening." Aunt Sybil was trying to hand three people coffee at once. "You young people must remember that poor Merlin is not growing any younger."

"That's not exactly unusual," murmured Freddy.

Fortunately, Aunt Sybil did not catch this rude aside. She continued, "Mornings bother him. He says the light hurts his eyes."

"Turning into Dracula, is he?" quipped my incorrigible cousin. He and Ben grinned at each other like a pair of delinquent schoolboys.

"Is that the explanation for all this subdued lighting?" Uncle Maurice was pacing ponderously up and down on the worn hearthrug, hands clasped behind his back.

"I am sorry you find the gas lighting oppressive." Aunt Sybil looked deeply wounded as she joined the group that had recircled the hearthrug.

Ben offered her his most charming smile. "Has a fuse blown? In a house of this age, so isolated, and with a snow-storm, I'd be surprised if one hadn't gone."

"Thank you for your concern, Mr Hamlet. But we are not suffering from any electrical deficiency. As I said, Merlin does not care for bright lights; but his motive for not using electricity on this floor is purely selfless. He may live somewhat removed from the world, but he does read the newspapers — not those dreadful scandal sheets trumpeting wife-swappers and sex-change operations, but *The Times* and the *Telegraph*. And Merlin feels that he must make a contribution to the energy crisis."

"Balderdash!" roared Uncle Maurice.

"I disagree." Ben turned and regarded him coldly. "I think the man is to be respected."

"Self-sacrifice is all very well," chimed in Aunt Astrid as though hers would necessarily be the last word on the subject, "so long as it does not become fanatical. While rocket ships are whizzing back and forth like long-distance lorries, I hope no one will have the temerity to ask me to give up the necessities becoming a gentlewoman."

"Don't worry, Auntie," consoled Freddy, "the days of the outside lavatory are long gone."

"Must everyone keep complaining?" Vanessa spoke for the first time in a while. (No doubt it takes a lot of concentrated effort to look gorgeous for hours on end.) "I thought we were all going to have such a heavenly weekend together." Moistening her dewy lips, she tilted her eyelashes alluringly up at Ben.

"I'm not complaining," I said sourly. "The dim lighting doesn't bother me. In fact, I like it."

"Naturally!" purred Vanessa. "We can only see half of you."

Silence thickened the air, and something dark and sinister took possession of my brain. "Really? That must be why Ben said he couldn't get enough of me that moonlit night when he proposed. Oh, I'm sorry, darling." I turned to my new fiancé with a deprecating lowering of my stunted lashes. "I know we meant to wait until Uncle Merlin was here before we broke our ecstatic news but I just couldn't resist. Isn't anyone going to congratulate us?"

"You're getting married?" intoned Aunt Astrid as if I had single-handedly turned a sacrament into an obscenity. The rest of the tableau had frozen. The relations all looked marvellously funny with their mouths hanging open. I wanted to laugh until I saw Ben's face. What a shame he wasn't enjoying himself. It's not every day that a man gets a new fiancée, without even asking.

"Well, this is very nice," said Aunt Sybil. "Not that I was ever that anxious to get married myself, but things are so much easier these days of course with divorce so readily available. Now we are all tired, so goodnight. Each of you must take a candle to light your way upstairs. You will find a light switch to the right when you reach the landing. I will see you all in the morning."

"Class dismissed!" whispered Freddy, reaching for the biggest candle. Force of habit, no doubt; as a child he had always grabbed for the cake with the cherry on top. The one I wanted. At the door I turned to see if Ben was following me ready to commit murder the moment we were happily alone, but he was saying a prolonged goodnight to Vanessa. If their candles got any closer they would both go up in smoke. To a vague murmur of belated congratulations I went disconsolately out into the hall and bumped smack into Uncle Maurice, who had been lurking by the stairs waiting for a word with me. He set our candles down on a small marble table and clasped my hands in his moist spongy ones. His face was very close to mine. I could smell his hair cream and his breath hot and heavy with port.

"Ellie, my dear," he said, "forgive an old buffer collaring you like this, but with your father chasing sheep in the Outback, I feel you need the advice and affection of a mature man of the world. Is this sudden engagement wise? A woman with your outstanding qualities could do rather better than your Mr Haskell. Something about that fellow I don't trust. A touch of the Arab there I would say."

"Come now, Uncle, what do you think he is going to do? Drop his candle and burn the house down so he can buy up the land cheap?" Ben was a shallow creature given over to the lure of Vanessa's flesh but one of us had to be loyal to our relationship.

"Now, now, Ellie." Uncle Maurice squeezed my hands again and chuckled reprovingly, a twinkle appearing in his bulging eyes. "Don't you think, my dear, you could call me Maurice? At my age, 'Uncle' makes a chap feel old. Besides, it is only a courtesy title. Our relationship is really quite distant. What was your mother to Merlin, a second cousin?"

"Something like that," I said, wondering how soon I could make my getaway. Uncle Maurice seemed to be having a little trouble breathing.

"Ellie," he wheezed, moving closer still. I could feel his waistcoat buttons pressing through the purple silk. "Some of my friends call me Maury, you know."

Before I could respond with "Oh really!" the drawing room door opened and Ben came out with Vanessa hanging onto his sleeve. Rather shamefacedly, he drew away from her.

"There you are, darling," I said. "Were you telling Vanessa that I want her to be my bridesmaid?"

My cousin paled and Uncle Maurice dropped my hands, backing towards the stairs. With a little less than his usual aplomb he picked up his candle and bade us goodnight. Vanessa trailed gracefully after him up the stairs.

When they had gone Ben said, "Don't glare at me. I had to be polite to the girl, didn't I? Mrs Swabucher's instructions were that I enchant your relations with my suavity. What she didn't advise me was that I was going to be trapped into an engagement."

"Oh, don't worry." I shrugged. "It doesn't have to be consummated."

"Nothing connected with marriage is funny."

"Fiddle! No one is going to handcuff you to the altar. This is an innocent pretence. Besides, you brought this on yourself salivating every time you looked at Vanessa. Not part of our deal."

"Do you know what you are?" Ben gave the tail of his tie a jerk which threatened to strangle him. His face was dangerously red. "You are trouble! I knew that the minute I first saw you looking like a typhoon in that purple shroud, and you have been nothing but a nightmare ever since. I wouldn't put it past you to sue me for breach of promise when I break off our fictitious engagement."

"You're not worth it." I made for the stairs. "You don't have any money to tempt me."

"Know something else," he said from behind me. "I don't understand why this farce is necessary. Other than having a fantastic face and figure, your cousin Vanessa is a zero. Talk about bored to yawns back there. While she was talking to me all I could think about was my bed."

"I'll bet," I said.

"Goodnight, my dears," called Aunt Sybil from below with what I am sure she hoped was gentle finality. She had told me where we would be sleeping so I was able to inform Ben that his room was the last but one on the left. "Not the last one," I warned him. "That is the dumb-waiter. Years ago it was used to bring up meals from the kitchen."

"There's a place I wouldn't care to visit." Ben shuddered. "After the grub we were served tonight, I picture cobwebs on the ceiling, slime on the walls, and the butler floating face down in a vat of beef tea."

"Ridiculous! He was pensioned off years ago. Either Uncle Merlin refuses to spend the money for servants or they are afraid to work here." If I had hoped for a lingering goodnight at my door, I was doomed to disappointment. Ben gave me a soldierly pat on the shoulder, informed me he was not an early riser, and disappeared down the corridor.

My bedroom was not a cheerful place. It seemed to be suffering from a bad case of the ague, the walls sweating patchily through mould-coloured wallpaper. The coverings on the great four-poster bed stank of age and the irritable little fire hissed and stuttered in the grate but did nothing to drive back the chill. Thank goodness I had possessed the foresight to pack my woollen jammies with the feet. This thought cheered me until I remembered they were securely packed away in my suitcase, which was still sitting in Ben's car.

Shuddering, I stripped down to my bra and undies, spread the purple monster over a chair — strategically placed to waylay any chance bursts of warmth from that sullen fire — and crawled like a skinned polar bear under the flea-ridden blankets. I was able to reach the light switch from the bed. The room shrank into darkness, but sleep like a spry old elf pranced just out of reach. I was afraid to stretch out my legs full length in case something soft and furry was nesting in the bed. The events of the day jostled and elbowed their way into my head, but out of the chaos came one realization: Though Ben had totally failed to live up to my expectations of the way a man from E.E. should conduct himself, five minutes into our first squabble I had felt completely at ease with him. Instead of counting sheep I played my favourite fantasy game, What if? What if I were painfully, emaciatedly thin, with a soul above cream cakes and Yorkshire pudding and big airy dumplings simmered in thick rich gravy? Oh hell! Given that luscious spread, who needed men!

A soft footfall sounded outside my door. The handle turned with a grunt. Ben? I could eat tomorrow; food was always available while . . . He was padding across the floor. A thump and a muffled yelp told me he had met the tallboy head on. My heart was slamming against my ribs and my temperature kept going up and down like a department store lift. "Scream," said the inner voice of decency and common sense. "So you can die not knowing?" asked its sparring partner. His hand was on the bedspread, an inch away from my exposed flesh. The sheet was lifting. I felt a pyjamaed leg rub briefly against mine. And it was all over. My hand found the light switch and the room blinked back to life.

I turned to spear Ben with my accusing, righteous (but grateful) eye.

"Uncle Maurice?" I quailed, yanking the blankets up around my neck. "Please explain yourself! You've got to the count of ten and then I start screaming."

CHAPTER FIVE

I should have known that the only man to come creeping into my room in the dead of night would be a lost soul returning from the bathroom. Uncle Maurice, looking quite ridiculous in lavender flannel pyjamas, apologized profusely for the intrusion and begged me not to mention the incident to Aunt Lulu. She would be most upset if she knew he had barged in on me and disturbed my rest. I swore that my lips were sealed and turned off the light. Now to try and sleep.

A noise awoke me, a threatening growling that jerked me upright, bleary-eyed and not at all in the mood for receiving midnight marauders. Another false alarm: The racket was only my growling stomach reminding me it was time for my favourite date — the two of us alone together — me and food. I tried to be strong. I reminded myself it would be more than greedy, it would be sneaky, to trek downstairs at two o'clock in the morning and invade Aunt Sybil's kitchen. My nose began to itch. Dust! Did Aunt Sybil never flick a duster, air a blanket, cook a decent meal? Resentment built. Those measly sandwiches! And stale, too! What a meal to serve people staggering in from the clutches of a raging blizzard! Besides, Freddy and Ben had scoffed most of them! Thumping my pillow with a fierce hand, I savoured my wrath. If Auntie couldn't cook, what was wrong with her buying a few sausage rolls from the baker's, and perhaps some Cornish pasties? My stomach was either applauding or cursing. Obviously it had decided to keep me up all night.

Moonlight reflecting off the snow cast a spiral of light into the otherwise darkened room. The illumination was sufficient for me to be able to read the face of my watch. Two-thirty. Hours before breakfast, and I did not have high hopes for that meal. Lumpy porridge and cold tea were not adequate sustenance for a growing girl. Climbing out of bed, I stood shivering as the chill air hit me. The fire had petered out and I was not surprised to discover that the purple horror was still more wet than damp. What was I to wear? Descending the hall stairs in my undies was out. There could be no greater anguish than being caught by Ben in my midriff bra and lace-up corset. Bumbling around in the moonlight, I managed to find the wardrobe. The inside stank of mothballs and old newspapers, but it contained no cast-off clothing other than a pair of button-shoes and a feather hat, which I mistook for a dead bird. Not much cover-up there. My hand found a shelf to one side and its search was rewarded. Under a furring of dust lay what proved to be a bedspread. It felt like chenille and, luckily, it seemed to be a double size.

Inching my door open, I peered out onto the landing. Several windows, particularly a huge stained-glass one at the top of the stairs, provided ominous shadows that crept along the walls. Only the promise of hot buttered toast and a decent cup of tea prodded me forward. One of those heartening theories about heavy people is that they are light on their feet, and I sincerely hoped it was true. I had crossed the narrow strip of carpeting and now had to deal with the stairs. My toga slipped and I tucked it back together. I felt like a liner being launched into shallow water. Steady as she goes!

The kitchen door swung inward with a slight shudder and I found the light switch at the first reach. The bulb was weak and the illumination it threw poor. Depressing as was the rest of the house, the kitchen was worse. Dingy grey linoleum and salmon-pink walls. They were not helped by the hunched assortment of cupboards, from which most of the paint and several of the doors were missing. The maze of tarnished copper piping extending up the walls from the rusty old-fashioned boiler was strung with greasy floor-cloths and stained dish-towels. Did Aunt Sybil sometimes confuse the two? Anyone with minimal housewifely instincts would have been revolted. I also looked at the room with a professional eye. Size and shape of the kitchen were both good, the windows large and facing south. Under that disgusting lino was probably a stone or brick floor. Already I was picturing it as it might be, with a navy blue Aga cooker, copper pans burnished to a warm glow, lots of greenery replacing the curtains, and a creamy wallpaper accented with navy and coral.

The vision faded and I was left staring at dirty crockery stacked precariously on the table, draining board, and other available surfaces. No wonder Uncle Merlin wanted the lights kept low.

I am not in favour of mandatory sterilization for all homes. Tobias had shredded my couch, and sometimes I did not make my bed for a week. But this filth was unbearable. The boiler, bless it, was still hot. After a valiant search among the cobwebs under the sink, I found a limp cardboard box that contained a slightly damp tin of cleanser, and a box of soap powder. They would have to do. Washing-up liquid was obviously not down on Aunt Sybil's list of life's necessities. Hoisting up the bedspread, I tied it in a knobby knot at the back of my neck, dared it to fall down, and started heaving refuse out of the sink.

Two hours later the dishes were washed, dried, and stacked as evenly as possible in the cupboards. The table had responded fairly well to scrubbing. Half the paint had peeled off the top, but what was underneath looked clean. Filling a pail with hot water, I poured in a bottle of bleach (so old the top had corroded), gingerly pried the cloths off the pipes, and watched them sink into the fumes.

Stifling a yawn, I opened and closed my eyes rapidly a few times to remind them I was still awake. How could I explain my interference to Aunt Sybil? Perhaps she would think the fairies had come. Biting down on another yawn, I filled the kettle, set it on the newly wiped cooker, and lit the gas. At last I was free to open the magic door.

The pantry was another room which should have exuded old-fashioned charm. Its marble shelves were built for hams and cheeses, pork pies and jellies. It should have sent forth an aroma rich in the promise of culinary delights. The truth was it stank. The odour of rancid fat mingled with the stench of bad meat and mice droppings. Crumbs were scattered on the shelves and spilt milk had dried to a yellow crust. Other than a half-eaten chicken, a bowl of curdled custard, and a basket of sprouting vegetables, the place looked like Mother Hubbard's — bare.

I found the breadbox. It was metal with a fairly secure lid, so I pulled out a loaf without too much foreboding and went out, closing the door behind me. The kettle was whistling, a high shrill peal which reminded me I still had to find the tea. As if annoyed that I did not come when called, the sound grew deeper, becoming a threatening rumble that set the saucepans bouncing about on the rack above the cooker and the row of cups jangling on their hooks beneath the cupboards. A lot of noise and vibration from one kettle. More like a steam train! I turned off the gas, and the noise went on briefly, then stopped. Thunder? I wondered, but the strip of sky glimpsed through the kitchen window, though flecked with tiny flakes of snow, looked clear enough. The rumpus must have been the hot water tank filling up. Where was that tea caddy?

Back to the pantry. As I opened the door, a slight movement caught my eye. Mice? I hate them, but if I didn't have my cup of . . . A form grew out of the shadows; arms extended, white gown flapping, it came slowly towards me. The ghost of Merlin's Court! My scream turned into a squeak which would have made me the laughing-stock of any mice that might be listening. I could not see the creature's face, but it had a white hood pulled over its head. That was not the worst part. It was laughing, horrible choking gasps of mirth that reduced me to gibbering terror. Any girlish heroine worth her salt would have swooned. I did almost as well; I tripped over the chenille and went down for the count, with the spectre's hollow words ringing in my ears: "By God, it's Aphrodite."

I should, by rights, have wakened to the pungent scent of smelling salts. Such was not my good fortune. Someone had me under the armpits and I was being dragged across the rutted floor, grazing my bottom and scaring me out of what little wits I had left.

"Lord save me, I'd rather drag an ox." Ben! How did he come into this? He certainly was not the pantry ghost. "This will have to do." He was stacking me up against a wall like a sack of flour. "If I try to hoist her into a chair I'll give myself a hernia — a double."

I'll wring his neck! But if I moved my arms the chenille would go completely. The only way to get even would be to report him to E.E. Another voice spoke, a foggy, barking, inhuman voice.

"What do you want from me — sympathy? Said she was your girl, didn't you? A man who takes on a woman twice his size should at least have muscles where his brain is supposed to be. Stop blithering around like a daffodil in the wind and bring her to her senses, if she has any. Douse her down with that pail by the sink. Looks like she's been meddling around in here disrupting the natural disorder. Damned interference."

The bleach! I had always wanted to be a blonde but not by such drastic measures. "Oh no, you don't!" My eyes flew open like a pair of window blinds. I shook myself free from Ben's grasp; flaying out with my fists I had the satisfaction of catching him a good one on the chin. "Fool!" I yelled, scrambling to my feet. "Drop that bucket and we'll have a hole in the floor that goes clear through to Australia." I turned and waved a furious schoolmistress finger at the scraggy figure in white. "Okay, you nasty Wee Willie Winkie, why don't you go off somewhere and chew on your tassel! I may not be a thing of beauty but look at you in that ridiculous headgear!"

Ben had developed a frantic twitch in one eye but I ignored him. I was incapable of thinking clearly, let alone deciphering optical Morse code. "Who the hell do you think you are?" I asked the scrawny spectre. "Leaping uninvited out of pantries in the middle of the night!"

He emitted a mirthless chuckle, baring glossy pink, toothless gums, then hissed out an evil whisper. "Don't you recognize me, my little pudding cheeks, naughty, naughty! You're going to make an old man cry. Great fool! I'm your host, Giselle, your dear, loving uncle Merlin."

"Isn't this chummy," smirked Ben into the raucous silence. "Mr Grantham was telling me while you were in the midst of your swoon that he often feels peckish in the middle of the night, and comes down for a snack by means of the dumb-waiter. I heard your screams of terror through my bedroom floor and came down to investigate, by the rather unimaginative means of the stairs."

"I didn't faint." I glared at them both. "I tripped. Perhaps I passed out later, when my head hit the floor, but that's not the same thing." I gave the chenille an upward tug. "And just suppose I *have* made a great fool of myself. If you had one ounce of decency, Uncle Merlin, you would accept some responsibility. I'm not used to seeing men shuffling around in the gloom of night decked out in white night-shirts and pixie hoods."

"Huh! Not used to seeing men in the middle of the night in *any* guise more like. Unless . . . have you told this London bloke that you are coming in for my money? Bark up another tree, girl! This night-cap keeps the body heat from escaping through the head while sleeping. Can't afford those electrical heating gadgets, especially tonight. One of my blood relations might sneak in and jimmy the wires."

"About that nocturnal snack," suggested Ben, over inspecting the cooker, "Mr Grantham, would you like me to whip you up a little something? Eggs Benedict, perhaps?"

"Ah, now I see it," wheezed dear old Uncle. "You're one of those, are you? Meet a lot of butterfly boys, do you, Ellie, in the decorating business?"

What a detestable sick-minded old man. I made a move for the door then thought better of retreat. I wasn't going to leave him gloating over his victory. "Do you know something? I think it's a good thing you have stayed holed up here all these years. The outside world is too good for you."

Uncle Merlin was seated in a chair and didn't move. For one rather scary moment I thought I had shocked him to death, and then I saw a flicker of icy amusement burning behind his hooded eyes.

"If you aren't divinely enthusiastic about eggs" — Ben outrageously fluttered his eyelashes at Uncle Merlin — "perhaps something a little more titillating, shall we say a nice little dish of curds and whey?" He added in his normal voice, "One way to get rid of all your damn spiders."

"Real men," barked Uncle Merlin, "don't eat gussied-up eggs and such for breakfast. We like our kippers. Follow your nose and you'll find a newspaper package in the drawer to the right of the sink. That's right, under the tea cloths. Hid it from Sybil. Those kippers were for Jonas and me. Friday nights we always play cards when she's safely in bed and can't look down her disapproving nose at us. Sybil doesn't mind gambling — gentlemen's activity — but she doesn't approve of my consorting with servants. Huh! If I thought of Jonas that way I would have pensioned him off donkey's years ago. I like the way he cheats at cards. Drat the old fool for getting himself laid up. Who wants his fish? Mine's the big one."

"As you have decreed kippers as men's food, Uncle, I think I will pop two slices of bread into this toaster that looks like a rat trap, in they go, take a cup of that tea Ben is brewing, and retire upstairs with a tray."

"What, and leave me at the mercy of this young thug? Upon your conscience, if you come down in the morning and find me with a meat skewer plunged through my heart! Where did she pick you up anyway, young feller? One of those desperate heart places. And what do you do, besides dangle a frying pan from your pretty little wrist?"

"He writes books." Furiously I scraped butter off a chipped saucer and smeared it over my toast. "Deliciously dirty ones, filthy actually, but not as filthy as this kitchen before I cleaned it up. Goodnight, Uncle dear, and don't choke on a bone just to please me."

* * *

Breakfast the following morning was atrocious. Thankfully Aunt Sybil was not present to hear the comments the meal aroused. She had brought in the food and was now taking a tray up to Uncle Merlin. Freddy sat stirring his porridge in circles like a child waiting for Mummy to say "one two three, all gone." Dropping his spoon, he muttered, "Either someone has already been very ill in my bowl or I am about to be."

My sentiments exactly. This was one meal I could forego, particularly as Aunt Lulu, her head a foam of soapy-looking curls, having just heard about The Engagement, was prodding a sullen-looking Ben for details. Lack of sleep had not improved his disposition. Excusing myself, I returned to my room where I found my suitcase sitting on a chest under the window. Ben had told me that he and Freddy had been out early and resuscitated the car, which was now drawn up against the wall of the old stable.

A diet even when unintentional should be accompanied by exercise. I would go for a walk in the snow. Off came the purple horror and I was happily reunited with my camel skirt, grey jersey, and serviceable brogues, woolly coat, and head-scarf. The mirror informed me I looked like someone's faithful old daily. Better that than a carnival bouncer. I consigned purple to the litter bin.

I had forgotten how close Merlin's Court was to the sea. The slapping surging rhythm of waves blended with the wind which bullied me along, wrapping my coat around my legs so tightly that walking became difficult. Certainly I had made a mess of my life, but I had no burning desire to end it by being blown off the cliff and dashed to powder on the jagged rocks below. I was turning to retrace my steps when I saw through the snow blowing off the trees, the bent figure of a man stumbling towards me, a dark scarf muffling his nose and mouth and a hat pulled down over his ears. This had to be the gardener — Jonas. Wasn't that his name? My efforts at walking were reduced to an exaggerated swagger, but I covered the ground as steadily as I could. As our paths met, the old man raised his battered hat, made a ducking motion of his head, and said, "Morning to you, miss," wheezed a short hacking cough and started to move on.

"Nasty day to be out," I said. "And you with a cold."

He squinted at me. "I've heard tell a good frost kills germs. But Mr Merlin, he'll not be out on a day like this. Might catch his death o' pneumony, and he's not one what likes to see others happy. Miss Giselle, that be you, ain't it? Aye, I know all the ins and outs o' the lot o' ye. Next to cheating at cards him likes a chin-wag about what 'e calls the maggots in the family pie. He! He! All came out at once, didn't ye? He weren't so sure about ye, but I bet him a quid ye'd be here. Brought a feller, too, is what I hear. A pornographist an' all! A nice clean-cut spinster like you!"

"We're engaged," I snarled, and battled my way back to the house. Aunt Sybil was in the kitchen when I went in by the side door. She was draping very holey dishcloths over the piping and did not look thrilled to see me. Probably afraid I would muddy the floor.

"I met the gardener," I said.

"Him! Lives at the cottage just inside the gates. Cliffside, it's called." She sniffed, maybe the bleach fumes from those cloths were opening up her sinuses. "You may not have noticed it last night with the weather so bad. Why Merlin keeps Jonas on, I don't know. Always ailing. But that's men for you — never happy unless they've something to moan about. Merlin's a different story, of course." Her bleach-wrinkled hands migrated to her hair, moving a strand.

"Jonas's cough sounded real enough and he was out and about." I shook myself out of my coat.

"Drawing attention to himself. And if it were not a cold it would be something else. Last summer it was waterworks trouble and before that varicose veins. Not a weed pulled in the garden, except to make up some home remedy potion, and Merlin insisting I fetch Jonas hot drinks of the stuff, morning, noon, and night." Her jowls quivered. "As if I don't have enough to do without pandering to hypochondriac servants. Oh, I know we have our duty to the lower classes — and if Jonas were the butler, something clean at least, I wouldn't mind so much."

What a dreadful snob. But I was wondering, behind the mask of evil recluse did Uncle Merlin have one or two salient qualities? At least he treated everyone with equal contempt and he seemed to care about Jonas. Or was that just because the man was a necessary amusement? "Uncle Merlin must appreciate his own health being good," I suggested.

Aunt Sybil fixed me with a look which said, "That's all you know." She made a great show of peeling potatoes. Skin flew in all directions under the onslaught of her knife. No one but she knew how Uncle Merlin liked his vegetables and my offer of help was firmly refused.

"Poor dear, he's lonely," she said. "He and Jonas are as thick as soup, always got their heads together over a crossword or cards and I worry because" — she fixed me with vague watery eyes — "besides the class thing, I don't feel Jonas is the best influence on Merlin, gets him to laughing and acting quite silly sometimes. So unsuitable. His father, dear Uncle Arthur, never said anything more than fetch and carry to the servants. But I have so little time for sitting, with trying to keep this house in shape and, as they say, this is a new generation."

Uncle Merlin part of the in crowd? Subject to peer pressure?

"Jonas looked pretty harmless," I said.

Aunt Sybil sniffed and continued slashing away with her knife.

Luncheon was another of life's experiences best forgotten, memorable only because I lost pounds. Vanessa was more poutingly adorable than ever, my fiancé sullen, and Uncle Merlin did not grace us with his presence. We were informed by Aunt Sybil, as though bestowing a great treat, that he would be down for tea.

Late afternoon moved into twilight. At the stroke of four from the grandfather clock in the hall, the relations assumed their positions.

Aunt Sybil hovered by the door like an enthralled fan waiting outside the theatre for her idol to appear. Slow muffled footsteps sounded in the hall. "Here he is," she cried. "My dear Merlin, I wouldn't let them start tea without you. We have all been waiting."

"I'll bet you have." Uncle Merlin's voice was strong though he leaned heavily on Aunt Sybil, a grey shadowy figure in the half-light. "Pack of vultures, the lot of you," he snorted venomously. "Swooping down to pick the flesh off my withered bones, but I'll fool you, every last one. I'm not dead yet, and we'll see who has the last laugh."

"Wicked old man," said Aunt Astrid, almost choking as she tugged at her pearls. "I expect he will leave everything to a cat home. He should be put away."

CHAPTER SIX

Our drive back to London the following afternoon was chilly; the weather was cool as well. Ben kept dwelling on my announcement of our engagement.

"Oh, stuff it, you pompous little prig." I'd had enough. My eyes were watering with cold and my left leg was in a coma. "What you resent is having Vanessa think you are desperate enough to settle for me. Don't worry, she won't think we are sleeping together. I told her you were impotent, a childhood mishap. When she learned you were half-Jewish she was easily convinced. Circumcision sounds like a simple operation, but the knife must slip sometimes. . . ."

"Hell, Ellie." Ben skidded neatly round a curve. "You're impossible, but I wouldn't have missed meeting you for anything. I almost hate taking your money."

"You'll manage. In what manner would you like me to terminate our engagement? Will a formal notice in *The Times* be sufficient?"

Ben grinned. "I can tell what kind of books you read. My mother reads the same drivel." His voice sank to a growl. "My dearest, we were never meant for one another. . . . I beg that you put me out of your life forever. And remember when you dampen your pillow with your tears, that I was never good enough for you. Somewhere, some day out upon the far horizon . . ."

"What? Another man? And give up the thrill of having my life blighted by hopeless passion? Not on your life. I am going home to my cat and life as a disappointed spinster."

Ben's little car threaded its way tidily through the London traffic. We had made surprisingly good time. I had almost adjusted to the numbness below the knees when Ben skimmed into a tiny slot between two parked cars and flipped off the engine. Back to 129 Queen Alexandra Place.

The interlude was over. I insisted that he not come up with me. We stood on the kerb like a couple of refugees stranded in the desolate wastes of Siberia, hands extended in farewell, the battered suitcase at my feet. We needed music, the poignant anguish of "Lara's Theme."

"Sorry about keeping the top down," said Ben, hands deep in his pockets.

"Not at all. I feel all crisped up, like a fresh lettuce."

"I suffer from claustrophobia."

"Nasty," I said. We stared at each other for those long moments that stretched like elastic until they snap. "Damn it, are you trying to turn this goodbye into a marathon for the *Guinness Book of Records?*"

"Sorry." He sounded huffy. Backs turned, we paced off in different directions. When I looked back he hadn't moved and I imagined he was thinking how funny I looked from the rear — just like Aunt Sybil.

The flat wasn't a bad place to come home to. Tobias greeted me with unusual warmth and a rasp of his rough pink tongue. He even followed me into the bathroom and watched me take a scalding bath from which I emerged gleaming pinkly through a haze of steam. Tobias closed his eyes. "Cut that out," I snapped. Yawning rudely, he disappeared round the door. "Go ahead, turn tail and run, you cad!" I called after him. "So what else is new?"

"Anyone home?"

Jill! She had the most unnerving habit of appearing out of nowhere. I should never have given her my spare key. Even my mirror hadn't seen me stripped to the buff for years so I wasn't giving anything human the chance. Grabbing a towel, I went out to the sitting room with the intention of telling her I was about to take a nap. But she foiled me by coming as the bearer of gifts. The casserole she carried might be stewed seaweed, but after Aunt Sybil's cooking it would taste like ambrosia.

"You're an angel" — I smiled — "and a dear friend. Put that down and I'll get the kettle going."

"A new recipe. Tuna and peanut butter fricassee."

I should have stayed at Merlin's Court.

* * *

Work helped. I went in early and stayed late. One of my most demanding clients, Lady Violet Witherspoon, was going through a midlife crisis that found relief in redecorating her cottage on the Norfolk Broads from top to bottom every six months.

After posting my cheque to E.E. I told myself that I was finished with Mr Bentley T. Haskell, but the man was unprincipled. He kept popping into my head with much the same impudent abandon with which Jill came tripping into my flat. During the day I was able to keep him at bay, but at night when I closed my eyes there he was, the rogue — turning on the charm. He was crazy about my hair, my eyes, my ears. "Such skinny little ears," he would whisper, his breath warm upon my neck, and I would melt with delight.

What a blessing, I would say in the cold light of day, that he is such an impossible man or I might have been upset at the prospect of never hearing from him again.

To prove how indifferent I was, I had the telephone reinstalled. Spending money was one way of keeping busy. On one of my empty Saturdays I went into the West End and bought a royal blue dressing gown and had Uncle Merlin's initials monogrammed on the pocket. His response was a curt note by Aunt Sybil saying I should have better things to do with my money than waste it on fripperies when I was about to be married.

"Ungrateful old." Unfortunately I was not done with my relatives. Vanessa rang. She knew I would be ecstatic to learn she had won another fabulous modelling assignment, and why had she not seen an announcement of my marriage in *The Times?*

That telephone call clinched my need to escape the pressures of life in the big city. The next morning I invited Lady Witherspoon to the showroom and suggested that her new drawing room might benefit from the Italian influence. Would she like me to make some purchases for the room? In Rome?

Dabbing her moist eyes with a lace handkerchief, she breathed, "And to think one's acquaintances are always complaining about slackness among the work force."

Professional integrity would not permit me to accept Lady Witherspoon's offer to defray all expenses, but her cheque — for which I put in many hours casing the fabric houses — did permit me to travel in more style than usual. Once arrived in that city of fabulous antiquity and sunshine, I settled into a small but charming hotel where the view was excellent and every meal a sonnet. With so many double chins bobbing over their fettuccine Alfredo, I began to feel that my proportions were quite reasonable and ordered thirds without a pang. What was even better, Ben slipped back where he belonged, within the pages of paperback romance, chapter — and book — closed. With only the merest tinge of regret — a girl likes to have her memories — I put the book on a high shelf in some inner corner of my mind and let it gather cobwebs. I called the airline and was on my way home.

London in early April was wet and grisly, the pavements dark and slick. The tall narrow house on Queen Alexandra Place stood hunched and indignant with cold. Grabbing his tip with fingers poking through the holey fingers of his knitted gloves, the taxi driver spun off into the fog. Jill was out, but I found Tobias looking well-fed and dapper on the bottom stair. "The one person in the world who really loves me!" I cried, bending to clasp him in a fond embrace. With a curl of his lip, the ungrateful feline lifted his tail, gave it an arrogant flick as if to say, "Don't come crawling back to me, you cat deserter," and marched upstairs.

I respected his grievance. After three weeks of Jill's cooking I might not be speaking either. Fitting my key in the lock, I shoved my suitcase over the threshold with one foot just as the phone rang.

"Have you been wetting on Miss Renshaw's doormat again?" I yelled after Tobias as he scooted into the kitchen. "If I have to listen to any more complaints from that old biddy . . ." I informed his hindquarters. "Hallo," I said, snatching the receiver and speaking in the tones of weary world traveller.

"Ellie, where the devil have you been?" snarled Ben. "I telephoned Jill and she said you were due back two days ago. I got this number from her and . . ."

The colossal cheek of the man coming back to haunt me when I had finally laid his ghost to rest! I cradled the phone in my hands and did an on-the-spot tap dance. He was grinding his teeth, those dear, small pearly teeth that had nibbled my ear in all those banished dreams. . . .

"Look," he said with exaggerated slowness, "I do know the sound of my voice leaves you breathless, but would you come out of your coma for one minute — just long enough for us to hold a rational conversation?"

Rational? I didn't like that word. I stopped tap dancing.

"You lost the cheque?"

"Must you keep harping on about money? I hate to criticize at a time like this, but I find it extremely vulgar. If you ever checked your bank statement, but of course women don't, you would have seen that I never cashed the pittance."

"Back up a minute." I sat down heavily on the arm of the sofa, almost crushing Tobias, who had crept up silently.

Needle-like claws shot into my posterior and I stood up abruptly. "What do you mean, at a time like this?"

Now he was the one to be silent.

Shoving Tobias rudely aside, I sat down again. "Break it to me gently. . . ." My voice came out in the uneven gasps of a ninety-year-old woman running the marathon. "You and Vanessa have been seeing each other on the sly, and now you're getting married?"

"No."

"Oh, well in that case. . . ." I swung poor Tobias over my shoulder and nuzzled my face into his soft warm fur.

"Ellie, I get the crazy feeling that you don't know."

"Mm?" I tickled Tobias under the chin.

"Uncle Merlin's dead."

"He can't be!" I expostulated. "The man is immortal — he predates the flood."

"Obituaries printed in *The Times* do not lie. Look," said Ben, "I'm sorry to be the one to break the news, but I . . ."

"Don't turn this into a Greek tragedy." My voice was muffled by Tobias's fur. "The man was a stranger to me. That weekend was the first time I had seen him for years." I paused to take a deep breath. "And he behaved in the most foul fashion — maybe that is why I felt sorry for him . . . afterwards."

"You're not snivelling, are you?" asked Ben accusingly. "Hang it all, Ellie, you're just like a big slobbering kid. I'm coming over."

"Thanks," I sniffed.

* * *

Persuading Ben to accompany me down to Merlin's Court was not all that difficult. Actually, I think the suggestion was his — after I had encouraged Tobias to be nice to him and had stressed the difficulties of travelling by public transportation. Ben was back in the escort business.

"About that business of our engagement?" We were standing in the hall saying goodnight when I brought up this ticklish subject. "So far I haven't done anything about breaking the news to the family that we are no longer a couple."

"Then we will have to continue the charade." Ben was wrapping a long striped scarf which looked like a souvenir from his schoolboy days around his neck. "We don't want to upstage the funeral by denouncing our relationship as a fraud. But I do expect you to do the right thing and throw me over the minute this family crisis is over, understood?"

"Absolutely! Cross my heart and hope to die." Such light-hearted foolish words.

"I wonder if Merlin shared your sentiments!" said Ben succinctly as he went out the door.

* * *

When we drove through the sagging iron gates up the weed-ridden gravel driveway just before noon the next day, Merlin's Court looked more than ever like an enchanted castle with a curse laid upon it by a belligerent fairy.

Someone had been watching for us. Aunt Sybil met us at the door, dressed in black. Her lips were drawn down at the corners, but her face was otherwise expressionless.

"Auntie, this must be so hard for you." I tried to hug her but she backed away.

"No fuss, dear, please. In Merlin's and my young days, grief was always considered a very private matter." Her broad hand smoothed one of the many ripples in her silk dress, and I thought she looked more like a rhinoceros than ever with her muggy skin and sagging jowls. And then her lips quivered. Poor old girl, with the possible exception of the gardener, she might well be the only friend Merlin ever possessed.

"Was the end very sudden?" I asked, handing Ben my coat so he could add it to the pile of other garments on the trestle table.

"Very. The doctor came in the morning and Merlin was gone in the afternoon. Pneumonia, it was. He went quite peacefully."

"I'm surprised. I would have expected Uncle Merlin to go out cursing the fact that he had been forced to see a doctor for the first time in, what was it, forty years?"

"Forty-five." Aunt Sybil registered restrained pride. "Merlin never was a man who fussed about his health, as I think I told you when you finally managed to come down and see him."

Unjust! This was no time to argue with a bereaved elderly woman, but Uncle Merlin had made his own choice when he marooned himself in this house like a hermit. He had never acknowledged my Christmas cards or shown the least interest in seeing me. Ben interpreted the sparkle in my eyes and silently gestured a memo to stay cool.

The other members of the clan had already gathered in the drawing room and were once more clustered around an inadequate fire.

"Darling, let me see your ring." Vanessa held out her hand for mine like an eager child, but she was looking at the man standing beside me, her delicate winged brows lifted enquiringly.

To give Ben his rather begrudging due, he did rise to the occasion and protect me from the enemy. "Ellie and I have had our share of arguments over an engagement ring," he said smoothly. "She insisted that the money could be put to better, more practical use. What was it you wanted?" He turned toward me and grinned to imply the sharing of an inside joke.

"A battery-operated electric blanket, sweetheart, so we can snuggle up and stay warm on our little jaunts in your car."

"Isn't she a sport," Ben beamed.

The words were not loverlike, but the man was trying. Freddy, who had been lounging on the floor looking shaggier than ever, stood up and made a strangling gesture around his mother's neck. "Lay off, Ma," he said. "That sherry's weak enough without you diluting it with your tears."

"He was too good, too good to live," whimpered Aunt Lulu. "His kind are always the first to go!"

"Don't be ridiculous," snapped Aunt Astrid. "The man was over seventy. He'd been here quite long enough."

"Yeah," agreed Freddy, "cut the cackle, Ma. You'll be singing a different tune a couple of hours from now when the will is read and you discover the old screw didn't leave you the bundle you've been expecting." Freddy swigged down his mother's sherry and reached for the decanter. "I wonder who will get the lolly."

Aunt Astrid drew herself up in her chair. "I wouldn't put it past the old fool to have left everything to charity, but if he had any sense he will have bequeathed his fortune to those who know how to spend it well. Vanessa and I have always appreciated the finer things in life." Aunt Astrid cast a disparaging glance at Freddy and me.

Vanessa twisted a stray curl around a long slim finger. "I'm sure I don't expect a penny," she demurred gently.

Freddy said something very vulgar.

Aunt Astrid rose out of her chair. "How dare you, you disgusting unkempt creature, how dare you insult my beautiful daughter?"

"And how dare you insult my tall, handsome son?" Aunt Lulu banged down her glass on top of a pile of old newspapers littering a fireside table. She seemed to sprout feathers like an angry chicken. "Who do you think you are, Lady Muck? Don't put on airs and graces with me! My mother remembered the day when your father drove a rag-and-bone cart through the streets of Bethnel Green. To hear you talk, he was in textiles! Ha! For all the fancy finishing schools and your la-de-da ways you and that daughter of yours are nothing but a pair of jumped-ups!"

The victims of this onslaught looked staggered, while the rest of us had trouble hiding our enjoyment. Uncle

Maurice made a token protest, but we could all see his heart wasn't in it. "Now, now, my dear. Enough said, don't get yourself het up."

"I will not be quiet!" shouted Aunt Lulu, getting her second wind. "If that woman had one ounce of breeding she would know that in the better families, an inheritance always passes through the male line."

"I'll drink to that!" smirked Freddy, pouring himself another glass.

"Insolence," gasped Aunt Astrid.

"Calm down, Mummy." Vanessa poured a glass of brandy and handed it to her trembling parent. "You are upsetting yourself over nothing. I am sure Uncle Merlin possessed enough of his faculties at the end to leave his fortune to the most deserving family members."

Uncle Maurice tucked his pudgy fingers into his waistcoat pockets, puffed out his chest like a penguin, and frowned. He was obviously about to say something remarkably astute. "Over the years," he intoned, "I have on a variety of occasions offered Merlin the benefit of my investment experience. True, he was at times inclined to be testy, but that was his manner. And as, in my opinion, Merlin would have selected as his legatee someone of financial background, I do think myself a likely candidate for the bulk . . ."

"Fiddlesticks!" Aunt Astrid swept out of her chair in one majestic movement. For a moment I cherished the exciting notion that she would fling her brandy glass in Maurice's face. Ben, too, I could see, was having a whale of a good time. Our eyes met and he lowered one lid in a discreet wink.

"I gather you are not even in the running," he whispered. "Pity! I always find heiresses so attractive."

"Come, Vanessa." Aunt Astrid had unfortunately decided not to make a vulgar scene. "We will not remain in this room any longer listening to such complete folly. Sound investment advice from you, Maurice? How singularly amusing! I think you had better put your own house in order. From the rumour I happened to overhear at my dressmaker's last week, your financial expertise has reduced you to dire straits."

"Don't you think," I said, "that everyone is being a trifle premature, not to say greedy? Remember, Aunt Astrid, you are the one who suggested that Uncle Merlin would probably leave everything to a cat home. Maybe he liked your idea, although I think it far more likely that he left his money to the one person who has stood by him all these years, Aunt Sybil."

Right on cue she came through the door. In her black felt hat with the shadowy brim clamped down over her grey hair, and her dark coat reaching almost to her lace-up shoes, Aunt Sybil looked like the nanny in a melodrama — the kind where all the children turn into ghouls and the parents have to run away from home. "I think" — she glanced at the clock above the mantelpiece — "that we should be leaving for the service. Those who wish to drive may, but I shall walk. The church is only five minutes away, and Merlin abhorred motorcars. His remains are being conveyed from the undertaker's in a horse-drawn carriage."

She added, "I believe the means of transportation chosen was not only because of a distaste for motor vehicles, but a matter of sentiment expressed in a written request to his lawyer. Mr Bragg will be returning with us after the funeral so you will have a chance to talk with him."

"Won't that be fun!" gloated Freddy in my ear.

A heavy mist had descended over the area since our arrival at the house. Our little party clustered close together as we manoeuvred our way down the narrow cliff path, which was rutted with crevices and pockmarks. A railing strategically placed where the sharp drop-off to the sea was dangerous would have given some feeling of security, if I had been able to see clearly three feet ahead. Before long I had wrenched my ankle, and Ben took my arm.

"If you keep dragging on me like this," came his disembodied voice, "you'll have us both down, and we will go rolling over the edge to find ourselves impaled on the rocks below."

"What a misery you are, seeing gloom at every turn."

"You're damn right," he agreed amicably. "I see something very gloomy coming around the curve at this very minute, a vapourish chariot pulled by two snorting stamping horses, driven by a phantom driver. . . ."

"He's there; we can't see him because of the mist," I explained patiently and almost tripped again — this time over Uncle Maurice, who had stopped short. "Can't you visualize the coffin rattling around inside the carriage?"

Ben did not return my friendly squeeze. "I'd much rather not," he said.

Uncle Merlin was buried in the family vault, a small chapel-like building standing close to the church.

I hated the raised tombs, the older ones topped with marble effigies, the newer ones by brass plates. The coffin was carried in, high on the undertakers' shoulders. No friend or relation rose up to share the burden. Uncle Merlin was dead and nobody, including me, really gave a hoot. Why couldn't he have been buried out in the churchyard where the grass would blow above him in the wind? I turned to see the old gardener standing hunched and sombre, separated by polite distance from the family. A tear sneaked out the corner of one eye and slid in slow motion down his wrinkled cheek. Was he wondering how soon his turn would come — another name ticked off the list? "I'm leaving," I told Ben.

I made myself useful back at the house tidying the drawing room, removing all the dirty cups and traces of stale food, and making tea. I had finished dusting the mantelpiece with a wad of scrunched-up newspaper when I heard a tramping in the hall. In addition to the family, we were joined by Dr Melrose, who had attended Uncle Merlin on his deathbed. He went around shaking hands and apologizing for not arriving until the funeral was almost concluded. "I'm sorry I was unable to better assist Mr Grantham," he remarked to Uncle Maurice. "Pneumonia was the crunch, but the man had a very serious heart condition. Very foolish of him not to have sought medical assistance sooner. He must have guessed."

"But if nothing could be done," said Aunt Astrid, "and bearing in mind that even with National Health, there is always some expense . . ."

The vicar, Mr Rowland Foxworth, arrived and offered condolences in his charming voice. He was a very attractive man with prematurely silvered brown hair, strong eyebrows, and warm grey eyes. He was much taller than Ben.

I cast a considering eye over Ben and went on pouring tea. Mr Foxworth and the doctor had barely left when the doorbell chimed, announcing the man we had all been waiting for, Mr Wilberforce Bragg, solicitor at law from the firm of Bragg, Wiseman & Smith.

To do the family justice, I think we presented quite a charming drawing room scene. No one was sitting sharpening his claws or ostentatiously smacking his lips. Mr Bragg was a man in his sixties, with a squashily plump figure, like very soft dough. His complexion was a ruddy network of purple veins, his hair did not look as though it had been combed for a week, and his jacket and trouser legs were an inch too short.

"I don't think his mother allowed enough room for growing," whispering Freddy as he cast a regretful eye on the sherry and helped himself to a cup of tea.

"May we begin?" Mr Bragg's liverish lips parted in what appeared to be a smile and he pushed a pair of half-moon glasses onto his nose. "Ladies and gentlemen, we are gathered here today . . ." A tap at the door interrupted him, and into the room shuffled the old gardener, flannel cap twisted in his gnarled old hands. His eyes shifted around the group. "I heard word that I were wanted here, your worship."

"You are Jonas Alfred Phipps? Quite right, my man, we do desire your presence." Mr Bragg nodded with the graciousness of a man who considers himself above class distinctions.

Aunt Astrid did not share this view of social tolerance. She watched, flinching, as the gardener wiped his muddy boots in the doorway, and inched her skirts away when he clumped behind her to take up his position at the edge of the group.

"Now if we are indeed ready," the solicitor hemmed, "I will begin the reading:

"'I, Merlin Percival Grantham, being of sound mind, hereby declare this to be my Last Will and Testament revoking all other wills and codicils.

"'Article First: I name the Stirling Trust Company Limited as executors under this Will and hereby direct them to settle all just claims against my estate.

"'Article Second: After the payment of all my just debts, I direct my executor to dispose of my estate as follows:

"'A. To Jonas Phipps, the only servant foolhardy enough to remain in my service, in gratitude for the amusement he has given me in turning my grounds into a showplace for weeds, I bequeath the sum of one thousand pounds and the right to live in the rooms above the stables on my property for the course of his life.'"

The recipient of this largesse ducked his head and said, "Thank ye kindly, your worship." Mr Bragg read on:

"'B. To my third cousin Maurice Flatts, whose only claim to distinction is his sprightly pursuit of women young enough to be his daughters, I bequeath a pair of fireside slippers.'"

Babble broke out, Aunt Lulu's voice shrilling above the others. "Throw it on the fire. Burn the will!" Uncle Maurice looked dangerously close to a heart attack. "Libellous! I'll, I'll sue!"

The solicitor raised his hand. "I must caution you, ladies and gentlemen, that whether I approve or disapprove of this document is irrelevant. Legally it is airtight. Anyone who tries to overset it will do so at great expense and with slim chance of success. On that point I feel quite secure. The will was prepared by me, and I flatter myself I am one of the foremost probate experts in this part of the country. Merlin Grantham's wishes will stand."

"You mean there is worse to come?" For once feckless Freddy sounded quite sober.

The lawyer ruffled the pages. "There will be no further interruptions or I will arrange for the will to be read in chambers, before his honour, Judge Abernathy.

"'C. To Louise Emily Flatts, who on one unforgettable occasion disgraced the family name by cheating at whist at the church hall, St. Mary's-at-the-Mill, I leave a deck of unmarked cards.

"'D. To my fourth cousin several times removed (alas, never permanently) Frederick George Flatts, who regards poverty as a mystical experience, I leave an empty wallet.

"'E. To my relative, Vanessa Fitz-Gerald, who thought it amusing to pose nude for the New Year's Eve "bash" at the Retired Rectors' Club, I leave something I hope she will find equally amusing — a pair of overalls.

"'F. To my relative, Astrid Rose Fitz-Gerald, who hastened her unfortunate husband's end by her constant nagging, extravagant use of charge cards, and insatiable sexual demands, I leave a year's supply of saccharin.'"

Her eyes fixed in a ghastly stare, Aunt Astrid emitted a scream, powerful enough to reach Uncle Merlin in his tomb, made an abortive lunge at the solicitor, and crumpled into a deep swoon.

"Mummy! I do wish you would act your age." Vanessa regarded her recumbent parent with scorn but made no move to revive her. With a slight tremor of her graceful hand she reached into her bag for a packet of cigarettes, lit one, and inhaled deeply. Aunt Lulu and Uncle Maurice both appeared unmoved by Aunt Astrid's recumbent form. The gardener stood looking at his boots. The rest of us clustered about the body, the lawyer *tetch-tetching* while Aunt Sybil produced an evil-looking bottle of smelling salts and jammed them under the sufferer's nose. Aunt Astrid returned briefly to life, shouting, "Kill him! Kill the swine," before sinking back into unconsciousness. Mr Bragg blanched, wondering perhaps whether she meant him or Uncle Merlin. By the consent of all those present, Aunt Astrid was placed on the sofa, covered with a wool rug, and left to sleep it off.

"If I may now continue." Mr Bragg inspected his pocket watch and cleared his throat.

"'G. To my cousin, Sybil Agatha Grantham, but for whose appalling cooking I might still be alive today, but mindful of her (unsolicited) devotion, I bequeath my property, Cliffside Cottage, and the sum of ten thousand pounds."

All eyes were now fixed on Aunt Sybil. She appeared to swallow, then I realized she was humming one of the funeral hymns. Well, she had lived in the man's house for over fifty years; she was used to his jibes. Humming was probably a mental kind of cotton wool in her ears. Mr Bragg turned a page and lifted a hand as though calling for order. My turn must be coming up next. What had dear old Unc left me, an application form for a new body? The fire had petered out, and I, usually such a warm-blooded filly, felt chilled to the bone. After another surreptitious glance at his watch, Mr Bragg continued:

"'H. To Giselle Simons and Bentley Haskell in equal shares, I leave all my remaining estate.'"

Someone gasped: Was it me or Ben?

"'Subject to the following conditions:

"'1. That Giselle Simons and Bentley Haskell shall reside at my residence for a period of six months from the date of my death.

"'2. That Giselle Simons shall divest herself of four and one-half stone, no less, in body weight, within said six months and can prove same by presentation of a doctor's certificate.

"'3. That Bentley Haskell shall write and complete a book of marketable length and submit same to a reputable publisher within said six months, and said manuscript shall contain not one word of blasphemy or obscenity. My esteemed solicitor, Mr Wilberforce Bragg, has agreed to read same masterpiece and to be present when it is delivered into the hands of the post office.

"'4. That Giselle Simons and Bentley Haskell, singly or together, shall within said six months discover the treasure connected with my house. The answer to this quest, described in a sealed letter to be held in the possession of my solicitor, Mr Wilberforce Bragg, to be opened six months from the date of my death. In the event that either Giselle or Bentley fails to attempt or meet all of the four conditions within this time span, their shares shall be both divested and shall be divided in equal shares among Maurice Flatts, Louise Emily Flatts, Frederick George Flatts, Vanessa Fitz-Gerald, and Astrid Rose Fitz-Gerald, or the survivor or survivors of them.'"

A stunned silence swamped the room. Freddy drew a ragged breath and raised a wineglass, twirling it in an exaggerated arc above his head. "A toast!" he cried. "To the late great Uncle Merlin, a very sporting gentleman. The game has just begun."

"Yes," agreed Vanessa, lips curving into an unsweet smile, "by fair means or foul!"

CHAPTER SEVEN

Ben and I decided not to return to London that night. We needed time to talk. Aunt Sybil in a rather formal voice agreed to stay on for a few days until the cottage could be prepared for her, but she went to her room when the front door slammed on the last of the other relatives, all of whom spurned our offer of hospitality for the night. As late afternoon darkened the windows, only the solicitor remained with us, and he was impatient to be off. He kept glancing at his watch.

"You will each be sent a copy of the will," Mr Bragg said. "And here is the memorandum your uncle left in my keeping regarding his funeral arrangements, which I have fulfilled to the best of my ability. As you can see, the terms, like those of the will, are eccentric."

I passed the paper to Ben and he read aloud: "I, Merlin Grantham, request that I be accorded the same manner of funeral given my mother, Abigail Grantham."

Ben whistled. "Sentimental old geezer, wasn't he?"

"I only met Mr Grantham once when he came about his will, and he was not well then, kept coughing into his handkerchief." Mr Bragg was looking round for his coat and gloves. "Naturally I did all I could, but the funeral arrangements posed an almost impossible task." He pursed his lips in dissatisfaction. "Miss Sybil Grantham remembers staying in this house at the time of her aunt's funeral, but she was only a child of five or six. She did recall the use of a horse and carriage but the other details are as dead as Merlin Grantham and his mother."

"Rather careless of Uncle Merlin to be so unspecific." I folded the paper over and pressed it between my fingers. "But I suspect he had other things on his mind — composing his list of schoolboy howlers for his Last Will and Testament."

"Reprehensible, but all perfectly legal." Mr Bragg buttoned his coat. "Do not be persuaded otherwise. I wish both of you good fortune. May you find the treasure and live happily ever after. Well, I must be off. As stated in the final paragraph of the will, you will be the recipients of the income from your uncle's investments during the interim, six month, period."

"Goodnight."

We followed him down the hall and shut him out into the rising wind and lowering skies. It was confrontation time.

"You can wipe that Cheshire cat expression off your face." Ben headed back into the drawing room. "I refuse to be inveigled into this farce or to compromise my integrity for the sake of . . ."

"You wouldn't be so noble if you thought you stood a chance of qualifying for the dough." Tossing a cushion off one of the fireside chairs, I sat down and smiled smugly across at Ben as he lounged in the wingback opposite.

"Hark who's talking! I'll bet my whole share of the take that I could fulfil my part of the bargain while you are still sinking your teeth into cream buns and murmuring" — his voice rose to a dreadful muffled twitter — "'Just one more teeny-weeny stuffing session and, cross my size forty-two chest, tomorrow or sometime next week I positively will — God's honour — go on my diet.'"

"There you go!" I cried triumphantly. "You are incapable of stringing two sentences together without the use of obscenity or blasphemy. Whereas I when motivated am a woman of willpower."

"Don't make me laugh!" Ben did just that — hateful snickering creature. "I don't suppose you've seen your knees since you were two years old."

"That piece of spite is not even original. I expect your writing is equally trite." Standing up, I declaimed with wide-flung arms, "'Our stalwart hero Porno Hardcore ripped the clothes from the protesting body of lithesome lovely Tessie Tease, pressed his rapacious hand upon her curvaceous beep, beep, beep and cried, "Gee, sugar cube, I'd really love to beep-beep your beep-beep-beep!"'"

Ben's lips quivered. "You have just made my point. I write spy stories and for them to be credible the characters must sound like real people. No one in this day and age shrieks, 'Oh naughty, naughty!' when an alligator stomps up the river bank and nips off their left leg."

"True," I said, slumping down again and absently reaching for a piece of leftover fruitcake, dry as the Sahara, "but there's an easy way round that problem. You transport your story to another era. The eighteenth century was a little raunchy; you'd do better in the Victorian reign, when being a gentleman did not necessarily mean you were impotent, or . . ."

Ben shook his head. "Too limiting for my medium. A spy story needs the fast action of wireless, air travel, chemical warfare, and all the intricacies of modern-day espionage, nuclear secrets, intrigue. . . ."

"All right." I cracked off another piece of fruitcake. "If you insist on remaining within the twentieth century your hero must be from another world."

"Tremendous," said Ben, pitching a scrunched-up piece of paper into the grate. "I'll make him a pointy-eared little green man from Mars, running on a transistor battery, who . . ."

"Must you take everything literally? By 'another world' I meant cast your hero in a different mould from Mr Average Spy with his upturned raincoat collar and limp trilby hat.

Make him a college professor with a passion for Keats, or an opera singer with laryngitis. Make him a woman."

Ben's eyes flashed. "Ellie," he said, "you have given me an idea."

I held out my hand. "Half the royalties?"

"Nothing doing." Ben stood up and began pacing between our two chairs. "At the end of the six months I want to be able to shake my fist at Uncle Merlin and tell him where he can put his inheritance. A roof over my head for a while is one thing but . . ."

A tap at the door interrupted my exuberant whoop of triumph at Ben's apparent capitulation. In came Jonas Phipps, head bent and the inevitable scuffed old hat dangling between his fingers. In the half-light all I could see of the gardener's face were the jutting grey eyebrows and bristly scrubbing-brush moustache. Electricity would be one of the first amenities I would install in Merlin's Court.

As a novice at the lady of the manor game I wondered how I should address this elderly retainer. Aunt Astrid would have said, "Don't stand there gawking all day. Out with it, my man!"

"Yes, Jonas," said Ben, offering his hand. "Is there something Miss Simons and I can do for you?"

"Be I to sleep up at the cottage as usual, sir? Now that it rightly belongs to Miss Grantham I don't want to do nowt to upset her, but what with there being no bed in the rooms over the stables and me lumbago acting up, sir, I was awondering . . ."

"No problem. Miss Grantham is spending the night in her old room. Ellie and I have not discussed the matter yet, but it seems a shame for the old lady to be uprooted — unless of course she would like the privacy of her own place. And I am sure you do not relish being evicted from your home. In any event you must remain at the cottage until a decision is made."

"I'll not go against the will, sir." Phipps was probably a simple soul, subject to a superstitious terror of falling foul of the legal system, to say nothing of the thwarted ghost of Uncle Merlin.

"Mr Phipps, have you eaten?" I asked. "I believe there is some cold roast beef in the kitchen."

"Nay, I cook me own meals, mistress. I'll be on my way and thank ye both for seeing me." Bowing over his hat, the old man backed out of the room.

"This is the life," yawned Ben, "complete with faithful servant and the spinster chaperone upstairs."

"Fear not," I said, "your virtue is safe with me. Tell me — was outward respectability the reason you suggested having Aunt Sybil remain here?"

"I think it rather a shame to oust the poor old girl when she has lived here forever. And yes, Ellie, I do feel that having someone else in the house would provide a little" — he searched for the word — "*balance.*"

"If you are so frightened for your virtue," I hissed, "you can always have an iron bolt installed on your bedroom door and shove a chest of drawers up against it."

Ben closed his eyes and ground his teeth. The muscles on his neck stood out like ropes. "Can we never have a conversation without you climbing up on your high horse? Two single people living in one house, even when there is no romantic attachment, has to be a sensitive situation."

"Very!" I gave the paltry fire a shove with the poker. "But this sensitive situation has its practical plusses — six months free room and board, to say nothing of the chance to win the grand prize: a half-share in my ancestral home, a substantial bank account, stocks and bonds, and who knows what else? All, Mr Bentley Haskell, because my uncle supposed you to be engaged to me."

"Are you suggesting," scowled Ben, "that should I wish to become endowed with all these worldly goods that I am honourably bound to offer you marriage?"

"Come to think of it" — I swung the poker menacingly in his direction — "such would be the right and proper course for a gentleman. Poor Uncle's wishes ought really to be considered a sacred duty. As a tribute to his memory,

I think I could be persuaded to sacrifice my finer feelings. Down on one knee, young man!"

Ben removed the poker from my clenched fingers and tried to repress a grin. "You are a fool," he said. Perversely the words sounded like a compliment but I didn't let flattery go to my head.

"But not so great a fool that I'd tie the knot with you. Frankly, you are not my type, and when I get skinny I intend to have my pick of the litter. That vicar is a possibility — handsome, intellectual, amusing — but I am in no rush."

"Personally, I thought him a shade too hearty." Ben's brief good humour evaporated and he returned the poker to the grate. "But your life is your own. I am glad we are laying our cards on the table. You see, there is this girl in London with whom I have an understanding."

"How quaint," I said lightly. "Sounds like one of those arrangements made by families when their infants are still in the cradle. Won't your sweet young thing object to your moving in with me?"

"Not under the circumstances. Susan is very accepting."

"She must be. Of course, she promises to benefit also from our arrangement. With a bit of luck I'll be able to hand you over with a handsome dowry."

"Susie . . . Susan isn't mercenary. You'd love her. But are the locals going to be as accepting of a young couple living together without benefit of clergy? Your vicar for one can hardly approve."

"Ben, you surprise me. I'm beginning to suspect that along with your other hang-ups you are also a latent conformist. Are you afraid of getting tossed out on your ear from the village pub by the local morals committee? Given the choice of having Aunt Sybil fussing underfoot or being accused of living in sin, I'll opt for the latter! Calm down, Lancelot, no one could seriously suspect me of being a vamp."

"For once," snorted Ben irritably, "I think you underestimate yourself. You've admitted you have designs on the unsuspecting vicar."

"True, but I intend to restrain them until I am reduced to a shadow of my former self. By that time you will have written your masterpiece and it will be time to put the house up for sale and divide the profits."

"Complaisant, aren't you? But, Ellie, you are overlooking the one condition of that will which may defeat even your ingenuity — the discovery of the treasure." Ben was pacing again. His eyes under black knitted brows glowed like blue-green opals. "If old Merlin had played by the rules he would have provided us with clues."

"What do you expect?" I jeered. "Rhymed couplets written in invisible ink on ivory-coloured parchment?"

"They would make a heck of a lot more sense than a random search of this warren of a house. We could spend months, tapping desperately on every piece of panelling and floorboard in frantic hope of an echo, or dismantling old bureaus and sideboards searching for a secret drawer."

I could see his point. Perhaps though, we were underestimating Uncle Merlin. Some instinct told me that we had not heard the last of the deceased.

"Oh, don't look so crestfallen." To my surprise Ben reached over and touched my face lightly, only a comradely gesture, unfortunately. "I know I sound like a defeatist," he continued, "but I must say that if I have to get involved in such a hare-brained scheme, I would sooner it was with you than anyone else. Together we will evolve some brilliant strategy."

Ben and I parted for the night on amiable terms, having decided we would return to London the following morning to settle our affairs. For me this would entail donating my furniture to the Salvation Army and informing my boss he should hang a Help Wanted sign in his studio window. Having mentally disposed of my former life, I lay in the big double bed which I had inhabited on my former visit and thought about Ben and his lady friend Susan. Was she, I wondered hopefully, a mythical creature invented to act out the role of emotional chaperone? Possibly, but a man as eminently attractive as Bentley Haskell was bound to have some woman in his life. The fiancée might exist, but would he remain loyal, faithful, and true to her memory during an absence of six months? He could hardly entertain the creature here at Merlin's Court while supposedly engaged to me, and treasure hunting would, I hoped, leave little time for trips up to London.

I fell asleep to dream of the new me. "Have you seen her?" chanted a chorus of animated dumplings. "My word, that girl is thin — emaciated. Really most unbecoming! Her stockings bag around the knees. You should have seen her when she was well-padded. She had such a pretty face!" This flattery was so enjoyable I hated to wake up. But my window had not latched properly and a strong draught was blowing over me. Struggling out of my happy fantasy, I padded across the room and parted the curtains. Tonight there was no moon. As I reached for the latch, a pinprick of light stabbed the darkness. The gardener must be awake at his cottage, perhaps going downstairs to make himself a cup of Ovaltine. A very sound idea. Reaching for my dressing gown, grateful that I was no longer reduced to a bedspread, I knotted the cord around my middle and went out onto the landing. At least this time I would not collide with Uncle Merlin in the pantry. Getting rid of that antiquated dumb-waiter would be one of my first projects. My hand moved down the smooth curve of the bannister rail; this beautiful staircase should be restored and preserved. Was Uncle Merlin manipulating me from the grave, knowing full well my professional instincts would be aroused? Mr Bragg had emphasized that substantial funds would be made available to us during our stay. And the house certainly would fetch a better price after even modest renovations. In its present state of dirt and decay, even squatters wouldn't want it.

The kitchen was worse than the last time. Unable to face it earlier that evening, I had steered clear by sending Ben to fix sandwiches for supper. Tomorrow, before we left, I would roll up my sleeves and boil water. At the moment I was not ready for an assault on squalor. I found a tin of biscuits and then made myself a cup of strong tea. The milk was sour so I did without. One could only be surprised that Uncle Merlin had not died from dysentery years before pneumonia claimed him. Aunt Sybil was the limit. The effect of my disapproval was uncanny: As if to defend herself against mental attack, she materialized, literally, on the doorstep. I heard a stamping noise and turned in my chair as the garden door opened.

"Aunt Sybil," I cried, "what are you doing wandering around outside in the middle of the night?"

She looked momentarily taken aback, patting her badly permed grey hair with a fluttering hand. "Oh, Giselle, it's you," she said as though there had been some doubt.

She allowed me to help her off with her damp black coat and watched as I folded it over a chair. "A girl of your age should sleep the night through. We old people are different. I catnap. When I can't get back to sleep, I go outside and walk about."

"You have to be careful," I said. "We don't want you catching pneumonia."

"Now, Giselle, don't fuss. I simply felt the need for a little air. Besides, I wanted to walk down and look at the cottage, but then I realized Jonas was still there."

She sat down and I poured her a cup of tea. As she drank I noticed that the skin on her hands was dry and cracked like a crumbling autumn leaf. "Aunt Sybil, you don't have to go. This is your home. Ben and I are the intruders."

"That's very kind, Giselle." Absently she hummed a snatch from the Merlin Grantham funeral theme before focussing her vague pale eyes on me. "But dear Merlin's wishes are mine always. His leaving you the house is no reflection upon his feelings for me. He felt this place would become too much for me. Time for me to take life easy and sit down with my knitting. Whatever he said in the will, Merlin always appreciated my efforts."

I tried not to let my eyes wander around the towering disorder. Aunt Sybil leaned back in her chair, her worn hands clasped over her rumpled, spotted dress. She was renouncing her role as lady of the manor and handing over the keys to the new generation.

"Well," I said, anxious to conceal my relief, "we will expect to see you here often for lunch or tea and we will come down to visit you."

"Merlin would expect that," she returned, "but let us wait until we are both settled. Speaking of settling down, will you and Mr Hamlet be married soon?"

"Not for a while." I rattled the teacups together and picked them up. "Ben feels we should wait until the end of the six months. We want our lives in order so we can enjoy the wedding."

"I see." Aunt Sybil nodded. What she thought she saw was a fortune hunter about to keep me dangling until he could be sure our marriage would prove a sound financial investment. "You do realize, don't you," she warned, "that people will talk with the two of you living here together? Even though Merlin and I are, were cousins I, too, got those winks and nudges from the villagers. Oh dearie, yes, but I never let them bother me. Why? Because I can proudly say that in all our years together your uncle never made an improper suggestion. Behave like a lady, Giselle, and you will always be quite safe with men."

Now I knew where I had gone wrong.

"Remember, dear, if you must lie down — except to sleep, that is — do it with a good book. The one I'm reading now is a sweet story about a girl who is kidnapped from a nunnery by a pirate with a one-legged parrot. Remind me to lend it to you some time. Of course I must say I prefer William Shakespeare for something a little deeper, but . . ."

The next morning I came downstairs to find Ben on the telephone. From his furtive "Goodbye" and speedy replacement of the receiver I sadly concluded he must have been talking to the other fiancée, but somehow I would make him forget her. On the road back to London I talked with him about Aunt Sybil.

"That woman frightens me; fifty years in that house and I may end up just like her, an elderly wallflower still wondering what the knight in shining armour might do if he ever got off his horse." Unwrapping a bar of chocolate, I took a sneaky bite while Ben kept his eyes on the road.

"Why don't you worry about something real for a change, like how you are going to fare on your lose-some win-some diet. Tell me, why are your cheeks bulging like a hamster? Do I have to keep after you every minute?"

"Sorry." I swallowed. "But I wonder how you would react if you had to lose four and a half stone, translated, that is sixty-three pounds, and six months into sixty-three goes . . ."

"About two and a half pounds a week. Here, give me the rest of that chocolate. Ruin my chances of this inheritance and I will personally turn you over to the relations and watch them tear you limb from limb."

"You terrify me. But what is adventure without the thrust of danger?" I folded the chocolate paper and placed it in the ashtray.

"Something I can live without."

What disturbed me about returning to Queen Alexandra Place was how little I had to leave behind and how little I had to collect.

"Are you taking the monster with you?" asked Jill. Tobias had just taken a yank out of her stockinged leg, so she was not feeling kindly towards him. "If so, I may decide not to visit you after all, Ellie darling."

"Oh, Jill, you must come." I blinked back a tear but she would not have seen it anyway, because her own eyes had misted over. "But leave my furry baby behind," I continued bracingly, "you must be joking. He is off to mouse heaven. Rodents multiply in every closet. We are both going to work our tails off."

* * *

And the prophecy was fulfilled. On arriving back at Merlin's Court we found Aunt Sybil had departed for Cliffside, leaving a record number of dirty dishes in the sink and her bedroom stacked with torn boxes, broken hangers, and newspapers dating back to the beginning of the century. What we needed was a giant bonfire set sufficiently back from the house so we did not all go up in smoke.

Manlike, Ben had already deposited his typewriter on the dining room table, and sat reaming paper between the rollers, surrounded by items he had casually moved to the floor, a chipped willow pattern soup tureen, a bobbled red velour cloth, several dusty egg cartons, magazines, candle-sticks, and a bust of Churchill with half his cigar knocked off.

I leaned up against the door-frame and chirruped sweetly, "Putting together a few items for the church bazaar?"

"What?" Ben rubbed a finger across his brow.

"Trying to place me? I am the other half of the 'Double Your Money' team — not the whole operation. Will you stop feeding that machine its breakfast, or do I have to knock your chair over?"

"What do you want from me!" Ben squinted, closed one eye, and carefully adjusted his margins. "I thought you'd be impressed by my self-discipline. Not half an hour in the house and here I am flexing my fingers ready to start on my puritan tale. You will be pleased to know I took your advice. My hero is a woman — a nun, at that — Sister Marie Grace, an American who infiltrates the C.I.A., cleverly disguised as a disco dancer. What do you think?"

"I think Sister What's-her-face can go to hell and you can hand over your car keys so I can go into the village and get in provisions for the siege. Meanwhile you can put on a pinny and start shovelling dirt. If I don't look out you will be placing your boots outside your bedroom door for cleaning."

"You didn't tell me you drove," said Ben, pleasantly interested.

"I also feed myself, take baths alone . . ."

"Message received and understood. The keys are hanging on a nail just inside the stable door; bring me back a loaf of malt bread, will you?"

I made the notation on my list.

"You'd better get away from that typewriter," I said, heading out the door. "It is programmed to explode in thirty seconds."

The stables were at the side of the house, separated from it by a courtyard overlooking the moat and a pseudo-Norman arch. Shrugging on a short woollen jacket, I picked up my bag, slung the strap over my shoulder and, wrapping my arms around myself for warmth, made the short dash across the slick, moss-covered flagstones. Pushing open the iron-studded door, my eyes took a moment to grow accustomed to the gloom. After only once cracking my head on a slanted beam and putting my hand through something soft and spongy (which proved to be a gigantic cobweb), I located the car keys and was leaving when something moved in one of the far corners.

A bat? But bats don't speak, unless you count the kind who transpose themselves into vampires for the express purpose of sucking the life blood out of defenceless maidens. This one was addressing me. I backed towards the door. The voice definitely had a sepulchral ring.

"Who be there?"

"And who be ye?" Swinging the door open behind me, I let in a shaft of watery sunlight. I could see his face, the grizzled hair, the bristly scrubbing-brush moustache. Not an unusual face. Hundreds of tramps hiding in barns all over the country probably looked very much like him — anonymous. "Jonas Phipps! Does everyone in this dreadful house walk on air? I never know who will pop up and terrify me next."

"Nay, don't say I scared ye, mistress. Were t'other way round. I were just coming down for airing when I heard this fair awful squeal, like pig having its innards carved open."

"That t'were, were — was me. I cracked my head on a beam." Reaching out I touched the book he had half hidden under his arm.

"I see you've been busy, Mr Phipps. May I see?"

"Naw, t'is just a trifling yarn, 'bout giddy young thing what gets put in't family way by some ne'er-do-well feller an' from then on t'is all downhill for poor lass."

"*Tess of the D'Urbervilles.*" I tilted my head and spelt out the title. "Cheerful little tale. If all the laughs are keeping you away from your polishing cloth I can tell you the ending is wonderful. She gets hanged."

Jonas grunted. "Might have known t'would have happy ending. Was hoping she'd get married instead. Come to speak of wedding bells on't peal, don't doubt you and master'll be taking a walk down churchyard soon?"

Here we went again. I explained patiently to Jonas that while the family was in mourning a wedding would be unseemly. He shook his head. "No call for fuss an' show. Me ma and da went out in their workaday clothes day they was churched, but t'were legal, in them days. Decent living counted for summat then. Mr Merlin would want ye wed, I'll tell ye that straight."

So he would have — the sadistic old devil.

* * *

Ben's car went like a leopard that suddenly finds its cage door open. I pressed my foot on the accelerator, honked twice on the horn to speed up Jonas's dawdling approach to the house, and zoomed down the driveway past Aunt Sybil's cottage, through the drooping iron gates and onto the cliff road. The looping turns took some negotiating but I was exhilarated, like a schoolgirl experiencing the first day of holiday freedom. Luckily I met no other cars, and although I passed a bus stop, no lumbering vehicle approached me with a load of holiday-makers. Moving over, whilst polite, might have meant parachuting over the cliff edge. When spring finally graced us with its presence, this view would be magnificent, but now the sea was sluggish and swollen, slapping out at the jutting rocks like a petulant grey-faced crone.

Contemplating nature, I took a turn a little sharply, swerved to avoid a telephone kiosk, put my foot down to steady the car with the brake, felt it start and buckle like an angry carthorse, and was thrown forward with a painful jolt against the steering column. The road lunged forward ready to hurl me into the sea. Grinding the wheel between my fingers, I held on for dear life and closed my eyes. I cannot say that the sum total of my past experience flashed before me, but I heard Vanessa's voice: The words were the ones she had spoken after Uncle Merlin's will was read, "By fair means or foul."

My eyes flew open. Let Vanessa have the house, the money, I'd even throw in Ben as a special bonus offer, if the car would stop shuddering towards the cliff edge. Taking my foot off the brake, I let the car slide at roller-coaster speed until I met a relatively flat strip of road, yanked on the emergency brake, and slammed the car in a wild flourish into the right-hand bank.

What I needed was a comforting slice of chocolate cake.

For ten minutes I sat taking deep breaths, explaining carefully to my jumping limbs that we were safe and still hanging together, everything properly attached and nothing badly bruised or broken. After this pep talk I felt strong enough to climb out and inspect the damage to Ben's pride and joy. Not that it mattered. Even if the car had survived without a scratch nothing would induce me to return to the driver's wheel, and let the leopard loose again.

Down on all fours, inspecting the paintwork, I heard plodding footsteps and realized I was not alone.

"I say, having a spot of bother?"

Of course not, I thought, I just chose this isolated place to do my morning exercises.

Around a curve in the road came a sporting-type woman about forty, wearing a bright yellow cardigan, wheeling a bicycle.

"Sorry, did I startle you?" she boomed. "This certainly is not the place for surprises, one nervous shudder and over the side one would go, ha-ha!"

The people a girl meets on a quiet drive in the country.

CHAPTER EIGHT

"Not to worry!" rasped my new acquaintance. "I'll have this blighter off before you can sing the first verse of 'God Save the Queen.' How's the spare?"

So much for murder plots. True to form I was the victim of something much more mundane, a blown tyre. Miss Jolly Hockey Sticks hummed blithely as she worked, ginger hair tucked uncompromisingly behind her ears and trouser legs riding up to show an expanse of purple and yellow argyle socks. With fingers deft and quick, she had the defective wheel on the ground within minutes and was moving the spare into place.

"This is most kind." I felt like a pigtailed new girl at school being taken under the kindly wing of a sixth-form prefect.

"Not at all. Not at all. 'We shall all pass through this world but once.' Each do our fair share and the planet won't fall apart, although can't say the same about your car — no offence, but the little she-devil looks like she's held together with paper clips and sticking plaster. Aha!" She lifted up the bonnet and peered inside. "Your sparkplugs need a clean, and if I'm not mistaken that radiator could erupt like a burst appendix at any minute, but at least your confrontation with the cliff hasn't done more than add a scratch or two — for character."

A little Austin moving up the hill paused and a face ballooned uncertainly through the window. Completely in command, Argyle Socks flagged the driver on. "Proceed with caution; sufficient room. We are well onto the bank. Take her up in second — steep grade ahead."

Petrified by the barrage of orders, the Austin shot backwards, stalled, coughed, and ploughed on with a horrendous crunch, whipping around the corner without a moment's pause.

"That, I am afraid, is the end of your bicycle," I said regretfully.

"Male drivers!" Socks shook her fist at the cloud of exhaust and picked up the flattened metal object as tenderly as a mother holding a battered child. "That's life." She patted the dismembered object awkwardly on what had once been a mudguard, laid it gently down on the verge, and blew noisily into a large plaid handkerchief. "A good friend," she explained, eyes averted.

"Is there anything I can do? I feel so responsible, but for your kindness your bike would be ali — here today, I mean now."

"Not to worry, brief sentimental lapse. Excuse me just a minute. That's better, back in control. Now if I could trouble you for a lift?"

"Of course." I had an idea. "We were travelling in opposite directions, but if you are not in a tearing hurry, come down to the village with me. Perhaps we can find a handy repairman who, with a few new parts, can put your bicycle back together. They," I said vaguely, "can do marvellous things nowadays."

"Kind thought, but must face facts. Only part salvageable is the bell, which I will keep as a small memento. Make a clean break has always been my motto. Once I reach a phone box, I will arrange to have someone come and pick up the remains." Argyle Socks again fished for the oversized handkerchief. A warmer personality than mine would have made some physical gesture of condolence — an arm around the shoulder, a sympathetic handshake. I stood fiddling with the buttons on my jacket.

"Excuse me!" Socks blew noisily. "Not usually given to embarrassing displays of sentiment. If you are ready we can now proceed. I would offer to drive for you, but there's truth to the old saying — leap back on the horse or you will never ride again. That's the spirit!"

The car heaved irritably as I did my U-turn, but it did not balk as we moved onto the hill. I let out the clutch, aware that Argyle Socks was totalling up points for and against. She would probably hand me a report card when we reached our destination.

"Where to?" I asked.

"Not far. Large house at the top of the hill, one quarter-mile past the churchyard and rectory, turn left at iron gates, gravel driveway . . ."

My foot hit the brake.

"Hoy there! Easy does it. Know the place?"

"I should do. I live there."

"Miss Ellie Simons? Providence again lends a hand. I am an applicant, arriving in answer to your advertisement in last night's issue of the local rag, *Daily Spokesman.*"

"My advertisement?"

"For housekeeper. Must tell you right off the bat, have absolutely no experience, not even sure what the job entails but if you want hard work, loyalty, stamina, and honesty that's me, Dorcas Critchley, at your service."

* * *

Ben was the master-mind behind the employment ad caper. When I introduced Dorcas to him on our arrival back at the house, he confessed to having been on the telephone to the newspaper when I came downstairs the morning we returned to London. He was so delighted with the success of his methods that he was quite blasé when I explained about the tyre and the few scratches on the side of his car. Muttering his amazement at the swift applicant response, he went off to fetch coffee and I followed him into the hall to hang up the coats.

"I left the salary open." He lowered his voice. "See what she wants and negotiate from there. Looks like a jolly sort. But don't be taken in. So do most bank robbers; ask for references."

"Don't be so suspicious. How many bank robbers would clamber off their bicycles to assist a benighted traveller? By the way, I have a feeling that, given half a chance, she will take that car of yours apart, bolt by bolt, and put it back together so it thinks it's a baby again. Be good and I may lend Miss Critchley to you when the inside jobs are done."

"The woman is not a fountain pen."

"You'd better be careful," I said. "You're catching something — humanity."

Other than Jill, I had never had a woman friend. Meeting Dorcas was another beginning. The decision to hire her had nothing to do with references. Not only had she assisted me in an hour of need, but under that gruff exterior she was like me, vulnerable. Her peculiarities of speech and manner were rather endearing. We would be a team.

Having produced a large envelope containing a three-page reference, Dorcas explained that she was by profession a games mistress and had been teaching at the Miriam Academy, an exclusive girls' boarding school about fifteen miles down the coast. The old head had recently retired and been replaced by a grim young woman who wanted to cut the sports programme in favour of extra Greek.

"Madness! Girls too cloistered as it is. Unhealthy! But nothing to be done. Had a set-to with her last week and decided to leave, not quite without funds so could manage for a time. Shook the woman's hand, parted amicably, but working together was out. Would always have been at loggerheads."

"She wrote you a glowing reference."

"Can't place too much store by that, I'm afraid. Woman only knew me for four weeks, had the records though. Also enclosed in that envelope, names and addresses of banker and clergymen. They won't object to enquiry."

"I'm sure they won't." I smiled. "Men ridicule women's intuition but the job is yours — if, of course, you still wish to stay, having seen something of the state of the house?"

Dorcas's long pale face so reminiscent of a kindly horse creased into a smile. "Never one to resist a challenge. One problem — can't promise to make this permanent. Start to miss the hockey field no doubt, but I won't leave you in the lurch. If I remained until September would that be satisfactory?"

"Perfect. None of us may be here after that." And I told her about Uncle Merlin's will.

At the end of my recital Dorcas slapped her hand on her trousered knee and leaned forward eagerly in her chair. "Marvellous. Always did adore a treasure hunt. Your Mr Haskell is right. To make chase sporting there should be clues. Haven't seen any folded bits of white paper propped up on the mantelpiece or hallstand, have you?"

"No, but I haven't had much time to look. We were in Uncle Merlin's bedroom yesterday but didn't give it a thorough combing. Perhaps tomorrow we could search there."

"Super! Great hoarders, men. So I've heard. Mother always said that Grandfather . . ."

"Yes?"

"Not important. Don't want to prose on about people you've never met, old-maidish behaviour — boring."

"What about me? I just bored you with a character sketch of all my relations."

"Different matter, relevant. Need to know who's who in case I catch any of them skulking around the house. Forgive my saying so, but don't like the sound of one of them, except possibly the boy Freddy — should have gone into the army. Mark my words, the rest will be up to tricks. But not to worry; between us we can foil any little schemes to do you out of your just inheritance."

"Have you ladies reached a decision?" Ben kicked the drawing room door open with his foot and came in carrying a tray of jangling crockery. "Good!" He nodded at our pleased faces. "Sorry there aren't any biscuits." He poured tea and handed cups round. "Our food situation, I regret to report, has now reached the famine stage. Super for you, Ellie, on your starvation programme, but I can now feel my spine when I touch my stomach."

"Complain, complain! Was it my fault this morning's shopping expedition had to be aborted?"

Ben shrugged suggestively. "All I know is that your driving wouldn't win you any gold cups. You screeched down the driveway at top speed, tearing up the gravel. . . ."

"Why is it" — I slammed down my cup, spilling half the contents — "that men have accidents and women make mistakes?"

Raking his fingers through his thick curly hair, Ben sucked in a hissing breath. "All I meant to suggest was that you probably picked up a nail or a chunk of glass. . . ."

"What I suggest" — Dorcas raised a restraining hand — "is that Ellie and I go down to the village now and do the shopping. No point in harsh words, you two. A little breathing space and Bob's your uncle, you'll be the best of friends again."

"Never!" I stood up, jamming the teacups back on the tray. "Dorcas, you have been very straightforward with me and as you will be closely involved with our lives here, I think it only fair to inform you that Ben and I are engaged in name only. Let's fetch our coats and I'll tell you the whole lurid story in the car."

"Good show! Wouldn't have missed this for the world. Life in this house is going to be more exciting than a tied game at the end of the first half."

"Don't hurry home, ladies." Ben picked up the tray and bowed us out of the room. "Phipps and I will do the washing up. You have fun."

"That's the ticket!" Dorcas gave him a friendly smack on the back, straightened her cardigan and followed me into the hall. "You can't complain," she said. "Not a bad lad; don't come down too hard on him. He'll iron out in time."

"That's what I'm afraid of." Picking up my bag, I checked to make sure I still had the shopping list. "If he improves drastically it will be like parting with a dog when he finally gets housebroken."

"Hard cheese! But never say die!" Dorcas administered one of her bracing slaps, adding, "Don't want to put you about, but perhaps we could pick up my suitcase and other gear. Left it at the station which isn't too far outside the . . ." She was still talking when we went out into the garden.

* * *

The village of Upper-Biddington-Marsh consisted of a bramble of small lanes dotted with picture-postcard thatched cottages, surrounded by walled gardens thick with fruit trees and rose bushes. Market Street was entered through a crumbling Roman archway and, apart from the modern traffic, might have looked much the same two centuries gone. A clock tower dominated the small square in the street's centre. Anxious to explore, we picked a parking place on the outskirts of the square, gathered up our shopping baskets, and stepped out onto the pavement.

"How about lunch?" I looked hungrily across the road to the Muffin Man bakery, nose twitching as a tempting aroma of hot meat pies wafted by on the wind.

"Not for me, thank you, never eat after I've been travelling, but don't let me stop you if you wish to indulge. Happy to join you for a cup of coffee."

"Better not. If the waitress came by juggling a couple of pies I might forget myself and bite off both her hands."

"Bad as that, is it? Never had a weight problem myself, but sympathize. Must be rough rowing."

"You're a pal," I said. "If you only knew how many people have told me that all I need is a little willpower! As though that were an item I could purchase at the grocery shop for fifty p. Speaking about my weight, I'm supposed to get a certificate from a doctor documenting my poundage at this time. Perhaps I could go along to the surgery now and take care of that little matter. I would hate to lose out on the will by default."

A woman with a toddler clinging to her skirts directed us to Dr Melrose's surgery. He received me warmly and readily signed the form recording my weight. To save me a trip to Mr Bragg's office he offered to post it for me. Our next port of call was the grocer's.

It seemed wrong somehow, when eating was to become a voyeur sport for me, that I should stagger to the car a half-hour later completely doubled under the weight of our purchases. Dorcas carried her share, she just had better posture. We took time out to review the rest of the shopping list. "Aspirin, sticking plaster, malt, and a few other precautionary items from the chemist." I turned over the paper to make sure I had not overlooked anything scribbled on the back, and read the words *Post Office.*

"A bit cryptic. Ben probably jotted that down this morning when I told him to read over the list and add whatever he needed. Trust him to expect me to have psychic powers. Does he want stamps, airmail envelopes, or what?"

"Meant to write the item down no doubt and got side-tracked," said Dorcas. "Often happens, the phone rings or someone comes to the door. . . . I'd play safe and go for a book of stamps, always useful."

"We would go to the chemist's first, I thought, and then I could phone Ben to find out what he wanted at the post office."

Our visit to the chemist's was short and not particularly sweet. The man in the white coat brusquely refused me any panacea that would have made my dieting less traumatic.

"Revolting man!" Clutching my little brown bag of aspirin and sticking plaster, I stalked out the door talking fiercely to Dorcas's back. "I despise spotty little men with skimpy ginger moustaches. That one looks like a goalkeeper on a dart team."

"Now, now! Wasn't the man's fault. Only doing his job. Unfortunate manner, but no point in wallowing. Sky looks a bit like rain. A good time for that liquid refreshment over at the Hounds and Hare, around the corner? Not usually one to frequent public houses, but I wouldn't say no to a ginger beer shandy."

"Sounds great to me." To the Hounds and Hare we duly went, all thoughts of telephoning Ben temporarily forgotten. A rather brassy-looking woman poured our drinks and then came round the bar to hover at our table. Arms akimbo over her tight black taffeta dress, she was obviously starved for a nosey natter. Newcomers must be a rare commodity in the village if two dowdy women excited such interest. Brassy would have been an asset to any police department. She quickly elicited our vital statistics: who we were, where we came from, and our connection with the village.

"Moved into that blooming big 'ouse, 'ave you? Ooh, in't you brave! I'd rather die than live up there. Fair give me the creeps, it would."

"Fortunately, you don't have to sacrifice yourself." Dorcas sounded very much the games mistress repressing a chatterbox pupil, until she ruined the effect of her quelling gaze by asking avidly, "Have you heard sinister rumours about the house? Anything mysterious — apparitions? Smugglers? Licentious carryings on in the olden days?"

"Don't know about them things." Brassy reached casually over to another table and handed Dorcas a coaster. "But me granny says she wouldn't set foot in that chamber of 'orrors if she was paid a thousand quid. The 'ouse of misery, she calls it. Worked there donkey's years ago as a maid she did. The old bag's eighty-three and sharp as a tack. Remembers back to the days when the old gent were a young lad. Eh, but that one turned out queer, didn't 'e, living like a bloody 'ermit and all? I 'eard tell 'is fingernails was two foot long and his. 'air all matted to 'is scalp like a scab." Brassy's pale yellow eyes behind the gummy mascaraed lashes bulged slightly with excitement. "Go on, you can tell me!" She smiled ingratiatingly. "Close-mouthed Sally they call me. I never spread nothink around. What was the old brute really like?"

"Enough of that, my girl!" Dorcas's long thin nose fairly quivered with indignation. "You are speaking of a person recently deceased." A gentle nudge of my foot told the defence league to cool it. I had no desire to dry up this source of information. Brassy's disclosures might be full of inaccuracies, but they could still provide some insights into life at Merlin's Court.

"Can't fault a person for being interested." Brassy gave her apron a pert twitch.

"Of course not," I said soothingly. "Especially when Merlin Grantham led such a secluded life. Isn't it true that no one from the village had seen him in years? Well, there you are! He became the local monster, sprouting horns and a tail. Even the family doesn't know why he shut himself off from the world, with my great-aunt Sybil standing guard at the gates."

"She's another funny old 'en, an' all." Brassy tilted the coffee pot and added a trickle to each cup. "Granny says Sybil Grantham was born with false teeth and an 'airnet on. She used to come to the 'ouse for long 'olidays when she was small. Strange, Mr Merlin didn't leave the place to 'er, but they always was an odd package was the Granthams. Makes me laugh, does me granny; she says Mr Merlin's father had a face fit to curdle a pint o' fresh cream and put a hen off laying. Made 'is wife's life a living 'ell. Passed on she did when the boy were young."

"I had forgotten that," I said.

Brassy pulled up a chair and joined us. Fishing into the pocket of her frilly white apron she unearthed a battered packet of American cigarettes and lit up. "Sad, i'nt it" — she blew smoke into our faces — "when a kid loses 'is mother. From what gets said in these parts I 'spect the late Mrs Grantham done 'erself in. Well, in them days, with a bugger for a 'usband, what else was a woman to do?"

"What indeed?" Dorcas and I looked at each other.

Brassy watched avidly while I searched in my purse for a tip. Feeling rather like an undercover agent sliding a little something into the hand of a paid informant, I handed her all my loose change. "Your granny sounds like a woman with a long memory." If I hoped this hint would encourage her to suggest a meeting with the old lady, I was to be disappointed. Brassy merely shrugged and tucked the coins in her pocket.

"Typical old age pensioner, can't remember where she last stuck the chamber pot but can tell you who was Lord Mayor of London in 1926. If Gran says that 'ouse is spooked, it is." She paused in gathering up the cups. "Haven't you never thought it weird that in a house that big there ain't no cats nor dogs? I saw a flick at the town 'all once, all about extra-sensory prescription it was; and animals have it worse than people. They won't go nowhere that the vibes ain't right. Think about it! Mr Merlin never as much as kept a Chihuahua about the place."

"Doesn't mean a thing," pooh-poohed Dorcas. "Not everyone is a canine friend. Chew up slippers, make puddles on the floor. Fond of the little beggars myself, but mustn't expect everyone and his great-aunt Maud to share the same tastes."

Brassy shook her head. "Even if the man 'ated dogs, every old 'ouse keeps a tabby cat about the place. I ain't never met a mouse yet that knew diddle about birth control."

Remembering the calling cards left by mice in the pantry, I began to think the lack of feline protection was a little strange. Buttoning my coat, I informed Brassy that the house now possessed a resident cat. "I brought my kitty down from London," I said, "and with all the hunting on the premises, he doesn't have to set a paw outside for entertainment. He thinks he's died and gone to heaven."

"Happen 'e will one of these days if you don't watch out." Brassy went off in search of more conversation in the form of new customers and Dorcas and I hurried out onto the pavement. The hour was nearly 5.00 and the street lamps were already lit, but it wasn't raining. We would, if we hurried, reach the post office before it closed; however, I would have to forget about telephoning Ben.

"Rubbishy superstition!" Dorcas swung her arms briskly as she marched down the street, the end of her tiger-striped scarf flapping out behind her. "Wouldn't give that woman's nonsense another thought if I were you."

"She didn't frighten me." Pushing open the door of the newsagent's, which housed the post office in its rear, we stepped over the threshold to the jangle of a small bell. "I'm not afraid that something dark and slimy is going to rise up through the night, clutch Tobias to its scaly breast and fly off with him, tucked between its ivory claws. But that woman did make one observation. . . . I think, subconsciously, I already realized that the drawing room lacked something."

"Pardon my saying so, but no extrasensory perception needed there." Dorcas closed the door behind us. "Room hasn't been properly cleaned in twenty years."

"But there should be dog hairs adding to the squalor and a scroungy mutt or two stretched out on the hearthrug, hogging all the heat from the fire."

"Sorry. Can't see where all this leads. But not to be ignored of course. Any information you collect will help build a psychological profile of Merlin Grantham, very important that you know what made the man tick."

Behind the post office grille a young man was sorting letters. He did not immediately look up. "What would really help" — I set my bag down on the counter and turned to face Dorcas — "would be talking to someone like that waitress's granny. As a former housemaid she could tell us not only about Uncle Merlin, but about his parents. They must have played a part in forming, or warping, his character, but I know next to nothing about them."

"May I be of assistance?" The young man straightened his horn-rimmed glasses looking, I thought irreverently, like a new priest eager to hear his first confession.

"A dozen twelve-pence stamps, please."

"Staying in the village on holiday, or just passing through?" The young man swung open a large green book and began unpeeling a strip of stamps.

"Neither. We live here, or I should say, a few miles outside the village. A relative of mine recently died. . . ."

The young man's jaw dropped slightly. "Is either of you ladies a Miss Ellie Simons? Yes? Well, I call that a real stroke of luck your walking in like this. We close in five minutes. Did you come by car?"

"Yes, but . . ."

"Hold on, I'll be right back."

The young man disappeared like a magician behind a long reddish-brown plush curtain and returned carrying a large flat package, wrapped in brown paper and bound with string. "Found it here leaning against the counter this morning," he explained. "No postage, only the names Mr Bentley Haskell and Miss Ellie Simons. Bit of a cheek really, I thought, no explanations, no stamps. The whole business rather put me on the spot. I recognized the names, you see. In a village this size there's always talk when new people move in, but technically" — he leaned earnestly forward — "rules and regulations being what they are, we are not supposed to encourage persons to cheat the Royal Mail. My supervisor gets back from his holiday tomorrow and I was going to ask him how we should handle the matter. Still, as you are here, I'll hand the package over and have you sign this receipt. A good thing you came by car — that hill's a regular puffer."

* * *

"Where," asked Dorcas, as we crossed the square, carefully carrying the package between us, "did you get the piece of paper on which you wrote your shopping list?"

"From the bureau in the drawing room. I tore it off a little pad. Why?"

"Because I am now certain Bentley did not write 'Post Office' on the back of that list; logical thing would have been to write postage stamps, or airmail letter forms, etc. No need to mention post office at all; such items are not found at the butcher's or the candlestick-maker's. Sorry to say it, but dimwits both of us. Tripped over Clue Number One without seeing it. Have to do better than this in the future."

"Funny!" I opened the car door and gently eased the package between the front and rear seats. "Only this morning you told me to be on the lookout for suspicious pieces of paper."

"Wasn't speaking literally," disclaimed Dorcas, taking her seat.

"The ploy was risky though. I might have written my list on a scrap of cardboard or a piece of paper towel."

"Treasure hunting is a game of chance, not an exact science. But I'd say the odds for success were good this time. Most natural thing in the world to look in that bureau for the right-sized piece of paper and tear off the top sheet."

I backed carefully out of our parking space. "Okay. Now we have to ask ourselves who is in cahoots with Uncle Merlin. That package did not shuffle into the post office on its own, and it seems sensible to assume that the note was written after his death. He would hardly have left it lying on his bureau collecting dust while he waited to die."

Dorcas nodded enthusiastically. "My guess is that on the day of the funeral, the go-between, who we will assume is a neutral person, possibly either the lawyer or the vicar, followed instructions and under cover of the general turmoil at the reading of the will, quietly replaced the old pad of paper with a new one."

"The doctor was also present for a while, but the person I think Uncle Merlin would have included in his little schemes is Aunt Sybil. Whether she agreed with him or not she would carry out every order and keep her mouth shut, which means there is no point in our trying to ferret anything out of her. She could have caught the bus down here this morning. There's a bus stop not too far from the gates. She could wait until the post office was busy, lean the package up against the counter, and walk out unnoticed."

"And she, more than anyone, had the opportunity to leave the note," agreed Dorcas.

We had reached the station, and the next five minutes were taken up with locating Dorcas's luggage and stowing it aboard. Back in the driver's seat I followed the wavering beam of the headlights up the ridge of the hill, still thinking about Uncle Merlin. "Something about this situation," I said to Dorcas, "strikes me as a little too pat. The family is called down for inspection, the stage is set, and the old man conveniently kicks the bucket. I know the doctor said he had a heart condition but . . ."

Dorcas's long thin nose quivered like a bloodhound on the breakfast trail. "Are you suggesting that Uncle Merlin took a leaf out of his mother's book and did himself in?"

"I wouldn't put it past the diabolical old fossil. He wasn't the type to sit around kicking his heels when he had cleverly arranged other people's lives to his satisfaction. The kicker is I really can't see how he could have accomplished it. The doctor did say pneumonia." I reached the iron gates and drove on down the driveway.

"An interesting theory." Dorcas nodded. "And murder would be even better, but I expect the truth is simpler. The man set his plans in motion and then closed his eyes in final sleep."

"Yes, even God would think twice about keeping Uncle Merlin in the waiting room beyond his appointed time." I drew the car up under the archway between the house and stables. "Help me out with this package, will you? The groceries can wait. We must find Ben and show him the Number One Clue."

"Hope he isn't one of those fanatics who refuse to cut string and insist on unravelling it knot by knot with their teeth," said Dorcas.

CHAPTER NINE

"Ladies and gentlemen," cried Ben, "let us start the bidding at one hundred and fifty thousand pounds for this remarkable painting, subject auburn-haired Edwardian lady holding lap-dog, artist unknown. Come on art lovers, all proceeds to the Bentley Haskell personal charity fund. Do I have a bid? Do I see a hand waving in the far corner . . . ?"

"That," I snapped, "was an obscene gesture indicating that if you don't climb down from that chair-cum-soapbox, I am going to tip you off."

The proceedings surrounding the opening of the package had rapidly degenerated to a mood of extreme giddiness, mainly because our expectations had been dashed. I think we had all expected a skull-and-crossbones map (laminated to a drawing board for easy viewing) signposted "To the Treasure." The reality was the portrait described by Ben. The auburn-haired lady might have considered herself lucky if her likeness fetched five pounds at a side-alley second-hand shop. We knew one thing about the artist — he wasn't descended from one of the Old Masters.

"I hope I write better than he painted!" Ben put the portrait down and rubbed his chin thoughtfully. "What's happened to Dorcas?"

"Your eloquence frightened her away," I said, sitting on the sofa with Tobias curled up on my lap. "She was afraid she might make a bid which she couldn't honour, so she went out to make tea."

"Is that it? Must have been my imagination then." Ben was still looking at the portrait. "I thought she looked a little uncomfortable when we undid the package. Wondered if she felt in the way."

"Embarrassed I would think by how awful it is, and afraid we would ask what she thought. . . . Here she comes now."

"Return of the wanderer. Will someone get the door?" carolled Dorcas from the hall.

"You shouldn't have," I protested, mouth watering when I saw what accompanied her. "Ben, look at those delicious ham and cheese sandwiches. Mm, and watercress, too! Dorcas, shame on you fetching in the groceries. That was Ben's job. We don't want his muscles to atrophy."

"Can't say the same about your jaw!" Ben reached for two sandwiches at once while Dorcas poured tea.

"Already I don't know what we would do without you, Dorcas." I ignored Ben's rudeness and slid my hand unobtrusively towards the edge of the plate.

"No, you don't." Ben reached out and slapped me away like a troublesome fly and then picked up a couple more sandwiches. "You get a tomato and a piece of cucumber. Half an hour ago you declared that food was of no consequence."

"Reduction is one thing, starvation is another," I retorted furiously.

"Here, here! Leave the girl alone, Bentley. Machinery has to be oiled if it is to work." Dorcas passed me a cup of tea. "Don't believe in skipping meals, three squares a day, that's my way. Never gain or lose an ounce. But can't all be alike, Ellie is a big girl. . . ."

"You said it, I didn't." The glutton, who was downing his ninth sandwich, grinned.

"Harassment never achieved a thing other than rebellion!" Dorcas turned staunchly towards him. "You write your book and let Ellie do what she has to do. She knows the score. Never did agree with all this pressure to turn women into rows of garden rakes. Look at me! Thin as bone. Does that make me a sex symbol? Huh! No man has ever wanted my figure."

For an earthquaking moment I thought from the glint in Ben's eye that he was about to make her an offer.

I finished my tea and refilled my cup. "I wonder what killed off our portrait lady?"

"Rabies, I would think." Ben looked content and replete lounging in his chair. "From the expression on that pug face he looks ready to chomp down at any minute."

"Having your likeness taken can't be much fun for a dog," I said. And, Tobias to show what he thought of canine models, yawned and leapt off my lap.

Ben picked up the portrait which he had leaned up against the coal scuttle. "Did women in those days always wear gloves?"

"Even in the bath — pretty nearly. One more fight against the lure of the flesh! I wonder if the Victorians and Edwardians ever thought about anything other than sex. But I have always liked the frothy hats and parasols."

"Actually" — Ben held the painting away from him — "I rather like her. The portrait is lousy, but she has a quality that appeals. She reminds me of someone."

"Oh really!" Dorcas spilled a little tea from the pot and was busy mopping it up, her face a little flushed. Clumsiness in a games mistress must be considered a major vice.

"Here, Ben, let me look." Reaching out impatiently I took the painting from him. "She certainly isn't a beauty, not even pretty — face is too long and flat and her nose too pointed. The hairdo doesn't help either. I always call that style the bird's nest."

"You're very critical." Ben sounded irritated.

"Not at all," I soothed. "I'm looking for the source of her charm because I agree with you there is something about her, something in the eyes. She's the kind they don't make any more." Finding the right words wasn't easy; the woman in the portrait was watching me, listening patiently. "An honest-to-goodness old-fashioned English lady," I floundered, "the type who made soup for everyone in the village and never turned a beggar away; but not a prig. There is humour and vulnerability as well as strength in that face. She wouldn't have been scared of gipsies, or afraid to blacken her hands at the stove, and she would have kicked off her shoes to share a cup of tea with her maid. . . ."

Ben looked impressed but said dryly, "Don't you think you are jumping to conclusions reading a whole character dossier from a very mediocre painting? We all agree that the artist should have joined his father's accounting firm or become a . . ."

"Chauvinist!" I said without rancour. "Why assume the artist was a man? If we are looking for an amateur, a female is a much likelier candidate. Girls of that era were all raised to work samplers, crochet, net purses and paint in water-colours and oils. Application, not talent, was considered the necessary requirement. And where would a dutiful daughter find a model? In the lady of the house, of course."

"I still think the style is masculine," objected Ben. Dorcas winced and shook her head slightly but apparently she had decided to stay out of the ring. Was Ben right, did she feel an intruder in the midst of this discussion? I got up and opened the door to let in Tobias, who was sharpening his claws on the woodwork. The grandfather clock in the hall chimed out the news that it was 9.30. Critiquing was turning into a lengthy business.

Ben grimaced but returned to his artistic commentary. "There are several other aspects concerning this portrait that I consider worthy of note. Ladies, are you ready?"

"I'm all ears," I said, returning to my seat. "Tobias, don't park on Uncle Ben's foot. He's a bit off you at present."

Ben ignored me. "The lady in the portrait lived in this house. You ask, naturally enough, how I cleverly divined this fact, which . . ."

Dorcas promptly raised her hand. I was glad she had decided to participate in "Questions and Answers." "Fireplace shown in background, very much out of proportion, but it is the one in this room. No mistaking carved cherubs worked into the wooden moulding. Quite unique, I would say."

"Very good," applauded Ben.

"The man thinks you are almost as clever as he is," I told Dorcas kindly.

"May we have a little hush!" Ben took the painting from me and paced up and down facing us, rotating it slowly so we could see all angles. "What I find interesting about the portrait is not its execution — we have all decided that is poor — but the fact that it is not titled or signed. Our artist may have wished to remain anonymous. I sympathize, but I do not think that is the explanation. Look again."

"It's not finished," I said slowly. "We have been looking at the woman, not at the background, and I suppose I put 'the something missing' down to the artist's inability to express what he saw, but when I get up close I can see that only the woman is completed and she doesn't have any feet."

"Not wishing to cast a blight on your observation" — Dorcas leaned forward — "but must ask, does it matter whether picture is finished or not? If a schoolgirl did indeed paint the piece, lack of perseverance is typical. Sun shines, out comes the tennis outfit and away go the paint pots and brushes."

"Agreed." Ben accepted the comment in good part. "But we have to assume the portrait is significant in some way, which means searching for straws. As clues go I'm not ecstatic about this one."

"Have you prodded the canvas to see if some message is tucked inside it? That's the way books do it. In *The Counterfeit Mona Lisa* the portrait has a false back, which fell off in the hero's hands," I suggested sleepily. I caught myself yawning. I still had to show Dorcas her room, which meant finding one with the smallest accumulation of dust and putting fresh sheets on the bed. Dorcas was collecting up the cups and saucers while Ben held up the portrait to the light for one last look.

"If you are hoping to find a hidden masterpiece shining through the top layer of paint, I think you are doomed to disappointment. I doubt if any of the artist's earlier efforts were superior to this one. And I can't see some amateur plastering his own work over a Renoir or Van Gogh."

"I don't know so much. Where Uncle Merlin is involved I think we must expect something lunatic. . . . We write off the picture as junk, store it in the attic, and six months from now we find . . ."

"Speaking of the attic." I yawned again. "That's another place I have to explore. So perhaps we should all get a little shut-eye. Ben, bring in Dorcas's luggage while I see about her room."

"Can't have you waiting on me." Dorcas attempted to take the tray out of my hands. "I'm here to work, not sit lazing around."

"Nonsense." Ben held the door open for her. "Ellie and I think of you as one of the family. More of a companion than a housekeeper."

Dorcas flushed, a painful mottled red which clashed with her hair. Seeing her embarrassment at a rather mild compliment, I shook my head. "She doesn't want to be one of those. Companions are always downtrodden grey ladies banished with their tatting box to the draughtiest corner of the room, and only tolerated because they are distantly related to the family." I spoke lightly but as I did so, a thought occurred. Another name applied to Dorcas's services in this house: "chaperone." Ben and I would no longer be alone at night. Was this, rather than a concern for my detergent hands, the reason he had placed the advertisement in the paper?

While Dorcas did the washing up, I went upstairs and collected bed linen. I gave her the room next to mine, Spartanly furnished with a single bed and a plain oak chest of drawers. When Ben came up with the cases I was spreading an eiderdown over the blankets. He agreed that the room was not very inviting but at least the wallpaper was not peeling damply from the walls, and the curtains did not crumble to dust at the touch of human hand. Dorcas, appearing moments later, seemed quite satisfied. "Certainly no worse than my cubicle at school. Shouldn't have made the bed up though, quite capable of fending for myself."

"Dorcas." I touched her gently on the arm and looked very directly into the hazel eyes under the shaggy brows. "Please climb down from your high horse. I have never been an employer, except once," — I sent Ben a smouldering sidelong glance — "and that is best forgotten. I thought we agreed earlier that this was going to be a team effort?"

Dorcas blinked rapidly, gave a slight sniff and, extending a hand, shook mine fiercely. "Never looked forward to anything more in my life. Together we'll win this game of hide-and-seek."

"And the best of British luck to all of us." Ben leaned against the door jamb. "Don't stay up too late, ladies, we don't want to spoil sport for the ghosts, shy creatures that they are. They won't start their prowling until everyone is tucked up in bed."

"The only person who prowls is Aunt Sybil," I said. "The night we moved in I caught her at it, and a couple of times since. A lot of elderly people have trouble sleeping."

"Ellie, you are so naive," scoffed Ben. "Under that frumpy old lady exterior Aunt Sybil is quite as weird as the rest of your batty relations. I expect the moon was full and she was stretching her vocal cords."

I was the one who had trouble sleeping that night. The day had been so eventful that hunger had remained at bay, a small plaintive hand tapping at the outside of my consciousness. Flat on my back with the light turned off starvation threatened to storm the citadel. Worse! I began to entertain lustful thoughts. I desired a roast beef sandwich with horse-radish and pickled onions with a wanton savagery that I had never felt for any man.

I have often read, in those "true life experience" magazines, how in moments of deepest crises people have been rescued from the chasm by a voice floating out of nowhere, with warnings such as: "Marge dearest, do not marry the man with the black handlebar moustache and the eagle talons where his hands should be. Fernando is a fortune-hunter who has murdered nineteen wives and wants to make an even number." My experience was not quite that uncanny but as I swung my legs over the side of the bed and fumbled for my bedroom slippers, I remembered some quite simple words Ben had spoken to Dorcas that evening, so ordinary in fact that at the time I had not attached any significance to them. I replayed them now: "Ellie and I think of you as one of the family."

Ben could as easily have said "part of the group" or "one of the gang" but he had said "family." He had linked himself with me, however momentarily, in a warmer bond. I lay back and held those fragile words to me like a flower, touching each syllable, each petal, gently, until one by one they fell away and drifted off into the night. Smiling into the darkness I wriggled into the hollow spot of my lumpy mattress and kissed the roast beef sandwich goodnight.

I awoke the following morning feeling rather more rational. Sentimentality looks a little silly in broad daylight, but my determination to stick with my diet had fixed. At breakfast I watched Dorcas and Ben chomping down on bacon and eggs without too strong a pang. Half a grapefruit didn't do much for my appetite but it promised (rather sourly) to do marvellous things for my figure.

Dorcas spread chunky orange marmalade on her toast. "Not much of a cook, I'm afraid, always thought cookery books harder to decipher than Greek but if you're not afraid of being poisoned, I'll do my best."

"Tell the expert," I said, taking a mouth-shuddering spoonful of grapefruit. "Ben's Cordon Bleu."

"No dice." The recipient of this soap-job looked up briefly from the book he was reading between mouthfuls. "I told you I'm retired. This morning was different, I gave Dorcas a hand with the 'fry' because she is new and . . ." He drank a sip of coffee and spluttered, "Yuck! Dorcas, what blend did you use for this witch's brew? Tobacco juice and ashes?"

"Instant."

"I give in!" said Ben. "If you can do this to hot water and a teaspoon of brown crystals I daren't think what you might do to dinner. You and Ellie can have the fun jobs like swabbing floors; I'll be the resident chef."

"Motion carried." I poured myself a glass of tomato juice and raised it in salute. "Don't think, Ben, that I fail to realize why I was never considered for the job. But I'm not resentful. Cooking is a very dangerous occupation in my state of transition and the less time I spend in the kitchen the better. On the subject of food, how is Jonas Phipps managing? I gather he has cooking facilities in his rooms, but what about shopping? I know there is a bus but . . ."

"Don't worry about the old boy." Ben rather reluctantly put his book down. "People of his age still manage to fend for themselves. Jonas doesn't exert himself more than need be, but good grief, he's no older than my father! Being seventy doesn't make a man an ancient monument."

"Neither is he a spring chicken," I said. "And cooking for himself he won't be getting his vitamins and minerals. We don't want him ending up run-down. I suggest we invite him to share breakfast and lunch with us; that way he will have two good meals a day and if he wants to eat bread and dripping for dinner it won't matter. A light meal at night is better for people his age anyway."

Dorcas nodded. "Kind thought. My grandmother always said . . ." She paused and took a sip of coffee — "a little more water in the stew and no one notices the extra mouth to feed."

After a round of fresh coffee, I called an organizational meeting. Ben, it was agreed, would not try to dazzle us with his culinary techniques that day. We would have a light lunch and supper. He wanted to spend the day with his book to make up for the unproductivity of yesterday.

"Baked beans on toast will do me fine." Dorcas was already rolling up her sleeves.

"All right." I put down my cup. "Dorcas, I think you and I should tackle Uncle Merlin's bedroom this morning. Everybody happy?"

My enthusiasm faltered a little when we reached the room and I took another look at the dust and detritus accumulated by half a century of neglect. But I reminded myself that buried beneath the cobwebs might be another clue, or at least an explanation of the clue we had already received. A man who hoarded laundry shirt boxes must have kept other souvenirs, like newspaper clippings or letters. The first order of the day was to take down the sagging maroon velvet curtains from the window, and let in light and air.

"Not worth cleaning!" snorted Dorcas in disgust. "Thick with moth, and stiff with dirt."

Sneezing violently, as a swirl of dust — equal to any desert sandstorm — blew out of the folds, we staggered under the enormous weight of the material. When we finally got the curtains unhooked we were faced with the question of where to put them. Mounted on chairs at both ends of the window, Dorcas and I looked at each other. Nodding like a pair of identical mechanical dolls, we flung open the casement and bailed the lot out. The same fate awaited the stained bedspread. Fifty or more years ago it had matched the curtains. In a sense it still did. Another eruption of dust almost choked us as we lumbered over to the window. Blankets and sheets followed.

"Mattress?" Dorcas raised a shaggy eyebrow.

"Right. Out it goes." By this time we had synchronized the old heave-ho routine to perfection. The mattress sailed out the window like a magic flying carpet.

"One blessing." Dorcas was brushing the grime from her hands onto her dungarees. "In the good old days they made windows a sensible size."

Stripped, the room looked a little indecent, naked. Dorcas and I divided up; she took on the huge wardrobe, and I pulled up the bedside chair and opened the mahogany desk. Two drawers revealed nothing of interest, other than a large assortment of old Christmas cards. Rather surprisingly, these were neatly grouped together by year and on some, comments had been noted: "Nice pair of carpet slippers this year" and "Another box of peppermint humbugs — doesn't the woman know they yank my teeth out." In addition to the Christmas cards I found several boxes of used cheque books — again nothing exciting there, other than the fact Uncle Merlin had on several occasions either given or lent money to both Aunt Astrid and Uncle Maurice. From the sums involved neither had done badly out of the old man while he lived.

In the third drawer was a large cardboard box bundled with bills. Thumbing through I found them all marked paid in full and the dates. One caught my eye; it was a subscription to a free veterinary clinic. I studied it briefly and put it down.

"Any major discoveries?"

"Not really. Except Uncle Merlin looks better on paper than he did in real life. Turns out he gave the relatives quite a bit of financial help, and here he is making donations to an animal home. You'd think if he liked the four-legged race that much he'd have had a pet of his own, which brings me back to what that waitress said about this house having the wrong atmosphere. . . . How about you, found anything?"

"Four boxes of those round laminated collars with studs."

"Hang onto them. They are antiques!"

At the back of the bill drawer was another cardboard box, smaller than the other and lighter. Lifting the lid I experienced a sudden premonition. This was important. I saw at once that the letters it contained were old, but what interested me more at first were the toys. They were small and worn, remnants, I supposed, of a child's visit long ago to Merlin's Court. Peeling open the top letter, I saw from the date that it was sixty years old and its tone was stilted, authoritative, pompous. Hardly today's informal letter from Daddy to his son away at boarding school.

Poor Merlin! (For the letter was addressed to him.) In one of those peculiar flashbacks which sometimes come from reading old letters, I could see him vividly — a knobby-kneed, ink-smeared schoolboy in short trousers, striped tie, and peaked cap. Stricken with a father such as his no wonder the kid had grown into an oddball. Arthur Grantham had always been a vague figure to me, the skipped step in the family ladder. I had gleaned more about him from Brassy the waitress yesterday than I had from my mother or the family.

The letters all bore the same message. Rearing a child was an awesome responsibility at best, and to a widower like Arthur Grantham a great trial. How "sharper than a serpent's tooth" it was to have raised a son who shared none of his father's talents or virtues and had the audacity to resemble his mother in taste and feeling. I was heartened to discover that Arthur admitted to one mistake in the course of his lifetime; he had married a woman unworthy of him. The sins of mother and son were dissected minutely.

I laid the fifth letter with its brethren and picked up the sixth wondering if I really wanted to read any more of this pompous piety. "Oh well, in for a penny . . ."

The letter began:

My dearest Merlin, happy as I am that you are enjoying your visit to the seaside, I must tell you that the days go slowly by without you. Think me very selfish, but I confess I am anxious for your return and so are the animals. I was sorry that Sybil's kitten got lost.

Uncle Arthur in a more affable mood? Turning the page, I read the signature — *Your loving Mother, Abigail Grantham.* This letter, dated four years prior to the others, had been folded into a small square. Making it, I thought, just the right size to tuck into a small clenched palm where no one could see it. A sort of security blanket for a little boy whose mother had died, and whose father did not like him much. The time-scarred toys in the box assumed a thoughtful new significance. They had not belonged to a child who had come to visit and forgotten them on his return home. The wooden camel with the broken hump and the painted train engine had been the playthings of the boy Merlin. I was sure of that. At the ripe old age of nine or ten when he was sent away to boarding school, his stiff-necked father probably ordered him to put away the trappings of childhood and immerse himself in Greek and Latin. My mental impression of Arthur Grantham was a man dipped in starch along with his linen, slicked-down hair parted in the middle, eyes like brown cough drops and a twirled wax moustache that never came unravelled.

What had the man really looked like? I riffled through the drawer again. Pulling open the others I had already searched, I left them stacked out like a row of steps in my haste. No photographs.

"Dorcas," I said to the wardrobe, "can you manage without me for a few minutes? Fine! Tell you about it anon!" Down to the bureau in the drawing room. From its state of chaos I knew this had been used by Aunt Sybil, but being the jackdaw she was I might find a wad of old snapshots under the litter. Besides, I remembered something about the bureau. In a rare benign mood during one of my childhood visits Uncle Merlin had shown me a secret. There was a false bottom to the main drawer. Slowly inching this out I held my breath. Nothing. Nothing but more old bills, a dilapidated telephone directory, and a yellowed travel brochure itemizing the charms of a tropical paradise. Had Uncle Merlin once planned a trip for his health? Somehow I could not envision him sitting under a striped umbrella wearing a pair of skimpy bathing trunks and oversized sunglasses. I was disappointed because the memory of the secret drawer had raised hopes of finding more than old bills. One day soon I would box up all this stuff and send it down to Aunt Sybil.

The stampeding movement of typewriter keys from the dining room across the hall informed me that Ben was hard at work. Lunch, therefore, was not imminent. I went through the kitchen to the alcove by the garden door and unhooked my raincoat from its peg. The day was overcast and thick with clouds. A buffeting wind laced with rain punched into me the moment I set foot outside. With my rain hood flapping about my ears, I ran across the courtyard. I caught a glimpse of Jonas staring round the stable door, dressed in a sou'wester and oilskin coat. Ben had set him to clean out the moat, which had become a dumping ground for litter, but the elements had forced him to retreat to dry ground.

Cupping my hands around my mouth, I bawled across the wind, "Come up to the house for lunch, Jonas."

"Aye, won't say no. Had a bellyful of me own cooking these last few days. Ain't nothing highfalutin, is it? I take me grub plain. If I want snails I've got plenty in the cabbage patch."

"You'll eat what you're given," I yelled, and I was off. I could feel old Jonas watching me. Goodness knows why. A fat girl running is not one of the lovelier sights of nature.

Aunt Sybil took her time answering the doorbell. Assuming she must have taken the bus down to the village, I was about to turn away when I heard her feet slapping down the hall in oversized carpet slippers. The cottage door opened an inch, then widened, rather tentatively, I thought.

"Oh, it's you, Giselle." Aunt Sybil sounded as though she had been hoping for someone else, the coalman perhaps on a day like this. Or the vicar? That might explain the uneven streak of lipstick across her mouth and the mismatched earrings protruding from her lobes.

I explained my search for old photographs and followed her into her overstuffed sitting room. Every surface was smothered with magazines, books, rusty tin canisters, or blobs of tangled knitting wool stabbed through with metal needles.

Aunt Sybil started to gesture vaguely that I sit down, but thought better of it. Standing about, I felt like a stranger, which in a way I was. I had never known her well.

"Sorry, Giselle, but I can't help you." She was glancing absently around the room. "I was devoted to Uncle Arthur, but at my age hanging onto mementoes becomes overly sentimental." (I refused to follow her gaze which must have absorbed the mass of useless paraphernalia, making Queen Victoria look like an amateur collector.) "I destroyed all old photographs years ago."

I was almost certain she was lying. And I could not blame her. She might well feel that Ben and I had more than enough without demanding a piece of her past as well. But as I made a move to go, she unbent a little. She did have some snapshots of Uncle Merlin, if I would care to see them? What surprised me was that she found them so fast and when she handed them to me they were neatly wrapped in tissue paper. Alas, the package was better than the products. Every one showed Uncle Merlin taken unawares in the garden, with half his head missing. "'Tact versus Truth" was an old family motto on my father's side. My enthusiastic response to headless Uncle Merlin brought its own reward. Aunt Sybil unbent still further and offered me a verbal glimpse of Uncle Arthur. "He was a dear, wonderful man," she volunteered, folding up the tissue package. "Would you like to know his pet name for me?" She flushed slightly at the remembered compliment and smoothed one of the inevitable wrinkles in her dress. "'His little ray of morning sunshine.' And in those days children were expected to behave — not slouch or wriggle — so you see, if Uncle Arthur thought me special it was a great compliment.

"Poor Uncle Arthur, he did not have an easy life," sighed Aunt Sybil. "You know he was widowed early?"

"Did Abigail Grantham suffer a lingering illness?"

"Oh no. Quite the reverse. At the time, you understand, I was very young and not then living in this house, so I remember nothing except that she went very suddenly. I came for the funeral, and that stands out in my memory but nothing about the cause of death. Just between us, perhaps it was a blessed release, for Uncle Arthur, too. Abigail, to put it as nicely as possible, was a bit of a social liability. Not out of the top drawer. And then, she was not the best influence on Merlin. Under her care he was growing up rather rowdy."

Aunt Sybil was such an infernal snob, I thought, but then her sagging cheeks puckered and I felt sorry for her. Had she resented Merlin's freedom to be naughty, while she had to be good to please? "So long ago," she murmured. "A few years after Abigail's death my parents died and Uncle Arthur took me into his home. Of course there was a little money which he managed for me, but I know he would have treated me the same if I had been a pauper. He was such a good man — always wearing the knees out in his trousers praying. And now," she squared her shoulders and I had to admire the courageous set of her heavy jaw, "another new start. And with more free time on my hands I have decided to take up some hobbies. Being of an artistic nature I've always been interested in sculpture, so I've decided to do each member of the family a head of Merlin for Christmas. I'm working in papier-mâché as I have so many old newspapers. What do you think" — she fixed her vague no-colour eyes disconcertingly on my face — "of my using a clear varnish instead of paint, to retain the literary symbolism?"

I could see myself whiling away a dull moment reading Uncle Merlin's head.

"And I've also decided to take up swimming," she continued before I was forced to comment. "Only last week I read about a woman of ninety-six who attempted a Channel crossing. She didn't make it but she did make a big splash in the papers and I am almost thirty years younger. Such an inexpensive hobby, too." She bent and picked up one of the tangled balls of wool. "I can knit myself a costume and with a pair of water wings from Woolworth's I will be all set."

She was certainly eccentric, but I had to give her a tremendous amount of credit coming to terms with grief by diving into the swim of things. Dorcas would approve.

What I wanted to dive into was lunch so I was delighted to be met by a taste-tingling aroma as I entered the kitchen at Merlin's Court. French onion soup! And with the added virtue, so the resident chef informed me, of possessing so small a number of calories they could be counted on one hand. Naturally, I would not get the toasted au gratin slice or the lemon pancakes with lingonberry sauce for dessert.

"Show-off!" I said, skimming bowls like Frisbees across the table. "While you have been puttering about the kitchen doing what women have been doing since time began, with no thanks at all, I have been searching for old family records. Looking for clues to the Number One Clue."

"Any discoveries?" Ben turned down the heat under his soup.

"Only that Merlin's parents, Uncle Arthur and Aunt Abigail, did not have the kind of marriage that is made in heaven, that Uncle A. liked Sybil more than his own son, so she believes. Merlin in his young days was a bit of a mischief."

"In his old days, too."

The kitchen door swung inwards, nearly catching me in the back. "Fe! Fi! Fo! Fum! I smell something good enough for an Englishman." Everyone seemed to be getting the same message at once. The back door opened and in trudged Jonas, water running off his mackintosh onto the floor.

"Dorcas," I said, after I had introduced her to the gardener, "let me take those shirt boxes. You needn't have brought them down. They should have gone out the window with the other rubbish. I was only joking about the collars being antiques."

"Don't think you would want these boxes thrown out," rasped Dorcas. "No collars in this lot. Full of old photographs."

"Give them here!" Ben outgrabbed me, literally tearing the box out of poor Dorcas's hands. The three of us huddled together. Only the gardener remained oblivious, sucking noisily on the soup Ben had poured for him, head bent.

"That's her!" Dorcas pointed to a brown, spotted snapshot. As she leaned forward a strand of limp red hair fell across one eye, giving her a piratical appearance. "The woman in the portrait and here's the name and date written on the back. Abigail Grantham."

CHAPTER TEN

This revelation, though interesting, hinted only that the treasure might in some way be connected with Abigail. Ben suggested the theory that she had hidden a hoard of jewellery before her death to prevent her husband passing it on to a second wife. I disagreed. According to Aunt Sybil, Abigail had not come from money and from the look of Uncle Arthur (his photos depicted him just the way I had imagined — middle hair-parting, waxed moustache and all), he was not the man to have squandered his money draping his wife in diamonds and pearls.

After spending the better part of the afternoon discarding other equally feeble brainstorms, we decided that our best course of action was to await the arrival of Clue Number Two. This is not to say that the next few weeks were idle or dull. The Reverend Mr Foxworth called several times. He was such an attractive man, but I am not a girl who can afford to be caught with a grimy moustache and her hair in a duster. As the days lengthened and warmed into spring, Dorcas and I continued our onslaught against grime. At times I grew tired of smelling like a bottle of all-purpose household cleaner, but by mid-May our accomplishments began to justify our efforts. I had contacted Mr Bragg, the solicitor, to arrange for the release of funds for repairs and redecorating. Far from chiding me for my eagerness to spend money before the end of the probationary six months, he admitted that the value of the property would be vastly increased by the application of my professional talents.

One thing I did not want was to continue working in the dark (literally). The gas lighting downstairs was ruining my eyes, and I telephoned the electricity board and made the necessary arrangements. Not only did we get proper illumination, but I was able to purchase that marvellous modern convenience, the vacuum cleaner, and plug it into action. Dorcas was a tower of strength. I began to feel guilty about her pushing herself so hard. The house, in its present state of decay, even with the progress we had made, was too much for one fat woman and one skinny one. Early one morning I told Dorcas to hand over her dustpan, no questions asked, fetch her coat, and go out to the car. This was the maids' day off.

"Am I invited?" Ben came out from the dining room, looking rumpled but disquietingly attractive in a frayed seaman's sweater. The only times he spoke to us during the mornings were when he had a bad case of writer's block. At times Sister Marie Grace was a great trial to her creator.

"Sorry, this is a hen party, but don't despair, we will be home for dinner. How about another triumph from the chef? I wrote a sonnet to that last beef roulade in my diary."

"I suppose you could call that one of my finer achievements," Ben smirked.

"Makes me feel terribly inferior, but keep up the good work." I tied on a head-scarf and made a face at the fatuous creep. "While you are at it, whip up some of those delectable potato scones. I know I can't eat them, but the smell is terrific."

* * *

The day was so blue and clear and the breeze coming off the sea so fresh and tangy I felt like a child playing truant.

Dorcas also was in high spirits, even her outfit was jaunty. She sported a navy and yellow jersey over trousers patterned in rather atrocious pyjama stripes.

"Where to, driver?" she asked as the car slid tidily into its parking place and we made ready to disembark.

"The Labour Exchange. I want to arrange for two charwomen to come up to the house every day for a couple of weeks to take us over the hump."

"Thought we were managing okay," protested Dorcas rather dolefully.

"So we are," I agreed. "But I want us to move on to more exciting projects. The attics are jammed with pieces I may want to move downstairs. We have already been in the house over a month, and there is an incredible amount to be done before our time runs out. I am itching to redo the kitchen, and you were saying the other day you would like to dig up the old herb garden. And then there is the moat half full of muddy rainwater and still floating debris. . . ."

Happily discussing future plans, we went through the Roman arch into the square. To our delight we found the day had presented us with another bonus. The area was crowded with wooden stalls. Men and women were hawking their wares, and elbow-shoving shoppers eagerly bartered over each held-up item. This was market day. "Want two quid for that, do yer?" bawled a red-faced woman with rollers poking through her head-scarf. "Come off it, mate! 'Alf the buttons is missing and the collar's on the wrong way round. Flaming cheek!"

Dorcas and I were tempted to linger, milling with the crowd, but business had to come first. We inched our way through the jostling throng and headed for the Labour Exchange, where we were treated like visiting royalty and given the names of several worthy matrons who would be happy to work on a temporary basis and could be trusted not to steal the silver. Having set the wheels of industry in motion, we visited the bank and armed with cash went down the road to the grocery.

Our duty done, my friend and I were free for the pursuit of pleasure. We were drawn back to the market area, fascinated by the patter of the stallsmen. All were artists in their own right.

"'Ere, you! The lovely lady with the gobs of long brown 'air!" A scrawny man with greasy black sideburns and eyes small and shiny bright as shoe buttons was standing behind row upon row of shampoo in bottles ranging in size and colour. He waved a wiry, tattooed arm in my direction. Mesmerized, I moved in front of two giggling schoolchildren, hoping that the eyes of the whole crowd were not upon me.

"That's the way, love, don't be shy. Nice 'air, wery nice," the man said to the crowd. "But, and no offence to the lovely young lady, wery dry. Been washing it in turpentine, 'ave you, duck?"

The crowd roared as I stood rooted to the spot with Dorcas panting in my ear.

"Which is a shame and all, but no reason to give up 'ope." My Svengali reached out and grabbed a large bottle in the shape of a mermaid, full of purple liquid. "Yours at a price, ladies and gentlemen, it would be wicked to refuse. Stand back, please, no pushing an' shoving. Only six bottles left, an' this one is for the little darlin' 'ere. And the best bit o' news yet is that this fantastic shampoo is fully guaranteed to make your 'air grow an extra inch a monf."

"More likely to make it all fall out in one day," stormed Dorcas, outraged, and receiving for her intervention a ribald cheer from the mob.

"I'll take a bottle." Hastily reaching into my purse I handed over a pound, explaining to anyone who cared to listen that it was my birthday in two days' time, and I might as well buy myself a present. Dorcas, not appeased, hustled me through the milling crowds when I bumped into a tall woman with a long greasy pony tail; at least I thought it was a woman. I really only saw the back of her — him — and a flash of gold earring.

"Haven't drunk anything out of that bottle, have you?" Dorcas slipped her arm through mine. "Look a bit queer."

"Just hungry," I said. The clock tower struck noon. The Hounds and Hare was the change of scene we needed. Brassy called over the bar to us that the 'ash was burnt but the meat pudding melted in the mouth.

"Suits me," said Dorcas. Demonstrating magnificent restraint, I ordered a salad and we headed for a window table. I was beginning to find discipline brought its own satisfaction, not very filling of course. And I was learning to savour every mouthful, even the Espresso coffee which, like the 'ash, tasted burnt.

Dorcas dropped three sugar lumps into her cup and our food arrived. "Uncle Merlin should have given you more time. Typical man to think if the world was made in seven days it could be put right in six."

"Well, he did give us months, not days. The trouble is the days are galloping by." I lowered my voice because I always eavesdrop in restaurants and for some reason today I had the paranoid feeling that others in the crowded room shared my habit.

"Speaking of time passing, is your birthday really the day after tomorrow?"

Reluctantly, I admitted it was. Before this confession could lead anywhere, Brassy wandered over to our table. She had mentioned us to Granny, unlocking a floodgate of memories about her days in service with the Granthams. If it would not be imposing or out of our way a short visit would be greatly appreciated, as Granny rarely went out of the house these days.

* * *

We stopped at a florist in the square and bought a bunch of daffodils. Granny lived in one of the lopsided terraced houses on the coast road beyond the village. The door was opened by a peachy-faced little dame whose hair, still more brown than grey, was neatly knotted at the back of her head.

I was sure Dorcas was thinking as I was that if we could look this well at eighty-odd we wouldn't be doing badly.

No explanations of who we were or why we had come seemed necessary, and the daffodils were gratefully accepted. We were promptly seated by a crisp red fire in the front parlour with its photographs on the sideboard and crocheted doilies on the polished wood. A plate of rock buns appeared (to have refused, one would have to be moronic) and we were told tea would not be a minute. In spite of the oceans of coffee I had just drunk, the sight of the black kettle sizzling on the hob was enchanting. I loved this little toadstool house. It was like slipping between the pages of a children's book where the hostess was a comfy little dormouse sitting beside her fire in dimity dress and white starched apron and cap.

As a young kitchen maid up at the house Granny must have worn such a costume. When we addressed her by her married name, Mrs Hodgkins, she insisted we call her Rose. She had been twelve when she went to work.

"Those were hard days," said Dorcas.

The old woman bent to scoop tea leaves from a small canister into the earthenware pot and filled it with steaming water from the kettle. "Times weren't easy, but I was fortunate in having a good mistress. Most days Mrs Grantham was down and in the kitchen when I arrived, and more days than not she'd say, 'Set yourself down by the stove, Rose, and have yourself a cup of tea.' Made me cry sometimes how kind she was. One day I came hobbling in, barely able to lift me feet, the chilblains was that bad what with the cold and wet shoes. Told me to take off me stockings she did and put on this ointment and a bandage. A great hand she was for mixing up remedies. The cook was furious, I remember that, because I was sent off to the morning room to sit and mend sheets. Though what the missus wanted with a cook I never did know. I've worked many places since, but I never met another like Mrs Grantham for coming up with something different. A great one to experiment, she was. Sent a recipe to me mum, she did, for fudge that you couldn't undercook or overcook, delicious it was."

"And Mr Grantham?" I put out my hands to take a cup.

"Dreadful man." Rose did not apologize for not mincing words. "The big-I-am type, puffed out like a parrot, always wanting to impress the neighbours. Most people in them days received afternoon callers once or twice a week, but Mr Grantham insisted the mistress be at home every day of the week. My word, she did used to get vexed having to be dressed up and sitting in the drawing room for hours on end, entertaining them dowagers and debutantes. She'd rather have been baking or gardening or out flying a kite with Master Merlin."

"Did they quarrel?"

"The mister and missus? Did they ever!" Rose straightened a doily on the arm of her chair. "Everything was show with Mr G. I mind a time a great lady come to the house, got stuck in a storm, she had. Motorcars didn't like bad weather in them days. And oh! you should have heard his nibs carrying on because the missus took her ladyship into the kitchen instead of the drawing room. They talked recipes and remedies and such. 'Dead common,' he called the missus, but her ladyship couldn't have taken no offence for she sent a thank-you letter and a little present — an Easter egg, for little Merlin, I suppose. I remember all that because it was about the time Mr G. got the notion to have the missus's picture done. Not because he was so devoted but because it were the done thing. Trouble was he weren't prepared to cough up for a proper artist — got a boy from the village, Miles Biddle. I remember his father was a clerk at the bank. Nice lad but his pictures was proper dreadful."

"So that's who did it. We were curious about the artist — we have the painting, but it was not finished." I looked at Dorcas for corroboration, but she was busy stirring her tea.

"The rows that painting caused. The missus wasn't good-looking. Weren't her fault, except according to Mr G. what he wanted was one of them ladies in tall white wigs with them bits of black confetti stuck on their faces — like Marie Antonetti before they took her head off. Said the missus looked more like a servant than mistress of a big house. Joan the parlour maid told me that bit (she was cleaning dust out of the drawing room keyhole, so she said), then mister got started on Miles Biddle, would have it that the lad didn't know his place."

"Really!" I said. Perhaps Aunt Sybil couldn't help being a snob; it was a genetic fault.

"All nonsense. Miles were too shy to be pushy — used to blush when missus spoke to him. Joan liked to take the mickey out of him, they was the same age, about twenty. She'd giggle and tell him what a prime bit of stuff he was, and off he'd scoot. Around the missus he was all right though. Too much so, according to Mr G. when he found the lad wasn't coming in through the tradesmen's entrance."

"And why not?" Dorcas bristled; I hoped she wasn't feeling demeaned by all this talk of back entrances. "He may have been an inferior artist, but he wasn't peddling trumperies door to door."

"Don't you worry none. The missus stood up for him. Said the lad was doing them the favour. Such a go-round, which she hated on account of young Merlin. Always her first thought he was. Used to have that cousin of his, Sylvia, or was it Sybil? over for long holidays to keep him company. Mucky little blighter she was. Her bedroom! The state of it. And when the missus would speak to her about it, she'd say the little dog had got in and done it. I ask you! Always so timid, but Mr G., he liked Miss Sybil, but wicked as it is to say, I've often found that his type of man — the ones with prayer calluses on their knees — have a thing about little girls."

Rose was refilling the teapot and I asked her why the portrait was never completed. Much to my disappointment she said she did not know. Shortly after the portrait was started it was discovered that Rose was suffering from tuberculosis and a year in a sanatorium was the result. When she was sent back home, she was told that Mrs Grantham had died. For years she had worried that she might have passed on her disease to her mistress, particularly as her mum had taken a clamp-lipped attitude on the subject of the death and had ordered Rose not to ask questions. But once she married she began to hear rumours that had nothing to do with TB. Abigail's death had been hushed up. Even the doctor would not talk, which could mean only one thing — suicide.

"And can't say as I blame her, poor dear lady," said Rose sadly. "Wouldn't be anything for her to fear in the next world, would there? Not after the hell her husband put her through on earth."

We left our new friend with promises of returning to visit her again soon. Outside on the pavement the sky was threaded with shades of pink and rose, deepening in places to damson and crimson. I love sunsets and was beginning to realize how much I had grown to care for Merlin's Court and the rugged strip of coastline, to say nothing of the village.

Ben was in the kitchen when we got back and, surprise! Freddy had telephoned to chat and afterthought, to hear how we were faring in tracking down the treasure.

"I told him nothing," said Ben. "Nothing to tell, and I am not seriously concerned that if he got wind of where to look Freddy would dig a tunnel under the house. I simply thought it politic to keep quiet."

"Did he say where he was? He wasn't ringing up from this area, was he?" I asked edgily. I was about to spill part of the armload of butter, cheese, and sausages I was attempting to stash in the new refrigerator while Dorcas hung up our coats. Anyway, I was relieved when Ben said Freddy had rung from home, miles away from here. He wouldn't be following up his phone call with a personal visit.

"His other reason for ringing was to ask for money." Ben took the sausages from me. "He seems to think we are under a moral obligation to keep him in the style to which he would like to become accustomed. I promised him twenty quid but that's his lot."

"How soon the *nouveau riche* forget. Remember, Galahad, when you were scrounging an existence on bread and dripping and selling your smile to pay the rent. Freddy's not a bad sort. Just because to us all hippies look alike doesn't mean he isn't an individual with his own worries."

"You're unusually magnanimous this evening." Ben brushed past me on his way to the table with the bubbling pot, almost branding me on the arm. "But let's get one thing clear from the beginning. I do not intend to support your sponging relatives for the rest of their natural (or should I say, unnatural) lives. Has my mother been on the phone trying to put the touch on you?"

"Now wait just a minute!" I slammed the refrigerator door with such emphasis the motor revved up. "How did your sainted mother get into this? Did she leave us a fortune? No. She tossed her sonny boy out on his ear — a prey to the benefice of the first rich old man to cross his path."

"So? No one's perfect," replied Ben equably as he lifted the casserole lid and inhaled deeply.

"Curing a cold?"

"No." Ben wrinkled his brow, and sniffed again. In the voice of one deeply concerned he asked, "Do you think I went a little heavy on the garlic? Perhaps I should have omitted that last squeeze of onion juice."

My mouth watered. I smiled slyly. "Now you mention it, I do detect a rather pungent quality not quite in keeping with that *pièce de résistance*, the steak smothered in béarnaise sauce that you conjured up for us last night. Hand me the ladle and . . ."

"Oh no, you don't." Ben replaced the lid. "Poulet en crême parmigiana is fatal to diets. You get a cos salad with fresh spring vegetables, chilled in lemon juice and tarragon."

In this enlightened age deprivation wasn't so bad, and possibly as male chauvinists went, neither was Ben. It was his indifference to my charms that I found infuriating. Why couldn't life be the way it was in the TV adverts: A girl changed her shampoo and men came buzzing round like flies round a jam jar. Perhaps if I tried the bottle I had bought at the market I would wake up tomorrow morning to find my name was Rapunzel. A chubby one, perhaps, but who would notice under all that floor-length hair? On the other hand, what hair I had might all disintegrate and leave me worse off than before. Such was Ben's prophecy when I gave him my impersonation of Uncle Ted's sales pitch.

"Look on the bright side," said the charming creature. "If your hair did fall out you would legitimately lose a few pounds. Whatever the charlatan told you, you certainly have a bountiful supply."

I was ninety-nine percent sure that was a compliment but I had to probe to verify. "My ends need trimming and I have been toying with the idea of going blond. What do you think?"

Ben tossed his wooden spoon into the sink. For a moment I thought he wasn't going to answer, then he looked at me and said slowly, "You have beautiful hair — the kind that should be left to itself, thick and shiny. You ought to wear it down sometimes."

What was such flattery worth when I practically wrung it out of him?

"Vanessa is the one in the family with gorgeous hair."

The cosy shared mood vanished and even the bubbling percolator could not bring it back. Why had I dragged Vanessa between us? Was it because hearing from Freddy had reminded me that she and all my relations must be praying to their dark gods that Ben and I would fail at Merlin's Court?

The thought plagued me even the following day. I had gone out into the grounds in search of Tobias, who had taken to straying farther afield than I liked. Nasty visions of boys with sling shots kept infiltrating my brain, so I abandoned my lavender furniture polish and went searching.

The afternoon sunshine was warmly fragrant with the scent of daffodils. They were almost over, but the last blooms gleamed soft and yellow. I was tempted to pick some for the house, but that would have invoked the ire of Jonas Phipps. None other than himself was ever allowed to cut flowers. I hoped Tobias had not sneaked into the cottage. I was not sure if cats frightened Aunt Sybil or if she merely disliked them. She would have considered it unseemly to display any strong emotion, even terror. My elderly aunt came out of the cottage in time to catch me spying through her sitting room window like a burglar.

"Anything wrong, Giselle?"

I burbled something incoherent about an afternoon walk and not wanting to disturb her if she was sleeping, ending in a rush with, "You haven't seen Tobias, have you?"

"The cat?" From Aunt Sybil's expression I gathered she considered it excessive to dignify animals with names. Her plump jowls bounced as she shook her head. "Don't you think, Giselle, that all this concern and devotion could be somewhat better spent?"

I stared at her.

"We can't all think alike." Her tone implied this was a pity. "But I never could see showering affection on dumb animals; affection should be given to people."

I almost forgot myself, so tempted was I to say bitterly that I never realized that human beings were each endowed with a premeasured amount of affection. Then I looked at her. She was a small dumpy woman in a frayed grey cardigan and thick lisle stockings that couldn't quite hide the lumpy varicose veins.

"Tobias is an old friend," I said mildly. "For a long time I didn't have many. Aunt Sybil, I know you have been lonely, since Uncle Merlin . . ."

"But that doesn't mean I have been sitting around moping. Merlin would not have wished that," she said huffily. "Those water wings Mr Hamlet kindly purchased for me, though the pink and yellow stripes are a bit loud, really help my technique in the water. I don't know why people would ever wish to swim without them. I'm onto the butterfly now. The breast stroke isn't the exercise for me. I'm quite well enough endowed. Vanessa takes after me in that area. Lovely figure, but then, she eats sensibly."

Why is it, I wondered, that people so often believe that if one eats sensibly, one will end up with perfect proportions?

With my luck I would discover I was pear-shaped. "Vanessa never said 'no' to a currant bun in her life," I said pettishly.

Aunt Sybil did not seem to hear me. "Such a lovely girl." She paused, looking vague. "I don't really see any harm in mentioning that she took me out to lunch yesterday. She, her mother, and Lulu all came down for the day, but they wouldn't go up to the main house. Afraid, I suppose, that they would not get a proper welcome. Perhaps I shouldn't have said anything. I think they asked me not to, but I wondered if you might have seen us. We saw you and that Dorcas woman at the Hounds and Hare, but the place was such a squash you may have missed us. Astrid had asked for a table in the corner away from the glare from the window."

That feeling of being watched, of someone listening . . . and earlier in the market, was that my imagination, too? "Did either Maurice or Freddy come?" I asked.

"We were expecting Freddy," she said, "but he didn't show up and Maurice can't afford time away from work. Up to his neck in debts." Clucking, her yellow false teeth slipped a little.

From the past came a memory — the day of the funeral and a snippet of conversation that I had put down to pure spite on the part of Aunt Astrid. She had said the rumour was out that Uncle Maurice was on the verge of bankruptcy. I would have to talk to Ben. Since the reading of the will, I had not been comfortable thinking about Uncle Maurice. The stuffy boorish middle-aged man had been denounced as a philanderer and seducer of young girls, and I had remembered with a maidenly blush his accidental arrival in my bed. But even the lecherous have to eat, and I did not like to think of Aunt Lulu having to forego her thrice-weekly outing to the hairdresser's. Yes, I would talk to Ben, and together we could consult Mr Bragg about the possibility of releasing some funds.

Aunt Sybil dutifully asked me in for tea, but I think she was relieved when I refused. I rather doubted that she had any clean cups. Leaving her, I continued my search for Tobias among the shrubbery, but without success. My hope was that he had returned to the house in my absence. I hurried down the gravel path to the house, when, rounding a curve, I came suddenly upon a tall, expansive oak. Surrounding the trunk was a wooden bench, and asleep on it was Jonas, his head nodding over a furry bundle — the errant Tobias. I would have been hard put to guess who was snoring or purring more loudly. I left them in peace and went into the house smiling. Poor Aunt Sybil! From the kitchen window I watched her come trotting through the garden, a basket on her arm, peering at the ground. Surely she wasn't . . . ? But I saw her bend and pick up something small and pop it into the basket. Aunt Sybil was having escargots for supper. Ugh!

I awoke the following morning with the knowledge that I had aged in the night. Another birthday hardly made me ecstatic and even the thought of breakfast (I lived for my three meals a day) did not cheer me as it usually did. Work was the tonic I needed. I would gobble down my cornflakes and set about peeling the wallpaper off one of the bathroom walls. Still a little downcast, I pushed open the kitchen door, and my ears were assailed by a somewhat shaky rendition of "Happy Birthday." Dorcas was flat, Jonas gravelly, and Ben, who was conducting with a wooden spoon, added a few artistic hums here and there. I leaned against the wall, overcome with emotion, not sure whether to laugh or cry.

"Oh, for God's sake, don't go all sentimental!" Ben threw the wooden spoon in the sink and clapped his hands. "Minions, bring forth the feast!" I was led to the place of honour, meaning I was the only one who got a place mat — the others had paper towels under their plates as a sign that this was an occasion. And a feast it was: grilled gammon, poached eggs, and baked tomatoes seasoned with herbs.

"You may even, as a special birthday treat," Ben pushed the tarnished silver toast rack in my direction, "have half a piece of toast." Bliss!

Dorcas was the tattletale. She had told Ben that this was my birthday, and yesterday afternoon while I was working in the attic (after finding Tobias), they had gone down into the village and each bought me a gift. Ben's came in a big square box and proved to be a bathroom scale. At last I could weigh in and check my progress. Dorcas handed me a small package which contained a pretty enamelled bracelet. It was churlish to wish they could have been reversed, and I stamped on the thought. Jonas rather grandly handed me three potted geraniums which I received with delight, saying they were what I needed to brighten up the deep tiled window-sill in the dining room, particularly when it was refurbished, which would be soon. The plasterers and carpenters were due the following week. Without moving a facial muscle the gardener graciously accepted my thanks. Reaching into the pocket of his rumpled flannel jacket, he slapped a flat narrow package wrapped in brown paper and string beside my plate.

"Jonas, you shouldn't have!" I cried, touched. "The flowers were quite sufficient."

"Aye, they were and all, didn't cost nowt but a bit o' time, and I'm not one to throw coppers away on nonsense like birthday presents."

The table was silent, all of us intent upon the gardener as he extended the pause, savouring the anticipation of his audience.

"Aunt Sybil?" I asked.

"Nay, not her." Jonas riveted us with his eyes. "Stranger came up hill at cockcrow this morning. I was about to tell him to his face no trespassing allowed when he handed me this here package. 'For the lady of the house,' he says, 'no questions asked, no lies told,' and off he goes quick as a weasel."

"Damn it," said Ben. "Open it, or I will."

With the paper off, I looked down at two narrow books, one bound in green leather and one in brown. I opened up the green one, hands trembling slightly, and read the words on the flyleaf: *The Housekeeping Account of Abigail Grantham.*

Snatching it from me, Ben thumbed rapidly through the pages, scanned some of the entries, and tossed it down in disgust, saying, "I thought women of her era kept diaries chockful of youthful indiscretions, unspoken passion for the curate, or a tryst in the shrubbery with the captain of the cricket team. This is nothing but an expense account — how much she paid for six dozen eggs, reminders to pay the milkman for the extra jug of milk he brought on Tuesday."

"You'll like the brown volume better," I said, closing it and passing it across the table. "That is Abigail's collection of recipes, all sorts of goodies, pheasant soup and eel pie. But I do agree with you, Ben. If this is Clue Number Two, old Merlin is sitting by the fire in his new abode laughing up his sleeve."

"Ee," chortled Jonas dourly, "'e will, at that. A prime sense of humour had Mr Merlin. No one can say he ain't had the last laugh on this one."

CHAPTER ELEVEN

A birthday deserved special concessions. I abandoned thoughts of scraping wallpaper and took the green-bound volume up to my bedroom. Ben wanted to peruse the recipes in the other book. I pulled the overstuffed armchair up to the window and sat down to read. Warm sunlight flooded down upon the upright, rather childlike writing on the lined pages. Ben, with typical male lack of perception, had seen only an accounting of monies paid to the butcher, the baker, and the woman who came in to sew. I caught a glimpse of another era: seven shillings and sixpence-ha'penny for a pair of buttoned boots and four pounds ten to the carpenter for an oak overmantel for the fireplace in the dining room. I began to visualize Abigail Grantham, a woman not much older than myself. She would have been about thirty at the time of these entries, a thrifty girl brought up in less-than-affluent family, bred on the premise that if one never spent more than nineteen shillings in the pound one would never be a pauper. Every penny that passed through her hands was carefully noted in clear black ink, but under the line "six linen shirts for Arthur" was another — "one smocked velvet Sunday suit for the doctor's youngest child and one pair of boots for the boy who delivers the milk." What economies did Abigail practise so her husband did not discover these gifts? He certainly would not have approved them. Two-pence was noted a few pages further on, for wax flowers bought from a gipsy woman. Was Abigail afraid that a curse might be put on her house if she refused? Her practical good sense made me think this unlikely. I turned another page. The first entry was "sixpence-farthing for a red and yellow kite." Rose had said Mrs Grantham enjoyed taking her small son outside on windy spring days. They moved before my eyes, the boy in a sailor suit and the woman in long skirts slapping about her ankles as they ran following the arching triangle across the grounds. The orderly woman with her neat bookkeeping had possessed a lighthearted side.

The next series of pages contained nothing of special interest, although I did get one idea of how Abigail might have practised economy. She seemed to buy an inordinate amount of dairy products — milk, cheese, particularly eggs — over the course of several months. I was on the point of checking to see if her butcher's bills were lower at this time, when I came upon a significant entry: "two pounds to Mr Miles Biddle towards payment of portrait, leaving three pounds due upon completion." Leafing through the succeeding pages I found no further reference to the artist. It would seem Uncle Arthur had not been pleased and had booted the young gentleman off the premises. The journal did not continue through the end of the year. It ended abruptly on the September 25 with a number of payments made to tradespeople, and one final notation: "nine pounds received from Mr Pullett for Mamma's garnet ring."

The Pulletts were the jewellers in the village. Why had Abigail needed money at the price of disposing of her mother's ring? Uncle Arthur, from the amounts deposited in his wife's keeping, had not been overly generous, but had provided her with sufficient means to support the household. Had I stumbled upon a hidden vice on the lady's part, a passion for dice or cards, or cream sherry? I could not accept this; Abigail came through as too disciplined in financial matters.

Perhaps she had given the money to a needy relative or friend. Was it a coincidence that this transaction was made as the journal ceased, or were the two related? Was Abigail ill and aware she was about to die, and did she feel the need to assist someone close to her while she still could? What bothered me was her handwriting. The last entry was as strong and firm as the first. Her passing must have been sudden. I remembered Rose and the suspicions she had voiced. Married to a man as truculent and obnoxious as Uncle Arthur, no woman could be faulted for sticking her head in the gas oven or taking a flying leap off a handy cliff, but reading the journal made it difficult for me to see Abigail as a suicide. Another darker suspicion came to me. More than ever it seemed vital to talk with someone who might be in touch with records from the past — old letters, journals such as this one. Mr Pullett was a possibility; so was the vicar. The rectory and this house had stood side by side on this clifftop for generations. The parish register! That would give me the date of Abigail's death, which I was sure was not marked on her tomb. Excitement surged within me.

Only half the book was taken up with entries. A long series of blank pages followed the last one dated September 25. Picking it up again, I inadvertently opened the volume at the wrong end. I found four or five sheets pasted with snippets of fabric and clipped corners of wallpaper samples. Underneath each item was written a description of its intended use. One such notation read: *Fabric for Queen Anne chair and sofa cushions, look for complementary damask stripe in rose and cream for the curtains and window seat covering.* Here were Abigail's plans for redecorating the drawing room. Had they ever been completed?

Sometimes new wallpaper was applied over old. If I peeled off a small strip in the corner of the drawing room, would I find the pattern Abigail had chosen underneath? Taking the book with me, I hurried across the room, pausing to open the bedside table where I kept a pair of scissors and a nail file. Not very workmanlike tools but . . . Something else waited for me inside that drawer — a large flat box of chocolates, done up in shining transparent red paper, which crackled when I touched it, and a silky green ribbon, under which was tucked a small white card. It said simply: *Happy Birthday*.

Dorcas, I thought, or Ben. Which one of them had decided I needed a little relaxation from the rigours of constant privation? The reason for secrecy was easy. Neither party would want the other to know I had been seduced from the straight and narrow. The closest I had come to cheating during the past weeks was when I had bought myself a flavoured lip gloss in Daiquiri Lime. The chocolates were a kind gesture, but a person in my situation was so vulnerable. Of late I had begun to fear that my ears might grow and I would start twitching like a rabbit if I chomped down on any more carrots and celery sticks — the fun food Ben kept on ice for me in the refrigerator. I fingered the box again.

To refuse one small nibble would be puritanical. Perhaps an orange-filled one? Doctors were always harping these days on the benefits of vitamin C. I hesitated. How typical it would be of Ben to present me with a bathroom scale with one hand and this calorie-loaded time bomb with the other! A small test to see how far I had come in terms of willpower and perseverance? Hateful man!

But what if Dorcas were the gentle giver? Under that hearty exterior she really was a very sensitive soul. To hurt such a friend would be unforgivable. Schoolteachers believed in the reward system, fair play and incentive, and I had been exemplary of late.

The first chocolate was delicious. The second was even better. But they naturally came from the top layer. What if the bottom row had grown a bit stale? If I wanted to put them out in a dish at teatime, I felt it my duty to check these out, too. Moist, succulent! I slid the wafer of paper between the layers and was just replacing the lid when I remembered that violet creams are not a general favourite. Virtuously I popped the offender into my mouth.

"Ellie," called a voice from below stairs. Dorcas! I returned the chocolates to the drawer, grabbed the green book, the nail file and scissors and ran out into the hall as though a legion of sugar-coated demons were after me.

"Wanted to know whether we should call the chimney sweep out for this week or next?" Dorcas wore a bright yellow duster tied serviceably round her flaming hair and her ruler-thin figure was encased in a grey serge boiler suit. She stood waiting for me in the hall.

"Next week, I think." How ridiculous to feel so culpable. As I passed the speckled mirror hanging above the trestle table, I took a furtive peek checking for tell-tale smears of chocolate.

All of this cloak-and-dagger stuff was unnecessary if Dorcas had put the box in my drawer. I decided to submit her to a test. "This has been a wonderful birthday." I looked meaningfully at her and stretched out the next words. "Thanks for being so sweet to me, Dorcas."

"Thought you would like the bracelet. Don't go in for fandangles myself, but had the notion a pretty trinket might be a boost; something towards your new image."

So much for that ploy! Dorcas had not looked the least conscious of any double entendre. She wanted me to look at the glass-fronted bookcase in the drawing room, afraid that this piece, like several others, might be afflicted with woodworm. I was easily diverted. We had been talking for several weeks about completely redoing this room. Now Abigail's journal had sparked added interest in the project. After inspecting the bookcase and agreeing with Dorcas that it was too far gone to be saved, I handed her the journal. She was as interested as I had been in the patterns pasted on the back pages.

"Shocking crime the way this room has been let go. Handsome woodwork, beautiful moulded ceiling. Don't find plaster work like that central ceiling rose these days. Frightful shame!" Dorcas gave the words almost Shakespearean anguish.

I looked around the room. "Aunt Sybil told me that Uncle Merlin never purchased a stick of furniture so one thing for which he cannot be blamed is the decorating scheme of things. After Abigail's death that asinine Arthur must have ripped out everything of his wife's choosing. From the samples in this book she would have hated everything about this room and the rest of the house. And it is not as though Uncle Arthur married again and had to defer to a new wife's judgment."

"Wiped out her memory with a pot of paint and yards of wallpaper," sighed Dorcas. "The question you have to answer, Ellie, is why?"

I looked around at the walls. "Hold on a minute. I want to try something." And sure enough, when I pried a strip of wallpaper loose with my nail file there, underneath, was Abigail's cream-worked silk paper, as shiny new as when first pasted to the wall. Of course, when we removed the porridge overlay en masse we would not reach it intact, but . . .

"Dorcas," I said, "I have made a decision. I am going to restore Abigail's room, make it hers again. When I was in the attic the other day I saw some beautiful pieces, including a walnut bureau and a Queen Anne chair, which may be the one Abigail mentioned in her journal." I paced about the room. "The colour of the paper is neutral, and was to be picked up in the damask stripe Abigail wanted for the curtains and window seat. Rose was the predominate shade there and in the brocade which was to be used to cover the Queen Anne chair. I wonder what other colours she used? Jade perhaps."

Dorcas's nose quivered with excitement. "Peacock blue," she suggested promptly.

Considering that Dorcas favoured the most unfortunate colour combinations in dress, I was surprised that she might be right. "Hold on!" I backed across the carpet which covered about half the room, until I stood on the dark oak surround. "Being the saving person he was — the attic is chock-full — what might Great-Uncle Arthur have done with Abigail's carpet?"

"Used it as an underlay instead of old newspapers or felt," replied Dorcas promptly, and again she was right.

Beverages had leaked through in a few places, but when revealed to the light Abigail's carpet looked new, the shades of its bird-of-paradise pattern warm and bright against the rich cream background.

"Dorcas!" I said solemnly. "Were any of your ancestors burnt at the stake? What primary accent colour do you see before you?"

"Nothing odd in that! Likely combination." Dorcas blushed dark red from the neck up, and kept looking down. "Peacock blue has always been a favourite with me."

The shuddering boom of the gong in the hall aroused us to the fact that every-day life does go on in the midst of great discoveries. Ben was summoning us to lunch.

Having eaten enough chocolates to fill my calorie quota for the coming month, I decided to cut back by skipping lunch and dinner. But when Ben slipped a puffy yellow omelette on my plate oozing gently at the edges with mushrooms, tomatoes, and small golden onions, and garnished with spears of broccoli, I hated to disappoint him — or me. After sacrificing my finer feelings to preserve Ben's culinary pride, I was disappointed that he did not share my excitement about Abigail and the drawing room. When he saw I was provoked he made matters infinitely worse by saying that if the purchase of new curtains and papering a few walls made me happy, then he was pleased.

"Ben, this is not trivial. I am not playing with doll's houses." His response was an irritating lift of his black eyebrows.

Pouring his coffee into his saucer, Jonas entered the arena with "Dunno how many years it's been since that room was done up proper." I waited until the old man had finished his last slurp, wiped his mouth with his serviette, and tucked it back into the neck of his knit jersey. "Well, Jonas." I looked into his face. "Are you also of the opinion that I should leave the dust in that room undisturbed? Perhaps I should. I suppose it does, by rights, belong in a museum. It certainly is old enough."

Jonas stared fiercely back at me, the hairs of his moustache damp with coffee. "Don't always be talking yourself down, girl. And don't let him do it neither. This house was a mouldering hovel till you arrived with your new broom."

Eyebrows bristling and his lower jaw jutting aggressively forward, Jonas tossed his serviette down on the table and stumped out the garden door, leaving three very surprised pairs of eyes fixed upon the place where he had sat.

"That fatal charm of yours again, Ellie." Ben's lips quirked. "Another admirer falls at your feet."

"Sneer all you want." I glowered at him. "You may think that if a girl doesn't look like Venus rising from the deep, she isn't worth a twist of salt in a bag of crisps, but not every male has your impossibly high standards."

"Now, now, Ellie," Dorcas intervened, "harmless jest. Take it in a sporting . . ."

"Please." I took a deep breath. "Do not talk to me about being a good sport and all that tommy-rot. Ben does this to me all the time, belittling me, making out that no rational person could possibly like me because I'm fat and ugly." Something soft and furry-warm wound itself around my leg. Tobias. I reached down for him and thankfully hid my flushed face against the fluff of his neck.

"Ellie." Ben's voice vibrated with kindly compassion. "You haven't done something you regret, have you? Don't be afraid, you can tell us. Dorcas and I are your friends."

Who did the idiot think he was? The concerned papa in a Gilbert and Sullivan operetta? Or did he know something about the chocolates?

I lifted my face from Tobias's fur. "Well, I haven't had an affair with old Jonas if that's what you're thinking."

"No, you idiot!" Ben's eyes laughed at me. "I meant had you eaten something you shouldn't have? Whenever you flare up at me in the old belligerent way, I wonder if you have just consumed a tin of condensed milk. People who fall off the wagon turn nasty because, dear Watson, they feel guilty."

What a disgustingly perceptive man he was, but unless he was inhumanly devious he had not sent those chocolates. I began to suspect Jonas, but I was saved from speaking in my own defence by Dorcas, who vouched that I had not been near the kitchen all morning. Having tried to stare each other down for a few protracted minutes, Ben and I reluctantly broke into grins and called a truce.

"I'm glad you decided to be civil because I have a treat planned for dinner."

"What?" I asked. Tobias was not as polite; he yawned mightily, showing glossy pink gums.

"Dessert actually — a café-au-lait mousse with Chantilly cream and shavings of bitter chocolate!" Ben leaned back in his chair and closed his eyes.

"Sublime!" I applauded, feeling totally unworthy after my chocolate binge.

Dorcas, who rarely ate desserts, said "Jolly good," but without much conviction.

"I found the recipe in Abigail Grantham's collection." Ben reached behind him for the little brown book which was lying on the Welsh dresser. "Some of the entries are quite fascinating. Of course there is also the usual stuff." He turned through the pages. "Seed cake, simnel cake, smoked haddock in egg custard, delicately seasoned with nutmeg. That's a nuisance." He stopped and ran a finger down the inside of the book. "A couple of pages are missing, we jump forward to soups and stews, nothing tremendously exciting there. My favourite is the brew guaranteed to sober up an unsteady bridegroom so he can walk a straight line down the aisle. Here's another gem, an after-shave lotion made from mashed dock leaves and dandelion juice! And which one of us has not craved a sure-fire method of taking scorch marks out of pillowcases, when some thoughtless guest snuffed out his candle between the sheets?"

"Sounds marvellous! May I see?" Dorcas took up the book and scoured the pages. "Listen to this — a cough remedy calling for two very ripe cucumbers, liquorice root, and a sampling of herbs commonly found in an English country garden — sage, mint, and . . ."

I left the two of them poring over instructions for preparing a rose-water and glycerine hand lotion. Not that I was uninterested in this other glimpse into the life of Abigail Grantham, but I wanted to go up into the attic and see what pieces of abandoned furniture I could discover that might have been evicted from the drawing room. It wasn't until sometime later that I remembered that I had not told Ben about the sale of Abigail's garnet ring, but it was probably not important. From the price paid for it, the jewel was of no great value. Unless it was a ruby masquerading as a lesser stone, this was not our treasure. And if it was, why had we been sent the two books, since the housekeeping journal alone would have been enough to point us in the right direction? I would have to take the recipes away from Ben and read them myself, looking for the missing link. Speculation may be good for the soul, but it was beginning to make my head spin. Time for a stretch of manual labour.

My afternoon among the cobwebs and open rafters passed happily. I was in my element browsing through trunks filled with discarded clothing and linens. In one I found a magnificent crocheted bedspread which I set aside with several embroidered cushions to take downstairs with me. Antiques are not my forte, but I know the basics. By the time mauve shadows began combing the windows, I had amassed a sizeable grouping, set out in the middle of a cleared area. It included two fireside wingback chairs, the Queen Anne chair (I was sure it was Abigail's), a lady's bureau of the same period, a carved gate-legged card table, a sewing cabinet with cabriole legs, a walnut tea trolley, and my most prized find — a sofa covered in a cream silk brocade that exactly matched the wallpaper we had uncovered in the drawing room. The fabric had rotted and it tore at the touch, but reupholstering in a similar pattern would present no problems. Nothing I had found constituted a real treasure, but I was pleased.

A tinny clashing of cymbals sauntered up through the floorboards. The dinner gong. Wiping my dusty hands on the back of my khaki slacks, I made my way to the lower regions. Stopping off at my bedroom to change my shirt, I decided to destroy the evidence that had been plaguing me. Those chocolates had to go. Where could I ditch them without being caught in the act? Pondering the problem I absently ate three more, and found myself looking at the solution. The box was now empty. I could scrunch it up and leave it in my wastepaper basket under a few old magazines until I had the opportunity of disposing of it permanently. Burial in the garden under cover of midnight was out because I might bump into Aunt Sybil on one of her nightly jaunts, but I would think of something stealthy. I was putting the wastepaper basket back down when I noticed a flat gift-wrapped package lying on top of my dressing table. Surely it hadn't been there when I was last in this room! What a day this was for surprises. This must be from Aunt Sybil. In her way she was a very conscientious old dear. Not another address book or dictionary, I hoped, as I tore off the paper.

This was neither. When I folded back the thin layer of tissue paper, I found an exquisite silver photograph frame. It was old — a very early one of its kind, and unlike the chocolates the sender had not chosen to remain anonymous. The plain white card said simply: *Ben*. Nothing else. No chirpy birthday greeting, no flowery sonnet composed by a rhyming computer. The gift spoke its own language. I knew what the frame was for. Ben remembered how I felt about that photograph of Abigail and had provided me with the perfect setting for it — a sentimental gesture from the man who claimed to be a cynic. With the tip of one finger I stroked the frame as tenderly as though it were a face. (Perhaps Ben had sent the chocolates, and the talk about eating on the sly was all a tease.) Tonight I must get him on his own and thank him properly in private. Even the bathroom scale was revealed in a more attractive light — he believed I was going to lose those 63 pounds even with a day off. I felt like a queen celebrating two birthdays: one official and one private.

A second irate summons of the gong forced me to set my daydreams aside for the moment. As I trod down the last stair the telephone burp-burped from its hiding place on the hall table. I groped for it under Dorcas's grey felt hat; the line crackled and seemed to go dead for a moment. My "Hallo" came back in a halting echo. "Is anyone there?" I asked, getting bored.

The voice was muffled, as though the speaker wore a thick woollen scarf wrapped across his mouth to ward off the cold. But this was May, an unusually clement one, too warm for thick woollies — "Tell me, dear, did you enjoy the chocolates?"

So Ben had not sent them, a pity but in a way a relief. That last helping of soft centres was beginning to make me feel somewhat queasy and I would have hated the slightest resentment to spoil the possibility of a new closeness.

"Absolutely delicious," I enthused. "I just finished the last one!" An electric pause while I waited for my fairy godparent to be revealed.

There was a throaty snorting laugh, and words so low I had to press my ear tight against the receiver to hear them: "Glutton, fat slobbering hog. I knew I only had to push the trough close enough and you would start to gobble." Wheezing, hiccupping, horrible laughter. The receiver slipped from my grasp. It hung down, slapping back and forth against the table legs like a dead pelican, while I doubled forward, clinging to the wall as a life support.

I was going to be very sick. The kitchen door swung open and footsteps pounded a path through my head. "Ellie, what's with you?" Ben stood a few feet away waving a metal spatula. "I know the house is in bad shape, but you don't have to shore it up with your bare hands. Hey." He bent forward, picked up the receiver, and stood looking at it. "Have you had bad news? My God, Ellie, you look positively green — here, hold on to me." He threw the spatula down.

"An obscene phone call, a rather nasty one." My mind was reeling. One thing I did not want was to have Ben touch me. I had the absurd idea that some of my shame would rub off on him. Pressing my fingers against my temples I backed away from him towards the stairs but I was not fast enough; he caught hold of me. I tried to pull away but my hands were trapped against his chest. I could feel the tenseness of his muscles under his light wool shirt, the steady beating of his heart. I could smell the spicy clean scent of his after-shave. My body for once in its uncooperative life did me a great big favour. I felt like a girl in one of those stupid adverts where someone in the background is singing, "And He Wears Wild Desire." I was responding to Ben's nearness with a feeling so new, so stupendous it blotted out everything else. Even the Voice. I yearned to move even closer.

"Ellie." Ben spoke the word caressingly against my hair. "Tell me all about it."

The moment shattered like a teacup dropped in the sink, not because he was uncaring; his voice, his touch told me he did care. My guilt kept me silent. I wanted only a place where I could hide away like a mole underground. The oldest excuse in the world. I told him I had a headache and had been lying down when the phone rang.

I don't think he believed it, but he did not press me. Dinner was not ready anyway; he had only rung the gong to invite me down for a birthday drink. Dorcas was out scouting for Tobias, who was missing again. If I felt better later on, I could have dinner on a tray in my room. Ben's concern made me want to cry. How he would despise me if he knew that I had played into the hands of the enemy. Glutton! I shuddered again at the memory. This lovely day with its discoveries about Abigail and Ben's sensitive gift was spoilt. I had not even thanked him for the photo frame. Tomorrow.

Lying on my bed I tried to puzzle out who would be the most likely suspect. Three of them had been down here and lunch with Aunt Sybil would not have taken all day. Had they pumped her about our movements? Was it possible that she knew something, had seen one of them slipping past her cottage to sneak into the house while Ben was busy at the typewriter and Dorcas and I were out? And if she had, would she tell me? They had made sure they were in her good books. The Voice might even have confided in her, explained the little practical joke, but no, I really couldn't see Aunt Sybil approving anything that might put a spoke in the wheel of Uncle Merlin's plans. Vanessa would always be my prime choice for villainy, but what about Freddy? His not joining the others as arranged did not let him off the hook. He might have come down as planned and then decided his time could be better spent . . . that feeling of being secretly observed at the Hounds and Hare . . . One point in Freddy's favour was that he had applied the direct approach for money. But then, a hand-out wasn't a handful, or better still, the whole flaming lot. Did he want the money for himself or for his father, who on the surface appeared the one in dire need? Perhaps if Ben and I offered Maurice a loan or a gift? Thinking about his other habits I realized that Maurice was a very greedy man. Look who was casting stones! Sighing, I sank back further against my pillow. I was left with Astrid and Lulu, both of whom, in their own ways, I felt could be extremely ruthless.

Dorcas came up an hour later. By that time my headache was real. She persuaded me to take a few sips of brandy out of an eggcup. She had found Tobias. No need to worry about that old scallywag; Ben was the one. She had never seen him so glum, he was in the kitchen taking out his frustrations whipping up another of Abigail's recipes. With those words of encouragement she tiptoed out of the room.

Eventually I sank into an uneasy doze broken by flashes of nightmare. I was tucking Freddy into a bed shaped like a bird's nest, at least I thought it was Freddy — I never really got a good look at his face — and Aunt Lulu was pecking at me with a long beak made out of playing cards. I bolted upright in bed with the sheets clutched protectively about me; the house sounded alive, bones grating in worn sockets. Footsteps softly padding. I was on the brink of crying out when reason returned. Ben often got up in the early hours to wrestle with a difficult chapter. The last I had heard of his dauntless heroine, Sister Marie Grace, she had been knotted into a sack and tossed into the Bongo River, pursued by a territory-conscious crocodile. Easing back under the bedclothes, I willed myself back to sleep.

I woke before the sun had fully risen. A pale grey light crept through the crack in the curtains. What did surprise me was how much better I felt. The enemy had won the first round, but I was eager to climb into the ring and come out swinging.

A quick hot bath further revived me. While dressing, I considered whether I should tell Ben what had happened. Crossing to the window, I opened the curtains and discovered I was not the first one up. In the breeze below me was the clothesline swelling with small, jaunty, clothes-pegged flaps of white, lifting and falling. Miniature sheets? Handkerchiefs? I had to find out.

Ben was coming across the landing when I left my room. He almost knocked me over in his haste to reach the stairs first.

"Out of my way," he yelled.

Ignoring this cheery morning greeting, I pelted after him. "What's wrong? Fire or flood? Have you left the kitchen sink overflowing, or . . . ?"

"Don't ask, don't speak to me, don't even come near me!" He sped across the hall, smashed into one of the suits of armour, kicked it clangingly aside, went through the side door and across the paved courtyard to halt abruptly under the clothesline strung between two trees. He emitted a howl of such hideous primitive anguish that I fell back a step. Following the direction of his eyes, I looked up and saw what he had seen. The squares of white strung in a row were not handkerchiefs, they were pieces of paper — typing paper.

"My book," panted Ben, rolling on the ground like a wounded dog. "A note was shoved under my bedroom door. I found it when I woke up. With your sense of humour, Ellie, you'll love the next part. It said, 'I didn't think you could write a clean book if you tried, so I washed every page in very hot water and bleach and hung them out to dry.'"

The enemy had struck from both sides. But surely all was not lost. The carbon copy! I spoke quietly but firmly to the creature on the ground. "Ben, calm down. You'll strangle yourself if you wrap your arms around your neck like that. Where did you keep your copy? Perhaps the person who perpetrated this atrocity didn't find it."

"Copy!" Ben surged to his feet with a bellow which I took for hope reborn. "I didn't make a copy. Call it laziness, call it artistic preoccupation, call it what you will! And do you know what else I, the Fool, did?"

I backed away from the savage display of sharp white teeth. "Don't bite me! I haven't had my rabies shots." This small touch of humour did not have the desired conciliatory effect. Ben continued to advance upon me. Grabbing my arm, he shook me until my head was ready to snap off like a poppy from a stalk. "Show some normal curiosity, ask in what other ways I aided and abetted the enemy."

My head continued to smack back and forth in frantic assent. Ben's eyes were so glazed I doubt that he even saw me. "Erasable bond" — he whapped me again. "I liked the ease with which I could rub out a superfluous word, a cumbersome line. Very handy stuff, that kind of typing paper, a little extra money but, for the lousy typist, worth it. I'll bet the creeping, crawling fiend who committed this crime must have been highly chuffed. When I think of how I agonized over every word — then one dunk and away they rolled. Look at these pages!" He ripped a couple off the line and a clothespin hurtled towards me, missing my nose by an inch as I ducked. "Clean and white! Shining bright! I think I'll go inside and write an accolade to the makers of bleach."

For the first time I realized how alike we were, hitting out angrily at others when the person we blamed most was ourselves. Damn it, I thought viciously as I stumped indoors, the trouble with acquiring your sex education through romantic novels is you don't realize that love is miserably hard work. Not that I was, theoretically, in love with Ben — physically attracted, yes — and when it came down to it that was a rotten alternative. Ben's body was as much off limits to me as any of my favourite foods, and the hunger pangs a damn sight worse. Sometimes lately I seemed to catch a glimpse of that hunger in his eyes, but now the only thing Ben was ravenous for was revenge.

Breakfast was a black-edged meal. Fortunately for Jonas, he missed it. Dorcas broke down when informed of the tragedy, but after blowing noisily into one of her plaid handkerchiefs, she squared her shoulders and rallied.

"Mustn't think of ourselves, Ellie," she urged bracingly as she plugged in the coffee pot and popped bread into the rattrap toaster. "Ben needs all the support we can give, if we are to get him back behind the typewriter before he loses his nerve."

The recipient of all this fellow feeling lay slumped across the table, his arms flung out. Every three minutes or so he would go into a spasm. His whole body would vibrate and his knees would jerk, heaving up the wooden table surface and causing the coffee cups, which Dorcas had set down, to slither away in different directions.

"Counter-attack! We will trounce the unseen foe!" Dorcas deftly retrieved a flying saucer as it was about to skim out of bounds. "We should organize. Make up a list of suspects, grading them according to motive and accessibility."

The head on the table lifted briefly and a mirthless chuckle contorted its features. He reminded me of the late Merlin Grantham. "If going by the latter," he said, "you two are prime suspects. Anyone want to confess? I won't kill you, at least not quickly." The sharp white teeth flared again.

"Ben!" I meticulously spread butter into every pore of his slice of toast. "Remember the old saying misery loves company? Well, this is going to cheer you no end. You were not the enemy's number one choice." I told him and Dorcas at a gallop about those sickening chocolates. Neither interrupted. Ben sat with his elbows on the table, his chin cupped in his hands, eyes closed. Was he listening? Or just being sensitive to my acute embarrassment? I told them about the phone call.

"Monstrous," stormed Dorcas. "But what we need to understand is how this was all accomplished and when. Sneaking into the house with those chocolates could be done pretty speedily, would require only minor risk of being caught. This is a big house. The attack on Ben would necessitate more time."

Reconstructing the plot against him seemed therapeutic for Ben. He was in shock. Later the real pain would set in. Now we had to keep him talking.

"Seems to me the pages must have been hung out an hour or so before dawn," Dorcas spoke up. "Working in pitch darkness extremely difficult. Even light from a torch might have alerted someone."

"Damn!" I exclaimed. "What a pity Aunt Sybil wasn't out on one of her night-time prowls and could have set up the alarm."

"Perhaps it is just as well she did not get in the way" — Ben grimaced — "or we might have found her strung up on the line too; we are dealing with someone completely mad."

"Diabolical but patient." Dorcas sat down again and stirred her cup. "Have to hand it to him — forgive the pronoun, a little chauvinism in all of us — perfect sense of timing. Waited until you, Ben, were more than halfway through the book and Ellie well underway with her diet before fattening her up for the slaughter."

"I think the attack on me was primarily psychological," I said. "Eating one box of chocolates would not put back all the weight I have, hopefully, lost. That ghastly phone call was aimed at making me feel unworthy to be thin. And you know! It is working. Here I am doing what I haven't done in weeks, shovelling sugar into my coffee, eating one slice of bread after another. But no more." I pushed my plate aside. "The enemy has made one big, fat error. If getting even means total abstinence, I'm ready."

"Good for you," said Ben wryly, dropping his head back down on his arms. "But don't kid yourself you are doing it for the inheritance. If you chain me to a chair day and night I can never write that book in the time left. Perhaps we don't have to fear another attack from the enemy — his job is done."

"And the third condition — the treasure?"

"Why bother looking now?"

It wasn't until sometime later that I wondered whether that wasn't exactly what the enemy wanted.

CHAPTER TWELVE

Whatever thoughts obsessed the mind of the unseen enemy, he seemed to give up on us for the present. The succeeding weeks passed without another attack. We might be living on false security but I could have been almost content, involved as I was with work in the house and my search for the identity of Abigail Grantham, if only Ben had not turned so aloof. He wasn't unpleasant, just politely distant. He was fine with Dorcas so I had to assume this attitude was separate from any depression over his book. To give the man his due, he had come to terms with his loss remarkably well, and for that Dorcas was partially responsible. She had refused to let him sit up in his room and mope.

"Sulk," she had growled, "and you know who will end up doing the cooking. Ellie's still busy sorting furniture in the attics. Know I should be able to make a tom-artichoke quiche or whatever, but don't know how to crack an egg let alone boil one."

That night dinner was on the table at the usual time, at the usual gourmet standard. Ben even looked moderately pleased with his raised pheasant pie.

"Well done," applauded Dorcas. "Tomorrow we will have you propped up back at the typewriter. Know writing isn't like knitting, you can't just pick up the dropped stitches but . . ."

"I've been wondering about that," said Ben. "While I was plucking that bird and wishing like hell I had the enemy in my hands I kept thinking, oh God, if only I had been blessed with a photographic memory — which gave me an idea of sorts. What if I could acquire one through hypnotism? I would need an expert, someone tiptop, not the usual run-of-the-mill non-smoking types, but where to look? We don't even have a damn phone book in this accursed house."

"I think we did, once," I responded vaguely, still thinking about his idea, "but it got boxed up with Aunt Sybil's junk and sent down to the cottage. Anyway, it was years out of date. Besides, I can do better for you than thumbing through the H section. Jill."

"Jill?" Ben eyed me without enthusiasm. "That funny little runt of a friend of yours? She's not a hypnotist."

"True, but she's bound to know one. She's into reincarnation and regression and all that stuff. If she can produce someone who is in the business of taking people back to former lives, your case — a matter of months — should be child's play. I'll write to Jill tomorrow."

I did. And I must say Ben was properly appreciative. It wasn't until later that he grew cool, I think. The change was so gradual it was hard to say when it began.

Fortunately in other respects I had some good moments. While lifting aside a pile of rugs in the attic I found the oak overmantel. Abigail's overmantel, the one mentioned in her ledger. I had Jonas polish it for me. Scowling, he rolled up his shirt sleeves. "Proper shameful this is, men being put to women's work." But I noticed he was humming under his breath, and unlike Aunt Sybil he didn't favour funeral dirges. Life eased all round the next day when the two rather condescending char-women arrived. On the following Wednesday an army of electricians, plumbers, carpenters, and painters began their work on the ground floor. The bedrooms and bathrooms would have to wait. In all probability Ben and I would no longer be at Merlin's Court when the time came to redo them. The greatest, immediate inconvenience was being unable to use the kitchen. The men installing the new cabinets and working surfaces seemed to consider it a great intrusion if one of us came in for a glass of lemonade, and with the dining room also out of commission, meals had to be eaten either in the old wash house or picnic fashion out-of-doors. Ben, whether to take his mind off his book (Jill had still not answered my letter) or because he could not help himself, had turned very temperamental about the kitchen. As soon as any decision was made, he would hear it over the start and stammer noise of his typewriter, and march out to alter it. He argued with the plumber, insulted the electrician who was installing the strip lighting, and hovered underfoot like an overanxious new father while the Aga cooker was being installed.

"Say, lady!" One beleaguered fellow mopped his brow with a damp handkerchief. "Don't yer 'ubby 'ave no place of work to visit?"

"No," I said, ignoring the little misunderstanding about our relationship. "He doesn't know what he wants to be when he grows up."

Unless we were prepared for a full-scale strike it seemed expedient that as many inhabitants as possible should clear out of the house each day. Naturally the thorn refused to budge, but Dorcas was always happy to don her felt hat and take her thermos of tea out to the walled herb garden, which she had made her special province. One morning I remembered my idea of checking the parish register for the date of Abigail's death. Walking through the hushed, silent churchyard bothered me, but I found the current register open on a lectern by the font, at the back of the church. The older volumes were stacked neatly underneath on a shelf. Within minutes I had found the recording of Uncle Arthur's death. Merlin must have been about twenty when his dead papa passed on to his just reward. I hope he liked warm weather, but I found no reference to his wife.

Musing, I left the church and drove down into the village. The tall, dapper gentleman behind the varnished counter at Pullett's Jewellers was deference itself; but he regretfully informed me that the firm's records dating back fifty years and more had been destroyed in a fire sometime back. So much for Abigail's garnet ring. Perhaps I had overreacted to her entry of its sale, but I still felt convinced that, if not the treasure, it was part of the puzzle. Her every-day life, revealed through the journals, continued to obsess me during the following weeks almost as much as my restoration of the house. Her house.

Shopping for other people's domiciles had always given me great pleasure, but buying for Merlin's Court was a joy. Often Dorcas would accompany me, and we would lunch in whatever picturesque inn caught our fancy. Eating sensibly was now becoming almost a habit and I was getting plenty of exercise sauntering through arcades and marketplaces, searching for the right objects to ornament the house in its renewal. The drawing room mantelpiece was causing me some problems. I did not want it to look top-heavy or overly fussy. What I needed were one or two fine pieces to accentuate the mood and colours of the room. One afternoon, ambling along in our usual stop-and-start fashion, we came upon a place called the China Cabinet, sandwiched between a row of mellow brick bow-fronted shops. Dorcas was the one who pointed. "That's it! The yellow Chinese vase with the peacock-blue leaf design. Put that on your mantelpiece with a pair of brass candlesticks and you'll be all set.." As soon as I saw it, I knew she was right. Dorcas had shown another of her rare flashes of artistic brilliance.

All this was great fun, and the house, having been stripped bare, was coming to life again like a tree after a long hard winter. The two worthy ladies from the Labour Exchange finished up their days with us by scrubbing every window with vinegar and newspaper until they winked like a hundred sparkling eyes. On the day they picked up their last payment and left, there was so little for me to do that I remembered my intention of talking with the vicar. I should have visited Mr Foxworth sooner to request his help, but I had begun to feel that a continued search for clues was a waste. Time was a runaway horse. Despite his daily stints at the typewriter, I knew Ben seriously doubted his ability to finish the book. Still no word from Jill, but he had gone off the idea of hypnosis anyway. He didn't have what it took to be a writer, Ben told me morosely. The spirit was willing but the prose was weak, as Jonas had kindly pointed out to him, adding that Thomas Hardy, Dickens, or any of the other greats could have polished off a rewrite of that blasted book during one of their tea breaks. Let's keep the enemy happy, said Ben. Forget about the inheritance, buried treasure, fifth-rate novels, and even diets.

But I did not want to forget about my diet. I had become quite fond of the tyrant; it was being nice to me. And I did not want to forget about Abigail, if for no other reason than I felt she would have been, was, my friend. Whatever else was or was not accomplished, I had to discover why and how she had died.

To ensure that the vicar did not write me off as just another crackpot who wanted to trace her family tree back to William the Conqueror, I took time over my toilette. Looking cool wasn't easy; we were in the midst of the summer's first heat wave. My hair was already clinging damply to my neck, so I lifted it into a thick twist which I pinned on top of my head before slipping into something from last summer's collection — a coffee-coloured smock. Something was very wrong. Instead of billowing out in a happy, frolicsome mushroom, the folds of the dress hung limp. The shoulders sagged and the neckline gaped. Nervously I placed a hand where my stomach usually was and inched towards the mirror. I was peering into it, my neck twisted, when Dorcas knocked and came in asking if I wanted thyme or parsley in the outer border.

"Both," I replied vaguely, lifting my eyebrows and sucking in my cheeks.

"Impossible. Foul up the whole system. Anything amiss? You seem distracted." Dorcas jolted down on the bed. "Ellie, are you looking for something?"

"Yes. I've just this minute noticed I'm missing one and a half chins and my cheeks aren't right either. They no longer have their friendly hamster bulge."

Dorcas nodded. "Realized for some time, but thought it best to say nothing. Afraid comment on the subject might throw you off your stroke. What do the scales say, or haven't you asked them? Aha!" She correctly read my reflection in the mirror. "Afraid of disappointment. Always better to know the truth, however unpalatable and, when the news is good, marvellous boost to the morale, keeps up the momentum."

Taking me by the elbow, Dorcas marched me forthwith into the bathroom and ordered me to climb on the scale. "No time for false modesty," she assured me, "all girls together." The needle swung into a curve, flickered, and stabilized. Awed, I looked down at the dial: over two stone. When did it all go?

"Congratulations!" Dorcas vigorously pumped my hand. "Now if only Ben can find inspiration and we can turn up another of Uncle Merlin's clues we will be all set."

Walking out into the courtyard, we discussed the ones already in our possession and I mentioned the thought that had been nudging at the back of my brain for a while. Uncle Merlin's instructions had been that we find the treasure connected with the house. He had not said *in* the house. This implied that the treasure might not be hidden within the structure itself but in the grounds or even farther afield.

We were now standing in the little walled herb garden. The sun beat down on our bare arms and the air was rich with the smell of newly turned earth and the fragrance of mint, hardy enough to have survived years of neglect. Dorcas loved this place; so must have Abigail. Many of her recipes depended on the sweet sun-savoured herbs she had nurtured here. Had this garden also been an island of escape from the tedious company of a critical husband, a place that was peculiarly her own? Bending, I picked up a handful of soil and rubbed it through my fingers. If Abigail had wanted to hide anything this would have been an ideal place. But again I might be assuming too much. In Abigail's day an herb garden usually fell to the sole province of the lady of the house and since then it had lain in total neglect. No one had plucked a sprig of mint here for years, until Dorcas came along wielding her gardening fork. As so often happened, she understood what I was thinking.

"Been wondering if this is the place, have you? Logical! Should have thought of it sooner. You go ahead and pay your call on the vicar. See what you can discover about Abigail, and I will proceed here; unless you feel it inappropriate for me to conduct the dig unattended — your treasure and all that. Appreciate your allowing me to participate, but you should be less trusting, Ellie — can't always judge a book by its cover — worked for a woman once, taught English Lit. Nicest person one could wish to meet, but feather-fingered — embezzled the Sports Day prize money."

Assuring her that I had no doubts of her integrity, I left Dorcas plunging her fork into the earth with workmanlike precision, and went off to visit the vicar. I found Rowland Foxworth in his study working on his Sunday sermon. I was ushered into this sanctum by Mrs Wood, his housekeeper — a sparrow of a woman who muttered, pushing open the study door, "If folks was meant to arrive unannounced the good Lord wouldn't have bothered inventing the telephone."

Thoroughly snubbed, I was apologizing to the vicar before he was halfway out of his chair. "I should have rung before coming over, but I didn't know the number off-hand and . . ."

"Please." He clasped both my hands warmly in his and beamed approval. "I am delighted to see you." The room gave evidence of the glum Mrs Wood's belief in the power of elbow grease, but the signs of Mr Foxworth's relaxed, tweedy personality were evident in the open book on the coffee table and the worn pipe spilling ash on the desk. Brushing his silvering hair back from his brow with a rather endearing, abstracted gesture, Mr Foxworth drew forward a leather chair for me and sat down opposite. "Ellie, what can I do for you? I have called several times and found you out, but even so you must think me very remiss in not seeing more of a new parishioner."

"And you must think me very remiss in not attending services." I looked into his kind grey eyes. "I am ashamed to admit it, but I have an uneasy feeling, not about the church itself really . . . but the graveyard. I didn't relish coming through it today, especially when I had to pass the family vault. Give me time and I will overcome the feeling."

"I appreciate the effort you made in coming to see me." He smiled, reaching for his pipe. "It would be good to see the old Grantham pew occupied. Miss Sybil Grantham does occasionally attend evensong, but as you know, your uncle viewed every clergyman as a bombastic hypocrite and refused to darken the doors of St. Anselm's."

"At least he agreed to a Christian burial, but I think that may have been to ensure he was not hustled out of this world without due pomp and pageantry." This topic was right where I wanted it.

The vicar smiled. "He certainly went out in style; I gather the horse and carriage was a sentimental gesture in remembrance of his mother. An unusual man, a pity he was such a confirmed hermit. When I was assigned this living three years ago I did call, but Miss Grantham was ordered not to let me over the threshold. Now tell me, can I help you in any way? Or may I hope this is a social visit?"

Nice man! I wasn't sure, being such a novice, but I thought I detected a decidedly unclerical gleam in his eyes. Ben might not want me, but he was not the only twig on the tree. Wickedly, I was tempted to test the strength of Mr Foxworth's virtue by doing an impromptu impersonation of Vanessa at her sexy, alluring best. But my diet had taught me restraint and I still possessed the naive notion that nice things happen only to girls who wait.

At that moment Mrs Wood entered the study, and grimly deposited a tray of tea things on the table between me and the vicar and left us with an affirmative slam of the door. While I poured, I told Rowland, as he insisted on being called, about Uncle Merlin's will and the treasure. He looked immensely interested.

"You may possibly have already considered the idea, but I would think that carriage might provide an excellent hiding place for something of value, under the seat or floor."

I told him that I had searched the Victorian conveyance to no avail before lending it, with Mr Bragg's approval, to the local historical society. It had been taking up rather a lot of space in the stable. "We have no horses. The ones used for the funeral were borrowed. But I do agree that Uncle Merlin's funeral arrangements are important because they were our first indication that the treasure was connected with Abigail Grantham, and in particular her death. Which is where I hope you may be able to help. I know I am delving back a very long way, but did the previous vicar say anything about her? Anything vaguely hush-hush or mysterious? Anything to suggest suicide?"

"No." He took a long thoughtful puff on his pipe. "But I do remember overhearing a discussion once among some of the older women at the Mothers' Union, something to the effect that Mr Merlin Grantham's mother had died under peculiar circumstances. Or am I being accurate? I think the statement was that no one quite knew how she had died. Not quite the same thing, is it?"

"No." I set my cup down and reached to refill it from the pot. "And the rumours concerning Abigail would be fuelled by Merlin's eccentric behaviour. Her former maid, an old woman called Rose, was the one who told me about the local suspicion that Abigail killed herself."

"What do you think?"

"That she was murdered by her husband, Arthur Grantham." There — I had said it at last; but the suspicion, voiced in the vicar's study with its air of rumpled comfort and quiet occupation, sounded melodramatic, almost sacrilegious. What right had I to cast aspersions upon a man long dead, who had doubtless been respected in this neighbourhood and a pillar of his church? The villagers whispered about his wife — not him. How could a man who parted his hair in the middle, waxed and twirled his moustache, and probably undressed in the wardrobe, be anything worse than a ponderous bore?

Rowland proved to have one rather serious fault. He was a realist; he wanted to know on what basis I suspected Arthur. "Why do you think he killed her?"

"Because if suicide is out, what other reason would there be for people whispering about her death sixty-odd years after the event? An event which, by the way, is not recorded in the parish register. Add to those facts another. Aunt Sybil, who visited the house regularly as a child when Abigail was alive and was present at the funeral, knows nothing other than that Abigail went very suddenly. I can't think of anything more sudden than murder."

"In those days there were a lot of twenty-four-hour killers, blood poisoning, bee stings, append—"

"Then why the mystery? Those aren't social diseases to be shoved under the rug. No, believe me, the most likely explanation is that hubby did her in. Oh, I admit he appears to have been a model of respectability, but those types are often the worst. The man was an exacting prig — demanding, carping — perhaps breakfast was late two days in a row, or maybe Abigail cooked a batch of jam that didn't jell. Who knows? Arthur's only problem would be convincing the doctor that Mrs Grantham had fainted dead away and never come round."

Rowland looked interested but not convinced so I pressed on. "Okay, doubting Thomas" — a biblical reference seemed polite when talking to a clergyman — "explain this: Why is there no record of Abigail's demise in the church register?"

Lighting his pipe, Rowland pulled thoughtfully on it for a moment. "I'm afraid that rather supports than hinders the suicide theory. From what I have heard, the vicar who held the living here at that time was from the school of fire and brimstone. If Abigail died by her own hand, he would have considered her memory one to be shunned, not recorded among the names of the righteous in the parish record."

He almost had me there, for a minute. Then I remembered something: my first meeting with Ben and his reason for demonstrating outside the Hallelujah Revival Chapel. The elders had refused to bury a child in consecrated ground because she had died without being christened. That quaint notion was a throw-back to the good old days when the unshriven, including suicides, had been buried outside the churchyard, in unconsecrated ground. If the old vicar had been the rigid puritan Rowland described, he would not have overlooked this blighting tradition.

Rowland perked up when I pointed out this detail. Whatever her sins, Abigail was tucked away inside the family vault. He wasn't quite a convert yet, but he did agree to consider, theoretically, the idea of murder. "I suppose," he said, "the doctor on the case may have suspected that all was not as it should be, but in dealing with a well-to-do family a humble GP might well have been afraid to call in the authorities and stir up a rumpus. To accuse a man of sterling reputation of contriving his wife's death would be pretty risky — unless there was a motive. We keep coming back to that, Ellie, the motive. The petty, every-day aggravations you suggested just aren't enough."

Downcast but not defeated, I confessed that my villainizing of Arthur Grantham was based mainly on my growing liking for Abigail, and my distrust of any man with eyes set close together.

If he saw anything ludicrous in this reasoning, Rowland was too much of a gentleman to say so. Tamping tobacco into his pipe, he reached for a match and asked how he could be of help in unravelling the truth.

"I don't know that you can," I said. "But you are my best hope. The vicarage is even older than our house, and our closest neighbour. Is it possible that some of the records kept by previous vicars are still here somewhere? If so, I wonder if you would be willing to see if you can find anything that would provide some insight into Abigail's life with Arthur? This may sound far-fetched, but I have a feeling that if we discover how Abigail died, we may also find the treasure."

Rowland assured me that he would be more than pleased to assist in the investigation, though he was, unfortunately, leaving the next day on a three-week visit to Israel. Immediately upon his return, he promised to search the filing system.

More boxes to be unearthed from cellars and attics! Such seemed to be the story of my life. The delay was disappointing, but I wished Rowland an enjoyable trip with good grace, and told him that I would invite him for dinner upon his return. He was, I thought as I walked home in a mood of sudden depression, likely to be our first and last guest at Merlin's Court.

* * *

The way things looked, all too soon we would be packing our bags and saying our goodbyes. Back to the old humdrum existence. I wondered how I would face life in another drab two-room flat with Tobias my only roommate, while Ben returned to the waiting arms of his long-suffering fiancée. When first mentioned, I had not seriously believed in the existence of this paragon. I had considered her a childish invention, produced on the spur of the moment by Ben to keep me from harbouring false hopes in his direction. Now I was not so sure. He had spoken of her rather often recently. Susan (or was it Sally) was an athletic marvel who could even balance her cheque book.

"She'll have to learn to juggle with it, too, if she has to support both of you," I told him on one embittered occasion, following a three-day attack of writer's block which he had blamed on my singing as I went about the house. Admittedly

I have an atrocious voice but he need not have compared it to whooping cough set loosely to music.

"Susan, unlike you, considers me perfect," Ben informed me coldly, before turning on his heel and stalking off. I really didn't think he had caught my parting thrust of "That's because she hasn't lived with you."

As he reached the door he turned. "Oh no?" He smiled, quirked an irritating eyebrow, and was gone.

* * *

Dorcas's spade was leaning abandoned against the herb garden wall. I found her in the washhouse, scouring dried earth from her hands and humming with raucous disregard for tune, worse even than mine, "Onward Christian Soldiers."

I tossed her a towel. "You sound happy."

"Whamo! Glad to see you back." Dorcas swung round and grabbed hold of my arm with a soapy hand. "Something rather stupendous has happened. Had a marvellous time working in the garden. Heat a bit grim, enough to blister a camel's hump, kept up the pace by singing, nothing like a good rousing hymn for . . ."

"You've found the treasure," I said, scarcely able to breathe.

"Sorry, can't win the prize for that one, but . . ." She unclasped the hand she wasn't using to hold on to me and in her palm lay a small oval-shaped locket on a slender gold chain, still encrusted with mud, although from its soapy condition, she had been cleaning it up.

"Pretty," I said without too much enthusiasm as my vision of a wooden chest spilling over with jewels worth a king's ransom faded. This was a cheap tinny piece, something I might have owned myself, or Aunt Sybil . . . no, she wore brooches the size of doorknobs. I looked up at Dorcas, my heart suddenly leaping about in my chest like someone doing the highland fling.

She read my eyes. "You've got it" — she nodded — "on the nose. Abigail's — see!" Inserting a grimy fingernail into the side of the locket she pried it open like a shell hiding a tiny sea animal. I expected to see a miniature photograph tucked into one side or a clipping of auburn hair, but the locket was empty. I didn't want to appear negative but . . .

"Look!" Pointing with her finger she showed me the finely traced engraving: *To Abigail From M.*

A present from Merlin to his mother? That seemed a pretty safe assumption but all other theories and conjectures led into a maze. Had Abigail deliberately buried the locket in the herb garden, and if so why? Or had she lost it while working there? I preferred not to think this might be another clue. Because if they were now being buried what hope did we have of actually tripping over the treasure? But for Dorcas, the herb garden would never have been touched. I had my hands full with the house, and I doubted if Ben knew a petunia from a dandelion.

Speaking of the blighted author, he came searching for us to announce that luncheon was being served al fresco under the large beech tree in the garden. He took a quick dekko at the locket, screwed up his eyes, and said that having worked in his Uncle Abe's pawn shop as a teenager he knew something about jewellery. This little number while not exactly the kind of thing to be given away with three bars of soap, was worth all of two quid. I half expected him to say take it or leave it, but he returned the locket to my hand with "Don't turn your nose up. That should make a nice little souvenir of your extended holiday at the seaside, if the family is prepared to sell."

Ben had spent the morning experimenting with the new Aga in the finally completed kitchen and had prepared a delicious repast of lobster stewed in wine, chilled to icy perfection and dressed in homemade mayonnaise, laced with capers. There were only three of us. Jonas refused to join us, informing Ben that he considered eating outdoors heathen folly. We spread a cloth on the lawn under the dappled shade of the beech tree.

"Must congratulate you, Ben," Dorcas said as Ben lifted spinach salad onto my plate, "absolutely lip-smacking, these little brown rolls — super! Forgive me, I must indulge once more."

Ben passed her the plate. Flattery did things for him; he looked more cheerful than I had seen him in days. With a touch of nonchalance he volunteered the information that a spoonful of treacle added to the yeast base was the secret for his rolls. "And I do think," he added, "that this rather understated salad with its lemon and sweet vermouth dressing is the perfect foil for the lobster — subtle but not insipid."

"Come off it!" I lay back against the warm grass and let the sun soak deep into my bones. "The only people who talk like that are those creeps who have just started making their own wine in the cellar." Lifting my glass of cider I intoned deeply while looking down the bridge of my nose. "Robust without being coarse, fragrant but not floral. Sensitive but not lacking in spirit . . ."

"Okay, I get the picture." Ben gave a rather unwilling grin and lay back on the grass; resting his head on his hands, he squinted into the sun. "I admit I can become rather fanatical on the subject of cookery." He turned his head and looked in my direction. "Rather like you and your Abigail craze."

"Before you make any more cracks on that subject," I replied thoughtfully, "aren't you somewhat hooked on the lady yourself? Isn't this lobster one of Abigail's recipes?"

Ben used the type of word to which Uncle Merlin had objected, rolled over, and apologized to Dorcas.

"Don't worry about me, heard far worse in the school lavatories." Dorcas tucked Tobias, who was eying the lobster greedily, firmly under one arm and buttered another roll. "Pity, recipes like this are not published any more, plenty of home-grown veg fresh from the garden, herbs to season, nothing out of a tin or from a packet. Bound to be more time-consuming but marvellous dividends! Loads more nutrition and flavour."

Ben sat up slowly. The sun filtering through the leaves gave him a greenish mottled appearance, and in the bright light his eyes looked dazed. For some reason I thought of

Lazarus rising from the dead. "The Edwardian Lady's Cookery Book," he muttered. Repeating the phrase sotto voce several times, he leapt suddenly to his feet, oversetting the lobster dish and causing Tobias to strike out at Dorcas with unsheathed claws and hurl himself across the lawn, his tail blown out like a dandelion clock. Ben ignored the scratch marks on Dorcas's arm and Tobias's frenzied retreat; eyes closed, hands pressed to his temples, he was a man awaiting another revelation from above. Apparently he got it. Launching into his own version of an Indian war dance he shouted out, "To hell with Sister Marie Grace!" and before we could ask what in heaven he was going on about, he vanished into the house.

"I say." Dorcas looked at me. "Was I responsible in some way for that display of exuberance? Hope I didn't say anything to unbalance the dear chap!"

"Quite the opposite; if I'm not mistaken what you have done is given Ben a new lease on life. The novel is dead. Our literary genius is about to write a cookery book, and why not? Uncle Merlin's will did not specify that the work had to be fiction. I wonder Ben never thought of utilizing his own field of expertise before."

I was proved right. When Dorcas and I carried the dishes back into the house we heard the sound of beautiful music, not the mechanical stammering of recent days, but the rapid clatter of the typewriter keys. The race was on.

Now he was once more a man with a mission, I hoped Ben would take a good long look at me and realize there was a new trim-line dish on the world menu — me. But he continued to treat me with marked coolness. He did tell me, when I hovered admiringly over his typewriter one day, that he was inserting anecdotes between the recipes and had written to a friend in London asking him to produce some pencil sketches in keeping with the era. But in the main his attitude was very strongly one of "don't bug me."

One thing I did admire was his commitment to see this thing through to the bitter end. He had given his word that he would remain at Merlin's Court for six months and he had kept to that even if I had done something horrendous to turn him against me. One day a flash of genius told me what that might be. I had never thanked him for the silver photo frame. Ignoring the No Admittance signals vibrating through the closed door of his work room, I went in to apologize.

"With all that wretched business about the chocolates and your book," I said, "other matters got brushed aside but I did love my present. Abigail's picture looks right at home in it. The more I learn about that woman, the more special I know she was. She wasn't pretty or—"

"My God," snapped Ben, thumping the back-spacer with his thumb, "what a creature you are for always harping on appearances. I'm beginning to have some serious doubts about that damned diet of yours — it's turning you into another bird-brained Narcissus, goggling in every mirror you pass. What's happened to your sense of values?"

"This coming from you?" Somehow I managed a creditable snicker as I glowered down at him. "Physical attributes don't impress you? Hypocrite! You never stopped smacking your lips the first time you saw Vanessa. When she and I were in the same room you never gave me a second glance and don't tell me it was her mind that held you in thrall!"

"I thought we were discussing Abigail." Back-spacing rapidly, Ben did not look up. "Somehow I got the notion that we were all agreed that she was the perfect example of how a woman does not have to be pretty, as you call it, to be beautiful. Remember when I first saw her portrait I said she reminded me of someone? At the time I wasn't sure who. For starters I thought of Dorcas — there is a similarity of colouring — but one night when you and I were sitting in the drawing room together, talking away, I realized that the person Abigail put me in mind of was you. Oh, don't panic, not in looks — in other ways."

"Like me?" I had to sit down on the nearest chair even though it was already occupied by a stack of paper. Being told I resembled Abigail was like being given a flower, especially when the words came from Ben. To be strong and fine, warm and alive as she had been . . . I couldn't think of anything more . . .

"We saw it by gas light, the lighting was poor, remember?" Ben pounded away on the keys. "And who knows, we may all have waxed too sentimental over that portrait."

I loathed him then. I loathed his rumpled dark hair and his faded sweater and his neat nimble fingers. I hoped they jammed between the keys and had to be amputated. What had I done to make him turn so hostile — spitting meanly at me the way Tobias did when I mistakenly gave him the wrong food?

"Why don't you run along like a good girl," Ben said. "Go and visit the vicar. I'm sure old Rolly will be delighted to see you. Oh, I forgot. He telephoned yesterday to reiterate his goodbyes. I gather he had previously offered them in person. Sorry I forgot to tell you."

* * *

By the next week the dining room was ready for use in its proper capacity and Ben had taken over the loggia as his study. It was rather crammed with displaced pieces of furniture, empty pots of paint, and wallpaper scraps, but he had installed his typewriter on a small table near the window and asked with wintry politeness to be left undisturbed. The closed door was as effective as writing on the wall.

One evening Dorcas and I decided to drive out to one of the hotels for dinner, partly because with Ben hard at work I had been doing the evening meal (and while I did much better than Dorcas, Ben had spoiled us), but mostly because I wanted an excuse to wear a rather super blue dress I had just purchased. Most of my clothes had been hanging on me like maternity smocks for some weeks, but superstition had prevented my buying new until now. I was still certain that once I boxed up all my old clothes and sent them to the Salvation Army, I would regain two stone overnight. But this evening I decided to burn my boats and bridges, too. Was it the subdued light in my bedroom (one of the bulbs was out) or the sapphire shade of the dress which kindly made my eyes two sizes bigger and the rest of me two sizes smaller, or that I had drawn my hair into a severe knot on top of my head which emphasized the emergence of cheekbones I had never known I possessed? To be truthful, when I looked in the mirror, I was quite taken with myself.

"You know something, baby doll" — I smoothed out an eyebrow — "you ain't half bad." On a tidal wave of new-found confidence I swept down the stairs, through the hall, knocked on the loggia door and, barely waiting for Ben's unenthusiastic permission to enter, I turned the door handle and went in.

His back was to me and without turning his head, he muttered, indistinctly, "Well?"

Advancing slowly I stood immediately behind him, wishing my knees had not taken up their old nervous rattle and, afraid that my voice would go on strike, I took a deep breath.

"Unless you have come on a matter of national importance, I do wish you would return later." Ben ran a hand through his hair, removed a pencil from his lips, and began scribbling something on a piece of scratch paper.

"I won't take that personally. Unless you have eyes in the back of your head, you can't know if it's me or Dorcas, or . . ."

"Don't be ridiculous, Ellie, all I need are ears on the side of my head. I would know those footsteps anywhere. You always sound like an army sergeant marching up and down the compound on inspection."

So much for my graceful floating entrance. Better get this thing over. What was needed was a small joke to help the job along.

"That's because I lost my glass slippers and had to borrow boots from one of the ugly sisters. This is your prime favourite of fairy-tale romance, Cinderella. Outside is Dorcas doing a nice impersonation of Fairy Godmother. But in order to go to the ball I still need our Charming escort, how about it, chum?"

Ben swung round in his chair. His eyes raked slowly over me, seeming to take in every inch of the blue silk dress, the sheer nylon stockings with nary a wrinkle, and my high-heeled navy sandals. Returning at last to my face, he took a long hard look as though studying a stranger before saying coldly and with complete finality, "I'm sorry, Ellie, I don't do that kind of work any more."

CHAPTER THIRTEEN

All those foolish hopes! The myth that Ben would fall a helpless victim to the charms of the updated, stream-lined version of Ellie Simons was at an end. Had I brought this on myself? In losing weight had I become arrogant, conceited, thoughtless, and complacent? Horrible thought! And, naturally, I would be the last to know. Those were not the sort of tidings one's best friend would hasten to pass along.

I did ask Dorcas for an honest appraisal, but her opinion was worse than useless. She assured me I was nicer than ever and Ben's behaviour was probably due to intense concentration. Total involvement with his book. I might have swallowed this if he was not being perfectly charming to Dorcas, Jonas, and even Aunt Sybil on her rare visits to the house.

"An exile in my own home," I confided sadly to Tobias. Things are getting rough when the only satisfactory male of one's acquaintance is a cat, and these days he, too, was something of a deserter, jumping onto Jonas's lap more readily than he did mine.

Most of the work on the ground floor was completed. The workmen had left and I now had only to wait for the delivery of the furniture, curtains, and carpets before putting the rooms back together. The drawing room looked exactly as

I had hoped it would. Bracket wall lights shed an amber glow over the cream silk wallpaper and the rich tones of the freshly cleaned carpet and dark oak surround. On the mantelpiece stood the tall brass candlesticks and Dorcas's yellow Chinese vase. My only regret was that Abigail's portrait could not hang above them in the place of honour. I mentioned this one day at lunch, adding that discounting the poor artwork the picture did have a special meaning for the house and it was a shame it had never been completed. Dorcas suggested taking it to a gallery or a small art shop for touching up. Jonas, who had been steadily wiping gravy off his plate with a crust of bread, looked up and announced that he'd always been thought by his teachers at school to be rather a dab hand with a paint box. Not that he'd picked up a brush in years, but he didn't doubt t'was the same as swimming or riding a bicycle — once push came to shove t'would all come back. Jonas had put us in a bind. To refuse would be a slap in the eye, but what if he bungled?

"Sure, Jonas," said Ben. "Go ahead. You certainly can't do worse than the original artist." Jonas was watching me with a sparkle in his wicked old eyes, daring me to say him nay, and Ben had not even cared to ask my opinion. Men! How I hated them and myself for not resisting their tyranny. Samson's strength had evaporated with the loss of his hair, mine with my lost inches. In more ways than one I was not half the girl I used to be.

On one point though, I did stand firm. I refused to succumb to the old trap of eating to console myself. What I needed was another project in the house, but one that would not require too much time. With the weeks stretching into months, we were now entering September. The sand was running to the bottom of the glass. The six months would be up on October 5. The vicar was still away, but I didn't fret about that. I had almost given up hope of his uncovering anything that would lead us to the cause of Abigail's death and through that knowledge to the treasure.

I began work on the master bedroom, unoccupied since Merlin's death. Stripping off the old wallpaper was a tedious business, but I refused Dorcas's offer of help knowing how anxious she was to spend as many hours as possible in the herb garden. I called Jonas into service and surprisingly he submitted to his indoor assignment with good grace. No sooner would I send him downstairs in search of a tape measure or a bottle of liquid soap than he would reappear. My nerves were not in the best state those days and once I almost fell off my ladder when he popped up behind me like genie from a bottle.

"Work agrees with the man" was Dorcas's explanation. "Got more spring in his step than when I first came. Colour healthier, too, lost the wax look he used to have. Madame Tussaud's wouldn't take him now, ha-ha!"

"He does seem more fit," I agreed. "For a man his age he can certainly move and he's doing a wonderful job with the garden. Uncle Merlin must not have brought out the best in him. I can't believe the improvement in the grounds this year."

"More than one change made at Merlin's Court, Ellie. I'm happier than I've been in donkey's years, and your Aunt Sybil is coming out of the sulks. Always a bit condescending with me but I take no notice. Asked her if she wanted those ancient newspapers left stacked in her old room for her papier-mâché heads. If not they could go on Jonas's bonfire. Had to laugh myself when I went through them. Not one copy of *The Times* or *Guardian*. Scandal sheets every one! Still, mustn't criticize. An hour on the tennis court would have left her too winded for such nonsense. But never too late. Glad she's taken up swimming, except, told me she sees no reason to waste water on her weekly bath now. Ah well, if she's in good spirits! Wanted to know how you were progressing with the toils of Hercules."

"You didn't tell her about the cookery book, did you?"

"Not a whisper. Mum's the word. Old girl might blab and we don't need another sabotage attempt. Can't see they'd have much luck with Ben tucking it under his mattress at night and keeping it with him at all times during the day, but better safe than sorry. Admire you for wanting that book to succeed even if the final requirement of the will is never fulfilled." She went out of the door murmuring, "Love is kind, love is not selfish, love is . . ."

Didn't the woman realize that I now had no feelings for Bentley Haskell other than a certain respect for his skill at the cooker? Stamping up and down on a ladder in a fit of impotent rage can be perilous to one's health, particularly when the phone startles one in the middle of a bounce. Fortunately I managed to catch hold of the picture rail as I swung out into mid-air, but my breath was still a bit quivery when I reached the hall and picked up the receiver, something I had not done without a pang of fear since my obscene call. But this time there was nothing to worry about. This was Rowland Foxworth telling me in the pleasant voice that warmed my ear, that he had enjoyed his visit to Israel but had missed his friends. And he had something for me of greater interest. He had found several boxes containing old sermons and other papers dating back to the vicar of St. Anselm's during Abigail's day. He would look through them and get back in touch with me.

"How about dinner next Thursday?" I suggested.

He told me he would be delighted and that 7.30 would be perfect. Some men were so easy to please. Social success went to my head.

Aunt Sybil appeared at the door several minutes later to ask if she might borrow *The Merchant of Venice* from the study and I could not resist boasting of my social engagement. A mistake. Before I could bite off my tongue I had asked her to join us; but what else could I have done when her eyes misted as she told me that she would like to entertain Mr Foxworth but for a single woman to entertain a man was bound to lead to gossip? Oh, horse feathers! I would have to wait until Aunt Sybil went home before talking with Rowland about Abigail. But it would be a chance for the old pet to dress up in her black silk.

Before she left, Aunt Sybil asked me if I had been having any problems with the family. Did she suspect something or was she making polite conversation? Probably the latter because when I asked her what she meant she went all vague and said, "You know — difficulties, thank you for the book. You don't read Shakespeare I gather, no spots or creases on any of the pages, that's television for you!" We didn't have television.

Over lunch that day Ben took a sarcastic enjoyment out of belittling my small dinner party when I advised him and Dorcas of the approaching event. "If this is to be a white tie affair," he scoffed, "I must regretfully decline your kind invite. My wardrobe does not extend to formal do's. But don't cancel your evening with the vicar on my account. I can always take a tray up to my room, unless you would like me to masquerade as the butler. Having done my stint as a waiter I am quite adept at balancing a silver tray on the tips of my fingers."

"Rubbish!" Dorcas held up a hand for order. "As housekeeper I will serve dinner. Don't possess one of those skittish parlour maid outfits but do own a black dress and can always run up a white apron on the old treadle machine in the sewing room."

A babble of refusal met her offer. Ben, feeling quite rightly that he had opened a can of worms by reminding Dorcas with his talk of butlers that she was officially an employee of the household, admitted he had been joking. He had every intention of sitting down with us to dinner, but only on the condition that she promised to do the same, thus sparing him an interminable evening endeavouring to entertain a man of the cloth without a friend's moral support.

Thanks a lot!

Before I could pick up cudgels in Rowland's defence, Jonas lay down his fork with a clatter that drew everyone's attention. Glaring at the pack of us from under his shaggy brows, he proclaimed that he was the one who should properly perform the task of serving dinner.

"Jonas," I demurred, "this whole discussion is ridiculous. No one need serve. This is not Buckingham Palace.

Admittedly the dining room is rather inconveniently placed, but I see no reason why I cannot . . ."

The gardener silenced me. "Madam," he roared, "your place is with your guests. Be about your business and leave me to tend to mine. Ain't now't shaming to a man in carrying a tray of soup plates. Always had a fancy to try my hand at it. Me old grandpa used to say 'a change is as good as a rest,' and at my time of life variety don't often come aknocking."

Having said his piece he picked up his fork and ploughed it back into his plate of stew as though digging up a bed of turnips, pausing only to suck the juice off the ends of his moustache. Ben grinned acidly. "Sounds as though we're in for a swell do. Perhaps you would prefer to have the food catered in, Ellie, or will my beef Wellington with an asparagus mousse for a starter be classy enough for his honour the vicar?"

Stoically I forbore to answer, but Dorcas piped in with the information that she was very partial to a cheese soufflé and if Ben thought . . . He didn't, saying that if the vicar were delayed by his errands of mercy and arrived late, the soufflé would be a cheese omelette and a rubbery one at that.

"Soufflés," I said flippantly, "like the tide wait for no man. Even you, Ben, with all your savvy can't alter that."

It seemed Ben and I couldn't be in the same room together for five minutes without friction. But neither he nor any other thorn was going to spoil my pleasure in my small dinner party. When the day dawned I had matters so well in hand that early in the afternoon I drove into town with Dorcas and both of us had our hair done. I wasn't quite sure about my friend's bouffant, having previously only seen her red locks resolutely thrust behind her ears. It certainly made her look taller. As for me, the girl drew my hair to one side and plaited it into a single, gleaming braid. "Stunning," she said, "in its simplicity."

Holding up the mirror so I could admire her handiwork, she asked, "Well, miss?"

"Fantastic!" But I wasn't sure. Who was that stranger behind the glass? What did she have in common with the real me — the fat girl of the shapeless clothes and serviceable shoes?

Ben did not see me until he passed me in the hall on his way upstairs to dress, and the only indication that he noticed any change in my appearance was a curt admonishment not to let my hair trail in the soup he had spent hours preparing. Pleasure in my appearance ebbed. The foxglove dress which clung to my new figure with petal-like softness seemed gaudy now. But pride in the house remained. As the grandfather clock struck seven I went down into the hall. Tonight the electric lights had been turned down by a dimmer switch. Candlelight flickered golden over the rich dark sheen of the wainscoted walls and the graceful curve of the bannister rail. A deep Turkish red rug warmed the stone floor. The two suits of armour blinked silver-bright — a testimonial to Jonas's skill with the polishing cloth. The carved trestle table, which until recently had been a dumping ground for overcoats and Wellington boots, stood empty except for the telephone and a blue Devonshire pottery bowl filled with autumn flowers and leaves.

Opening the dining room door, I stood admiring Abigail's overmantel above the fireplace, the deep bay window, its ledge bright with my birthday geraniums, and the ancient black oak table reflecting in its brightly polished surface, the Indian tree dinner service, old silver, and sparkling crystal. My tour led me next to the kitchen, where Ben's copper saucepans simmered on the Aga top. Pots of herbs hung from the ceiling to form a curtain at the small window. In an alcove away from the draught sat a wicker basket stuffed with a plump cushion where Tobias could curl up on cold nights — when he was home, that is. He had taken to visiting Jonas quite a lot of an evening. The room was the way I had imagined it could be on that first night when I had come down here to forage for something to eat: the navy blue Aga, the quarry-tiled floor, the wallpaper's neutral cream . . . a room that spoke of warmth and cleanliness.

The clock in the hall struck again — 7.15. Slowly I retraced my steps. I savoured the thought of going into

Abigail's drawing room, where a fire had been lit in the hearth and the flare from its coals bathed the silk-papered walls in a dancing rosy light. For a moment I thought I saw her, but it was only Dorcas with her puffy hairdo holding Tobias on her lap. A knock at the door startled me, intruding on the stillness. In came Jonas looking rather formidable with his grizzled hair flattened down, sporting a shiny black suit. True, the mouldering gardening boots sneaking out from under his trouser turn-ups did rather lessen the effect of all this grandeur, but I was impressed by his obvious efforts. He carried something in both hands, and before I could speak he handed Abigail's portrait to me and switched on the light.

I was almost afraid to look. I had never been very keen on letting the old man tamper with the canvas. It had changed subtly; the colours softened, it offered the same unreal, luminous quality of the room seen through firelight. Jonas, in addition to filling in the details necessary to complete the portrait, had brushed the entire canvas with a translucent glaze. The haunting effect was of Abigail glimpsed through an ocean mist or behind a frosted pane of glass — always out of reach.

"Jonas," I said sombrely, "you are a genius."

"Now't to brag on't," grumped the old man. "Not enough to have Mr Botticelli turning in't grave, any road."

* * *

I was standing on a chair tapping a picture hook into position above the fireplace when the door opened once again and Ben ushered in Rowland Foxworth. Dorcas and I had been so busy arguing whether or not I was off centre that we had failed to hear the doorbell.

"Don't get down," expostulated the vicar, smiling up at me while patting his pockets as if to make sure he still had his pipe and tobacco safe and sound. "You look absolutely charming."

"Permission to dismount?" I asked, smiling into his eyes. "I don't think I'm the type to remain on a pedestal too long without toppling off."

"I would be more than happy to catch you," replied the vicar gallantly and, reaching for my hand, he helped me down. For a fraction of a second our eyes held, then he released me, turning to speak some pleasantry to Dorcas, who blushed fierily while making an abortive attempt at running her fingers through her starched hairdo.

"Tell me how he does it," whispered Ben under cover of helping me put away the hammer in the bureau drawer. Batting his eyelids, he bared his teeth in a hideous impersonation of an ingratiating smile. "If our Dorcas is susceptible to the cleric's charms no woman is safe."

With patience at an end, I kicked my persecutor sharply in the shin. "Ah, the doorbell," I cried, drowning out his moan of pain. "That must be Aunt Sybil."

Dinner was superb. The asparagus mousse melted in the mouth, the soup was steaming hot and redolent of fresh herbs and garden veg. The beef Welly was done to perfection — the meat pink and juicy, the golden crust flaking at the touch of a fork. Jonas moved around the table with commendable loftiness, missing his footing only once, whereupon he neatly retrieved the two or three spilt brussels sprouts which had landed on Aunt Sybil's shelflike chest. Without batting an eye he proceeded royally on his way. But everyone else was at his worst. Ben acted as though he had swallowed arsenic. Dorcas, whom I had always believed to be above such distractions as men, turned salmon pink and coy each time the vicar spoke to her. In a different way Aunt Sybil seemed equally in awe of this kindly gentleman. Where Dorcas was tongue-tied, she twittered on about nothing, in the most embarrassingly trite way.

"Whatever you say, my dear vicar," she replied to some statement he had made and to which I had not been paying attention. "Far be it from me to argue with a man. We women must accept the truth that we are not the intellectual equals of your . . ." Aunt Sybil lowered her eyes and coughed discreetly, "sex."

Dorcas promptly rediscovered her voice. "Pig swill, never heard such a piece of outmoded piffle in years. Most repressive attitude — not at all healthy."

"Why don't we return to the drawing room," I suggested, rising hastily. Ben was ignoring my frantic mime that he help maintain the peace. At that moment the doorbell chimed again and the atmosphere became charged with something extra — anticipation that bordered foolishly on disquiet. We were expecting no one else.

"Who the devil?" Ben wondered out loud as we went to find out.

Freddy! He stood surrounded by a nimbus of light from the outdoor lantern. His hair and beard, lifted by the wind, made him look more roguish and disreputable than ever. "Greetings, folks. How about a night's free lodging?" he leered. Ben and I, united in spirit for the first time in weeks, eyed each other. What did this arrival forbode? If anything?

Dropping his knapsack by the stairs, Freddy, never one to mince words, asked if I had bequeathed one-half of my body to science and if he was in time for dinner. The only person noticeably touched by these words was Aunt Sybil, who murmured, "Poor boy, I worry about you sometimes, if you get enough rest. Shall I make you a sandwich?"

My initial impulse on witnessing Freddy's barely repressed shudder was to let him wallow in this horrible fate in hopes he would decide not to extend his visit. But curses! Charity prevailed, and I asked Jonas, who had been standing at a discreet distance, to bring some beef Wellington and whatever else he could salvage into the drawing room.

"Where did you pick up the feudal retainer?" Freddy slipped his arm through mine with cousinly good will and we led the small procession back to the fire. "He looks like a ghoul dressed up to go to a birthday party." His voice sank to a hoarse whisper. "And who is that astringent female with the plaster of Paris hairdo?"

"Freddy," I responded, after angrily checking to see if Dorcas had overheard him, "if you want us to feed and house you for the night, you must make a supreme effort to speak nicely of your fellow human beings."

"Is that what they are?" he asked in feigned wonderment. "Sorry!" He stood taking inventory. "I see you have been dipping into the family purse revamping the joint." His eyes continued to rove about until they reached the portrait above the fireplace. "And who is that, the ghoul's mother?"

"That's Abigail Grantham," I answered coldly. "Uncle Merlin's mother."

"Not much to look at, was she?" Freddy swung round to include all of us in his observation. The door clicked inward and in shuffled Jonas carrying a loaded tray. I was about to take it from him when Aunt Sybil spoke, and I thought it rude to cross in front of her. "A very plain woman," she agreed, reaching up to pat down her badly permed hair. "Oh, I know we can't all have the looks, and that you will say, dear vicar, that handsome is as handsome does, but I have always thought that when a woman employs time to snare a husband she should employ some more to show appreciation and respect. Man did not put the word *obey* in the marriage service for woman to take it out. And Abigail, although I will admit her apple charlotte was second to none, did give poor Uncle Arthur a lot of headaches. Far too familiar with the help, for one thing, and look at the effect that had on poor impressionable Merlin. I tried everything to discourage his unfortunate, unprofessional relationship with that coarse, disreputable gardener. . . ."

Rowland coughed and cleared his throat, but whether he would have spoken into the volcanic silence we were not destined to discover. A harsh, gravelly voice, rasping with fury, severed the air like a rusty guillotine. My shock was so profound I had difficulty believing this was Jonas speaking.

"Madam!" He ground out the word, eyebrows meeting like a pair of furious furry caterpillars. "What do you know about a woman who was wife and mother — a dried-up, man-hungry spinster like you?"

Aunt Sybil's face turned a dangerous shade of purple, seeping as quickly out to deathbed white. "How dare you!" She clutched a hand to her heaving silk chest. "Merlin"

— she took a deep breath and stammered, "Merlin would never have permitted you to talk to me so."

"Wouldn't he?" The tray rattled in Jonas's blue-veined hands. "And nor would he have allowed an old frump like you to speak ill of his mother." With these words he banged the tray down on the coffee table, bowed to the astonished company, and thundered from the room.

"Ee, by gum." Freddy rubbed his hands together in glee. "Ain't it fun to be 'ome!"

Aunt Sybil was not at all well. I was quite frightened for her and urged her to let me fetch a doctor. Like a small bewildered child, she asked only to be taken home so she could sleep. Ben went immediately to fetch her coat, saying he would escort her to the cottage, but on his return Rowland insisted he would be happy to perform the office. "Although," he continued, "I will expect a small reward for my services — perhaps you will offer me a small glass of brandy, Miss Grantham, and take one with me." Aunt Sybil did not return his smile. "Ellie" — Rowland was patting his jacket pockets and peering about the room as he spoke — "I seem to have mislaid my pipe and tobacco pouch."

"I expect you left them in the dining room, shall we go and look?"

Sure enough we found these articles beside the place where he had been sitting, but I was glad of this brief opportunity of talking with the vicar alone. After thanking him for his concern for Aunt Sybil, I apologized for Jonas's incredible rudeness. "He's a dreadful old man at the best of times," I sighed. "Whatever his other vices, Merlin wasn't a snob, and Aunt Sybil should keep her nose out."

Rowland tapped his pipe on the ashtray and put it back in his pocket. "What I consider interesting is that the confrontation concerned Abigail Grantham. I only hope I excite as much influence when I've been dead for half a century. Clergymen are not supposed to be superstitious, but I almost wonder if her personality lingers in this house."

"I'm glad you understand." I fiddled with a water glass on the table. "I don't believe the house is haunted, exactly, either — but what happened to Abigail somehow changed its character. Uncle Merlin's years of neglect and Aunt Sybil's deplorable housekeeping did their part, but I still feel the corrosion began when Arthur Grantham ripped out or papered over every trace of his wife's presence."

Rowland nodded. "So far I am still exhuming the thousand and one sermons written by the late Reverend Geoffrey Hempstead, all extremely lengthy and of the hell-fire and brimstone variety. Much as I dislike decrying a predecessor, Hempstead was a fanatic."

We crossed the hall to the drawing room and stood briefly outside the closed door. "One wonders," I said, "how the worthy Mr Hempstead addressed truly hardened sinners. They got the works, I assume, eternity in a Turkish bath?"

The vicar placed his hand on the doorknob. "Unless they could be brought to their knees in abject repentance. To prevent other family members from being similarly corrupted he strongly recommended the spiritually deceased member be torn off like so much rotten flesh and cast out upon the world. I found several themes of this nature, many deploring drunkenness and one relating to a woman taken in adultery. Apparently, the husband had done the Christian thing and shown her the door." Rowland smiled. "You will be relieved to know the church has mellowed over the years. I for one don't expect apprentice angels."

Minutes later as Rowland left the house with Aunt Sybil, he pressed my hand significantly and reminded me that he would be in touch.

"Is something naughty going on between you and the cleric?" Freddy asked, as he poured himself a glass of Benedictine and slouched down before the fire. "Can't say I blame the chap now you've shed the flab. Sporting of Ben not to mind, but living together often does that to a relationship. The ardour cools, and both parties start looking for a change of playpen — someone who doesn't hog the bathroom in the mornings or polish off the last crumb of cereal in the box. . . . And why not? If both parties are mature and open-minded . . ."

Before I could respond to this view of the sexual revolution, Dorcas ruffled up like an angry chicken. "Young man, I refuse to stand here and listen to you insult my friends. Everything here is on the up and up. If it were not, young man, I can assure you I would not have remained a single night under this roof. Why should you believe me, you ask? Because, my fine friend, I am a gentlewoman, a games mistress, and a Girl Guide! Need I say more?"

"Not a word!" whispered Freddy.

"The trouble with your kind" — Dorcas eyed Freddy's pony tail and earring with strong disapproval — "is that now hippies are passé. You don't have a clue what to do with the rest of your life. Do yourself a favour, my boy, take up jogging."

Dorcas's pep talk must have done Freddy some good. He behaved like a model guest from that moment. He even made his own bed the next morning, but Ben and I were nonetheless relieved when he informed us at breakfast that he would be scooting off after lunch. If he was mixing business with pleasure, checking up on our activities in order to lay them waste, he had not allowed himself much time. Still, Ben had hidden his manuscript in one of the suits of armour in the hall. During breakfast Freddy did remark reproachfully that I now ate like a sparrow and asked if I had lost all the weight necessary to meet my goal. I answered truthfully — no — and hastily turned the subject before he could enquire how close I was to success. The morning passed quickly and relatively easily. Ben reminded Freddy that Aunt Sybil had asked him to stop at the cottage before he left.

"Maybe she is going to spot you a loan," suggested Ben as he pointedly began removing eggy plates from the table.

"Really." Freddy cocked an eyebrow. "Of course she was in such a tizz; what do you think, should I toddle down and see her now instead of waiting until my hour of departure? Yes, I think I owe the old buzzard something for teaching me over the years the meaning of good food." Not like Freddy to be so gallant, but he was so hard to figure. I told him Aunt Sybil would be in the middle of her swimming practice down in the cove and he nobly said he would go and give her a private lesson in survival fitness if Ben would lend him a pair of trunks. He hoped she would not insist on paying him but, if she did, he would give her his special discount rate.

As matters turned out, Aunt Sybil did not have to part with her money. She was neither in the water nor at home, Freddy informed us, looking peeved as he trod sand into the hall. I was rather worried. I hoped Aunt Sybil's absence did not indicate that she had fallen ill and gone to visit Dr Melrose.

Freddy demanded a house tour and as we stood on the half-landing on the stairs looking up at the huge stained-glass window, he slowly ran a hand down the smooth surface of the bannister. "Know something, Ellie," he said, "I'm kinda impressed. You've brought something here," he said. "Something honest. One of the reasons I prefer the outdoors is that there most things are alive, the trees, the sheep with the wool still on their backs — but this" — he stroked the bannister again — "isn't dead. Cripes, I must be going soft. . . . I wonder, if you have already unburied the treasure, if it isn't something tangible at all — just good vibes."

I was touched, but Freddy was clever. Was he hoping I would say, "But it is an actual something — last week we found a postage stamp printed and run through the meter during the reign of Cleopatra." I continued the grand tour. "Uncle Merlin's old room." I flung open the door. "As you see, we have retained the woodwork and hung new paper. The curtains and bedspread should be here any hour. The other bedrooms all require redecorating and the floors sanding and I would like to make the dumb-waiter into a linen cupboard and . . ." Happily babbling on I did not mind that Freddy was unusually silent. It took a lot to shut him up.

* * *

No harm done from this visit, I thought, watching Freddy buzz out of sight on his motorbike early that afternoon. We had given him precious little to report. But as the day lengthened I began to feel curiously uneasy. A storm was brewing. A sullen wind stirred the trees to tapping on the windowpanes, setting my teeth on edge. So much so that when Jonas stepped out of the kitchen (I could have sworn he was working upstairs in one of the bedrooms) I squealed, lashing out at him in a wrathful tirade.

"What are you up to, snooping and prowling up behind people like a burglar practising for his stealth test? Aren't you satisfied with insulting harmless old women? If my aunt has a heart attack and dies, I will hold you responsible, Mr Phipps."

"If she does, won't be from a lifetime of hard work keeping her tongue in her mouth. She's not like you. I'm not one to throw posies but ye be a rare lass. I know what's got your craw — that lad coming down to spy out the lie of the land, but ye've nowt to fear with me about. The buzzards may be out there, hovering, but I'll swat 'em down like flies before they touch a hair of your head."

Was Jonas trying to cheer me or scare me to death? I'd scare him if Aunt Sybil hadn't fully recovered her health and spirits. But Dorcas and I found that Aunt Sybil was still not home. After our repeated knocks had met with profound silence, we took the key down from the side window ledge and let ourselves in through the front door. Six papier-mâché heads of Uncle Merlin grinned lopsidedly at us from the mantelpiece, but such was our only greeting, until we found the note on the pillow of Aunt Sybil's unmade bed. Very Victorian. But she had not eloped with Rowland Foxworth or run off to a nunnery. She had, so her distinctive spidery handwriting informed us, gone to visit an old friend for a while. After last night she had felt the need to get away.

"Makes sense," said Ben when I told him. "Would have made more sense if she had notified us in person, but she wants us to worry about her. Sad. She's old, and as Jonas implied, probably never had a man take her to the pictures, let alone try something sinful when the lights went out."

"Some of us learn to live with that handicap," I said. But I was sorry for poor Aunt Sybil and a little troubled.

"She'll be fine," said Dorcas bracingly. "Glad to know she's got a friend she can visit, somehow didn't think she had any."

One afternoon, about a week later, I had been shopping in the village and returned to some good news.

"Aunt Sybil just rang," Ben said. "You've been worrying about nothing. She couldn't say much because the line was bad, but she wants us to meet her and her friend for lunch at the Windhaven Hotel, in Shipley, this Saturday. We are even, get this, to bring Dorcas. Sounds like she feels a little guilty about her remarks concerning servants in front of Dorcas."

"Either that, or she wants us to bring her as a chaperone, in case you lose control and try and get me in the back seat of the car now we both would fit."

"You're incorrigible," said Ben, "but I am relieved about dear Aunt Sybil, she sounded chipper, too, so I guess we can count her back in the world of the living."

CHAPTER FOURTEEN

The Windhaven Hotel was situated above the promenade of the small seaside resort of Shipley. It had an air of faded grandeur, like an elderly aristocrat who slips a fine lace shawl across her shoulders to hide the darns in her outmoded gown. Dorcas, preferring to work in the herb garden, had declined to join us, but Ben and I were greeted like gentry by a hunched minion sporting old world livery and an obsequious smile, and ushered across the worn red carpeting of the reception hall.

Ben and I were served a superb lunch in the high-ceilinged Regency Room. Nothing was lacking on the heavy parchment menu. Nothing was lacking whatever, except Aunt Sybil. She had agreed to meet us at 12.30. When she had not arrived by one o'clock, I was not unduly concerned. The delay meant Ben and I could indulge in our second glass of Dubonnet. By the time I had reached my fourth, the reason for our being there seemed immaterial. Time to order solid sustenance. Not being a regular drinker, I had not learnt the basic rules — like when to stop. By the time we had finished our five-course lunch, one of which was a bottle of wine, I was feeling lovely and floaty and only vaguely melancholy about Aunt Sybil's absence. She would have been rather in the way in this cosy little rowing boat for two which swished ever so slowly up and down on the red sea — oops — carpet. The boat took a lunge and I had to take hold of Ben's hand to stop myself falling overboard.

"You don't think something could have happened to her?" I slurred.

"Such as?" Seen through a golden haze Ben looked as mouth-wateringly delicious as every bite of that delicious repast.

I toyed with my coffee spoon, and moistened my lips. "Could sh-sh, Sybil, have fallen off a bus or . . . ?"

"My guess is that she has mistaken the day. Or she may have been taken ill after we left home and been unable to put us off."

"I'm sure you're right." I wanted to drop my head down on the table and have a five-minute snooze, especially if Ben would join me.

"We'll wait a while longer in case she did get on the wrong bus or train and ended up fifty miles from here." He turned his best profile to the waitress and as on our first dining-out experience brought the waitress hurrying to his side. He ordered Irish coffee for both of us, seemingly unaware of my condition.

He was aware by the time he guided me out into the reception room half an hour later. The carpet was all soft, spongy waves flowing up against the double entry doors, and I was taking dainty little bites out of Ben's shoulder. The seagulls inside my head were telling me to do it.

"Behave," Ben hissed as a waiter passed us with an elevated purse-lipped stare.

"I can't help myself." I sagged against the man from E.E. as we swam through those double doors and got slugged in the face by the feisty salt wind with the sting of rain in its tail. "Ben," I said meekly, "if you don't take me in your arms here and now and kiss me with disgusting animal passion I will pitch myself down these steps and some innocent bystander is going to have to scrape me up with a spatula."

"Don't be an ass." He sounded strange, and a long way off. "You don't want to be a cheap thrill for all those holiday-makers down there."

"No." I turned my body against him and twined my fingers through his hair as though I had been doing that sort of thing all my life, instead of just reading about it in paperback. "I want to be a cheap thrill for you, you elusive little Pimpernel. What's wrong with me? Don't you care at all? Don't I rave about your cooking? Don't I appreciate how you slave at keeping grease spots off the kitchen wallpaper? Don't you realize that under this brittle facade I really am worried about Aunt Sybil? We don't know anything about this friend of hers, where she is. . . ." I think I was crying in nicely maudlin fashion, but I couldn't hear too well, over those damned seagulls — the ones racketing around inside my head.

"Oh, Ellie, the things I have to do to shut you up." His breath brushed my face lightly, and he kissed me. It was possible that I had got this far under false pretences, that I had intentionally misrepresented my state of inebriation. I could not have been officially soused when his lips first met mine because I was really drunk now. I was floating, flying, seagulling on gossamer wings towards ecstasy.

"Disgusting!" a voice roared in my ears, and in exquisite slow motion I lifted my lips away from Ben's, opened my eyes, and met the glare of a purple-faced little man in a pork-pie hat.

"Sir," I said, "you have made my day, my life, actually. My greatest ambition has always been to make an obscene spectacle of myself."

"Does that mean," said Ben, "that you have changed your mind about those steps? Good, then let us go home and see if there is any word from your aunt. The drive back will take an hour and those clouds are shouting rain."

The clouds weren't the only blurred objects about to spill over. My eyes threatened deluge equal to Noah's flood. Why had Ben done this to me, treated my drunken overtures as nothing more than a shallow display of momentary lust?

Why hadn't he kissed me again to show the pork-pie man where to get off? Why had he refused to take advantage of me? I was capable of decent restraint, I could have waited until he got me to the car for something more meaningful.

Happily, the louse was not troubling to make polite conversation. He was listening to ribald rock and roll lyrics blasting from the car wireless and puffing away on a pipe, a new affectation. If only he knew how ridiculous he looked! Not a patch on the dear vicar, who was tall, kind, rational, and in every way ideal husband material. Poor Rowland, I really would have to give him a chance to declare himself. He deserved a nice girl like me. If I could not love him, because my heart had already been bestowed on the unfeeling creature humming cheerily away beside me, I could at least revamp his house, wash his socks, and be a mother to his children. My mind dwelt on a row of miniature Rowlands who paraded before my inward eye, all wearing tweed jackets, sharp creases in their knee-length trousers, and hand-knitted socks, courtesy of Aunt Sybil. A shutter came down, the small paragons vanished and were instantly replaced by a swarming tangle of boys and girls all with dark hair, tanned skins, and brilliant blue-green eyes — shinning down the bannisters, cartwheeling through the hall, creating a havoc of noisy laughter, muddy floors, and overturned chairs, under the approving eye of their gymnastics tutor, Auntie Dorcas. How sad for the precious poppets that their father, wicked philanderer that he was, refused to do the decent thing and marry their mother.

Reaction set in. Temper gave way to depression as I considered that what I was suffering now would be nothing to the emptiness I would experience when Ben took his final walk — out of my life. At least now I could see him, wallow in his indifference. Why not test the powers of my endurance by turning the knife a little deeper? "I wonder what Vanessa will think of the new me?" I asked. "For years I have been telling myself she is not half the woman I am, but that line is a little redundant now."

"Why do you do this?" Ben's voice cut through the rapturous howling of rock music.

"Do what, pray tell?"

"Sneer at the way you were six months ago. You remind me of one of those born-again religious fanatics who view their past existence as so much dirty laundry. Tell me, Ellie, do you really see yourself as totally reincarnated?"

"You've always thought there was plenty of room for improvement." I tilted my head back against the seat and let the salt wind blow against my face. Now I had an excuse for the stinging around my eyes.

"Have I?" Ben spun the wheel rather too sharply as we made a turn and the car gave an angry bounce. "What I have thought is that comparing yourself with someone like Vanessa is totally ridiculous. I told you what I thought of her at our first meeting."

"Yes, that making a pass at her was irresistible."

We had just passed the vicarage. Reaching over, Ben snapped off the radio. "Home sweet home," he said. "Do you plan to conclude this halcyon day by sulking in your room?" With an angry flourish he swung between the iron gates, failing to negotiate the towering mound of dry cement that had not been there when we left.

"What the hell is that?" he bawled through the swirl of fine grey dust that blew up against the windscreen.

"If you ever paid attention to the mundane details of our every-day life you would remember that I arranged to have the gate supports fixed and at the same time resurface Aunt Sybil's foot path. What galls me is that this was supposed to have been delivered and the work done last week. And it is not as though Messrs. Grimsby and Strumpet, Stone Masons, have been caught up in mass-producing tombstones. They told me summer is usually their slow season for cemetery work."

Ben had backed up, manoeuvred around the pyramid, and stopped at the edge of the driveway. "While I'm cleaning off the windscreen," he said, quite mildly, showing how little our tiff had meant to him, "why don't you check Aunt Sybil's cottage? One reason she did not show today might be that she has decided to return home, making a luncheon meeting with us superfluous."

"Smart thinking," I said coldly, and climbed out of the car. The cottage stood unlit and forlorn, but as I peered through the curtains, I had the odd feeling that Ben might be right in that Aunt Sybil had returned. Had something stirred, a shadow perhaps, to give me that sense of someone within? Whatever it was, no one answered my repeated knocks, and I told myself in no uncertain terms that I was becoming a basket case.

Ben parked the car under the archway and I went into the hall, where I met Dorcas coming downstairs wrapped from neck to foot in a plaid mustard-and-green dressing gown which would have turned anyone bilious. She looked like death warmed up. Groggily she informed me that she had been felled by a splitting headache and had been forced to take to her bed for the whole afternoon. She was still a bit woolly with sleep but feeling more the thing. At first the attack had been so severe she had felt disoriented and could barely remember climbing the stairs.

"Funny," said Dorcas, rubbing a hand across her face, "had been feeling fine, getting on with the garden. Only stopped to take a five-minute time-out with a cupper from the thermos, then went to get up and felt like my head was full of glass splinters and my legs had left home. Must have been the storm coming on. Only time I get headaches is when the weather is about to change. By the way, Ellie, some woman rang up for you just after you left, told her you were out, but rang off before I got her name."

"Sounds like Jill," I said. "Always in a mad rush. I hope she calls back." When I told Dorcas about Aunt Sybil not keeping our lunch date, she said she was not sure if she would have heard even if the phone had rung after she was taken bad. Too far under. But not to worry, she was back on her feet and on her way to the kitchen to serve Tobias his supper

— if she could find him. Shortly after Ben and I left she had seen him exiting from an open window; with the weather about to turn nasty she was anxious to see if he had returned.

"Sorry about all this." Dorcas rubbed a finger across her brow as if trying to erase the memory of pain. "That headache hit me for six, nothing to be done but seal the room in darkness, crawl into bed, and try to sleep it off." She winced and rubbed her forehead again. "Thought I heard Tobias yowling as I got up. Hope he hasn't been in a fight."

"Dorcas, you are the limit." Opening up the bottle of brandy that stood on the glass cabinet, I poured a generous measure and insisted the invalid knock it back. "Here you are worrying about that gadabout cat, when you should be flat on your back in bed. Relax. To set your mind at ease, I will hunt him down."

"Make me feel a lot better." Dorcas pursed her lips, scrunched up her face, and took a tentative sip. "Do more for me than this brandy — can't abide spirits — knowing Tobias is in the house."

Ordering Dorcas to stay put, I went into the kitchen, filled Tobias's bowl, rattled it suggestively a few times and when this ploy failed, went through the house, opening doors and calling for the old rascal. Ben was in the dining room setting the table.

"Dorcas still feeling lousy?" he asked.

"Migraine," I replied succinctly. "And she's working herself into a fizzle because Tobias may be prowling around outside, and it's beginning to thunder."

"Then there's nothing to get worked up about." Ben laid down another fork. "Tobias won't linger outside once his whiskers get wet. He'll turn tail and gallop home."

But Tobias did not come in. As another vibrating roll of thunder tore the skies apart, I slipped on one of the raincoats hanging in the alcove by the garden door, picked up a torch, and ducked out into the courtyard. Its frail beam was useless. The gale bore down upon me, whirling me this way and that. Not looking where I was going, I almost tripped over the edge of the courtyard into the moat. I was saved from a damp spill by a brief flare of light, a sizzle of lightning making an angry red graph against the black.

"Tobias!" I called, but my voice didn't travel. It hung in the air unable to penetrate the wind.

"Are you totally insane!" I couldn't see Ben, but his hand caught me roughly by the arm and yanked me backwards. "That lightning came down damn close to the house. Forget your bloody cat, he's got eight more lives than you have."

"I can't leave him out here," I sniffled. "He'll be scared out of his wits."

"If he had any, he wouldn't be out here."

"Bug off, I have to find him."

I tried to pull away, but Tarzan had me fast. "Dear Lord," prayed Ben, "what sins have I committed that you cast this affliction upon me?" With these pious words he threw me over his shoulder like Santa's sack of goodies and staggered back to the house, where he tossed me unceremoniously on the drawing room couch and ordered poor Dorcas to watch me. "Get out of that coat, you stupid girl. I'll go and fix you and the invalid a hot drink."

Dorcas finally was persuaded to go to bed, on the understanding that I would awaken her, whatever the hour, if and when Tobias reappeared. For the first time in several months Ben and I sat through an evening together. Saying he did not trust me to leave the drawing room, he brought our dinner in on trays along with a pot of strong black coffee. "If you are going to wait up half the night you need a stimulant." He handed me the cup and poured in a swig of brandy. To my amazement, he solicitously attempted to cheer me up. "That cat's an ingrate."

"He's never stayed out through a storm before." Unable to finish my cup of coffee, I put it down and went to pull back the curtains, staring into the sullen darkness.

"You won't see anything out there." Ben sounded thoroughly exasperated. "Okay, all right! No sacrifice is too much for Lancelot here! I will don my Wellingtons and mackintosh and sally forth into the raging elements. Don't thank me!" He raised an imperious hand. "I enjoy a leisurely walk after dinner. Getting drenched will be an added bonus — I won't need a bath tonight." He sounded like Aunt Sybil.

Hopes raised, I paced, waiting for Ben's return. The gilt hands of the Buhl clock on the Queen Anne desk scarcely moved. It was stupid to feel this panicky about a cat, especially one used to fending for himself in the heart of London. Probably at this very minute he was holed up somewhere warm and dry. The stables — Jonas! What a fool I was not to have thought of him before. Tobias often paid the gardener a visit in his rooms. Would Ben think to try there? Possibly, and yet . . . I cast a vengeful glare at the clock; the suspense was suffocating me.

This time I did not take a raincoat. Head down, I ran the short distance across the courtyard. Even so, I was dragged back by the wind, my movements laboured as though I were a swimmer in turgid waters. Lifting the latch on the stable door was a battle. "Tobias," I called, just in case he was hiding there. Which was silly; if he had made it this far he would have gone up to Jonas. Remembering the light switch at the bottom of the wooden steps I groped my way until my fingers caught on the nub of the switch. The stables sputtered into wavering yellow light.

"Hell and damnation! Who's blundering about down there in the middle of the night, can't a man get a mite o' sleep?" Jonas came strumming down the steps, moustache bristling, grey hair rumpled aggressively. When he saw me he paused, but didn't look any too pleased. "If you've come running round to see if I'm still alive and kicking you can about turn and go home. A bolt or two o' lightning don't bother me none. Like it, I do. Always have, and I don't need to be mollycoddled by a young thing who sees herself as Florence Nightingale. . . ."

"Why, you conceited old prune." I am ashamed to say I lost my temper completely and insulted a defenceless old man. "I'm not here to see you, but to ask if you have seen my cat, who let me tell you is worth a dozen men like you or Ben or . . ."

Jonas's eyebrows leapt up into his forehead. "Tobias? Missing, is he? In this weather?" As I nodded miserably, Jonas went spryly back up the stairs shouting abruptly over his shoulder that he would fetch his boots and jacket and be right down. He had reached the top step when the stable door blew in. At first I thought it was the wind, but then I saw Ben, and I knew from his eyes that there was no need to continue the search party. I knew even before I looked down and saw the sodden bundle he carried.

"You found him," I said almost matter-of-factly.

"In the moat." Ben's voice was wretched, and I was calm enough to feel sorry for him. I couldn't think about Tobias, my furry pal, the warm body snuffling onto my lap on cold winter nights. The sobs started and wouldn't stop. Jonas was beside me, patting my shoulder.

"Hold tight, girl. I know this is rough, but . . ."

"Ellie, I'm sorry," stammered Ben, not moving from the open doorway. "And the worst of it is this wasn't an accident. Someone deliberately set out to get Tobias out of the way. He was tied inside a sack. With all the debris floating in that moat, I didn't see him at once. If I hadn't dragged you back into the house earlier . . . if I'd helped you search . . ."

"Enough of that," growled Jonas. "If we stand here up'n till Doomsday chastising ourselves, we can't bring the little fellow back. Ye're sure he's dead then, Mr Bentley?"

"Damn it, Phipps," muttered Ben, "I'm not a coroner, but if something doesn't move, is stone cold and . . ."

I started to shudder again and Jonas told Ben to get me back to the house. He would take care of Tobias.

The telephone was ringing when we entered the kitchen. Ben refused to answer it. "I'm not leaving you, even to go as far as the hall," he said. Having put the kettle on to boil, he sat me down at the table, and after a while the phone stopped buzzing. Not that it mattered. Nothing mattered. Tobias my chum was dead. Ben was just being kind. People treat total strangers like blood relatives in times of tragedy. Ben hadn't even liked Tobias. But he hadn't hated him. Someone else had, though. Here was a question that did matter: Who?

Ben ladled sugar into a cup of strong tea and stirred it around. "Ellie, I want to do something, but I don't know what. I wish I could make you understand how sorry I am." Leaving the cup he came up behind me and placed his hands gently on my shoulders. "If I could get hold of the person who hurt you this way — you loved Tobias so much." Ben stopped speaking, perhaps sensing I was not really listening. The pressure of his hands tightened and he pulled me back against him. He was trying to comfort me the way he had after the obscene phone call, but this time my body did not respond. I didn't want to be comforted and pulled away. With a wry half-laugh in his voice he continued, "The fuss you made of him, sometimes I've felt quite jealous of Tobias."

"Don't make jokes now," I said, reaching for the cup of tea.

"I'm sorry, Ellie, that sounded flippant and it wasn't meant — I'm not helping, am I? What I want to do is stop you from thinking."

"But I must. Don't you see that we are dealing with the same evil person who destroyed your book and sent the chocolates? This is infinitely more sadistic but it's the same type of sickness. What could be gained by murdering my cat?"

"Fear," said Ben.

The kitchen door opened from the hallway, and Dorcas came in, her hair spiking up all over her head and her face drawn. "Thought I might find you down here, Ellie, tapped on your door and no response."

"Dorcas, you should have stayed in bed." I looked down at my hands, hoping she'd go back upstairs so I wouldn't have to tell her tonight. I also wished Ben would let go of my shoulders. I wanted to be alone, removed from any contact with this horrid wicked world.

"Couldn't sleep," Dorcas stated baldly. "Just received an unpleasant phone call — rather frightening. Never have considered myself the nervy sort, but felt as though a hedgehog were crawling down my spine. Kept reciting nursery rhymes this voice did, sort of snuffled. Remember thinking adenoids needed removing, kept chanting Humpty Dumpty sat on a wall, Little Miss Muffet sat on a tuffet. Was on the brink of asking to speak to the brat's mother and telling her what I thought of children babbling into telephones, when it giggled and whispered in a husky, unmistakably adult voice, 'Ding dong bell, Pussie isn't well.' That's when I got the prickles. Heard people speak about evil — always said I'd never seen it. Tonight I heard it."

"Ben, tell Dorcas," I said, rising and pulling out a chair for her. I gripped it hard to steady my hands. Before he could comply, a thunderous knocking jarred the back door, and he went to open it.

Jonas stood in the glare of light thrown from the small outside lantern. He reminded me of an old walrus, grey moustache dripping rain and matted tweed coat. The only humanizing effect was the striped pyjama legs stuffed into the inevitable muddy boots. "Can't stand here all night." Moustache twitching fiercely, he scowled into the kitchen. "What is this, a wake — sitting about idly sipping tea? Where is the warm milk and rum?"

"Warm milk?" Ben said as he closed the door. "Have you changed your drinking habits? I thought you were addicted to Ovaltine."

"So I am," came the surly reply. "But this fellow likes his milk." Folding back his coat collar, the old man looked down, his face a concertina of wrinkles. Jonas was smiling into Tobias's glazed but watchful amber eyes.

* * *

None of us saw our beds before dawn. Jonas was not modest. Assuming the dignified mien of an ancient prophet who neither cultivates nor abjures the adulation of the masses, he told us about his successful attempt at artificial respiration, which had probably worked because Tobias was suffering more from shock and cold than drowning.

"Seems to me the old fellow must have kept pretty much afloat, probably landed on a piece of junk floating around in the water. That mud puddle moat is awash with dead branches broke off trees. But more like it were that old bicycle tyre that must have belonged to Mrs Abigail."

"The would-be killer is not going to appreciate being foiled by a floating bicycle tyre." Ben poured another round of tea.

The centre of all the attention was curled up on my lap, warm and safe — apparently emotionally unscathed. "Ben," I asked, "what did you mean when you said earlier that the motive might be fear?"

"Ours, not the assassin's. I don't suppose he's suffered a qualm — quite the contrary. The enemy wants us to squirm — to start looking back over our shoulders into the shadows. What happened to Tobias is a warning. The next victims will be us."

"You mean . . ." I was afraid to finish the question.

Ben continued to scratch behind Tobias's ear. "Don't panic. I'm not seriously suggesting we will all get bundled into sacks and dumped into the moat." He looked up, his eyes deadly serious. "But I think we can expect a threat so menacing that the temptation to leave this house will begin to seem irresistible. Another thing, I don't think we will have too long to wait before this next move is made. Remember, the six months will be up in just under two weeks."

Jonas grunted. "You've been seeing too many Alfred Hitchcock movies, young man."

"That's fine coming from you." I forgot temporarily that this was the hero who had saved my baby's life. "What was all that stuff you fed me the other day after Freddy left? All your talk about vultures swooping down to pick our bones."

"Aye, lass, but that were just to put you on your guard when your relations come tapping you for money. They are a parcel of vultures, but they've not the courage to do you or Mr Ben bodily harm as them murder yarns phrase it."

"I wish I could agree with you." Ben rubbed his fingers across his eyes as though struggling to see more clearly. "My view is that we are dealing with a sadist who has moved beyond the bounds of simple greed. One of your relations, Ellie, no longer falls under the heading of lovable eccentric. Foisting those chocolates on you, laundering my manuscript, attempting to execute your cat, and then calling to gloat by reciting some perverted nursery rhyme. These have to be the actions of someone who is more than a little mad."

"Afraid you may be right." Dorcas jammed her hair behind her ears, obviously positioning herself for the fray ahead. "I say we rally the team, pull up our socks, and plan our strategy. Hate to be a pessimist, but have a feeling if we lose this match we may all wake up one morning with our throats cut."

Three pairs of eyes looked steadily at her.

"Sorry about that! Well, it would be one way of making medical history." She stood up, headache forgotten, and went to fill the kettle. "More tea anyone?"

CHAPTER FIFTEEN

"The trouble with this family," I sighed in exasperation as I stirred milk into my tea and refused another helping of the pale and weeping omelette Dorcas had rustled up in an attempt to restore our shattered nerves, "is that no one person stands head and shoulders above the others as an obvious candidate. Most people can produce one weird relative but not a single member of the Grantham clan is normal. So where do we start?"

"Hate to shove my nose in where it may not be wanted." As if to give lie to this protestation, Dorcas's jutting appendage began to throb like an antenna. "But if they are indeed a bunch of oddballs, all tarred with the same brush, so to speak, how about the possibility of conspiracy?" Anticipating a veto from one member of her audience she hastened to add, "Wouldn't alter Ben's theory that one of the group is completely bonkers. Madness usually is diabolical, to the point of genius. Been thinking, odd Sybil not showing up for lunch and still no phone message. What if our unknown foe faked that conversation with Ben, the one inviting you to lunch?"

"I can't be sure," said Ben, "the line was bad."

"Was it?" Dorcas grimaced. "Seem to remember Ellie saying something of the sort regarding her little natter with enemy over the chocolates. Suspicious. As suspicious as Sybil inviting me to tag along today, didn't quite ring true at the time. We've been a gullible lot. Another thing — that headache of mine, told you it came on minutes after I drank a cup of tea."

"What of it?" Jonas wiped a smear of omelette off his moustache. "Aren't telling us you'd tippled it up, are you?"

"Not booze," snorted Dorcas. "Something even stronger. I'm saying our secret pal put some shut-eye medicine in my flask. When, you ask? Got that figured out, too. Remember that phone call I told you about, Ellie, unidentified person asking for you?"

"Say no more," I sighed. "While you were in the house answering the phone, someone was drugging your tea. That lousy telephone certainly seems to have thrown in its lot with the enemy. And speaking of team efforts, we are talking about two people here: one behind the herb garden wall and one keeping you occupied. This is giving me the creeps. We are dealing with organized crime."

"We have all been closely watched." Dorcas nodded. "All our habits noted, right down to my taking a flask of tea with me when I work in the garden."

"Have to hand it to you, you're a shrewd woman, Miss Dorcas," conceded Jonas. "Which happens to be just as well. Ye'll never catch a husband with your cooking. One thing: Tobias weren't dropped in that there moat while you was lying on your bed in a drugged stupor and Mr Bentley and Miss Ellie at the seaside eating snails for lunch what I could have got 'em a lot cheaper from the garden, like I used to do for Miss Sybil, very fond of them she is with vinegar . . ."

"Will you kindly get to the point about Tobias." Ben sounded more asleep than awake.

"Elementary, Mr H., as in Holmes, if you 'aven't read the books, Tobias couldn't have been in that water more than half an hour, tops. If he had been I'd be out making a wooden box for him right now. What do you say to them apples? Why go to all the trouble to rid you people from the house when the deed weren't done till you was home agin?"

"He had to be caught before he could be put in the moat," I said, "and on a good day that could take our secret foe all afternoon. You gave him/her a good run for their money, didn't you, precious?" I reached down and gave the hero of the hour an approving stroke. "Besides, if the execution had been carried out in daylight the chances of discovery would have been greater. And by the way, why didn't the enemy take steps to remove Jonas from the premises this afternoon?"

Ben yawned wide enough to swallow half the room. "Because, as aforesaid, the ubiquitous party under discussion knows all there is to know about our little peccadilloes. He could feel perfectly secure in the knowledge that Jonas, with his snoopy employers off the premises, would be holed up in his loft with a book and that even the Judgement Day roll call would not bring him outside."

Fatigue was making me edgy. "Ben, please stop prancing about the kitchen in circles, my head feels like a boxing bag. Vanessa will always retain her place in my affections as prime suspect. I know you don't think that a girl so lovely can be all bad, but she would slice up her own mother and serve her between slices of bread if she was short of roast beef for a sandwich."

"A personal antipathy" — Ben tumbled into his chair and closed his eyes — "is not constructive, neither is it evidence. They all have the same motive. Now I am not swayed by prejudice, I like Freddy but I still have to point the finger at him as my first choice. If I'm wrong I will be delighted, but he is the only one who has made contact in the last months, and what's more—" he hesitated and looked down at the table — "we only have Freddy's word that he did not see Aunt Sybil that morning before he left. The person who invited us for lunch knew not only that Aunt Sybil was gone, but that she was staying with a friend."

"Not such a brilliant guess, where else would she be? If you had ever been apprenticed to Perry Mason you would know that the person most recently on the scene of the crime is always innocent. Whatever else he is, Freddy is not a fool. If he were the one, he would lie low."

"Oh, come off it." Ben yawned again. "We are talking about someone desperate, and we had better be talking about someone who makes a few mistakes or you and I are in big trouble."

"Okay." I nodded wearily. "Let's not you and I bicker over whom we most want it to be. We should at least consider all the possibilities. I have a bit of trouble picturing Aunt Astrid or Lulu chasing Tobias all around the house and up and down the garden path, but each in her own way is a very ruthless woman."

"I'd say they are rather alike," said Ben, "in one very important area — their obsessive devotion to their children, and then last but not least we have Uncle Maurice."

"Who is I think basically a very acquisitive man." I yawned.

* * *

Daylight was beginning to outline the trees beyond the window. Somehow Jonas managed to look more chipper than the rest of us. He reached over and took Tobias from me. "Here's the fellow who could tell a rare tale if he had the words. Have you thought, Miss Ellie, that the attacker may still ha' been in't grounds when you and Mr Ben went looking for the old tiger? The poor chap could'na ha' been in that water above ten minutes, I reckon, or he'd ha' been a gonner, knotted up in that there sack."

Dorcas tried to flatten her hair behind her ears and stifled a yawn. "Horrid to think he or she was out there lurking in the dark. You couldn't have seen an elephant if you'd met it in that rain, Ellie. Blighter will have got a thorough drenching, hope he catches pneumonia."

"What we should do" — Ben lifted his head briefly — "is to stage another family reunion — invite everyone back here, and note which one has suddenly developed a severe cold."

"That's not a bad idea," I said. "Reassemble the suspects and see what information we can pry loose; try and turn one against the other. How about it?" But Ben was snoring. Another illusion shattered.

Jonas gamely offered to assist the master of the house up to bed. Dorcas and I shuffled the dishes into the sink. Memories of Aunt Sybil's grimy reign forbade me leaving them overnight.

"I've been thinking about that phone call." I rinsed off a cup and handed it to Dorcas. "He or she must have used that public call box halfway down the hill on the coast road."

"Why?"

"Elementary. If Jonas is right, and I suspect he is, that the attempt on Tobias's life was made only minutes before we found him, the assailant could not have gone far. Even if the getaway car was parked, and hidden reasonably close by, getting to it in this driving rain would have eaten up at least five minutes — and the phone was ringing when we came into the house."

Dorcas set the cup down carefully on the counter. "Have you thought," she said, "that the unknown might have used the one in Aunt Sybil's cottage? No secret, that key hidden on the ledge."

"You may be right," I said. "When I checked at the cottage tonight I had the sneaking feeling that someone was there, pressed up against a wall, watching through a chink in the curtains. Or that's what I now think that I thought. Aunt Sybil has that old lady habit so I had the feeling that she might be back, until she did not answer my knock."

"Lucky for the unknown, Aunt Sybil being gone. Almost makes one wonder. . . . As you say, notorious habit of women her age, peeking out from behind their lace curtains . . . those middle of the night promenades of hers, wonder if the enemy has noticed, and found them a nuisance. Now Jonas I can understand being disregarded as a threat by any member of your family. No offence, but, if anything, like Sybil they would consider gardeners a breed below their notice.

Housekeepers too, I would have thought, but then I am living in the house."

"Returning to Aunt Sybil." I wiped a smudge off the counter. "You don't think that someone might have threatened her and that is why she left?"

"Wouldn't surprise me. Perhaps not an actual threat, merely a suggestion that her health would benefit from a few weeks away. She may have refused till that row with Jonas made the idea more tempting."

"We're getting rather carried away by our imaginations, aren't we?" I folded my damp cloth and kicked off my shoes. I was beginning to feel as though I had been up since the dawn of time.

Dorcas was still full of beans. "If someone did persuade Sybil to go away, they could have asked her to keep their involvement a secret, you know."

"And Aunt Sybil would enjoy knowing we were worrying about her."

"Pity in a way, her being offstage. Because otherwise would have said she was most likely candidate for a junior partnership in the conspiracy. Don't see her in the starring role — motive not strong enough, unfortunately. Didn't come out of that will smelling like a rose, but didn't do too badly."

I had wondered about Aunt Sybil's possible involvement before. As the person most deserving of consideration, I felt she had been the one most shabbily treated in the will. Uncle Merlin should not have made those cracks about her loyalty and her cooking. She had reason to dislike me. My opinion of her housekeeping had been implicit in my prompt assault upon the cobwebs and grimy accumulation of years of neglect. Under the circumstances she might well feel an allegiance with the cast-offs. And Aunt Sybil did not like cats.

"But to understand Aunt Sybil you have to understand how she felt about Uncle Merlin. To the outside world he may have been a scurrilous old curmudgeon, but Aunt Sybil's entire mission in life was to trot after him with his slippers in her mouth. Merlin may have had a difficult childhood which warped his outlook on life, but even that doesn't excuse his condemning Aunt Sybil to a life of emotional serfdom."

"The woman could have upped and left." Dorcas did not sound too sympathetic. "Enjoy being martyrs some people — no guts."

"Aunt Sybil certainly had none where Uncle Merlin was concerned, but in other areas she is tough. Look how she has developed new interests, and is plunging forward with her life. People are so complex. Aunt Sybil's weakness where Uncle Merlin was concerned would be her strength against anyone who might wish to thwart his final decree. If the old man had deemed it fitting that she be entombed alive alongside him she would have telephoned the undertaker, ordered her coffin, climbed in, and pulled the lid down. They weren't just cousins, circumstances had made them closer than the usual brother and sister. No — Sybil would not support these attacks."

"Then it has to be Jonas," Dorcas chortled. "Looks the part, foul temper, fanatical devotion to his late master, what more could you want?"

I gave her a laughing nudge towards the door. "Lack of sleep is getting to you. Jonas is the one who saved Tobias. I would no more suspect him than you, old stick."

Dorcas looked thoughtful. "Don't be too trusting, Ellie. Suggest you keep a sharp look over your shoulder from now on. Tobias has more lives to risk than you do." Sleepily I agreed to be careful. Not until later did I realize that in peering behind, one often steps right into the snare, laid ready and waiting.

Rain was still falling when we rose late the following morning, and the temptation to return to bed with a good book and a cup of hot chocolate was strong, but a walk to the vicarage would blow the cobwebs out of my head. Dorcas was unusually quiet during breakfast, finally admitting to the return of her headache, so I saw no point in asking her to take a walk with me. Instead she volunteered to take Tobias up to her room and watch him until my return. After fetching my raincoat and scarf, I decided it would be only polite to let Ben know my whereabouts for the next hour or so. I found him in the loggia wrestling with a ball of string and a brown paper package. Removing a pair of scissors clamped between his teeth, he informed me that I was in time to say goodbye. The cad! He was bunking off, leaving me to the mercy of cutthroats and kidnappers!

"Don't be stupid," he said. "I am not leaving. The book is. This household work of art goes into the pillar-box today. I'm not taking any more chances with its safety."

"Congratulations! You finished it." I almost hugged him, but he backed away and perhaps it was just as well, as he had those scissors back between his teeth.

"Will you restrain yourself," he mumbled through his metal fangs, "or at least be of some use." Thrusting my finger down on the string to hold it in place, he proceeded to tie a knot which threatened to cut off my circulation.

"Ouch! Ben, don't be such a grump, it gets monotonous. You must be excited about this."

He spat out the scissors and continued working on the string. "In a way, but in another I feel I have sold out — same as you."

"Me?"

"Sure. You have conformed to other people's ideas of how you should look, all for monetary gain which is not likely to be forthcoming."

And this was the man who had fed me all those salads until I began to see green? Crumbling a piece of brown paper into a ball I tossed it across the room. "Ben," I said, "you have skirted around the issue of my new image several times, why don't you come straight out and tell me what really bothers you about the way I now look."

"Nothing." Ben gave the string another yank. "You look great. But you don't need my round of applause. You've done as superb a job of making yourself over as you have with the house. In both instances, however, you had the raw material with which to work. All Merlin's neglect and Aunt Sybil's rotten housekeeping couldn't kill the charm of this house. That's what I remember when I think of that night we met, the house hidden under a mantle of dirt and decay and you hidden under that appalling purple shroud, and me being intrigued by you both." He was concentrating very hard on the string.

I had to put both hands on the table to steady myself. "You were — intrigued by me?"

"Absolutely," he said. "I thought you were the funniest, gutsiest person I had ever met."

"Thanks." Completely deflated, I scrunched up another piece of paper. Why couldn't he have said bewitching, breath-taking, wildly sensual? "Fat people often shine in the areas you mention," I agreed. "They're part of the package like being light on one's feet and having beautiful skin."

"You see why I liked you better the old way, when you weren't quite so bitter?"

"Or when my emotions were better hidden. What I do see is that you resent my being thin because you can no longer consider me inferior."

Ben deliberately strangled an innocent piece of string, then glared up at me. "You're the one who doesn't put a proper value on yourself. When I tell you you have a fine mind you are insulted — you only want to be told you have a body to rival a film star's!"

"Only because this is all so new to me," I threw back at him. "I feel like a child who had just received a fabulous toy. I want everyone to admire it."

"Careful! You may find everyone wants to play with it!"

"You're revolting. It is true that but for Uncle Merlin's will I might never have lost the weight, but I don't think that means I have sold out. If it does, I don't mind. I am much happier with myself than before so why can't you and I say 'happy endings.'"

"Or beginnings." Ben pushed down a curly strand of hair which had got poked up in the air. "In our case they're one and the same, aren't they?"

"Meaning?" I asked on bated breath.

"Meaning that in a very short time you and I will pick up our separate lives where we left them before good old Eligibility took over."

"I suppose so." I bent a stray paper clip into a perverted shape. "What are your plans, another novel?"

"I have been toying with the idea of opening my own restaurant, using an Edwardian theme and . . ."

"Ben, what a tremendous idea. And what a way to promote your cookery book! Perhaps you could find an old inn, think of the fun in renovating such a place — we could use some of the furniture from the attic and we could call it Abigail's."

"We?" Ben's voice came out hoarse and I wondered if he had suddenly developed a cold; his eyes looked . . . strained. Poor man, just look what he had done to that string — he had practically crocheted it. He glanced away from me and all sympathy vanished as he said, "I imagined you were bent on returning to London and taking the swinging set by storm."

"I don't think so," I said as evenly as I could manage. "This place has attractions of its own for me, quite unconnected with the house."

Ben tossed his parcel down on the table, scowling at it in disgust. A tear had appeared on one corner and he began picking at it irritably. "If that is the case I suggest you start practising your singing, immediately. I am sure your beloved vicar will not mind your being off key and a verse behind everyone else. Some people might think your other talents wasted, but I know you will be a great credit to the Ladies' Circle."

"Have you quite finished?" I fumed.

"All taken care of." The dimwit seemed to think I was talking about his cookery book. Reaching for his tweed jacket, which he had thrown over a chair, he said, "I've telephoned Mr Bragg's office and he is going to meet me there, look over the manuscript and then go with me to the post office to witness its launching. Let's hope it doesn't sink to the bottom of some slush pile never to be seen again."

I smiled evilly. "I wouldn't worry about its acceptance — it's a shoo-in, but don't you think you have been a smudge too efficient?"

"How?"

"Shouldn't you have waited to wrap the book until after Mr Bragg had seen it?"

His angry roar was music to my ears. Ducking hastily to the door, I left him yanking viciously at the knotted string, cursing that his scissors had disappeared. Very quietly I dropped them on the trestle table in the hall and beat a quick retreat. As I crossed the dripping garden, the ground sucked noisily at my feet but the wet didn't bother me. If I could drive Ben to mad irritation, perhaps he did have some feeling for me. Hope springs eternal in the foolish female breast. Heavy-footed but suddenly light of heart, I plodded on down the driveway, skirted the virginal cement pile near Aunt Sybil's, now covered in a rubber tarp, and on to the coast road. Here the gale picked up force, lifting me along like an empty paper bag.

I found Jonas at work in the small coppice a couple of hundred yards from the gates, heaping debris on an already towering mound of battered boxes, broken chairs, tattered bedspreads, and soggy mattresses. He was poking at a scrap of pink and yellow, which looked like the corner of a plastic tablecloth, edging out from the middle of the pile.

He was a pretty spry old geezer for a man over seventy — hardly the ailing creature Aunt Sybil had described to me last winter. Dorcas was right, he had changed during the last months. Perhaps having young people in the house had mellowed him; either that or he thrived on suspense.

Jonas's lumpy old trilby was seized by a sudden gust, bounced beyond his grasp, and skimmed like a gull over the cliff edge, out to sea.

"And that could be you, miss, if you walk too close to the edge," said he dryly.

I did watch my step as I ploughed on towards the vicarage and went through the lych-gate into the churchyard, my mind travelling over the list of suspects.

The newer tombstones were glossy white marble. Sharply lettered in black, they rose staunch and upright from the ground while their older brethren slumped at uneasy angles, ready to keel over at any moment. Through the drenched and trembling foliage of the trees I could see the dark and squat enclosure that was the Grantham family vault.

The uneasy revulsion that had touched me when I entered the building for Uncle Merlin's funeral returned now, but like the child who feels the urge to stick his finger through the lion's cage, I felt compelled to return, even as I told myself to trot as fast as I could to the rectory. Perhaps Uncle Merlin and his father deserved to lie here, but not Abigail, not the young woman who had raced across the lawn following the flight of a red-and-yellow kite, with a small boy clinging to her skirts. Her name was tersely inscribed on the brass plate affixed to her tomb, no verse, no record of her age or date of death and not one word of bereavement or affection. She lay in her raised stone enclosure, flanked by those of her husband, who had despised her, and the son who had apparently loved her as a boy. She would lie in the dark for eternity.

Such gloomy thoughts were making me jittery. Was that a footstep outside the door? A mausoleum has never been first on my list of favourite places in which to be attacked. Uneasily I stared out into the churchyard. A short way off a twig snapped — a breaking drumstick in the hands of giggling children. Here even the thought of laughter was sinister, amused, furtive, with nothing childlike or jolly about it, like the voice on the telephone. Just as eerie was my conjuring of Uncle Merlin's ghost, he who had proved himself the master of the last laugh. My fevered imagination got a good shot of him. Peering out at me from a fiery inferno, his death mask face leered. "A rare fool you've made of yourself, Ellie girl. Haven't found the treasure, can't get your man, and now you've the whole pack out after you, nipping at your heels. Don't you hear them baying off among the trees? After her, doggies!"

Blinking rapidly to banish the nightmare ghoul and hugging the door for moral support, I took a deep breath. Unfortunately, before I could swallow, another thought clobbered me between the eyes. Ghosts weren't fun people to have around, but they did have a reputation for being vapourish and frail, without the muscle necessary to do bodily harm. The enemy, as of last night, had been very much alive. Was he or she out in the graveyard now, slinking low between the tombstones, panting for fresh blood — animal, vegetable, or human?

"Is anyone out there?" I croaked, which was ridiculous. I could hardly expect the truth from the enemy.

Silence answered and I didn't believe a word of it. Time for a quick getaway. Stumbling down the steps, I ducked my head and ran. For the first time, I regretted my lost weight. A few months ago I need only have fallen on the enemy to have rendered him powerless. Perhaps if I had accepted Jill's offer to teach me judo, I might now have saved myself. A shadow swooping towards me sent me into hysterics. Uttering a frightened squawk, wings flapping wildly, the seagull backed off, and I staggered on my way. The mist was thickening. Even in broad daylight I consider a sense of direction a skill comparable with reading Chaucer in the original. Now I was wandering in narrowing circles, bumbling into tombstones and straggling branches that scraped my face and caught at my hair. I was a prisoner held fast. Desperately I strove to unravel the knot, but the strip of hair would not tear loose. Fingers vibrating, numb with cold, I tore at the branch, trying to break it in two. Arms raised to my head, I was defenceless, completely vulnerable — when the hands came out to get me.

"I surrender."

In the face of capture I was instantly icy calm and calculating. Let the enemy think I was willing to go peacefully.

"Ellie, is that you?" asked the voice of Rowland Foxworth.

* * *

After he freed me from the clutches of that evil tree, he explained to me that he had been returning from a call upon one of his parishioners, when he had heard a scrambling sound and followed its direction.

"How long were you ensnared?" he asked as he opened the vicarage door and waited for me to enter.

"How long is eternity?" I asked.

Rowland had a wonderfully calming effect on me. The hour I spent in his study, sipping the hot cocoa brought in by a grudging Mrs Wood and toasting my toes at his fireside, did much to restore my faith in mankind. And yet, when I told him about recent happenings, Rowland warned me to take no one at face value. "You are surrounded by people who six months ago were strangers to you. Jonas is as much an eccentric and hermit as his past employer, and what do you really know of this woman Dorcas?"

I laughed. "Thank you for being concerned, but surely you cannot believe that Jonas is a mass murderer who has been holed up at Merlin's Court for the past forty years? And as for Dorcas, I would trust her with my life."

"Ellie, let us hope that does not prove necessary. Of course you have your fiancé. By the way, how long have you known him?"

"Ages," I said, and it certainly seemed that way.

Rowland's expression was hard to read but he went on to tell me that he had been plodding through the Reverend Hempstead's collection of sermons and private papers, but had found nothing about the Granthams.

"You couldn't let me have the box of papers?" I asked.

He shook his head, explaining that the bishop had very rigid rules about church property, but as soon as he had anything to report he would be in touch.

With that I had to be content. But when I got back to Merlin's Court I found Ben was still out, which depressed me. Even though Rowland had walked me home I had still experienced the sensation of being watched. Even Jonas's appearance minutes later did not cheer me. He started grousing about the lack of food in sight. "Most folks my age" — he was pulling off his boots — "get Meals on Wheels."

"Your own wheels aren't rusted out yet. The cook's taken the afternoon off, but cheer up. I'll give you a crash course in how to work a tin opener. Consider it occupational therapy for a man of your declining years."

Jonas was riled. "I'm not on me last legs and don't plan to be yet. Miss Dorcas be the one what's failin' — still proper poorly. I saw her a while gone when I came in for more rubbish to burn. Said she'd keep to her room this afternoon."

I was worried about Dorcas but decided against tapping on her door to ask how she was feeling. Sleep was the best medicine, and if she had dozed off I did not want to wake her. The house was beginning to wrap itself around me. Merlin's Court was my friend. Even with Ben gone it would not let anything happen to me. I went upstairs, stripped off my damp clothes, and steeped in a hot scented bath for an hour, rubbed myself dry with a warm fluffy towel — the new heater in the bathroom was paradise — and felt ready to face whatever the world had in store.

Dressed in a pair of blue jeans (a concession to the fact that I now had a waist) and a plaid shirt, I straightened and dusted my bedroom, wiped down the bath, and polished the already sparkling taps. The master bedroom was still waiting for its new curtains and bedspread, but was otherwise in spotless order. Dorcas and Ben always did their own rooms. Now what? I had been meaning to measure the dumb-waiter and look it over to see if a solid floor could be put in to convert it into a linen cupboard.

I went along the landing, opened the door to the dumb-waiter and reached for the light cord. Somehow it had become looped high on the rope pulley and even stretching my arm to the limit I was unable to reach it. I considered fetching a chair, but vanity stopped me and literally proved my downfall. I was sure the wooden platform with its heavy slats would support skinny me. Stepping confidently aboard I held onto the hand rope with one hand and reached for the light cord with the other. An ominous creaking filtered into my ears. Too late I tried to back off; the platform plummeted wildly to one side, spinning me dizzily off balance. With feet fighting empty air, I clutched desperately for a stronger hold on the rope. I was going down.

* * *

"I don't think she's dead," remarked an encouraging voice.

"Then she's giving a damn good impersonation." That was Ben, and I was amazed at how furious he sounded.

The pantry. The thought was hazy — a puff of smoke — I had to catch hold of it by its wispy little tail before it got away. No wonder Ben, poor Ben, was angry with me. I'd crash-landed in the pantry. It was the landing station for Dumb-Waiter Number 9. Clumsy, clumsy, missed the runway and bounced off the creamed salmon mousse. Poor Ben! But he wasn't angry with me. Cupping my poor broken head, which had severed from my body in mid-flight, in his exquisitely tender hands, he pressed his lips down on mine. Slowly, deliciously, my body reunited. Arms, legs, feet, hands all floated back together, and — huge relief — everything was working. I could feel every inch: the tingle that started at my toes crept upwards in a searing wave. For an eternity I lay there savouring, relishing the knowledge that I was alive and Ben was kissing me. After a while though it did seem only fair to set the poor man's mind at ease by telling him that this dazzling performance did not have to be our swan song.

"Hallo," I said, prying open my eyes. My lids were fractured, but otherwise I was in great shape.

"Will you shut up," ordered Ben. "This mouth-to-mouth resuscitation requires perfect timing."

Dr Melrose was duly summoned and after much poking and prodding announced that no bones were broken, and I could consider myself a very lucky young lady. A mild concussion appeared to be the sum total of my injuries, for which he prescribed a sedative and bed rest for the next three or four days. "And in future, Miss Simons," he admonished as he put on his hat and picked up his little black bag, "stay away from circus tricks — unless of course you wish to hobble through life as the Hunchback of Notre Dame."

Solemnly I promised to be a model of discretion in future. But as I said to Dorcas when she brought me a tray of soup later that afternoon, from now on neither Ben nor I could move a muscle without danger of the whole world caving in upon us. All that morning I had sensed a presence behind me, and had kept turning to look over my shoulder, but I had not thought to look immediately ahead when I opened up the dumb-waiter. Someone had tampered with the rope, Dorcas confirmed. Jonas and Ben checked after the doctor left and found a clean cut across half the width, then a jagged tear where the rest had wrenched free. I told them how it had been looped up high so I would have to reach for it.

I lay in bed the rest of that day and the next, my bruised and aching head propped up by a heap of pillows. Ben came in to see me several times, once to bring me a postcard from Aunt Sybil, postmarked from a resort thirty miles away, but with no mention of the aborted luncheon. It seems we had been duped, decoyed, and made to look like fools; but we weren't dead yet. Both nights I had one of those half-waking dreams that are difficult to distinguish from reality. I felt Ben lean over me, brush my hair back with his long cool fingers, and press his lips lovingly and gently against the side of my mouth. On the second occasion I started up in dazed pleasure to see my bedroom door softly close and heard footsteps disappearing stealthily down the hall. Dorcas must have come in to check on me; I slipped back into sleep.

Tobias was my constant companion. He snuggled warmly across my middle — fellow victim of the assassin's machinations. Someone was desperate enough to dispose of at least one of the inhabitants of Merlin's Court permanently if they would not leave voluntarily. If either Ben or I took up residence in the family vault before the completion of the six months, the estate would revert to the family, excluding Aunt Sybil, on a technicality.

"Worst possible thing for you," Dorcas fumed when I tried to discuss the situation with her over my lunch tray. "Should be resting, not churning yourself up into a froth."

"No doubt the murderer agrees with you." I put down my soup spoon. "Lying here like a trussed chicken makes for very easy prey. Dorcas, if this were a detective story, who would be the prime suspect?"

"Me, of course — appearing out of nowhere, references all phonies, old grudge against the family. Uncle Merlin had got my father sentenced to life imprisonment in a dank Cornish jail . . . or, I know about the treasure and . . ."

"Very funny," I said. "Next candidate, please."

"Obvious — our dashing swarthy hero, also with a murky past, Bentley T. Haskell, Esquire."

"Dorcas, Ben comes from a very solid background, his parents are decent, honest people."

"They may be," sighed my friend. "But you have to look at this from the perspective of the police should they enter the picture. Here is a man you picked up at an escort service, who charmed you into deluding a senile old man that you were engaged to be married, he is now ensconced in this house with you. . . ."

"Wait a minute!" I sat up in bed so quickly I wrenched my neck painfully. "I'm the one who proposed to Ben!"

"No matter. Dead people don't make reliable witnesses. An adventurer, that's how he'll appear to Chief Inspector, Scotland Yard. Cutting out the hopes of all those devoted relations! Can't you see the headline, 'Playboy and Sometime Escort Murders Fake Fiancée'?"

"Not without a motive," I said. "Ben doesn't have one — without me he gets nothing. The will stipulated that this must be a joint effort."

Dorcas still looked unconvinced when my bedroom door opened and Ben came in. "You ladies having a nice chat?"

"Super! Watson here and I have just wound up the case. Dorcas, handcuff him to my bed. Then go to the telephone and dial our local friendly police station. Take your time."

Warning of his imminent peril left Ben cold. He said, "If you women would spend less time fantasizing and look at the evidence, we might make some headway!"

I was determined we would not call in the police until we could prove the identity of the villain.

"Okay, Mr Instant Analysis." I watched as he moved to the end of my bed and stood resting his hands on the foot rail. "You tell us."

"Don't be cheeky," he said reprovingly. "I may not have the answers but I sure as hell have a lot of questions. How, for instance, did the enemy know that you would be stupid enough to climb into that dumb-waiter?"

I'd had ample time to mull this one over. Confession is supposedly good for the soul so I took a deep breath and announced, "When I was giving blabber-mouth Freddy the grand tour of the house, I mentioned that I was considering turning our archaic feature into a linen cupboard."

Ben did not take this news too critically. "Even so, you might not have got round to doing anything about it. As a method of bumping someone off, it strikes me as haphazard, sloppy."

"That's not quite the way I would describe my recent brush with death!" I tried to draw myself up in bed and sank back painfully with a little help from Dorcas. "Besides, if we accept your theory that we are wrestling with a full-scale lunatic, can we expect computerlike calculation?"

"Madness," said Ben, "has a nasty habit of going hand in hand with incredible cunning. How else can it turn a relatively normal face to the world?"

My skin prickled, but I replied calmly enough, "Are you implying that we are overlooking something?"

"Exactly!" Ben's eyes glistened under the knitted black brows, and I suspected that on some perverted level he was enjoying himself. "Although," he continued, "some pieces of the jigsaw are beginning to fit into place. For instance, booby-trapping the dumb-waiter was the prime reason for the enemy's visit last Sunday. Kidnapping Tobias was an added bonus but I doubt if it was part of the original plan. That cat of yours happened to be in the wrong place at the wrong time. Right from the start I had difficulty with the idea that our mystery guest had made his elaborate plans in the hopes of tracking down that mangy ball of fur. The moving target we called him, remember? We should have seen the drowning in the moat for what it was — a side issue."

"I'll have to explain to Tobias," I said sarcastically, "that he wasn't the star of this drama at all, just a bit player."

"Oh, he was more than that." Ben met my glare blandly. "He acted as the enemy's calling card. In addition to his other psychological problems, this weirdo is an egomaniac — hence the telephone calls gloating over his cleverness. Tobias floating in his sack was tangible proof of who was winning this battle of wits."

"Will you shut up!" I snarled. "You're actually getting a kick out of facing off against the enemy."

"Come now." Dorcas, who had been sitting very quietly as though lost in thought, roused herself. "Mustn't excite yourself, doctor's orders."

"Try and see it this way," Ben reasoned. "For months you have been fascinated with Abigail, trying to establish some order to what you knew about her, hoping it would lead you to the treasure. For me, even with the incentive of the inheritance, the trail never blazed the way it did for you. Somehow the whole notion seemed a bit fanciful. You were happy fitting the pieces together so I left you to it. But now we are dealing with another kind of chase and I don't want to be carried out on a stretcher without knowing how, and why, and whom." He moved to the side of the bed and lightly touched my hand. "I think the time has indeed come for a return of all suspects to the scene of the crime. How about a family reunion this weekend?"

"Have a heart," grated Dorcas, "the girl's still on her sickbed."

Ben's eyes met mine. "Bring me my crutches," I cried. "What a deplorable hostess I am, lolling in bed with guests expected any day."

CHAPTER SIXTEEN

Surveillance. That was the key to success and safety. Ben repeated this maxim often. While discreetly watching the suspects, we would as carefully watch each other. During the day Dorcas would be on permanent duty, unobtrusively keeping tabs on Ben and me in the event that either of us was left alone at any time with one of the suspects.

"Nothing too obvious," Ben warned her. "Keep a low profile. You don't knit, by any chance? In works of fiction, genteel lady spies always sit tucked away in dark corners clicking away with their needles. No one ever notices them."

"Nor old people neither." Jonas nodded sagely, stroking his moustache. "Folks don't look at us twice. Don't want to be reminded that one day they'll end up in the same boat. Fat, thin, tall, short, raving beauty or ugly enough to sink ships, we all wrinkle up and look alike."

"Okay, Jonas." Ben grinned. "Never let it be said life doesn't start at seventy. A life of espionage opens up before you, but for cripe's sake be subtle, don't keep trotting through the house with a watering hose and a bag of fertilizer."

Jonas cast a knowing eye out the kitchen window where, for the first time in a week, the sky was a clear limpid blue. "Looks like rain, I'd best come inside and do the silver."

"If you keep this up," said Ben, patting the old man on the back, "we'll give you a shilling a week raise and elevate you to butler. Dorcas, I want you to camp down on a mattress at the side of Ellie's bed. That way you can sleep in relays. I'll give Freddy my room and move into the one next to yours, Ellie, so you have nothing to fear. You do agree that the doors should be left unlocked to give the enemy ample opportunity to stage his attack when the lights go out?"

These prep sessions did little to still my foreboding. What if, as Dorcas had suggested, we were the victims of a conspiracy? If I had serious misgivings about one or more of our guests busily planning the social event of the season — a double funeral for Ben and me — Dorcas was even more upset. Since the night of Tobias's near-tragedy, her brisk and chipper manner had paled, and my accident following so closely had left Dorcas a very troubled woman. I would come across her at intervals during the day, sitting limply, staring into space.

On the Friday evening a half-hour before the guests were due, she followed me into the drawing room and begged me to speak to Ben and have him call the whole thing off. "Ellie, this is madness!" She caught hold of my arm and pushed me down into a chair, as though hoping to hold me captive long enough to bring me to my senses. "Must put a stop to it. You're building a volcano. Evil bubbling away under the surface now, but it's gathering force, ready to erupt — destroying everyone in this house."

Poor Dorcas, my devoted friend. She didn't even sound like herself, and her eyes were glazed and feverish. I did hope she wasn't coming down with another of her headaches. I squeezed her hand and told her to go upstairs and rest. Even had I wanted to, I could not stop the relentless march of feet drumming to our front door. My kin were already on their way. I had taken one precaution. That morning I had driven into the village to visit Rose, Brassy's grandmother, and left Tobias in her keeping.

Dorcas did not go upstairs and rest. A short time later I saw her through the window in what appeared to be earnest conversation with Jonas. After a minute or two they moved away in the direction of the stables. Comparing strategies, I thought. What a loyal pair they were. Somewhat consoled, I went upstairs to dress.

Red for courage. I slipped on the flame-coloured dress, and smoothed a touch of the same shade gloss over my lips. Dorcas returned to the house. Apparently she had taken Ben's knitting request seriously, for she emerged from her room with a yard-long purple and citrus wool strip flung over her arm, needles jutting out one end like a psychedelic tiger baring its teeth.

She seemed in rather better spirits when we walked down the stairs together. "Only things I knit, scarves," she confessed as I admired her handiwork. "Tried a jumper once, but the pattern lost me when it reached the armholes. Couldn't make head nor tail of all that decreasing, increasing nonsense — slip one, drop one, loop the loop — lost patience. That jumper became another scarf. Rather wide but warm."

I was glad to hear her sound more like her old self. The talk with Jonas must have done her good. "Never fear," she whispered as we entered the drawing room, "I shall be right behind you at all times."

"Don't overdo it," I whispered back. "You just took off part of my heel."

Whatever their other vices, lateness was not a family trait. The guests all arrived within minutes of each other at seven o'clock, were shown to their rooms, given an opportunity to freshen up and unpack if they wished, and by eight were all assembled in the drawing room. They talked among themselves sipping sherry while Jonas did his stuff with the silver tray heaped with cheese straws and mushrooms à la grecque. Freddy looked at them with dismay. "Don't tell me," he said. "Aunt Sybil didn't make these and I've been dreaming of her tantalizing titbits all day."

"She's away at the moment, visiting friends," I said. But Freddy quickly swallowed his disappointment along with a mushroom while greasily juggling four others.

"Will you stop that!" Uncle Maurice turned on him. "Makes you look like a sea lion at the circus."

Aunt Lulu murmured, "Don't get on at the boy, dear," as she turned over a china ornament to check its maker.

Freddy ignored them both. Arching his neck he tossed and caught another mushroom in his mouth. His hair trailed back in a pirate's pigtail, and he wore a turquoise figure of a naked woman swinging from one ear. A conservative middle-class jury would have branded him the felon, but I wasn't sure I could convict him on "appearance." Aunt Astrid with her regal crown of white hair and her high-necked buttoned blouse pinned with its cameo brooch, and Vanessa, more gorgeous than ever in a daffodil-yellow silk suit, appeared the perfect mother and daughter combination. Uncle Maurice epitomized the man who always returns his library books on time, while Aunt Lulu represented the women of the world who take their iron capsules every day, serve liver every Thursday, and always shop at the January sales. Yet, all of these paragons had hidden their guilty little peccadilloes until publication in Uncle Merlin's will.

"And to what," enquired Aunt Astrid, "do we owe the privilege of this belated invitation?"

"Darling." Vanessa turned her perfect profile towards her mother. "Don't be dense. Ellie couldn't resist showing off her creative homemaking talents and her youthful — prepuberty — figure."

I saw Dorcas's head come up sharply like a pointer on the scent, but her fingers kept clicking away at the needles, lips mouthing knit one, purl two. Her eyes caught mine and moved on around the circle, the guard dog sitting in its darkened corner.

I smiled at Vanessa. "Darling, in all of us — even you — there is a fat girl waiting to come out."

"Come now." Ben picked up the silver tray which Jonas had set down when he left the room. "Ellie felt the time had come for a little celebration."

"Aren't you counting your guppies a little early?" asked Freddy amiably as he reached for another fistful of canapés. "The money isn't yours yet, old chap."

"We're not talking about the money." Ben set the tray down again and reached for a cheese straw. "We're celebrating our having survived the last six months. That hasn't always been easy."

No one choked on his food, dropped his wine-glass, or began to twitch. I was disappointed. A crashing boom from the gong in the hall announced that dinner was served.

This meal promptly struck a false note when Ben discovered that Jonas had heated the jellied madrilene intended to be served over ice. Unruffled by his boss's baleful glare, the old man elbowed his way round the table, pouring the wine. "Cold soup," he chortled, wheezing down the back of Aunt Astrid's neck as he stooped to fill her glass, "on purpose! Hrumph!"

No complaints, however, could be justly levelled against the rolled roast stuffed with layers of smoked ham and oyster dressing. Uncle Maurice never laid his fork down, but Aunt Astrid whispered audibly to Vanessa, "All this prissy foreign cooking! I told you there was something very peculiar about that young man. No wonder he hasn't rushed to marry her."

Dessert came and went. The remainder of the evening proved uneventful. Uncle Maurice, who had sat on his dignity until the brandy was poured, mellowed with each glass. So much so that when we all parted for the night, he clapped Ben on the shoulder, saying, "Shocking disappointment, that will, but the time comes when wounded feelings have to be set aside. If you would like any investment advice, dear boy, I am your man — for a very reasonable percentage."

As agreed, Dorcas stayed in my room, and we took turns sleeping, but morning found us alive and well. I took the last watch; to while away the hour before dawn, I read through Abigail's two journals again. The household ledger told me she had been a thrifty but generous woman, often buying items of clothing for the village children. Perhaps to cover these expenditures she had purchased little meat but large amounts of dairy products for several months. The recipe listing showed that she had been Ben's type of cook — an artist.

As Ben had informed me when he first looked at the journals, a couple of pages were missing from the recipe collection. I had surmised that Abigail had found them unsatisfactory and had removed them but . . . I suddenly shot away from my pillows into a sitting position. Abigail was not like that. She would not have made the entries in her neat round hand without previous experimentation with each dish. Besides, those entries had not been neatly clipped out with scissors, they had been ripped off leaving a ragged edge. Again, not Abigail's way. Those missing entries had to mean something. Were they the final clue? I could have strangled myself with my bare hands. All those weeks and months wasted, and Ben — a fat lot of help he had been. Where, where could those pages be hidden? Calm down, think. They came from the S section, therefore to be found filed under stove, sofa, soup tureen — damn, what I needed was a dictionary, an encyclopaedia or . . . a telephone directory.

A bell buzzed inside my head. Ben and I had always used the lazy expedient of asking the operator for information. The house had owned a phone book, outdated and falling to shreds, but . . . the secret drawer. I could see myself in instant replay the morning I went looking for photographs of Uncle Arthur, and mentally writing off the old bills, the travel brochures, and the obsolete phone book as more of Aunt Sybil's stuff to be sent down to the cottage. Aunt Sybil had the directory! Could I justify breaking in and searching the premises? Dear Aunt Sybil, bless that wonderful Victorian virtue that never permitted her to throw anything away. The phone book was most likely a futile last-ditch grab at straws, but as soon as I could get out of the house Dorcas and I would go and retrieve it. I went down to tackle the kitchen, which had been left to Jonas's ministrations last night. The best that could be said was that he had done better than Aunt Sybil.

I reached for a damp cloth to wipe off the sticky counter top, picked up a dish of butter left out to attract any mice who might come back now Tobias was gone on his holidays, turned and saw the refrigerator. The door was smeared all over in sticky red streaks. What now? Jonas writing reminders to himself? I'd strangle him. Wringing out my cloth I turned to wipe off the mess and stopped.

At close range the letters separated and cleared; I found I was squeezing that cloth so hard water spattered onto my bare feet. "*Who is Dorcas? What is she?*"

I was standing immobile when she came in.

"Couldn't sleep," Dorcas said, "thought you might . . ."

"Look." The accusation screamed at us in angry red blotches from the refrigerator. Dorcas dragged out a chair and sat down, hands riffling through her already untidy hair.

"What does it mean?" I asked, and was afraid for her to answer. Unwillingly I was remembering Rowland Foxworth's words. Six months ago Dorcas was a stranger. And even now there were a lot of gaps in what I knew of her. What was I doing? Friends trusted each other. "Tell me," I said.

Dorcas squared her shoulders and looked me straight in the eye. "Obvious, someone knows who I am."

"A Russian spy?" I joked feebly. Perhaps this was a nightmare brought on by emotional stress and I would soon wake up.

"Sorry, Ellie. Haven't been quite straight with you from the beginning. That business about wanting a change from teaching for a while was true, but had my own reasons for coming here. You might say I have a connection with this house."

"Dorcas, this doesn't mean . . ." I couldn't continue, my throat was closing. For the first time I realized that it was rather odd Dorcas had never spoken about her past. On the day of her arrival and on one or two other occasions she had started to say something about one of her grandparents but had cut herself short, saying she didn't want to bore me. Not a word about mother, father, brother, or sister.

"Mustn't believe I'm engaged in this murderous, heinous plot against you, Ellie. You're like a sister to me. Think the world of you and Ben."

Ben had said that criminals often had the nicest faces. "Then tell me," I begged, "what's the big dark secret?"

"Can't. Sorry, Ellie, other factors involved. Have to play the game by the rules up to the end."

Whose end? "Dorcas," I said quietly, "we're not on the hockey field now, murder isn't a sporting proposition. If your secret, the secret the enemy has discovered, has any bearing on whether or not I will stay alive, I need to hear it."

"No connection at all. You have my word, Ellie, that in due course I will tell all. Have a feeling you will be more pleased than not. What we mustn't do is fall into the enemy's trap. Plain as the nose on your face, trying to foist a quarrel on us with this poison pen business. But undervalued our friendship. We are still friends, aren't we, Ellie?"

I said yes, and I meant it. If I couldn't trust Dorcas, who was left?

Vanessa came yawning into the kitchen, demanding a cup of coffee, and without another word Dorcas left. She didn't come down for breakfast in answer to the gong and I understood. Neither of us would be completely comfortable in each other's presence until those questions *Who is Dorcas? What is she?* were answered. "Where's Dorcas," Ben muttered out of the corner of his mouth as he passed me the marmalade. He thought she was slacking off on her guard duty.

"Are you enquiring about the housekeeper?" sniffed Aunt Astrid. "I saw the woman walking in the garden about fifteen minutes ago. The help these days! Out admiring the flowers when she should be dusting the furniture or making beds."

Ben might be irritated with Dorcas, but he wasn't about to let someone else take swipes at her. "Dorcas is more friend than housekeeper," he said.

As matters progressed I had no opportunity of speaking with Ben alone that morning, and I saw nothing of Dorcas.

The ladies autocratically demanded a tour of the house, and Ben's security system necessitated that the men tag along. Aunt Astrid nosily opened Dorcas's door when we reached her bedroom, but it was empty. "Perhaps she went into the village," I said, and tried to concentrate on Uncle Maurice's suggestions for further improvements to the house.

"Well, Ellie, you have made a passable job of this house," huffed Aunt Astrid, "but you should have used more mauve."

After elevenses the men and Aunt Lulu settled down at the card table for a game of bridge; Aunt Astrid sat with her embroidery hoop in a corner by the window and Vanessa said she would do something meaningful — varnish her nails. Jonas could have the dubious honour of watching her while I crept off to the cottage. So much for my plan of taking Dorcas with me. Where the hell was she? Who was she?

Aunt Sybil's sitting room looked worse than I remembered — the fireside rug dragged out at a slippery angle, the coffee table still littered with dirty crockery, and an overturned teacup by a chair. Looked like Chief Inspector, New Scotland Yard, had already searched the premises. I really would have to come and give this place a clean whether Aunt Sybil was offended or not. The mantelpiece was edge-to-edge rubble, newspaper clippings, tangled balls of string, and stacks of magazines. I searched through these just on the off chance that the phone book had been inserted somewhere. Forward and onwards. Gingerly I removed a greasy paper bag from my path across the room. All four corners of the sitting room were stacked with boxes and spilt contents, but these turned up nothing useful. The kitchen was an impossibility, my stomach could not face more than a cursory glance through cupboards. I did check the fridge; Aunt Sybil might have used the phone book to drain the lettuce. Passing the cellar door I found it locked, but it was unlikely she would have taken one box down there when all the others had been incorporated into her decorating scheme. I hesitated at her bedroom door (snooping through this most personal room bothered me), but I reminded myself that I had already been in here the morning I found her note. Nothing could have changed, and nothing had; crossing the floor was like tiptoeing through a mine field. But, miraculously, on the dressing table sat a box, *the* box. Right on top I spied a travel brochure and immediately underneath sat the phone directory. Instantly I got cold feet. This was a wild goose chase — how likely was it that my mind and Uncle Merlin's ran on parallel lines? With fingers trembling, I opened up to the S section; sure enough, neatly taped down were the missing pages to Abigail's recipe journal. I scanned them rapidly. That was it! I could not wait to show Ben this find. Knowing him, he would very likely conclude that our search was completed, that these pages contained not just another clue, but the stuff of which treasures are made. Somehow, I didn't think so, not because this wasn't very special, but I could not perceive Uncle Merlin ripping those pages out of his mother's book — even in the interests of mystery. So many pieces of the puzzle were still missing.

The clock in the hall struck noon as I returned to the house, just before a storm broke loose. I found Uncle Maurice and Aunt Lulu at the card table. None of them had seen Vanessa, Aunt Astrid was upstairs putting away her embroidery, and Ben had gone to make lunch. Saying I would check up on that meal I went to the kitchen, eager to tell Ben my news and show him . . . but he was not at his usual place of business. On the table lay a note from Dorcas saying she was leaving for a while, and would be in touch when she had thought matters over. How could she? Had Ben seen this?

I found him in the dining room. Vanessa was with him. They were sitting very cosily together. The vamp was fingering one of his shirt buttons and I caught the throaty gurgle of her laughter. And I thought I had ceased being a joke. . . .

I left the door hanging open and backed into the hall. This day was turning into a crash course in betrayal. Where did I go from here? Six months earlier I would have dived straight for the refrigerator. If ever a girl needed half a dozen chocolate éclairs and a hunk of Gorgonzola, this was it. Why bother telling Ben about my discovery of what must be the final clue? My only hope of retaining my sanity was to get out of this house. Unfortunately my paralysed limbs refused to heed the call to action; I was still standing in the hall when Vanessa burst out of the dining room, almost knocking me over. "Horrible!" she screamed.

What had Ben tried?

"A man's face pressed against the window, all contorted and flattened, squishy eyes, no nose, ugh!" Shuddering wildly she fled upstairs.

Why wasn't the gallant lover galloping in hot pursuit? Not waiting for an answer, I charged out into the rain. Like Vanessa, I wasn't watching and went sprawling into Jonas. Slouched hat pulled over his eyes, water spouting off his bushy eyebrows, he was a sight to unnerve even the undistraught.

"You!" I accused. "You were the face at the window."

"Only doing me job." Jonas tried to look guileless but the unholy glee dancing behind his eyes betrayed him. "Thought them window frames might warp in all this damp, best check 'em out, I says." He sobered suddenly, "Hey, lass. Nowt's tha' bad. Thought you had a mite more pluck than to bolt the burrow over some dippy female making fish eyes at . . ."

I made to brush past him. "Please, Jonas. I no longer believe in Father Christmas. Ben is a monumental rat. Heaven only knows who Dorcas is, or where she is. The way this day is going, I'll find you've posted a notice in the personal column of the local newspaper announcing you're the son of Jack the Ripper."

Jonas caught hold of my arm. "Dorcas gone? I think you'd best come inside, girl."

"And do what, drink a cup of Ovaltine?" I yelled. "To hell with Ovaltine. To hell with the lot of you. And Jonas" — I wrenched my arm away from him — "if you are thinking of leaving my employment, I hope you will have the decency to give notice, not leave a bread and butter note."

The going wasn't easy. Like the small child who runs away from home, I had no clear destination in mind. My feet slipped, sloshing through mud puddles as I crossed the grass to reach the driveway. I never paused to wonder if anyone was watching me. The rain was pelting down. I passed the mound of cement by the gates, which was beginning to look like a permanent monument. Where could I go? To the vicar? He had promised to be in touch — another man who had failed me. I had reached Jonas's refuse heap, the iron wheels of his wooden cart still tilted up against the mound of soaked mattresses and worm-eaten wooden chests, and I knew that I could not face a trip through the churchyard even to sit in Rowland's warm study. Staring miserably down at that pile of discarded junk, my life in abstract, one rain-darkened scrap of pink and yellow stripe caught my eye. Flashback, Jonas poking this into place on the heap the last time I saw him here, and that vague, ticklish feeling of something wrong, something where it should not be. Bending now, I pulled the striped rubber thing out with my hands, and with strangely thudding heart looked down at the false cheer of its bright colours. "Loud" was the term Aunt Sybil had used, but she had been fond of her water wings, too fond to have tossed them away, unless they had acquired a puncture. Testing. I blew, and they ballooned into gaudy shape. I moved the stopper on its rubber string and plugged it into place. So? What had I proved? Aunt Sybil could have tired of them, thought they made her look too young. But she had said she could not imagine why anyone would swim without them. Calm down, I ordered my jangling nerves. Nothing has happened to Aunt Sybil. What reason would anyone have to harm her? We'd had that postcard from her. Sure, and we had also had that phone call. No, no! I was taking something perfectly ordinary — water wings owned by an elderly woman — and turning them into a murder clue. I was sick of clues, I was sick of my own hysteria. Staring down at the surging waves below me, I decided to go home, if I didn't get blown over the cliff first. What if . . .? But no, if someone had wanted to be rid of Aunt Sybil they would simply have removed her wings and . . . I had to stop these gruesome thoughts.

A footstep sounded close by and instinctively, I stepped backwards. Heart skidding, I turned. At first I thought it was Jonas. He was wearing the slouched hat and long shaggy tweed coat, but Ben was underneath.

"Ellie," he said.

I held up my hands, warding him off. "Stay away from me, you lecher!"

"Watch out, idiot, do you want to go over the edge?" He grabbed hold of me, hands pinning my waist. His face gleamed with rain — and something I couldn't place. Whatever it was, it wasn't guilt. Bentley T. Haskell didn't know the meaning of the word. I wanted to wrench myself away from him, but those fine blue-green eyes held me even more securely than his hands. There were some holds that even judo experts like Jill did not know about. A man had no right to eyelashes that long. But life was looking up. I had perfected the trick of hating this revolting creature just as he deserved.

"What is this?" asked the man in frustrated exasperation. I had to admire his rendering of innocent perplexity. "I feel as though I've walked into an excerpt from *Wuthering Heights*. Tortured, lovesick maiden throwing herself upon the mercy of the raging elements, in hopes that Heathcliff will come charging to the rescue."

"Heathcliff!" For once my voice did not cave in under pressure. "You megalomaniac, is that how you envision yourself?"

From the sudden blaze of blue-green fire behind those lashes, I saw I had shocked him. He released his hold of me, his hands falling awkwardly to the sides of his trailing coat. I was free, and immediately realized how cold I was. I would die from pneumonia and save our apprentice killer a lot of trouble.

"Me?" said Ben in a voice that managed to sound genuinely surprised. "We're not talking about me." He kicked a pebble aside and watched it go thumping over the cliff edge like an erratic heartbeat, then looked at me from under the brim of that terrible hat. "We're talking about you and the noble vicar — your boy friend."

"Rowland!" Stunned, I took another of those instinctive steps backwards. Had he called to make a formal offer for my hand while I was gone? Quickly, Ben grasped hold of me and pulled me onto safer ground. Were his hands trembling or was it me? Looking up I decided it was Ben. He was not his usual arrogant self; perhaps Vanessa had turned him down. Maybe there was a spark of goodness under all that superfluous beauty.

"Who else but Rowland?" Ben answered in his morbid monotone, rather like someone practising for a foreign language exam. "If you only knew, Ellie, how I have come to hate that man." Here his tone did perk up a little. "I have even toyed with the idea of taking a series of private lessons from the killer in our midst when we finally unmask him. Nothing would give me greater pleasure than to put dear Rowland away."

"Why?" I asked loudly so Ben would not hear the roar of my heart.

"He's taller than me, and . . .?"

"Don't stall." The rain was coming down more heavily, dripping down my neck, stinging my face. But I could not have wiped it away even if Ben had released my hands.

"Okay," snarled Ben, "make me grovel at your feet — you love the man, damn him. Case closed. The fellow is a cheat and a thief, but I'm worse. I am the fool who left the door open for him. But don't worry, Ellie darling, I may not be a pedigreed gentleman like your Rowland, but where your happiness is concerned I'll behave like one — even if it kills me. I'll even bake the wedding cake."

"Very sporting of you." Moments earlier I had been frozen to the marrow, now I was warm all over, deliciously so. An emotion totally new to me was searing molten blood through my veins. Power. A thousand chocolate éclairs could never have made me feel like this. I was sorry Ben was suffering. But the man had brought this upon himself. "Perhaps we should make it a double wedding?" I suggested, tilting my face up so my lips brushed his chin. "You and Vanessa would make a charming background for Rowland and me."

"Vanessa?" Ben shook his head in bewilderment, almost sending that dilapidated felt hat flying; poor Jonas had already lost one that way so I reached up and patted the monster firmly down on Ben's head. "How did Vanessa get dragged into this?" he scowled. "The last I heard she was your chief suspect. I may feel vaguely suicidal right now but I can think of easier deaths than permitting Vanessa to kill me with boredom — should she have nothing worse in mind."

"Boring?" My sophisticated sneer lacked something but my squeak had the ring of fury to lend it eloquence. "I saw you and my boring cousin snoogling away in that disgusting way."

"What?"

"Surprised, ha? I saw the two of you not half an hour ago in the dining room. Try a denial." The wind chose that moment to let forth an anguished wuthering. If this had been a film the sound effects could not have been better.

"I have no intention of denying anything. I was performing my duty as instructed, infiltrating the enemy."

"And loving every minute of what secrets you could uncover."

"Nothing of the sort; if Vanessa happens to find me attractive . . ."

I cut him short. "You never fail to amaze me. I recognize that vanity is a genetic male flaw, but you have a terminal case."

"You're wrong about that." Ben's face came back into focus and I saw him with a clarity that comes when a light is turned on in a dark room. "I know I appear somewhat conceited but, Ellie, you of all people should know it is just a cover. And from where I stand now" — he looked so pathetic and vulnerable in that dreadful hat my heart ached for him — "they're all justified, every one of my neuroses. Can you wonder that my parents disowned me? They were right — I've never accomplished anything worth a damn."

He was undeserving, but somehow my hands had moved and were pressed against the sodden roughness of his coat. I could feel the jolting of his heart against my fingers and the next moment his hands came up and moved through my streaming hair. I remember thinking what a blessing I had kept it long — romance demands long flowing locks of its heroines. And then everything stopped. Everything went quiet.

"You're a superb cook," I said.

"So are most of the housewives in England, and all they ever get is 'the grub's not bad.'"

"They haven't all written books on the subject."

"Neither would I have done, but for Uncle Merlin and his majestic will."

"So? I know you said once that you and I had both sold out, but the motive does not diminish the achievement. You are the one who turned a collection of forgotten recipes into a book and I am the one who killed off all those superfluous pounds. And you are wrong about something else, Ben. I never saw you as insecure. To me thin people never had any meaningful problems. I'm sorry."

"You're sorry. Oh, Ellie!" The pressure of his fingers tightened on my hair. "I'm the one who is sorry, now when it is too late."

Too late? Where had I got the warped idea that something spectacular was beginning for us, that Vanessa and Rowland and the London fiancée were bit players soon to be ushered off into the wings? Now he was going to tell me that he was suffering from some rare incurable disease and had three months to live. Fear made me clutch at the collar of his coat. Why had I never realized before what a beautiful chin he had, so strong yet tender?

"Much too late," he repeated, and the misery surging through the words flowed into me and settled like an ice cube in the pit of my stomach. "If I were to tell you now that I love you, you would never believe me, Ellie."

The ice melted. "Oh, but I would," I insisted and to minimize the belligerence of my tone I stroked his wet cheek comfortingly. "So long as you swear on Uncle Merlin's grave that you did not say the same thing to Vanessa within the last hour. You didn't, did you, darling?"

"Of course not," answered my hero with magnificent repugnance. "But, Ellie, lovely, wonderful witty Ellie, you'd have to be out of your mind to believe me when I tell you that I am wildly, madly crazy about you."

"Fortunately, as you well know, insanity seems to run in my family," I said as my arms crept up around his neck, and with the traditional half-stifled moan of impassioned love scenes everywhere, his lips came down on mine, warm, possessive, and tasting of rain and sea air. The sun must have come out for my whole body was burning with a fierce golden light, sending delicious spirals of pleasure all the way down to my cramped feet. Our coats slapped around our legs and the brim of Ben's hat scraped my forehead, but the annoyances were incidental. Alas, too soon joy ended. Ben lifted his head and looked at me sadly. "This is how it could have been if only I had confessed my love before you went and got so skinny."

"You don't think less is more?" Even as I spoke I was doing rapid mental arithmetic wondering how long it would take me to put all those pounds back on, and was I prepared to make this sacrifice even for Ben? "I know that recently you have thought me too caught up in appearances, but already I am . . ."

"That was nonsense, you're fine," he replied with an unflattering lack of enthusiasm. "But you must be asking yourself if your new body is what I am after, and to be perfectly honest, it is sort of a bonus — I love the way you look in that fiery-coloured dress. . . ."

"But?"

"I knew that first day we drove down here to Merlin's Court that you were rare, that I would never again meet anyone like you. The inheritance was never the attraction — lust for wealth, believe it or not, was never one of my vices. I told myself it was the challenge that appealed. But I wasn't honest with myself about the nature of the challenge. Like a lot of other fools I have always gone for women like Vanessa to boost my ego. Before you lost much weight I discovered that the image no longer mattered a damn, that to me you were beautiful. But being the insecure person I am and not having any idea how you felt about me, I decided it would be better to wait until the six months were up before telling you that I loved you. That way if you turned me down flat we could both have walked off into the sunset without too much embarrassment."

"Wonderfully eighteenth century," I said, pulling the horrible hat down to warm his ears.

"Sure. And then you had to complicate matters by turning into a sylph with the vicar languishing after you all over the place. The man positively oozed integrity. You'd believe him when he told you it was your soul he loved. So what hope was there for me? Restraint now read as indifference, until the packaging changed."

"I get it." The pieces of the puzzle were beginning to slot into place. "You deliberately set up a wall between us so I would not guess what passion lurked behind your dark inscrutable gaze."

"But I did have my relapses. I even copied Rowland's pipe, but it never provided me with the honest, stable authority it gave him, so I went back to ignoring you in the hope that emotional distance would cure me of my craving for you."

"I understand all about cravings," I said, leaning my face against his wet shoulder. "Part of me will always hunger for the wrong foods but I have to tell you that I am not prepared to eat myself back to my old proportions so you can prove the integrity of your love."

"I knew this was hopeless," sighed Ben, drawing me back into his arms for one long anguished kiss.

"No, it isn't," I contradicted when I came up for air. "You and I both have a lot to learn about love and I think we had better start with trust. I am going to accept your word that you would love me whatever my dress size, and you have to believe that I view Rowland Foxworth as a very kindly, not unattractive, purely platonic friend. Agreed?"

"Anything you say," whispered Ben. "Oh, Ellie darling, I do love you so," and he kissed me again, and this time all the shadows were gone. When I opened my eyes I found the rain had definitely stopped and the sun was doing its pale watery best to shine on our happiness. I had forgotten the menace waiting at the house and even Dorcas's departure had become a vague worry to be dealt with later.

"You haven't raised my hopes for nothing. You are going to marry me, aren't you?" asked Ben with the appropriate blend of hope and quiet desperation.

"Only after you formally jilt your mysterious fiancée, poor Susan, unless of course you invented her to keep me in line."

"Not quite," said Ben, "I invented her to keep me in line."

"Then as a reward for your chivalry I will marry you. But I must confess I am doing so for your body — not your mind. Wild unadulterated passion is going to be my new addiction, low in calories, good for the waistline. Although" — I paused — "as a connoisseur of sexiness yourself, you don't look so great in that outfit."

"What's wrong with it?" Ben looked down at the coat trailing low on the ground, its tails flapping spastically about his legs. "Jonas insisted on lending me this coat when he told me you had run off. I don't think he wanted me catching pneumonia before I caught up with you."

"He was right, bless him." I put my hands in Ben's. Jonas must not have told him about Dorcas, and I couldn't. Nothing must spoil this moment — not the enemy, not Aunt Sybil, not even Dorcas.

We stood quietly like that. I was wishing that no one was waiting for us back at the house. If we could have been on our own I would have taken a bath, put on my green velvet dressing gown, and come down to the fire and Ben.

We could have shared a glass of brandy and then . . . after all, we were engaged.

"I know what you are thinking," Ben smiled. "Aunt Astrid would definitely not approve. A pity — that sheepskin hearthrug was really one of your more practical purchases. Never mind, darling, we have all the time in the world, as soon as we can send the relatives packing."

"All the time in the world," I agreed, kissing him again to make sure we weren't getting out of practice. My mother had always warned me not to tempt fate and Ben and I had wilfully gone and done it again. I think in that instant I had a premonition, but it was too late. We never saw what hit us — literally. A staggering pain ripped through my thighs, buckling my knees. The world tilted at a crazy lopsided angle. In slow motion my life flashed before me. I was reliving the horror of the dumb-waiter. But this was not to be an instant replay watched from the security of an armchair. This was life, or more accurately, death. I was going over the edge of the cliff and I was taking my beloved with me.

"Ben!" I screamed. This could not happen. We had been so happy, I couldn't lose him so soon.

Only the wind and rain and the waiting, pulsing sea answered. "Ben," I screamed again, and far above a seagull mockingly echoed my cry.

"I'm right below you," he answered tersely. "No, don't look down, don't even breathe." A small scurry of stones dislodged by our scrabbling feet placed a compelling emphasis upon his advice. Spread-eagled, I clung to the face of the cliff, my fingers grappling for a firmer hold on the gnarled shrubbery which, with a precarious foothold on a narrow ledge, was all that kept me from slithering down that jagged incline into the foaming mouth of the sea.

Ben was on a similar ridge, his head a yard or so below my feet. If I went so would he. That knowledge kept me frozen. The muscles in my arms began to bunch and spasm, but I held on. We were doomed, of course; if we yelled for help the killer might hear and toss a boulder down to shut us up, and if we did nothing our pitiful grip upon life would slacken.

My foot slipped and another ominous shower of stones ricocheted down the cliff.

"We have to risk it," Ben said. "We have to call for help."

I tried. I opened my mouth but no sound came. Ben meanwhile made enough noise for both of us. I screwed my eyes shut, and braced myself against the impending avalanche.

"Is anyone down there?" came a voice from above. "My word, Ellie, Ben. What has happened? What are you doing down there?"

"Trust a parson to be a complete fool," Ben snarled. "What the hell do you think we're doing? Playing hide-and-seek? Fetch a rope, Foxworth, and hurry — unless you want to start digging up your churchyard for two more."

* * *

He saved us. Until my dying day, which through his good offices has been postponed indefinitely, I will owe Rowland Foxworth a debt I can never repay.

"Don't go overboard on the gratitude bit," Ben whispered in my ear when Rowland left us in his study while he requested the dour Mrs Wood to make us some hot cocoa. "No need to develop a martyr complex, or you'll find yourself marrying the fellow as a reward for services rendered."

"Nonsense," I chattered, still shivering. "Our troth is plighted in granite, a bit loose and crumbly, but . . ."

"All this consorting with clergymen is very bad for me," sighed Ben. He adjusted the wool travelling rug that was wrapped around my knees. For a man who had narrowly escaped death, he looked very dashing in Rowland's rubbed silk dressing gown. The same could not be said for me in Mrs Wood's washerwoman-style print dress.

"Yes, if I don't watch it," Ben continued, "I'll be catching religion. Foxworth appearing on the scene in the nick of time almost makes a believer out of me. His timing was nothing short of miraculous."

"Good," I replied, "because I insist on a church wedding. Which reminds me, I will have to sit down and write a letter to your parents, telling them you have mended your ways and if they want to be around when the grandchildren start arriving, they had better bury the hatchet."

Rowland's explanation for being on the coast road was simple. He had been on his way to pay us a visit. "I had news for you that seemed too good to be passed over the phone." He handed us our cocoa. "One mystery at least is solved. I have discovered what became of Abigail Grantham. In the light of what has happened, this now seems trivial, but I promised to inform you the moment I discovered anything."

Ben took a proprietary seat on the arm of my chair. "Let me guess. She was pushed over a cliff?"

Rowland shook his head. He was looking for his pipe. I removed the small lumpy object I had been sitting on and handed it to him. "Speaking of cliffs," he said, "I think you are committing a dangerous error in not notifying the police that an attempt has been made on your lives, and not the first either."

"And tell them what?" asked Ben. "That Ellie fell through a dumb-waiter? That we moved too close to the edge of the cliff?"

"The weapon?" suggested Rowland.

"Jonas's wooden cart. Sunk to the bottom of the sea without a trace, no doubt. But even if we could produce it, what would that prove? That it ran loose from its moorings and in the process sent us flying? A starry-eyed couple so wrapped up in each other they forgot the warnings posted up and down the coast road: 'Danger, Sharp Drop-Off'? The detective-inspector would wink at the chief constable and they'd fold up their notebooks and go home."

"Very likely," Rowland agreed reluctantly, as he struck a match to his pipe, "but calling in the police might provide some measure of safety for you and Ellie. The killer might back off if he felt the eyes of the law upon him."

"You're right," said Ben, "which is why I intend to inform our guests that we have telephoned the police from this house and they have promised to mount guard in the grounds throughout the night, and at the first sign of trouble will beat the doors down."

Rowland looked unconvinced. "How will that help, when you and Ellie are inside with this maniac?"

"I think it might." I slipped my hand into Ben's and felt secure enough to face an army of would-be assassins. Rather haltingly I told them about Dorcas, starting with the red scrawl on the refrigerator to my conversation with her and my discovery of her note. And then, almost as though both matters were related, I mentioned finding Aunt Sybil's abandoned water wings.

A curl of smoke crept up from the bowl of Rowland's pipe. "I don't like any of this," he said.

"The trouble is" — Ben rubbed his forehead — "grown women can come and go as they please. This plethora of farewell notes does have me rather worried but, again, would the police even be willing to check and confirm that Sybil and Dorcas are all right? We can't even tell them where to look."

"They must have taken public transportation." The vicar leaned forward and tapped his pipe into the ashtray. "Right. I know people at the train and bus stations; I will make some immediate enquiries. With that red hair I would think Miss Dorcas quite easy to spot, and the same goes for Miss Grantham, who rarely travels. This place is so small — I am sure I can come up with some information."

"Thank you," said Ben and I together. I didn't care what secrets Dorcas had kept from me. I did not care who or what she was. She was my friend and I wanted her back so I could tell her what she meant to me.

"And please, Ben, whatever you do, don't let Ellie sleep alone tonight," urged Rowland.

Ben raised one of his eloquent black brows. "Vicar, you shock me!" He grinned. "Sorry, I couldn't resist. This tension is making us all slightly daffy. If we are not reacting appropriately it is because we cannot absorb what is happening. Will you rest easier if we promise to sit up all night and keep each other company? Tomorrow the guests go home and within a few days the six months will be up."

"And what happens then" — I looked eagerly at Rowland — "may depend largely on what you have discovered about Abigail. Please tell us. How did she die?"

"She didn't."

Ben and I stared at him.

"Not at least when she is supposed to have done. For all I know Abigail Grantham lived to a ripe old age, but not in the company of her husband and son."

"But the funeral?" I couldn't assimilate this new idea. "Remember Uncle Merlin's request that his funeral be a repeat performance of the one given his mother? We thought it eerie at the time: gothic, that outmoded horse and carriage swaying along the coast road through the mist."

"Yes." Ben's eyes narrowed, and I felt a tremor of excitement run through his fingers into mine. The room was very still, apart from the rain strumming against the windowpanes and the curtains, stirred by a draught of air, billowing and falling. Rowland was warming to his role of master story-teller.

"There was a funeral," he agreed, savouring our patent expectancy. "But no body. Ellie, you were right about Arthur Grantham in one sense. He was the worst kind of Christian: sanctimonious, hypocritical, vengeful. But he was not a murderer. The burial ceremony was a symbolic expulsion of evil. Abigail was not dead, not literally, but he had already consigned her to the flames of hell. He had discovered her in what he considered a compromising situation with the young artist who had been painting her portrait, Miles Biddle was his name, I think. To Arthur, Abigail was dead. To prove this, he buried her in spirit, if not in fact. I imagine the gesture did much to soothe his wounded pride."

"How well did his pride survive if all the neighbours knew his wife preferred another man?" I asked.

"They didn't," said Rowland. "Arthur kept the scandal under wraps. The funeral served a secondary purpose. Instead of living out his days an object of sympathy and perhaps ridicule, he became a widower. There were rumours, of course, but he bribed the doctor and the undertaker to support his story that his wife had passed away unexpectedly."

"In a sense he wasn't lying about that," answered Ben. "I suppose an underpaid doctor and undertaker wouldn't be too hard to silence if the price was right. They probably clammed up so tight on the subject of Abigail that their very silence fuelled rumours that there was something funny about the business."

"The vicar." I pulled the travelling rug up to warm me. "Was he in on Arthur's little fraud?"

"Oh yes." Rowland struck another match to his pipe. "The Reverend Geoffrey Hempstead was bought with a stained-glass window for the south wall of the church — you'll have seen it, quite exceptional. At the time I imagine he felt justified in supporting Arthur Grantham in casting out his wife. Ellie, I think I told you I had found some of Mr Hempstead's sermons, one condemning a child for 'stealing' flowers and another castigating a woman caught in adultery. Whether he was referring to Abigail I don't know, but the harshness of his views was clear. He must have applauded the ruthlessness of Arthur's action, relished the zeal with which a sinner was purged from the lives of her husband and son. The difference between the two men was, I think, that Hempstead was not a hypocrite. His conscience flayed his own soul as mercilessly as it did those of his parishioners. He couldn't bring himself to falsify the parish register by recording her death. He wrote a letter confessing his worldly greed to his bishop. Along with it I found the reply, objurgating him for being party to a false funeral. The details are all there. The bishop dwelt on them at length."

"Strange." I shivered slightly. "We began with a funeral — Uncle Merlin's — and we end with one. For this is the end of the trail, isn't it?" I looked up at the two men. "If Abigail isn't inside that coffin, I think we can guess what is. The term buried treasure is quite literal in this case."

CHAPTER SEVENTEEN

We found Abigail's treasure. Rowland felt some qualms about not contacting his bishop for permission to open up the tomb, but his curiosity was as strong as ours, and he was no more anxious for delay than Ben or I. He came with us to the vault. At the bottom of the coffin we found, neatly arranged, Abigail's personal possessions, her clothes — not grand or many in number — a kite, a sewing box, hairbrushes and combs and a monstrous relic of Arthur Grantham's punitive tactics, the remains of a pitifully small skeleton and a brown leather collar.

"He killed her dog — that fierce little pug in the portrait." My hands gripped the side of the coffin. "Small wonder Merlin never had a pet about the house."

"We now know why he grew up shunning the human race." Ben lifted out an envelope which had been tucked down under the clothes. "What a scene for a boy of nine to witness — his mother's banishment and mock interment and her dog killed."

"I would like to hope that his father at least shielded Merlin from the truth," said Rowland, still looking down at the fragile heap of bones.

"Some hope." Ben's expression was dour. "Good old Art must have relished giving his son the news that Abigail had reaped her just deserts. Let's just be thankful that somehow Merlin managed to save the portrait and the journals."

"Gracious," I said, "I've been meaning to tell you about those, but, oh never mind — first things first, what's in that envelope? Open it up, please."

"Sounds like a night at the Oscars," quipped Ben, but I noticed his hands were not quite steady as he pulled out a single sheet of paper and started reading aloud:

> *"Dear Mrs Grantham, you had to break a lot of eggs to perfect your infallible recipe. My chef is ecstatic. He tells me our house has a new treasure, so I hope you will accept one of our old ones, a trinket given to Elizabeth by Philip of Spain. H.M. gave it to my ancestress, another lady-in-waiting, because she was peeved at P. when his gift arrived. Thank you for tea and cosy chat.*
> *Laura Wallingford-Chase'"*

"Oh,"

I sighed, "how simple everything is when properly explained."

"Precisely what I was thinking." Ben nodded at Rowland. "Don't tell me, dear chap, that you don't grasp the situation at a glance. Tell him, Ellie dearest, put the man out of his misery."

"Are you sure I won't bore either of you? Well, first the recipe in question is for an unsinkable soufflé. Don't swoon from ecstasy, Ben. . . ."

"The word is panic. Is this universally important discovery still in existence, is it . . .?"

"Safe? Naturally. I only found it today, but it is safely hidden from all prying eyes. You shall have it, my boy, never fear. Next question. Who is Laura Wallingford-Chase? Again my computer brain has the answer stored away. And in knowing who she is, I think I also know what the treasure is."

"But, my dear Ellie, where is the treasure?" asked Rowland and Ben like twin parrots.

"In the sewing box, I would think. It looks about the right size. Why don't you open it up and have a peek?" He did as he was told and sure enough let out a whistle of disbelief.

"Stop gawking and hand it over." I made a grab for the box, looked inside, and tightened my grip. What if I sneezed and dropped the sewing box with this inside? "It is so exquisitely fragile I'm afraid to touch it. If I breathe too hard it may shatter like . . ."

"An egg," supplied Ben, "like all the eggs Abigail had to shatter to perfect her recipe. But this egg is solid gold, less a few emeralds here and there. Laura What's-her-face must have been related to Midas if she considered this a trinket. You say you know who she was, computer brain, tell."

"Rose, Abigail's former maid, was the one who told me. At the time, being a bit slow on the uptake, I didn't quite put two and two together but now . . . Rose told me that once upon a time, a wealthy, aristocratic lady got stuck outside Merlin's Court during a storm and that Abigail entertained her in the kitchen very simply but hospitably and that she gave her ladyship one of her recipes. For which kind favour Abigail later received a warm thank-you letter and an Easter egg. Rose thought it was for the little boy, but she must never have seen it."

"Being a man of simple tastes," said Ben, "I must say I would have preferred chocolate but . . . this ornithological offering must be priceless, though not as valuable to me as the soufflé, should I ever open my restaurant." He looked down at the egg glowing in golden oval splendour like a sun sprinkled with tiny emerald stars. "I'm sorry the secret is not ours alone. Her ladyship's descendants must have been in the know for sixty years. I wonder if they are the kind of people who can be bought off."

"Be quiet," I said. "Look, the egg is in two halves like a locket, careful — don't shove while I open it; we don't want to scramble the insides."

What was inside was a delicately wrought platinum branch on which perched a shimmering blue bird, wings spanned for flight, amber beak lifted as if in song.

"That bird," I explained patiently to the men, a species not reared to appreciate the finer things in life, "that there bird is sapphire and the eyes emeralds."

"Your engagement ring is going to look pretty chintzy after this," sighed Ben.

"I don't think I want to talk about rings right now." I shut the bird away inside the egg. "To think that Abigail owned this magnificent piece of art and she was forced to sell her mother's garnet ring to start a new life." I turned to Rowland. "You may think poorly of her going off with another man, but she was a remarkable woman. Even when her situation was desperate she took the time to make the notation in her housekeeping ledger that she had sold that ring. When items went missing in those days, one of the maids usually took the rap. Abigail didn't take any chances."

Rowland smiled, and I thought again what an incredibly nice man he was. He deserved a loving, helpful wife, someone with plenty of energy. Jill — he would meet her at the wedding, and who knew what might develop with a little help from his friends? "How about a brief prayer for her, that whatever became of her, Abigail Grantham may rest in peace?" he suggested.

And Bentley T. Haskell, atheist, agreed.

* * *

"An attempt on your lives, and who, may I ask, are the culprits?" shrilled Aunt Astrid, when Ben informed her and the others why we were late for tea. "Police surrounding the house! I have never been so mortified in my life! Fetch my coat, Vanessa, we are leaving. I refuse to remain another minute in a place where I am accused of murder."

"But not single-handedly," Freddy comforted her. "We are, I presume," — he winked grotesquely at me — "all in this together? What a lark. I've always wanted to be involved in a conspiracy. Will someone fill me in on what I have missed so far?"

Uncle Maurice snorted. "Shut up," he ordered his son, "and stop snivelling, Lulu. If what Ellie and Ben claim is true . . ."

"Do you want to see my bruises?" I asked irately.

Vanessa feigned shock. "Darling, a lady never takes her knickers down in the drawing room."

Uncle Maurice spoke over her. "I was not doubting your veracity, simply weighing the facts. Here, sit down, Ellie. You should be off your feet."

"She's not having a baby," mocked Freddy.

"No," agreed Aunt Lulu, drying her eyes, "babies take nine months, and from the sound of things, she may not have that long to live."

"That's an unnecessarily pessimistic view." Uncle Maurice patted me on the shoulder and helped me heavily into a chair. "Ben, hope you won't think I'm nitpicking when I say the word murder has a damned nasty ring to it. I prefer to think of these admittedly unfortunate episodes as practical jokes that went rather too far. Now, if the perpetrator would sportingly own up, I am sure we can keep all this unpleasantness within the family."

He looked around hopefully. No one blushingly raised his hand or lowered guilty eyes. "Very well," continued Uncle Maurice as though speaking to children in a classroom where the blackboard eraser was missing, "no purpose will be served in any of us walking out tonight. In fact, quite the opposite. While we remain together we all have alibis. Astrid, if you wish to stage a tantrum, that is your business. I for one have no desire to paddle my car through a rainstorm — at two miles an hour I'd be lucky to reach home by tomorrow afternoon."

"I take it, then" — Ben smiled affably — "that we can count on all of you for dinner tonight?" Receiving the nod of assent, if not approval, he and I went out into the kitchen.

"I do hope," he said, kissing me, "that the old saying about marrying the family isn't true. Uncle Maurice was the only one who offered even a backhanded word of sympathy for our ordeal."

"Too busy worrying about their own necks." I pressed my face against his, then drew away, watching him carefully. "You seem remarkably sanguine. Is there something you're not telling me? I get the feeling you are not so worried about our shrinking life expectancy any more."

"Are you beginning to read my mind already? I thought that only came after years of marriage." He caressed my cheek. "There is someone I must talk with, then if my theory is correct, I will tell you why we are no longer in danger — if in fact we ever were — except through bungling error."

"What?"

"I don't think you and I were ever the intended victims of this plot. We just kept getting in the way. So many aspects did not make sense because we were looking at this business from the wrong angle. This afternoon I realized where we had gone wrong in the first place, which changed everything."

"Does this have anything to do with Dorcas?"

"No," said Ben. "I am worried about her, too; where she fits in I don't know, so we have no idea whether she may have placed herself in some kind of danger. Keep hoping that Rowland has some news for us soon."

"If you would only tell me what you suspect," I urged.

"Not until we have fed the mob in the drawing room, got them tucked away in bed, and not before I have spoken to my source. Chances are that I could still be wrong. I haven't been right often — so far."

The doorbell buzzed, and we both raced out into the hall, hoping desperately that this would be Dorcas, or Aunt Sybil at least. Freddy was ahead of us and he had the door thrown open against the wild wet night and was inviting someone in — a short, skinny female, someone with spiky greenish hair.

"Jill," I cried, rushing to hug her.

"Gosh, you look fab." She started patting me down the sides as if to see if I had the missing parts stashed somewhere on my person. "Hi, Ben, sorry I didn't get back to you and Ellie about the hypnosis bit. I've been off meditating with my guru in the Scottish highlands — Tibet is financially out these days — but he turned out to have a disgustingly physical mentality, besides he said he was a vegetarian and I caught him eating flies. But the spider did teach me something — hypnotism; I had already taken a correspondence course on the subject, but anyway that is principally why I am here, to help. I'm not too late, am I?"

How could I tell my sweet guileless friend that she had entered a house of murder? As it happened I didn't have to say much to her at all. Freddy seemed to have fallen victim to her mesmeric powers. He couldn't take his eyes off her and she seemed equally smitten with him. Talk about One Enchanted Evening. One mutual gasp of spiritual recognition and they both went into the trance state, which did not help the social aspect of the evening. They neither spoke to each other nor to anyone else. The evening dragged on, I almost said at funeral pace, but lately I had felt that the march to the grave was a hurried affair. At last everyone began yawning in unison, and they all, except Aunt Astrid, said they would seek their beds. Freddy did return to the world of reality at that point to tell her that if she sat up armed with her needle and thread after everyone had retired people might wonder what dark thoughts kept her from sleeping.

"I will never" — Aunt Astrid lifted her head and swooped out into the hall — "darken these doors again."

Things were looking up. Ben and I, alone at last, went into the kitchen. What a day this had been — beginning with that question regarding Dorcas's true identity. Had she taken off because she felt my faith in her was shaken beyond repair?

Ben was putting on his coat. "Stay here," he ordered. "I'll be back in a flash. Put the kettle on, I'm bringing Jonas back for a cupper."

So our trusty gardener was the source. What could Jonas tell us? I had barely set the kettle on the Aga top when Ben was back, alone, eyes blazing grimly in his rain slick face.

"Hurry," he yelled. "Grab a coat. We may already be too late. Here, take mine." He yanked it off, throwing it over my shoulders. His panic was contagious.

"Where are we going? Where is Jonas?"

Ben grabbed my hand and dragged me through the garden door into the driving rain, hurtling me across the sopping lawn. "Another farewell note — this time saying Jonas has gone to visit his mother."

"But that's ludicrous. Jonas doesn't have a mother. She's dead."

"Exactly, her address is Tombstone Villa."

"Then, oh God, Ben — those other notes!" I wasn't running. My feet were sliding along under me as Ben dragged me behind him.

"No time," he cried. "We may already be too late. What a fool I have been. I guessed this afternoon, but I thought we were safe to wait a few hours, until I could talk to Jonas without interruption."

We had turned right through the iron gates onto the coast road and had now entered the churchyard, weaving in and out among the stones. "Here," said Ben, and my feet stumbled to a standstill. We were at the family vault.

"Here? But Jonas's mother is not . . ." I stopped because I knew Ben was right. We had reached our destination. Evil was all around us.

"Ellie," said Ben curtly, "I want you to leave me here and run to the vicarage. Rouse Foxworth and get the police out here."

"Sorry." I refused through clenched teeth, trying to still their chattering. "I'm coming with you. Two of us have double the chance. You know who the killer is, don't you?"

"Yes, but you are not coming."

"Try to stop me." I kissed him quickly and hand in hand we went into the vault. I expected total darkness. Ben had a torch with him, but he did not need to turn it on. The icy stone room was flickeringly alive with shadowed candlelight. We saw Jonas at once — laid out stiffly on top of Abigail's tomb. Feet together, hands folded on his chest. Oh God, I thought, he's already dead. I loved Jonas. A distended shadow moved in the corner of the room. As we watched, a woman stepped out into the shivering light, carrying a lifted spade.

"Aunt Sybil!" I must have said the words out loud for she looked up, mildly irritated as she had seemed sometimes when I arrived unannounced at the cottage. "I did hope," she said reprovingly, "that I would be able to finish up here before you two turned up. I should have known you would come poking your noses in. That's why I left that note on Merlin's door. I hoped that if you found him gone you would run around like chickens with their heads cut off, but you smarty-pants had already guessed. I saw you go in here with the vicar this afternoon, after your little accident, but I could not wait to see you come out. I had to make my plans for Merlin here."

"Merlin?" I said, "Auntie dear, this is Jonas, not Merlin. You are just a little confused."

"No, she's not." Ben spoke up calmly as though this were a cocktail party. "Jonas is the one who died six months ago, not Merlin. It must have been quite simple really, two old men whom no one ever saw, both with a macabre sense of humour, deciding that when the gardener with his serious heart condition died his master would step into his muddy boots. That way Merlin could watch the outcome of his Last Will and Testament. The doctor signed the death certificate in happy ignorance, and Mr Bragg admitted he had only seen Merlin once, for the writing of the will, and that he was all muffled up in thick scarves."

"Do we really see old people as all alike?" I asked sadly, looking at Uncle Merlin's rigid form. "Of course he grew the moustache, and when we saw him that night in the kitchen he had his teeth out and was wearing the stupid night-cap, but I should have known. Even with the lights turned down and meeting Jonas outside with the snow blowing."

"Now, Ellie, don't go on so," said Ben in an inane voice. "We must apologize to Aunt Sybil for this untimely intrusion. What exactly are we interrupting?"

"I decided that in view of his devotion to his mother, wicked adulteress that she was, I would set him over her tomb and make an effigy out of him. Not that Abigail is buried here as you already know." Aunt Sybil smiled slyly. "She was carrying on with that weak-kneed artist boy, little more than a teenager he was and she over thirty. Poor Uncle Arthur, he was so mortified. But I helped make things up to him. When I came for the funeral I found her dog and killed it for him. Even the nicest men tend to be a bit squeamish but it wasn't the first time for me. I had a cat once, and it wouldn't let me dress it up in a bonnet and shawl so I drowned it. Merlin was staying with us at the seaside at the time, and oh, the silly tears! He wasn't quite certain — whether it was an accident, I mean. Boys are so dense. I hoped he would remember when I sank that horrid old tom of yours in the moat, but there are none so blind as those that will not see. He never even knew his mother tried to contact him all those years. I took care of that. I sent all the letters back marked 'Refused' and after a while they stopped coming."

"Uncle Arthur admired your . . ." Ben struggled for the word, "fortitude?"

"Oh yes, he thought me absolutely sweet." Aunt Sybil smoothed out the cement mixture with the back of her spade. "I do hope this doesn't crack. Life is full of mixed blessings. If those workmen had come when promised to fix the iron gates, I wouldn't have had this stuff on hand. I would have had to think of some other way of disposing of poor Merlin. And what a pity; this seems so apropos. Now what was I saying about Uncle Arthur? Ah, I remember, he doted on me and I suppose I was in love with him, too. I always hoped that poor Merlin would grow into a man like his father, but no spine and, fortunately, no imagination. Half a century I wasted trying to mould him, loving the man I wanted him to be. You see I had been given a glimpse of what I wanted. Dear Uncle Arthur, he loved the way I managed the house."

"Later, didn't you ever think of moving away, making a new life for yourself?" Ben was inching forward. I was reminded of the childhood game of statues. Each time Aunt Sybil looked up, he froze.

"What, and leave Merlin?" Aunt Sybil looked positively shocked. "I loved him, or thought I did. Lately I have begun to wonder if my feelings were a prolonged infatuation. You didn't understand the kind of love I had for him, did you? And that's where you made your mistake. Animal passion isn't rational, it changes. To hatred in this case. I felt the first stirrings when he and Jonas sat chuckling over their masquerade; I had been so happy when I realized that vulgar common man was dying. Merlin had fetched a London specialist to see him, and then they had to go and spoil it all. Jonas took the news that his number was up very well. . . . He'd always thought he had something the matter with him so he was bound to be pleased. In a joking way he said his only regret was that he couldn't be at his own funeral. That gave them the idea. Merlin had me write and invite all the family down so he could choose his heirs. The treasure hunt and all the other hocus-pocus was an added inspiration. He took one of his peculiar fancies to you both. Thought you had spunk."

"What did Uncle Merlin plan to do at the end of six months, rise from the dead?" My fear was evaporating. I felt slightly fuzzy. Why was I standing in a room full of tombs, communing with a mad woman while she cemented up the ex-love of her life. "Is he," my voice quavered slightly, "still alive?"

"Oh yes." She nodded cheerfully. "Only drugged. That's half the fun. I'm hoping he will come round just before I cover up his face. You were asking about Merlin's plans. He told me nothing about the treasure or those childish clues, but I think that originally he intended to let the dice fall where they might. If you accomplished the goals set for you, the house and money would be yours, exactly as the will said. But I told you he wasn't a realist. He became fond of you. He said Ellie had restored the house to the way it was in his mother's day. As though I didn't work my fingers to the bone. He made a new life without me, he didn't need me; now, if he had been dead I could have understood. . . . Well, enough of that. Whatever happened he didn't want you to leave. If you were not eligible for the inheritance, he was going to face the legal consequences and return like Lazarus to establish your rights of property."

"Aunt Sybil," Ben said admiringly, "you really are an incredible woman, pulling the wool over our eyes as you did, disappearing so that instead of being suspicious of you we would worry about your safety. And all the time you were hiding out in your own cottage, weren't you?"

Aunt Sybil nodded and giggled. "So much fun. But it wasn't you I wanted to worry about me, it was him. I left those water wings on the ground near his bonfire so he would think I had drowned, but what did he care? And what could I expect after the way he spoke to me at your dinner party? Before that, I had done a couple of things to show I was not pleased with the new arrangement but after that night I definitely decided to kill him."

"You always seemed so devoted to him," I said.

"I was." She dropped another load of cement on top of Uncle Merlin and patted it into shape. "Stupid, of course. These one-sided affairs are never meant to last. For years I used to dream about going to the South of France on my honeymoon."

So that was the reason for the travel brochures in the secret drawer.

"I've had my days of being hurt, now it's his turn." The wicked eyes looked out of the bland face. "Does this look even? I want his knees to look right, knobby and disjointed."

"Perfect," I said.

Aunt Sybil looked relieved. "As you young people would say, I'm into total honesty now. Goodness knows I deluded myself for years. That miserable man wasted my life." She hummed as she trimmed a rough edge. "My mother died before she could warn me about the selfishness of men. I didn't mind going to the cottage, I dared to hope that it would become our love nest; every time a knock sounded at the door I hoped it was him."

"Those times when I stopped at the cottage I had the feeling you were disappointed — that you hoped I was someone else," I said.

She continued smoothing cement. "I even flirted with that twerp the vicar at your party to make Merlin jealous, silly me. And very foolishly I imagined that if you and Mr Hamlet gave up and left, life would return to the old pattern. Merlin never suspected I was the one who put those chocolates in your room, Ellie, and washed that really stupid book. If you had wanted lessons in pornography you should have come to the expert — me. Wasn't it clever of me to invite Freddy to come and look things over at the house? Told him not to say anything, but that I was worried about you. Knew he'd panic, that his father, being so desperate for money, had been up to something. And I wanted you to suspect him. You see, I was worried that one of you might begin to wonder about me, but you foolish dopes" — she reached out and aimed a playful poke at us — "you were so easily duped it took the fun away."

"Sorry." We were now standing directly across the tomb from her. I dug my fingers through the wet cement and squeezed part of Uncle Merlin's hand.

"I do wish I had a palette knife," murmured Aunt Sybil. "Yes, my feelings for Merlin changed. You giddy young things don't realize that a woman scorned is the same at any age. Until that night of your dinner party I forced myself to overlook his cavalier treatment of me, but when he insulted me in front of the vicar for calling his mother what she was, and referred to me as a dried-up spinster, I knew he had to die. In the heat of the moment I almost called him by his own name, but later I was calm; I planned it all, luring you from the house, so I could jimmy the dumb-waiter and if possible snare the cat. Dorcas, old stick-in-the-mud, was a problem, but I fixed her tea. I asked Lulu to telephone at a precise time and keep the woman in conversation for several minutes. She was too stupid to ask why."

"Perhaps she guessed what you were up to, and approved your marvellous methodical scheme," said Ben.

"Oh, I would like to think so," sighed Aunt Sybil. "One does so like to be appreciated. I was rather proud of the dumb-waiter. I knew Merlin was still in the habit of using it."

"Of course," I said. "He did have that uncanny habit of popping up where least expected." Aunt Sybil had worked her way up to Merlin's chin.

"That was one of the things that bothered me." Ben seemed determined to keep her talking. "The chance of Ellie or me stepping inside that contraption was so slim."

"Yes, but she had to be such a busy little bee." Aunt Sybil looked sullen and then brightened. "I took the cat as an extra treat. Merlin was meant to find it when he came out of the stables in the morning. But fate was unkind. This afternoon, too, how could I have foreseen when I crept up from behind and pushed that cart that Mr Hamlyn had borrowed Merlin's hat and coat. I was so sure I had finished him off at last, and if Ellie went too that was the icing on the cake. Oh well, if at first you don't succeed, try, try, and try again! Don't you think I've made a lovely job of him?"

"Superlative!" came our unanimous response.

Aunt Sybil stood back and admired her handiwork. "Is there anything else you two meddlers want cleared up? Any more questions? Good. I would like you to know that whilst I did resent your moving into my home, once I began to hate Merlin I scarcely gave you a thought. Petty jealousies seemed so insignificant. I do hope you understand."

"Oh, we do." Ben and I nodded in fervent agreement.

"Because," Aunt Sybil cosily smiled, "I would not like your taking my having to kill you personally." She came slashing towards us with the spade. Ben dived for her legs, but she was too quick; whamming down on his head she shrieked with gleeful laughter. "One down and one to go," she chortled as he grunted and rolled over. "My, doesn't time fly when one is having fun!"

Out of the corner of my eye I saw the granite figure of Uncle Merlin rise slowly upon his tombstone bed. "Run,

Ellie," he crackled. Aunt Sybil turned ready to flatten the mummified Lazarus. For now she had abandoned me, and I was free to make a break to try and find some help, but I couldn't let her drive that sheet of metal down on Uncle Merlin's head. I was amazed at her strength as I leapt on her back. We wrestled frantically, both of us clinging to the handle of the spade. If only I had taken Jill's judo lessons more seriously! Aunt Sybil was winning, dragging me backwards with her. We almost tripped over Ben's inert body. I felt Merlin's agonized gaze upon us, powerless to intervene. We were at the door locked in a hideous embrace. Despite her age and rotund build, she was as spry as a cat. I could not hold on much longer. My hands were slimy as cold cream on the wooden handle. It slipped from my grasp.

Something thumped into the back of my head. At first I thought it was the spade until I realized that the metal blade was still pointing towards the floor. "Don't move," ordered a familiar voice, and I realized the blow had been struck by the door opening inward. "Drop your weapon. I am fully armed. Don't suppose I mentioned it, never one to boast, but our school represented England for archery. Didn't take me a minute to make this bow from a curtain rail and some twine. Knitting needles make marvellous arrows."

"Would you mind telling me," I asked sharply, "which one of us you intend to shoot?"

"Neither of you, if you behave sensibly. Ellie, move away from Sybil."

"More interference," snapped Aunt Sybil, sounding genuinely peeved. "I was so certain you were tied up safe and sound in my cellar, and here you come butting your long nose into my business. Oh! And things were going so well."

"To a Girl Guide leader," said Dorcas austerely, "knots are child's play once that drug you gave me wore off. Climbing out that tiny window was something else, but I managed in time. Now will you please drop that spade? That's right. Ellie, you take it and see if you can dig out Uncle Merlin, he's beginning to set."

"How did you know he's Merlin and not Jonas? And what about Ben? He's an unwitting victim, not like that devious old man who brought much of this on himself."

"If you really love Ben" — Dorcas ignored my first question — "you'll let him sleep this one off." Standing legs apart she pointed the arrow at Aunt Sybil's chest. "He's going to have a killing headache when he wakes up."

"How you do remind me of your grandmother," Aunt Sybil remarked nastily. She turned her head slightly towards me. "You do realize that she is a by-blow of that nefarious relationship between Abigail and the artist. I recognized the likeness at once, same long nose, scraggy build, and gingery hair. How did you like my little note on the refrigerator door? 'Who is Dorcas? What is she?' My own version of dear Willie Shakespeare's lovely poem. That's one way clever Dick here guessed. She remembered my passion for the Bard, and came hoppity-hop knocking on my parlour door, or rather she sneaked in with my spare key, and then you know what she noticed? That someone had been in the cottage. Those heads of Merlin weren't on the mantelpiece as they had been on the day you came to the cottage and found my note. Of course not, I took them down a week ago and ground them up in my blender. What is old eagle-eye? She's the granddaughter of a whoring slut and a baby-faced homewrecker."

The bow quivered in Dorcas's hand, but she steadied it. "Do not sully the memory of my dear grandparents with your unsavoury comments. Two finer people never lived."

Aunt Sybil took her advantage. "Really?" she asked blandly. "And did your mother enjoy being a bastard?" Dorcas gasped, her arrow slipped long enough for Aunt Sybil to ram her into the wall and make good her escape through the door.

"After her," bellowed Dorcas, clambering back on her feet.

"I'm ready," shouted a cement-caked Uncle Merlin.

We must have made a weird trio as we pounded into the churchyard, one red-headed woman pointing a makeshift bow and arrow, a crumbling granite man, and a young woman wielding a spade, all in pursuit of a stout elderly lady dodging among the tombstones. What would have happened if deliverance had not arrived in humble guise — Freddy and Jill vaulting tombstones in perfect Olympic form — I will never know.

"Don't hurt her," cried Freddy to his teammate. "She probably can't help it. This may have been coming on since she hit thirty."

Jill said later that she subdued Aunt Sybil by the ultimate nonviolent weapon — hypnosis. True, she barely touched her. As Jill leapt, arms lifted and outstretched, eyes blazing, hair spiking, she looked like an avenging angel from the land of fire and brimstone, and when she screamed, "Look into my eyes," Aunt Sybil fainted.

EPILOGUE

I experienced a wave of sadness when Aunt Sybil was taken, babbling incoherently, to a small private hospital where it seemed likely she would spend her final years. A remorseful Uncle Merlin would make payment for past sins by visiting her every Sunday and taking her flowers from the garden. He could do this in safety because Aunt Sybil was a little girl again living with her beloved Uncle Arthur. For her, Merlin Grantham no longer existed. In a sense she was right.

As he sat up in bed in the early hours of the morning, sipping his favourite Ovaltine, he told me he had decided to continue on as Jonas Phipps. "He was a great friend," he said, "and in bequeathing me his name he gave me a new beginning, a new life. God bless you, Jonas." He lifted his mug and looked upwards. "I'll try and do you proud."

"Well, it looks like you may have plenty of opportunity." I bent forward and kissed his still pale cheek. "Dr Melrose spoke to us after examining you and he says your constitution is remarkable. You should live to be a hundred."

"I wouldn't mind having a crack at it, if you and Ben and Dorcas would agree to stay on here." He looked at me sheepishly over the rim of his cup. "Sybil was right. I have been a blind wilful old fool, playing games with life and death. I should have known. She was peculiar even as a child. Dorcas tried to warn me last night. Seems she had begun to remember things my mother had told her about Sybil."

"The future is what counts. One of the first changes we are going to see around here will be officially naming this house Merlin's Court. I think your mother would like that."

The old man smiled. "You brought her home, Ellie. Everywhere I look there are reminders of her, and now Dorcas can talk to me about her and fill in all those lost years. When she left, the only things I had of hers were the portrait and the journals. I hid them so my father would not destroy them along with everything else. He had already ripped out the soufflé recipe because he knew my mother regarded it as her highest achievement as a cook, but I rescued those pages from the fireplace, and a few months ago — well, you know the rest."

"Admit it," I said, "you've had a lot of fun. Dorcas and I thought Aunt Sybil had planted the clues, but you did that yourself, didn't you? Well, the fun and games are over. I'll be here to watch over you and keep you on the primrose path, with occasional time off for good behaviour."

"Sounds like I'm in for a rough time," he grumped, almost back to his old self, "but I've done my share of watching, too. That day you went into the churchyard I was right behind you. I was having some doubts about that will. I tried to look after you, but it's true there is no fool like an old fool. Going down to Sybil's cottage and tackling her about Dorcas's disappearance nearly cost all of us our lives besides what being bumped over to the vault in a wheel barrow will have done to my lumbago."

I bent and kissed his cheek, which was beginning to show a little more colour. "For all your wicked ways, I do love you. Goodnight, Jonas."

Neither Freddy nor Jill was in the kitchen when I went down stairs. They had gone for an early morning jog, but I had already thanked them for our rescue. As they had explained it to me, they had both felt restless and decided to take a browse outside. They had met in the garden and Freddy had told Jill that he was worried about the whole situation, especially about Sybil. When they reached the churchyard, they heard the hubbub and took action. What surprised me was that lethargic Freddy had cared enough to get involved — another of those groundless assumptions based on the way people look. I was as guilty as all the rest and I should have known better. Freddy had told me that he had come down for the luncheon with Aunt Sybil and the others, that day just before my birthday, but before it was time to go to the Hounds and Hare he had walked through the marketplace, seen me happily chatting with Dorcas, and decided he didn't want to spend an hour listening to people gripe about my manipulative powers. I remembered how I had bumped into a tall person with a pony tail, and the vague uneasy feeling I had experienced. Somehow I had always hoped Freddy was not the one, and now it was time for his reward. Ben and I would pay off his father's debts, and if Freddy should ever get married, we'd see he was all right. As I went through the kitchen door I wondered if Jill could get him to cut his hair.

Dorcas was administering a potent brew of hot whisky and spices to my favourite casualty. Ben was looking very rakish in the bandage supplied by Dr Melrose and assured me he was well on the road to recovery. Sitting chummily at the table it was hard to believe that the night's terrifying events had ever happened. It was time for Dorcas to tell her story. When she had read the advertisement for housekeeper she could not resist returning to her grandmother's old home, but fearing that due to the old scandal she might not have been welcome, she had kept her identity a secret.

"Wasn't easy though. Hated deceiving you and Ben, but couldn't switch mid-stream once I knew the treasure was connected with Grandma. You know my convictions about always playing the game fair and square. Telling you who I was would have seemed like cheating. Once you knew Gram hadn't died here you'd soon have put two and two together. Can't tell you the moral battle I fought, wanting to speak out but knowing you'd want to play by the rules. Felt horribly uncomfortable when the portrait was unwrapped. Thought you might recognize the likeness, said it reminded you of someone, didn't you, Ellie? And me sitting not two feet away. The living image of Abigail, I am, so Gramps used to say. Then Ben told me I was to be treated like one of the family — felt such a fraud."

"But you saved us." I reached across and held her hand. "Dorcas, don't leave us. We need you, don't we, Ben?"

"We certainly do," he said. "With Ellie and me floating on clouds we need someone with her feet on the ground to look after us."

"I suppose," Dorcas replied, eyes blurring, "that the village school could do with a games mistress, and if the cottage is vacant, and if Uncle Merlin agrees . . ."

"He wants you here. He can't wait to talk with you about his mother. Dorcas, what did happen to Abigail?"

"She and my grandfather, Miles, had a good life. They never were having an affair under her husband's nose. He admired her, and one day when Arthur ill-treated her, Miles put his arm round her and got caught in the act. For her birthday he had given her the locket. Silly thing to have done, I suppose, but as Gramps told me, he looked upon her as the finest lady that ever lived. Gram didn't want to hurt his feelings by returning it, but knew what Arthur would think if he found out, so she buried it in the herb garden."

"So the 'M' was for Miles, not Merlin," I said. "Another clue we walked right past. Dorcas, your grandparents were happy, weren't they?"

"Gram said she never got over losing her son, but in every other way her life was good. Gramps, I suppose, deep down already loved her and she grew to care for him very deeply. Remembering her and Gramps walking arm in arm in their garden on a summer evening . . ." Dorcas pulled out one of her enormous handkerchiefs and blew loudly.

"Uncle Merlin will want you to have the locket," I said.

"Would like that, but mustn't get mushy. They had my mother and started a business, very prosperous, too. Mrs

Biddle's Best Jams, everyone knows the slogan, 'I'd Walk Miles for a Pot of Mrs Biddle's Jam.'"

"Do we have some?" I asked eagerly. "Strawberry is my favourite on a crusty slice of bread with lashings of butter. . . ."

"Nothing doing," frowned the man from Eligibility Escorts. "You have better things to do with your time than stuff your face — helping Dorcas refurnish the cottage, writing to my parents and your father, sewing your wedding dress."

"Don't be silly, darling, I can't possibly finish a dress by the end of the week, even if I could learn to thread a needle. Dorcas and I will go shopping, and what will you be doing, my hero?"

"Checking into starting that restaurant I spoke with you about. I hear the Hounds and Hare is up for sale. Then I may tackle another book. What do you think about a gothic horror with an overweight heroine, a devilishly handsome hero, and . . .?"

"You stick to your cooking," I said, leaning forward and kissing him to soften the chauvinist sting. "I'll write the story of Merlin's Court."

THE END

THE JOFFE BOOKS STORY

We began in 2014 when Jasper agreed to publish his mum's much-rejected romance novel and it became a bestseller.

Since then we've grown into the largest independent publisher in the UK. We're extremely proud to publish some of the very best writers in the world, including Joy Ellis, Faith Martin, Caro Ramsay, Helen Forrester, Simon Brett and Robert Goddard. Everyone at Joffe Books loves reading and we never forget that it all begins with the magic of an author telling a story.

We are proud to publish talented first-time authors, as well as established writers whose books we love introducing to a new generation of readers.

We have been shortlisted for Independent Publisher of the Year at the British Book Awards three times, in 2020, 2021 and 2022, and for the Diversity and Inclusivity Award at the Independent Publishing Awards in 2022.

We built this company with your help, and we love to hear from you, so please email us about absolutely anything bookish at feedback@joffebooks.com

If you want to receive free books every Friday and hear about all our new releases, join our mailing list: www.joffebooks.com/contact

And when you tell your friends about us, just remember: it's pronounced Joffe as in coffee or toffee!

ALSO BY DOROTHY CANNELL

THE ELLIE HASKELL MYSTERIES
Book 1: THE THIN WOMAN

Printed in Great Britain
by Amazon

23926436R00162